THICKER
THAN
WATER

Other Novels by Annie Cook:

THE TEAPOT COTTAGE SERIES
No Small Change (#1)
The Power Of Notes And Spells (#2)
When It's Meant To Happen (#3)
Ruin, Reins and Redemption (#4)

~ * ~

A Moral Swerve

~ * ~

THICKER THAN WATER

A NOVEL BY
ANNIE COOK

Copyright © 2024 Annie Cook

All rights reserved, including the right to reproduce this book, or portions thereof in any form. No part of this text may be reproduced, transmitted, downloaded, decompiled, reverse engineered, or stored, in any form or introduced into any information storage and retrieval system, in any form or by any means, whether electronic or mechanical without the express written permission of the author.

This is a work of fiction. Names and characters are the product of the author's imagination and any resemblance to actual persons, living or dead, is entirely coincidental.

The views expressed in this work are solely those of the author and do not necessarily reflect the views of the publisher, and the publisher hereby disclaims any responsibility for them.

ISBN: 978-1-917425-29-2

www.Anniecookwriter.com

Trigger Warning:

This book contains references to unlawful killing, homophobia, repressed memories, incest and child abuse.

To the unimaginably brave ones:

The ones who have shared their stories with me.

The ones who have found the courage to stand up tall and walk forward from terrible childhood trauma.

The ones who are still on that journey.

The ones who have yet to start.

Walk towards the light that heals and nourishes the soul, and don't let anything stop you.

Chapter One
- *Ruth* -

Most people can remember where they were, or what they were doing, when a momentous world event occurred. When John F Kennedy was assassinated, back in 1963, my grandparents were having a pie and a pint in their local pub, after doing some early Christmas shopping. When the death of Princess Diana in a Paris car crash exploded all over the news, my parents were on a cheap late-summer package holiday in Tenerife. When the world learned about the 9/11 catastrophe at the twin towers in New York, I'd just gone back to school after popping home for lunch. And, while my sister was being murdered, I was at the cinema. As some twisted, sick psycho was choking the last of the life from my poor, lovely but long-lost Rebekah, I was sipping coke and crunching popcorn, and laughing at something silly on the silver screen. I don't even remember now, what it was; some stupid joke that Gina and I found funny.

 I always switch my phone off when I go to the cinema. I'm not one of those people who feels forced to stay connected to the outside world when I'm doing something that doesn't involve it. I don't find it hard at all, to keep away from my social media accounts for more than five minutes in case I miss the fact that someone's posted a picture of their boring breakfast, or – God forbid – commented on something I said myself. I prefer to switch off entirely, and be disengaged from everything but the movie. I've never seen the point in paying decent money to see something and then not giving it my full attention.

 So it was only later, as we were coming out, that I turned my phone back on and saw two missed calls from Rebekah.

No messages; just two missed calls, fourteen minutes apart. Did I ring her back? No.

When the detectives asked me why I didn't return Rebekah's calls that she made to me, around an hour before she was strangled, I invited them to consider a certain scenario. I asked them to picture a member of their immediate family who despised them and everything they stood for, who never missed an opportunity (and sometimes actually created one) to torment them with phone calls, voice and email messages, and slanging matches in public places. Then I asked them both; 'if that person had called you twice, randomly, out of the blue, as so often happens when they are blind drunk or raging, and wanting to unleash yet another tirade upon you, would *you* have rung them back?'

They regarded me impassively at first, with faces like stone. Then predictably, like heat-seeking missiles, they homed in on the family rift. That's always the first logical angle to go at things from, of course, when there's been a murder. As I understand it, most murders are committed by family members or close friends. It makes perfect sense, I suppose. If you love someone enough, they can probably sometimes make you mad enough to want to kill them. But, while Rebekah never failed to upset me, cause me to lose my composure, or actually piss me off, the though never even entered my head to want to throttle her.

They asked me endless questions though, about my incredibly dysfunctional family, which quickly became annoying since not much of what they wanted to know even seemed relevant to the matter at hand. But they did have the grace to stop short of suggesting I might have killed Rebekah myself. A very neat, cinema-shaped alibi plugs that particular hole in their investigative process, and the CCTV set up outside the place offers no evidence of me furtively sneaking out of the movie and coming back an hour or so later.

So I haven't made it onto the list of suspects, and they seemed a bit disappointed about that. It's not a cut-and-dried, family-feud-based crime involving me then, unfortunately for them. It means they have a bit more work to do.

While a surprising number of murders *are* familial, sadly Rebekah's isn't one of them, or so it seems, since I do believe my father is too feeble of that particular kind of spirit and my mother's too miserly with her energy to use it to strangle someone. In any case, if they'd had the choice and the resources, I'm the one they'd have chosen to choke; Rebel Ruth, the daughter who wouldn't conform, always bunking off church, disappointing the family in too many ways to count. I was the black sheep who brought irrevocable mortification to the fine upstanding vicar and his mild-mannered wife, and their other poor daughter Rebekah, the erstwhile, now-gone golden child, who couldn't put a foot wrong until she went and got herself killed.

If Rebekah had been the one to run off and undertake the 'abomination' of a marriage to another woman, I'm sure they'd have found a way to forgive her. But it was me who committed that unpalatable sin, and since tolerance for me has never been in strong supply, forgiveness was never going to raise its head above the still, stagnant water of the frigid family pond. So much for Christian values, vicar! Loving thy neighbour, the acceptance and prayer for redemption of all the human flaws and frailties?

I might be a lot of things, but I've never been a hypocrite like you.

I've been with my wife Gina for nearly twenty years but, sadly, it doesn't seem to matter that I'm happy. It doesn't seem to matter at all, that she fulfils me in a way I once thought I'd never be. It doesn't seem to matter that we've made a happy home, that we're raising a beautiful happy child, that we support one another's careers, that we have wonderful, enriching circles of friends, both gay and straight. None of that matters, even though it's what parents are supposed to want for their kids. If I had all that with a man by my side, I would probably be closer to acceptable. Because I have it with Gina I'm *persona non grata* to my prudish parents, who flatly refuse to acknowledge me anymore. And Rebekah torments me with monotonous regularity, presumably out of some sort of misguided sexual fear.

At least she used to. She won't be tormenting me anymore, will she, being dead and all that?

Don't get me wrong. I'm sad beyond belief, that my little sister is dead, and I am utterly shocked at her murder. But I have to be honest. Rebekah was always mean to me and my own little family, to the point of being cruel. I still loved her in spite of all that but, as much as I wish she wasn't dead, a tiny, traitorous part of me is glad she can't hurl insults at me anymore. On being informed of her death, even the tragic, outrageous and scarcely believable circumstances surrounding it were not enough to prevent a small spark of relief from flaring inside me briefly, before the magnitude of what happened sank in, and heartbreak took its place. And there is, still, the tiniest vestige of hope that this unspeakable event might draw what's left of my fragmented 'family of origin' back together; that perhaps we might somehow be reunited by the appalling tragedy that's ripped us all in half. Time will tell, of course, but in truth I'm not holding my breath. My parents probably now just see themselves as childless.

Our friends have always struggled to say the right thing, in response to the rejection I've always had from my family. Everyone who truly cares wants to try to make it hurt a little less, usually falling on that inevitable, timeworn statement about it being the family's loss. But, what they fail to understand, is that it's not just *their* loss. It's mine too. It's my loss too, and I feel it every day. But if I say that, it leaves people literally lost for words. They go all flummoxed and fidgety, they lose the ability to speak, and that much discomfort is more than I can bear to be responsible for. So I never say it to anyone except Gina. She gets it. She gets *me*.

As I've told the detectives, repeatedly, I don't know much at all about my sister's adult life. I knew everything there was to know about her when we were little, growing up, dreaming of white weddings (but not the husbands, at least not in my case) and theorising about how many kids, cats and dogs we'd have, and what our place in the world would one day be. We shared everything, in the early years, before sexuality became first the wonder then the wedge between us. Nowadays, after years of growing apart, in entirely different directions and with entirely different destinations in mind, all I can tell them about Rebekah is that she evolved into a tortured soul. As a grown-up, she has always struggled and failed to find peace, and I don't know why.

So I can't be of much help, but the detectives have a few leads. They're chasing down some boyfriend, apparently; a bloke she blew off recently, after reaching her usual low threshold of boredom, or dissatisfaction, or both. Rebekah has a short attention span and an even shorter fuse. She quickly gets fed up, and she never hesitates to say so. Most times, when her latent prima donna makes an appearance, people who know her well simply shrug their shoulders, walk away from her, and come back when she's cooled down a bit. But I could see how an ex might get upset at being tossed aside when his amusement value had faded. I could see how a man prone to volatility or outrage might suffer from wounded pride and lose his temper with her, when she decides she's had enough and seeks to chuck him in the bin, without a backward glance.

But I have to stop thinking about her in the present tense, don't I? I have to remember that while I was simply sitting in a cinema, holding hands with the love of my life, chomping on popcorn and blissfully unaware, a massive part of my present simply slid by and turned into my past.

The funeral is tomorrow, and I am under no illusions. It will be horrible. It's taken a long time to get Rebekah's body released. Typical, I believe, where there's been a murder. They need to make sure that every last vestige of medical and forensic evidence has been meticulously scraped from her, and identified, and recorded. They don't want to miss anything, and that's entirely as it should be, but the wait has been interminable. All I've wanted to do is lay her to rest.

Maybe I'll never know why she rang me on the night she was killed, and whether or not I could have prevented it from happening if I'd answered or rung her back. I have to find a way to live with that, and I guess I'll eventually figure out how to do it.

Gina took the cringingly apologetic call from my father's put-upon secretary, requesting that I not attend my sister's funeral; that I spare the family any further anguish at this difficult time. But Gina put the poor woman straight, as only Gina can. My lovely, animated, effervescent, voluble, gorgeous Italian wife, who feels and communicates things like only true Italians can, told her in no uncertain terms to scuttle back to my father and tell him to *'dove il sole non splende,'* because I would be there.

We would *both* be there, audaciously and abominably *in flagrante* as a lesbian couple, and any further anguish the family might feel, over and above that of having to say farewell to a murdered daughter, would be of their own creation if they chose to make an ugly scene involving the one that remained. Like all behaviour, Gina patiently explained into the telephone in the most beautiful Italian accent, being embarrassed, resentful or small-minded is always an active choice. My parents had a choice.

Gina is prepared to do battle. Personally, I'm just expecting to be ignored. No more, no less. Given the magnitude and horror of the occasion, I doubt if my parents would want to add to it by openly drawing attention to the family rift. They will, in all likelihood, simply choose to pretend I'm not there.

I can cope with that. Gina can too, although whether she actually *will* is another story. She's a lot less adept than I am at hiding her true feelings. Gina wears her heart on her sleeve and believe me, it's a very full heart. She is passionate, honest to a cringing fault, and remarkably intolerant of stupidity or ignorance. She is fiercely loyal, especially to me, and although she appreciates the need for restraint tomorrow, it will be interesting to see her reaction to being treated as invisible. She is typically anything but. You can't forget Gina, once you've met her, and maybe that's the problem. It would be a lot easier to ignore what you might class as a 'repulsive relationship' if one of the parties involved wasn't larger than life and insanely beautiful to boot. Someone like Gina leaves a brand-mark on your brain.

She is fascinating to most men, and many struggle with the concept that one so beautiful, such an object of desire for them, does not in fact want them. Our equally beautiful daughter Chiara is the product of a misguided attempt six years ago by a friend of one of Gina's brothers to 'cure her' of being gay. It happened on a weekend when Gina had gone home to Italy to visit her family. She got a lot more than she planned for, that weekend, and I call it what it was – a rape. Gina is more forgiving however, having made the bargain with the man in question that she wouldn't drag his name through the mud and bring disgrace to his fine upstanding Italian family if he relinquished all rights to the child.

She quietly pointed out to him that everyone who was *anyone* in their local community knew her sexual status and would cheerfully stand up in court to say so. She also suggested that the prospect of opening the door to her four Italian 'baying-for-blood' brothers was probably something he should be at pains to avoid, if he wanted his shameful 'tackle' to remain attached. Few men with an ounce of common sense would want to go through any of that, and – entirely predictably – that 'man' (I'd have called him something a lot less flattering, but that's just me), well, he picked up a pen and signed away his child with lightning speed. Self-preservation is a powerful thing, and Gina knew it.

She looks on the bright side of the violation, because despite the circumstances Chiara is of course a truly beautiful gift, and I've got to grips now with the acceptance of how she came to us. She is as much mine as Gina's, we have the paperwork to say so, and we named her together. Chiara means 'light,' in Italian, and this beloved, beautiful, cherished child was the light that came out of a dark act, so it was a fitting name as well as a beautiful one. It somewhat sweetens the bitter pill of my beloved being raped by someone she grew up with; someone she'd once liked and trusted.

Do my parents know they have an adopted grandchild? Yes, they do. Are they interested? Not in the slightest. While I wouldn't want to second-guess them (because we've never even had the conversation), I'm assuming the presence of Chiara just adds to their total confusion about the mechanics of a relationship between two women who don't fancy men, yet one gets pregnant anyway and both go on to raise the child. Even as a vicar, my father knows an immaculate conception is a bit too much of a stretch, especially for one so 'evil' and corruptive as Gina Giordano! Apparently it's her fault, that I have surrendered to the devil-driven darkness within me and let it take hold.

Chiara will not be coming with us tomorrow. It is completely inappropriate to put our adorable, gentle child through the ghastly and traumatic funeral of someone who would never even acknowledge her existence. Having her there is also too much of an in-your-face statement for my parents to have to deal with, on what will already be the most miserable day of their lives. And I do still respect them that far. It's not my intention to cause a scene. All I want is to be permitted to pay my last respects to my departed sister because despite the turbulent, fraught and frustrating relationship we ended up having, if you could even call it one, I loved her with every last piece of my broken heart.

The detectives will be there, of course. Apparently it's standard practice, where there's been a murder but no conviction at the time of the victim's funeral. It is surprisingly common for perpetrators to attend the funerals of their victims, or so I'm told. Sick perversion, getting off on the misery and anguish they've caused, or sometimes even just to reassure themselves that they're not under suspicion. Go figure.

So the police show up, and generally just observe everyone in the act of grieving, just in case there's someone present for whom it really might be just an act. I wonder how many funerals they end up at, for people they don't know, and I wonder how many crocodile tears they witness.

I want my sister's murderer found and brought to justice. It's what my parents want too, but even with that, the common ground of grief and loss at either end of the great divide is not a solid enough foundation on which to build a bridge. They don't want me at the funeral. There is no olive tree with a branch to be extended; at least not from that side of the gulf. I have a field full of olive trees growing gently in my own heart, and I would give every last one of them up for peace and truce, but it doesn't make a blind bit of difference.

As much as Rebekah persecuted me, she loved me too, I'm sure of it. The opposite of love isn't the hatred she tried so hard to hurl at me. The opposite of love is indifference, and I could never accuse her of that. Rebekah was never ambivalent about me. It was either blind love or blind hate, with her, and turned on their head they are both more or less the same emotion – caring beyond reason, railing against what the mind cannot accept, fighting like a dog to protect yourself from being wounded by what you can't understand. But Rebekah's love had limits, it's how she was made. It's like going down a road expecting to end up somewhere, but finding a blunt dead-end. No throughfare. She can't transcend her prejudices to love without limits. Or couldn't. Past tense, remember?

So while I could accept Rebekah, with all her short ends and jagged edges, she could no more accept me than she could cease to breathe. Except that she did, in the end, didn't she? She did cease to breathe, and in the worst possible way. My poor tormented sister was actively prevented from breathing by some monstrous person who failed to appreciate all she had to live for, all she had to fix, all she could one day have been, experienced and done with her life.

It is intolerable. The grief is like a billiard ball, hard in the back of my throat, with another sitting solid in my gut, and I don't know if they will ever go away. Maybe one day I'll get to a place where I can think of her, and all we have lost, all we could have had but didn't, without feeling those hard lumps lodged inside me. Maybe when they catch her killer, I may get a chance. But maybe not. Maybe what doesn't get said, what doesn't get fixed in life, maybe it never goes away in death either. Maybe our unresolved issues, mine and Rebekah's, will just hang here, silent in the ether, stalking me from the shadows, shrouding me until my own dying day. And then what? Is there an after-life, a place we can meet as little lights or sparks, to effect a workable truce? Or is this it, what we have now, forevermore?

Most people expect me to have, as the daughter of a vicar, a belief system that can provide solace and reassurance at times like this. Drawing strength from God, and all that, and all the while remembering (as we are repeatedly told) that this God tends to work in 'mysterious ways.' Well, they might be surprised to learn that I have no truck with any kind of God who can produce and tolerate a bigot for a mouthpiece. And let's not forget the small matter of families being randomly and sometimes repeatedly robbed of loved ones through war, genocide or other types of death, or family feud, with us all being expected to simply accept that it's all part of some higher, divine plan designed to make us better people. I don't know what the fuck that is, and good luck to the people who believe it, but I'm not one of them.

Gina, the staunch Italian Catholic who has never once challenged my lack of faith, or forced her own upon me, has sorted out our funeral clothes. Bless her; I'm still too numb myself, to think about what Rebekah might have approved of, or what my parents are likely to think. Gina is inherently stylish; it's part of her Italian-ness, and she's a very famous clothing designer, so there's really no excuse for getting it wrong. Not that she would. Panache is in her DNA, this talented, wonderful woman who, as a wedding gift, presented me with the most stunning surprise imaginable; a breathtakingly beautiful capsule wardrobe of clothes she had made herself, especially for me; one-off pieces in incredible styles, fabrics and colours that would never be replicated for anyone else.

Gina *always* knows what to wear, so she has organised everything for us both. For me it's a heavy silk, black Giordano suit; a unique, designed-just-for-me skirt and jacket, beautifully tailored and timeless, but functional too. It's the kind of thing you could wear to work, to a wedding, to a party, or to a funeral, depending on the accessories you'd choose to put with it. Tomorrow it will be an understated soft pink cashmere camisole, and a single strand of pearls. Black shoes of course; I've always thought it disrespectful to wear any other colour at a funeral.

Gina will wear her slate grey trouser suit with a dark blue satin shirt, and no jewellery. Even at that, my darling, stunning, olive-skinned wife with her sloe eyes and her glorious waist-length waterfall of springy raven curls won't be able to avoid drawing attention to herself. She looks like the Romany gypsy of everyone's dreams. Even straight women would roll in the hay with Gina. Many of them have said so. It's just the way it is. There's never been a single day, in the last two decades I have known her, when I haven't pinched myself at the fact that she chose me.

I'm starting to feel a bit sorry for the poor detectives. They have to repeat everything they say twice; once to my parents and once to me, and that must be tremendously annoying for them. But over the days, as they develop more insight and gather more information, they have taken to running it by me first, before they let my parents know anything. I get to decide exactly what gets communicated, and how, to Mum and Dad. Without them realising it, I get the chance to protect them a little, which I think is for the best. I get a sense that the police have already learned there are certain things my parents will take well, and certain things they will struggle with; for example Rebekah's pathology and toxicology reports showing high levels of alcohol and cocaine in her system.

In addition, and even less comfortably for the family, there was evidence of four different strains of sperm located in various places, in Rebekah's body. All 'deposited' at around the same time. So she was either gang-raped, or she had quite a party with a few male friends. In the absence of any evidence of struggle, it looks more like the latter, and that's not the kind of thing my narrow-minded, straight-laced, prudish parents who adored their faultless golden girl could comfortably hear or think about. Learning these things about her would be too much for them. It's really hard for *me*, as broad-minded and worldly as I think I am, to hear something like that about someone I love, regardless of our estrangement.

For the detectives, that kind of information makes an investigation a lot more complicated. It substantially widens their field of enquiry, and creates a lot of extra work for the investigative team. It's a frustration they have to manage and, as time goes by, I'm not sure how well they'll be able to keep absorbing it. They are already noticeably fed up.

For me though, this onslaught of appalling and distressing detail has a much bigger impact. It creates complete and utter turmoil, like a cyclone starting up and gaining strength in my brain. I know so little about Rebekah's adult life, yet I'm struggling hard with the notion that she'd take any kind of illegal drug, or that she'd have sex with at least four men at once. It makes me desperately sad because, even if she was a willing participant, it's the kind of scenario I just can't imagine anyone being truly happy in, no matter what might be going on in their lives.

It's shocking, and it's confusing too, because Rebekah always seemed like such a prude. She dumped countless boyfriends just because they wanted to sleep with her. It seemed like she was never 'ready,' never *comfortable* with sex, in any shape or form, although we never really talked about it, in those days before I met Gina and my own uncertain future suddenly became reassuringly clear at the ripe old age of eighteen. All sex repulsed Rebekah it seemed, and she apparently found the idea of two women together so intolerable she couldn't even be content to simply ignore me and my wife. She was so revolted by us she actually made it her business to torment us at every turn.

As reactions went, it was extreme. But I never dug into it in any detail. Rebekah wouldn't have allowed that, even if I'd tried. I just had to acknowledge her prejudice, and try to find a way to let it wash over me. That would have been a lot easier if she'd simply kept away from us, but she didn't. She constantly harangued us, with nasty phone calls, emails and texts, and the occasional belligerent public appearance that always left us feeling frustrated and embarrassed.

Gina thinks Rebekah had other issues, and that we were just the most convenient outlet for some other, deep-seated, indefinable misery within her. I always rejected that idea, but now I'm not so sure I should have. Maybe Gina was right. Maybe there was more going on than we ever imagined, and maybe we *were* just the outlet. I simply assumed that Rebekah hated the way I have chosen to live my life, and felt the need to torment me about it, well-fuelled by my parents' disapproval. I never thought about the situation as being any more complicated than that.

So then, in my ever-recurring process of licking the wounds inflicted by my sister, had I missed something significant about her, and could I have saved her if I'd known what it was?

Rebekah's autopsy seems so incredible to me. The detectives do believe the sex to have been consensual. Pathology reports show that there were no wounds or marks anywhere on her body consistent with a sexual attack, and the 'event' occurred around 24 hours *before* she was murdered.

Equally weird was the fact that even her death was simple, almost as if that was consensual also. Again, there was no sign of a fight or even much of a tussle taking place. Her nose had bled profusely but that was, apparently, a typical bodily response to strangulation. There was evidence of slightly deranged bedding consistent with someone moving about a *little*, but nothing to suggest she had fought for her life. It had clearly been quick, whoever did it, and they were vicious with it. They'd snapped her neck.

The police say the semen is a significant part of their investigation, but I haven't a clue how they follow that up. They said they will start by running the DNA from each of the strains through their existing database of criminals, and see what comes up. If nothing does, I'd say they'll have a hard job ahead of them. But nothing about Rebekah's life was ever simple, so why would her death be?

Chapter Two
- Gina -

It is a grey, grey day today. Just the type of day that you see in a bleak foreign film when there is a funeral to take place; grey, miserable, everybody with stone-wall faces. And I am certain it will rain. What a *stereotipo!* A textbook day to bury the dead.

Ruthie is grieving, and not just for her dead little sister. It will be a tough day for her, faced with the miserable mother and the weak-chinned father incapable of practicing what he preaches to his smug, self-satisfied congregation on Sunday mornings. They are all burying Rebekah today. It is a shared family heartache, but will they share it as a family? No, they will not.

So yes, a tough day it will be. Me, I don't care about the dead Rebekah. I don't care about the pathetic parents, so mean of spirit; that mother with the mouth like the cat's arse, who lets her hypocrite husband decide everything for her, like who she talks to and who she ignores. He probably even tells *la stupida* what to wear! The woman has no spine. I have no time for her. And I told them so, those police, when they questioned me. I told them I don't care about anything that happens in that stupid shitty family, only how it affects my Ruthie.

Maybe they were hoping I killed Rebekah so they could wrap up their case, all nice and neat, and go onto something else. But of course I didn't kill her. On the night she was strangled I was doing something far more interesting. But, *mio Dio*, I gotta be honest. There were plenty of times when I *wanted* to kill that stupid *puta*. I told them that too; that I could gladly have killed her, many times, for how she made Ruthie suffer.

They asked me if I was glad that Rebekah is dead. I told them the truth; I honestly don't care. I am *indifferente* and nothing more. I told them I am glad she will never bother Ruthie anymore, but that's it. No more and no less. *È la vita.*

That family can burn in hell, for all it matters to me. They are bigoted, intolerant scum. Ruthie is the only one I care about. So of course I will go to this joke, this funeral, for *her*. I will look at the two-faced, stupid parents as they go through their motions of grief and I will hide the disgust if I can. And if I can't hide the disgust, so be it. Let them say and do what they want, to me. That won't matter. But if they openly insult my wife on this miserable grey day, let's see what happens then.

So a dark suit and *camica* today. Black shoes too, on Ruthie's insistence. But scarlet slutty underwear, and only I will know. My way of showing my disrespect. If I could, I would wear shiny red heels and a sequin dress, and tap-dance on Rebekah's coffin. But sadly I cannot, so a whore's underwear will have to do, as my statement for her. Take that, Rebekah. Take my scarlet satin bra with the big holes where my nipples thrust through, take my cheap *mutandine* with the missing crotch. Take this disgusting underwear that I went out to a sleaze shop yesterday and bought just for you, and shove it all up your tight, dead-bitch ass.

Since it sadly cannot go into Rebekah's stupid little coffin, this *oribile* slutty underwear only fit for *le prostitute* can go instead into the bin tonight. Trash into trash. It is filthy, degrading, uncomfortable underwear that has no place in my life, but for today, it is completely *perfetto* for the occasion, as we sit there, trying to stay awake through a boring drone of Rebekah's pointless fucked-up life.

And that is how I will pay my disrespects. Because, you see, she was *detestabile* to me. I was born without sisters, but I have longed for one, all my life. Four brothers, *mio Dio!* And I once held the hope that Rebekah might one day be the sister, that she may one day finally accept Ruthie and me and be a part of our beautiful little family, since her own was so foul and mean. We tried and tried, so many times with her; inviting her to dinner, asking her to meet with us for coffee and things like that. Ruthie and me, we talked about it, and we even invited her to be *Madrina* to our beautiful Chiara but, *la cagna,* she ignored our gesture of sisterhood. She did not understand the importance of what we offered to her. She did not appreciate such a privilege. And instead of getting better, everything just got worse. The bigotry, the *vetriolo*, it all became too much.

Eventually, Rebekah and I, we had to concede to being *nemici* – sworn enemies. No chance of a sister for me. Or for her. Instead of having two sisters she threw them both away, and a niece as well. Chiara, our adorable child, was treated like she didn't exist.

It always seemed to me that Rebekah's anger was a closer, more focussed emotion than hatred. It was almost like a jealousy, like a scorned, left-behind lover, *amante gelosa*, who throws a shadow on the new relationship of the lost partner, but Ruthie says no, I have it all wrong. So I don't know.

What I do know is that the dislike turned into hatred and was sealed with one matter, and it was my doing. Do I regret it? No, because one way or another it would have come to that anyway. The restaurant thing was just one of what would have been a dozen different *provocare* that brought us to a point of no return.

Ruthie and I were in the Banyan Tree, having dinner. Suddenly, in walked a drunk and staggering Rebekah, shouting at us both, calling us all kinds of *volgare* names. She screamed and swore at us that we did not think of the family we disgraced.

Well, for me that kind of stupid behaviour just rolls off my shoulders. I ignore such *cattiveria*, because I do not believe it worth a response, but Ruthie was taking it hard and a manager was coming, so me? I put a stop to it all. I stood up, grabbed Rebekah, spun her around and marched her like a frog into the street. I twisted one of her arms up her back and I leaned into her, and I said into her ear, low so nobody else could hear, 'fuck off you pathetic bitch and leave your sister alone. She does not want you in her life like this. And you are right. We don't think about you!'

I said some other things to her too, graphic things that made her choke with disgust, and I have prayed to *la Madre Maria* for forgiveness for those. But *la stupida* needed to stop harassing us for once and for all. It was becoming unbearable for Ruthie. I said what I had to, and let go of her scrawny arm, and she scuttled away like a crab across the sand. I never saw her again, and neither did Ruthie, and we were better for it. She continued to torment Ruthie from afar in stupid ways, in random stupid bursts, right to the end of her own stupid life, but she never put herself in front of us again.

That night, back in the restaurant, Ruthie wanted to leave but I said no, we did not have to run away, with our tails between our legs like a couple of *cani battuti*. We had done nothing wrong, and we had nothing to be ashamed for. So we didn't leave. We stayed and we had our meal. The waiters were nice to us, and it turned out to be a beautiful evening, not at all ruined by the stupid Rebekah. I would not give her the satisfaction of that.

Ruthie asked me what I said to her sister outside and I told her it didn't matter, because it didn't. Shocking Rebekah was just my way of hitting back, because gay people have to contend all the time with others sniggering about the way we have sex, and it is *tedioso* that they so seldom manage to think of gay relationships in any other context at all.

But the truth is that sex is only a small part of things for me and Ruthie. What we are is so much more than that. It is *cerebrale* too; the love of mind, heart and soul, of sacrifice and protection, cherishing and honouring. If Ruthie was *sfigurata* in an accident I would still cherish and adore her. I wanna be old with her, no matter what life throws at us. As I see the new wrinkles come, and I watch her hair as it starts to go grey at the temples, way too early, I feel the march of time and I celebrate it all because being the one she has chosen, to pass this time with her; it is the greatest privilege of my life. That *puta* Rebekah and her pitiable *dogmatico* kind would never understand.

I didn't even wanna look at that whore in her coffin. I went with Ruthie to the funeral home while she looked at her, but I wouldn't do it. That bigoted bitch was nothing to me.

So the taxi is here. Ruthie looks lost, and small, and so sad. I know that she is nervous also, because she is chewing the skin around her thumbnail, which is something she does when she is anxious. She doesn't know she is doing it, most of the time. She gets *irritato* when I tell her, but more so if I don't and it starts to bleed. When that happens she always looks so surprised, like someone else has done it to her, not herself. It is amusing to me, that expression, but I can't let her see or she would be even more upset.

So we are ready to go, to this stupid pointless funeral, Ruthie in her black suit and pink *canottiera* too nice for that family, and me in my own suit and filthy-cheap, *pessimo* whore's underwear, still too nice for that family.

And of course it has started to rain. What a shame. I was praying for sunshine, the kind of day that hurts the eyes with its glory, the brightness of sun that makes a mockery of sadness and despair. I don't wanna see that family get the weather that fits their miserable occasion so perfectly. But they do. They do not deserve the sombreness of rain today, but they get it.

As we arrive at the church and get out of the taxi, a solitary bell is ringing, slow and sad. It sounds so lonely. People dressed mostly in black or grey are making their way inside, all with their heads down, and so we do the same. As much as I wanna be defiant today, *provocatorio*, the feeling here is very subdued and awkward, almost like nobody wants to be here and nobody knows what to say. It feels disrespectful to *myself* to be defiant for the sake of it today, so I will be on good behaviour, but we'll see how long that lasts if someone is mean to my Ruthie.

There is no sign of the parents. I guess they will come in last. As we take our seats in the fourth row from the front, Ruthie sees Rebekah's coffin and chokes back a sob. I have made sure there are plenty of tissues in her *borsa*, so she will be ok. She won't have to stand or sit here with her nose running, with her grief so inelegant. She would hate that, so I have made sure it won't happen.

A few people extend their hands or their arms to Ruthie, and she accepts the good gestures of people who are not bigots, who do not condemn her for her choices. I turn to look at who is here, and I am happy to see that a few of our own friends have come, to show support and perhaps defiance too, since some of them are gay and they know the situation with Ruthie's family. They are standing at the back, waiting to see what seats will be free once the service begins. It is a respect this family does not deserve, and it says so much more about our lovely friends than it does about Ruthie's deplorable parents with their *intolleranza* born of a fear they are too cowardly to confront.

And here they come; Mrs Cat's-Arse Face and Mr Bigot *Ipocrita*. Down the central isle they walk, arm in arm, almost like a bride and groom, except there are no smiles and they are dressed down; the vicar with his dog collar shining white at the front of his black shirt. His black suit hangs off him. It only fits where it touches, and his shoes need to be polished. This man, this vicar, he looks so shabby for his dead daughter.

The mother is wearing a black wool dress with no shape, like some kind of tunic. It looks exactly like a bin bag. She has put no thought into it, like she dragged it out from somewhere in the back of her boring wardrobe and slung it on in the hope that it would do. But it doesn't do. It looks a mess. The woman is a mess; she has not even had the grace to style her hair or wear any make-up. Not that the dead, disrespectful Rebekah deserves anyone to make an effort for her funeral. I don't believe she does.

Our clothes, mine and Ruthie's, we wear them for ourselves, because we would no more go out looking inappropriate than we would go out in our *pigiama*. Our outfits today are appropriate for *us*, because that is who we are. Only my disgusting underwear is appropriate for Rebekah the slut. So even though the slovenly parents have clearly failed to see it, maybe they are actually giving their dead daughter nothing better than she deserves. *Giustizia poetica*, it almost makes me laugh.

As they walk by us, the mother looks directly into my eyes. Her expression of horror is priceless, and I meet it by raising my eyebrows and smiling at her as if to say, 'Well, Cat's-Arse, speak to me if you dare.'

She does not dare. Instead she goes rigid on her vicar's arm, and he feels it and looks up. I know I have an expression of triumph on my face, but I refuse to remove it. He looks at me, and his mouth disappears into the thinnest of lines, almost like he has no mouth at all through which to speak his religion. He refuses to look at Ruthie, there by my side, even though she is staring hard at both of them and willing them to meet her gaze. I can feel it myself, so they must surely feel it too, but do they acknowledge their own flesh and blood?

Santa Maria madre di Dio, no. They do not. Instead, they are swiftly ushered into the front pew on the other side of the aisle. They cannot see us anymore but we can still see them.

Ruthie and Rebekah's father will not be taking his own daughter's funeral service. Another vicar is doing it and he steps down from his place alongside the coffin to offer the father a hug. As we watch, the father-vicar looks at the other, says something in his ear, and then gestures directly to us. We can see the other vicar trying to reason with and placate him, but in the end he shakes his head and comes over to us, asking in a low voice if we would please see him at the back of the church for a private word before the service gets underway.

Ruthie is confused and hurt, as it is clear – at least to us – that this 'word' will be about asking us to leave. Me, I am *furioso*. I try to remember that we are in a place of worship, and I work to hold onto my temper.

'Father, I am sorry but we are not gonna leave. We have as much right as anyone else to be here. Ruthie has the right to be here to pay her last respects to her dead sister, no? Why would you let a bigot stand in her way?'

This vicar has the grace to look ashamed. He looks at Ruthie who is now crying quietly, looks back at the father who now refuses to look at this vicar at all, and he heaves a great sigh and quietly says, 'I understand the problems, but it might be in your best interests to leave now, and perhaps come back later when everyone has gone, and I can pray with you both for Rebekah.'

'Are you a bigot, Father?' I enquire in a voice loud enough for all to hear. A few people turn around to watch the scene.

He looks uncomfortable, then smiles nervously and says, 'Absolutely not, my dear.'

'So everyone is welcome here in your church, yes?'

He sighs again, and turns and walks away without answering me, and this to me is *intollerabile*. I feel my temper fly away as I say louder, 'Father, I asked you a question.'

He stops and turns, looks at me miserably as everyone else turns to stare – everyone, that is, except the parents who are busy staring at something miniscule but fascinating on the opposite wall.

I step out of our pew and into the aisle, and I raise my head to this vicar and I say in a loud voice 'Father, tell me please. Regardless of race, gender, colour, creed or *sessualità*, is everyone welcome in your church?'

He has no choice but to tough it out, this sad vicar that Ruthie's father has sought to use as a puppet. He nods slowly, raises his hand and pronounces, 'Everyone who shows respect to the Father, the Son, and the Holy Spirit is welcome in this church.'

'Then since I am a Catholic, Father, with every respect for all three, and for the Mother Mary also, I am welcome in your church, yes?'

The vicar glances at Ruthie and Rebekah's parents, who are still staring at the wall, then he nods graciously and says 'Yes, my children, you are welcome in my church.'

'Then it is settled,' I say.

And so the funeral begins. Like all funerals, it is sad, with lots of lament, but with some people sharing happy memories of a woman I don't recognise from the descriptions they give. It's like I am at a funeral for someone else, not the Rebekah I knew. There are no references or inferences to a screaming bitch. I know it is not a nice thing, to speak badly of the dead, but the rosy picture people paint of this unknown, golden Rebekah is a long way from the black-hearted woman I knew, the intolerant, mean, ugly sister of my beautiful wife.

It is *farsesca* to me, all this praise for one face, with nothing said about the other, as if the person they are all talking about in such glowing terms was incapable of meanness. Well, wherever her halo went, I never saw it. I guess nobody but me and Ruthie saw the other side of *la cagna* Rebekah.

I wanna stand up there at the front and deliver a eulogy of my own to her, but it would not be a nice one and I would probably be thrown out of the church so like I say, if only for Ruthie, I will behave myself today. As long as nobody pushes either of us too far.

As the stupid event draws to an end and the last miserable dirge is played on the ancient organ, playing music that makes you wanna slash your own wrists, people start to leave the church. Ruthie blows her nose into one of her tissues as we start to walk out. She has kept her composure well. *Mia cara*, I am so proud of her. Even though her heart is in turmoil, she has held it together far better than I think I would have done myself, under the circumstances.

As we make it outside, some of our friends are waiting to hug Ruthie and give their condolences. They don't hang around, but before they go, they tell us they will be in the Royal Oak pub, back in town, if we wanna join them for a drink when we are ready.

Rebekah is to be buried in this churchyard; the event is about to take place. The mother stalks past us with her cat's-arse face, up towards the little rise where the open face of the grave is waiting like a dirty black mouth to receive the coffin of Rebekah. The father is nowhere to be seen. He was crying in the church so perhaps he is in the *bagno*, wiping his eyes.

Before I can grab hold of her, Ruthie is off, marching behind her mother, and she reaches her at the point where they both stand right at the edge of the open grave. Ruthie puts her hand on her mother's shoulder, but *la stupida* shrugs it off and turns away. I am horrified to watch, as others do also, as she loses her balance. With a short, sharp scream, she falls the six feet down, into her daughter's grave. Other people are screaming now too, and I am trying not to laugh, but then I see Ruthie's distress as she looks down at the shrivelled little woman in the boring black tunic, down below the surface of the ground.

I start to run, and I make it up the rise to Ruthie's side, just as two grave diggers are hauling the mother up, since she has ignored Ruthie's hand. She is covered in mud from the grave, and it looks like she landed on her ass, down there. Her cheap shoes are soaked and ruined, her hose are laddered beyond belief, and I know I have to hold it together now but I know too, that for sure I will be laughing my *own* ass off later, at this *scena ridicola* you couldn't make up if you sat for a week and thought about it.

From out of nowhere, the father arrives. He has been told of what happened and he is making sure his wife is ok, which she is, although she is shaking and crying like a stupid adolescent girl. She is covered in the clinging dark grey clay, and streaked with filth of other colours. But *il disgraziato vicario* then rounds on Ruthie with an almighty roar and lunges towards her. I see what is coming and I step in front of her and I brace myself to end up down in the grave as well, thinking that if I go I will be grabbing hold of this *uomo stupido* and taking him down there with me. But it doesn't happen.

The big bigot vicar, he stops dead in his tracks before me like a horse that stalls at a jump, as I stare him down, but he doesn't stop shouting, and he is threatening to kill Ruthie.

'You can try to kill her, you stupid, small-minded bastard, but you'll have to get through me first. So come on. Try!' I cannot resist spitting the last word into his face, and he falls silent. He is *rosso* with rage and revulsion, but he suddenly has nothing to do and nothing to say. His jaw is working and his stinking breath is hard, but that is as bad as it gets. My spit clings to his face but he doesn't try to wipe it off.

'No, Vicar? No strength to fight this dyke, huh? Just as well for you, you partisan coward turd, because one more move towards Ruthie and I will break your stupid halfwit neck and throw you into this grave to lie there forever with your crazy dead-bitch daughter.'

The mother, who has tried and failed to recover her composure, is standing next to him, still crying and caked in filth, and she steps forward and hisses around me to Ruthie;

'Dirty little tramp. We told you not to come, but would you listen? No you wouldn't, because you never knew how to listen, did you? You never cared about anyone else's feelings but your own, did you, you selfish bitch?'

I hear the sound of a loud slap, and a series of gasps from the people around us. Then I look down at my stinging hand and I realise I have myself just slapped the mother in her stupid, dirty, mud-caked face. You can hear a pin drop at the graveside. Even the thunder has stopped rumbling. We are all like statues, frozen in miserable time. Everyone is stunned, including Ruthie, including the parents, the other vicar, the other funeral-goers, and me. *Nobody* is more stunned than me, that I have done this today, at my wife's sister's funeral. Yes, the mother had it coming, but this was not the time or the place. I am *mortificato*, but will I let them see it? No, I will not. So I draw myself up and I stand defiant.

The other vicar steps up and says to me quietly, 'You are no longer welcome at this church. Please leave.'

'Don't worry, Father, I am happy to go. I would rather be anywhere else but here.'

'I told you to get rid of them,' I can hear Ruthie's father muttering in a shaky voice as she takes my arm and we begin to walk away. He moves to come after us but the detectives step forward and block his way, forcing him to stop and let us go. Ruthie and I walk in silence back down to the church and I find my phone to call a taxi. While we wait for it to arrive, a heavy-set man in a smart, well-made, dark grey suit that is perhaps just a little too tight for him in places, hurries up to us. I remember seeing him in the church, and I brace myself for more abuse, but instead he throws out his arms and draws Ruthie into a big bear hug that almost knocks his glasses off his face.

'Uncle Colin,' I hear Ruthie mumble, into his shoulder; 'you came, all the way from Houston! It's so good to see you! How many years has it been?'

He steps back smiling, still holding her arms, and says 'Too many! I'm over here for a conference and the timing coincided with being able to attend for poor Rebekah. But it's great to see *you*, Ruth! My goodness, how you've grown!

'And don't you worry about upsetting those two old fools,' he says to me, with a twinkle in his eye. 'They deserve every spit, slap and shove they ever get. It's not much fun having a hypocrite for a brother, let me tell you. He might be a man of the cloth, but he's a pretty poor example.' He sticks out his hand to me and I shake it.

'Colin Stenton, bigot-less and quite removed brother of said Vicar Michael Stenton, and generally absent uncle of Ruth and poor Rebekah, God rest her soul. I live in the States, have done for decades.'

'Gina Giordano, loving wife of Ruthie. We live in Guildford, not so far from here, actually.'

'It's good to meet you Gina Giordano, loving wife of Ruthie, with the most beautiful accent I've ever heard in my life. I think you're adorable. But I also think you'd both better scarper before things get any worse around here.'

He nods in the direction of the grave, where Rebekah's coffin sits waiting to be lowered into the earth. Ruth's father is stalking down from it towards us, abandoning his precious dead daughter about to be put into the ground. He is shaking his fist at us and the Uncle Colin, and shouting something I can't hear.

I will fight with this stupid man again if I have to, but I really just wanna get Ruthie away from here, so it is with big relief that I see the taxi coming for us, and I push her towards it.

The father is still ranting, but I ignore it and we get into the taxi. I look back to see the Uncle Colin standing in front of him, pushing him back as he tries to keep coming forward, and the two of them appear to be properly fighting as the taxi pulls away.

Ruthie is crying openly now, and I apologise, over and over again, as I let my shame come forward for what I have done. But she shakes her head.

'It's not you, Gina. I don't blame you. I'd have done the same thing if I'd been you. She was goading us, they both were. There was no way we could have avoided a scene. It had to happen. They don't want me in their lives. They will never want us in their lives. It's over. All hope is gone.'

And all of a sudden I am crying too, as I tell the taxi driver to take us to the Royal Oak where we will find solace with our friends. I finally appreciate just what my darling beautiful Ruthie feels she has lost, through no fault of her own, and how much it really hurts.

Chapter Three
- *Ruth* -

Well, that was one hell of a fucking spectacle, and I don't know whether to laugh or keep crying. Someone once jokingly told me that all the best weddings and funerals have a bit of a ding-dong involved, but that was an absolute doozy. Gina is ridiculously contrite at having slapped my mother but, like I've said several times already, I'd have done exactly the same thing to anyone who openly threatened or abused *her* in front of *me*, even if it was her own mother. It's what you do. You defend the person you love against being hurt or bullied by someone else, and it doesn't matter who they are. Just because people are flesh and blood, or close in other ways, that doesn't give them the right to be abusive or disrespectful to your partner. I would never stand for that, and I'm not surprised that Gina didn't.

    I hadn't even done anything wrong! All I did was try to reach out to my mother. It wasn't my fault, that she lost her balance and fell into the bloody grave, for Christ's sake. It wasn't like I pushed her. She simply slipped and fell, and everyone there saw how it happened, but it's the kind of thing you see happening on TV soap operas. You never imagine in a million years it will happen for real, and certainly not to *your* family. But mine's not what you'd call a normal, well-functioning family, is it? So there you go.

    Gina is off the hook, as far as I'm concerned, but she's a bit worried about an assault charge from my parents. I am too, if I'm honest, because everyone there also saw the slap, including the detectives. So even though it was provoked, it's still an assault that was witnessed by the police! They could press charges themselves if they felt so inclined, however my guess is that they would seek to avoid it. The situation of them already having their hands full with the still-unsolved family murder is complicated enough. Adding an assault charge to another person in the mix, with another emotionally charged occasion at the heart of it, isn't going to help move things forward.

Emotions do run high at funerals; I know that, and so do the detectives. But this could go one of two ways with my parents. Given that my father is a vicar, laying an assault charge against his daughter's wife may not go down at all well and he may choose to take the route of practicing what he preaches for a change, and turning the other cheek. I'm sure the detectives would advise him to do that, since my mother wasn't exactly beaten to a pulp. She was soundly slapped on her own cheek, yes, but just once, which many people might actually argue she deserved. However, Dad was more enraged than I've ever seen him, disproportionately so in fact, so they may just decide to press charges. We'll have to wait and see.

As we join friends in the pub, I go to the bar and order the drinks while Gina fills everyone in on the events at the graveside. I get back to the table to cries of incredulity from our friends as she describes the scenes at the graveside, and we're just getting settled when my phone rings. It's the detectives, informing me that they need to speak to Gina urgently. Bloody hell; by anyone's standards, that was quick. So much for respect for the grieving; I guess that's too much to ask.

'Tell them to come here if they wanna talk to me,' she says, with a typical Italian shrug. 'I'm not gonna drag my ass to their stupid station unless they arrest me and make me go there.'

Gina's casual Italian arrogance is sometimes remarkable, but it's always funny. Smirking, I relay her reaction to them and miraculously they agree to come trailing over to the pub. Nobody could say today's been boring for them, could they?

So within half an hour they turn up and Gina goes outside in the rain to talk to them. She refuses my offer of being with her for it, but I can see what's going on outside the window.

She is animated, and is shaking her head at them, but after a while her shoulders slump and she gives them a slight nod. She then turns abruptly on her heel and comes back into the pub.

Apparently my mother is demanding a written apology and if she gets it they will not press charges. Gina is to write a letter of apology, get it to the detectives for them to pass on to her within 48 hours, and if that's done the matter will be dropped. If Gina doesn't comply, she will be charged with assault. She did initially refuse to apologise but then thought better of it.

We all raise a toast to 'peace-keeping Gina,' proclaiming the apology to be the easiest course of action, and we theorise that my parents probably wouldn't press charges anyway, even without the apology, with the good vicar wanting to be seen in the best light as the all-forgiving, grieving yet still magnanimous Man of the Cloth. We're all unwilling to consider the gamble, but we're united in concluding that the whole matter was a silly mind-game on their part, aimed to get the better of Gina, to put her in her place.

They succeeded, yes, but we all agree on it being a pretty pathetic win for them, and a small price to pay for a bit of peace. And of course, since Gina doesn't give a toss about them anyway, it will hardly be a sincere apology. She'll still get the last laugh because once she has recovered her dignity (which will probably take about eight more minutes) she will be roaring with laughter, and for a long time to come, at the memory of my muddied mother and the image of her landing on her clad-in-black backside at the bottom of Rebekah's boggy grave, already half-filled with water from a morning's torrential rain.

Gina will be howling in no time, and all indignant thoughts will simply evaporate. It's all about attitude, after all, and hers is a lot healthier than that of my ridiculously uptight parents. I've never known Gina to hold a serious grudge. When outraged or angry she erupts brightly, like a glorious flaring firework. She says her piece, usually in a fast volley of indecipherable Italian, and then she goes back to being her normal, generous, delightful self.

This is a woman who feels everything keenly, and she really knows how to love. It's her primary emotion. Gina's hugs are warm and all-enveloping. Her smile is ready and infectious. She would feed the entire world, given the chance, and she is the most forgiving person I know. But her scorn is also something spectacular to behold. She can be scathing enough to make paint peel. In full flight she is like the female equivalent of the proverbial Italian stallion – powerful, intimidating, and utterly unassailable. She says what she means and she means what she says. There isn't an insincere bone in Gina's body but, she can pretend when she has to, and in this case she will. Mum and Dad will get their letter, and hopefully that will be the end of it.

Just when I think we may be on the home straight and able to finally relax and enjoy a drink with people who really care about us, and salvage something from the horrible day, the detectives waltz back in and ask to speak to *me* privately. With a sigh, I grab my umbrella and follow them outside into the torrential downpour where they inform me that they have found Rebekah's ex-boyfriend, but he has a cast iron alibi for the night she was strangled. He was at work, and a hundred and nineteen other people can prove it. The detectives did take a DNA sample from him, which he willingly gave, it seems.

I can see how disappointed they are that this lead hasn't panned out, and I feel wretched too. I think we were all pinning our hopes on the 'ex' being the culprit, so we could draw a line under the whole sorry mess and move on. But, alas, it is not to be. We are back to square one. On this day, this awful, sad, ridiculous day, the last thing I needed was more bad news.

The boyfriend couldn't tell them much about Rebekah's movements in the last days and weeks of her life. They'd been finished for a few months by the time she was murdered, and despite his alleged efforts to contact her, she would never return his calls, so he finally gave up. When questioned, he said their relationship had hit the deck because she started refusing to be intimate with him. It had gone on for months, with no explanation, and he'd finally called it quits with her. He had no idea who she might have been seeing around the time of her death, and he wasn't able to fill in any of the existing gaps in the enquiry. His and Rebekah's phone records both appear to support his claim that the pair were not in contact in the weeks before her murder. He was as devastated, shocked and angry as the rest of us, to hear the horrible news, but he's as clean as a brand-new whistle, from what they can tell.

So we are all still none the wiser about what happened, or why, or who was responsible. The fact that Rebekah's phone yields no significant clues about her plans over the last days of her life is frustrating beyond belief. Other than the missed calls she made to me, there are only two other calls on her phone for that night, one made to our father earlier in the evening, and one back from him, about half an hour before her first missed call to me. When questioned he said she rang hoping to see him and Mum for dinner and he called her back to confirm it for the following week. My parents were looking forward to seeing her, it seems, and it's just another item on my long list of things to try to accept; that I will never be invited to dinner, that Mum and Dad would rather sit in solitary silence at a yawning empty table than lay a space at it for me.

The detectives leave, apologising for having no more information. I do feel for them. Investigations of this type are probably difficult enough without having to contend with the minefield of a family feud threaded through it. But I wish they had more to go on. It's unacceptable, that the person who murdered my sister is still out there walking around. It could even be someone we know, but I can't let myself dwell on that because it's a very slippery slope, down into a seething pit of paranoia, and regarding everyone I encounter as suspicious. I'm a relatively trusting person. I have to stay true to myself and not let this so-far failed mission, to find Rebekah's killer, mess any more with my head.

We make a semblance of effort to relax and have fun at the pub, but it doesn't really work. Gina is still berating herself for having slapped a grieving woman at a funeral (circumstances notwithstanding) and is struggling more than usual to regain her happy equilibrium. I'm pissed off that Rebekah's killer is still unidentified and at large, and our friends don't really know what to say to lighten the mood. This day has taxed us all to our limits. We've all run out of steam.

So we call a couple of taxis, drain our drinks, have a much-needed group hug, and head for home. I'm looking forward to seeing Chiara, who has been spending the afternoon with our neighbours, Bryan and Adie Bostock. She has probably been horribly indulged, and will no doubt be supremely sleepy and happy. All I want to do now is sit in a comfy armchair, snuggle my sleepy daughter, inhale her wonderful Chiara-ness, pull my scattered thoughts together, and let sanity resurface for what's left of the day.

Chapter Four
- *Gina* -

What a fucking day. I am so glad it is finally *finito*. I was not hungry tonight but Ruthie made poached eggs on toast for us. It is one of our favourite mini-meals, and after eating it I do feel better. But what a fucking day. It is a day we are both glad to see the riddance of.

Ruthie's mother, *la megera*, what a horrible person she is! I'm sorry I slapped her, but only because it might make things more difficult for Ruthie. If it was up to me, I would have slapped her again, and again after that, and thrown her back into that sodden clay-pit they call a grave, and I would have left her there. And that father of hers; he is one crazy *bastardo*. Yet again, I am finding it hard to imagine that my beautiful gentle Ruthie came from that crazy, fucked-up family.

So; I have to apologise to Cats-Arse? And she wants it in writing? Well that is easy for me, because I don't have to stand in front of her and pretend to be *sincero,* which is not an easy thing for me. Better to write it and pull faces while I do it, and imagine throwing *la stupida* back down into the dirt, so she gets a letter that sounds sincere but is laughing at her more than she will ever know. She looked such a mess today after falling into that grave. *Donna ridente*, everyone will remember her like that, with a kilo of mud hanging off her. At least it made that boring black dress look a little interesting for a minute. *Cagna triste*, she really showed herself, hissing and spitting like a mud-caked viper. Yes, it is a day we are glad to see the riddance of. There will never be another day quite like today.

Ruthie has been laughing tonight, which is wonderful to see. She came into our bedroom, and caught me taking off my slutty-tits bra and *volgare* crotchless pants as I was changing my clothes. I did not have chance to take it all off and hide it in the trash before she saw it. I was *mortificato*, to be seen in such horrible things that had started to give me a rash with the cheap chafing lace, and my face was burning with shame.

I told Ruthie she was never meant to see them, nobody was; that I wore them only for Rebekah. I expected her to be angry or troubled by my big *flagrante* intent to be disrespectful, but she thought it was funny to see me in such terrible underwear.

'It's kind of a turn-on', she said to me laughing, 'you look fantastic, actually. Keep it on, darling. Let me make love to you in it. You can be my cheap bitch for the night, if you want.'

But I was sure she really didn't mean that, since Ruthie adores fine things like silk pants and lace camisoles. She would never wanna wear or even see something that a whore would wear. I looked at her and I couldn't tell if she was serious or not, but then she bellowed with laughter, so I started laughing too, and then we were both *isterico* for a little bit. The image of her mother like a dug-up corpse, caked in mud and bristling with *indignazione*, it really had me going, and Ruthie howling at my underwear; the laughter would not stop.

It lightened things a little, and we needed that. Ruthie has been very burdened by the death of Rebekah. She is upset that there are yet no leads to finding the person who killed her sister. As much as I have no care that Rebekah is dead, I do hope they find out soon, who killed her, so that Ruthie can find some peace. And in spite of everything, I hope that Rebekah can finally be at peace too. Such *un'anima torturata*, it is sad that she could not find the truce in life with Ruthie. I wonder what was really going on in that crazy screwball head.

The police are very slow. It takes a while I guess for DNA results to come through, but it will be interesting to me to see who that *povera ragazza stupida* was screwing, if they can find out. They are trying to see if there is a DNA match with anyone on their files with a criminal record. Rebekah fucking a criminal, or maybe even four? That is a pretty sharp stick in the eye for the pious, pathetic vicar and his Cat's Arse wife.

And of course if there is no criminal man involved, maybe there will be no DNA match, and the situation will go on and on. How do the police find someone they have no suspicion about? Not just one man, but four they need to find. It is a big task.

Ruthie is struggling to believe it all, and I am a little, but not quite so much as she, because it looks a little different to me. There was big stuff going on with Rebekah. I always felt it, so this is not the biggest surprise we could get, at least not for me. It is obvious now that she was a *cavalla nera*, and we might find out soon just how dark. But no self-respecting grown woman I know would have party sex. And it must have been party sex, because it certainly didn't look like rape, and with cocaine and alcohol involved it was probably more like fun. Rebekah must have been high as a kite, and letting all those men screw her every which way, all at once, it was probably a fine time for all of them. Unimaginable to me, and even harder and more horrible for poor Ruthie to know it, about her little sister.

It's the kind of thing you see in a low-class porn film; a woman with lots of men, everyone moaning and screaming, begging for more, like it's fun. Maybe it is, but maybe they're only being paid to act like that and it's all just for the cameras and the people who buy it and watch it. So what was it like for Rebekah? *Consensuale*, the police said. So, no porn film, acted out for money. There was no big money at Rebekah's flat, or in her *borsa*, or even in her bank account, so it looks like it was just fun. That's what it seems like to me. She was one fucked-up bitch.

Chapter Five
- Ruth -

I jolt awake to the sounds of breaking glass and someone shouting, but I can't make out what they've said. The house is suddenly deathly quiet again, and I can tell by Gina's deep rhythmic breathing that the noises haven't woken her. She is soundly sleeping. I lie here in bed for a minute or two, stock still, heart pounding. My ears strain to hear any further sound, but there's nothing.

I get up and pad stealthily across to Chiara's room to make sure she wasn't disturbed either but, like her mother, our child generally sleeps like a stone. She is curled up with her dark hair fanned out across her pillow with Craney, her old, loved-up, one-eyed, half-bald giraffe, tucked tightly under her chin. She has somehow managed to kick the duvet off herself, but I feel a chill in the air so I gently cover her again.

It seems nobody but me has heard anything. I stand at the top of the stairs for a moment or two, straining to hear the slightest sound. Although I can hear nothing, I venture quietly downstairs anyway, in the heavy darkness. There's a torch in the hallway, hanging just behind the front door and I lift it silently off its hook and continue through the house, half-holding my breath and bracing myself for all kinds of unhappy possibilities as I go.

However, after a few minutes of quiet exploration, I'm mystified. Despite what I heard, which was very definite, nothing appears to be amiss. I head back to bed, but I feel too unsettled to go back to sleep, particularly when nothing seems to be out of place. I'm feeling a little bit weird about that, and I start to worry if anything's wrong at the neighbours; that maybe somebody has broken in there. As I'm lying there in the dark, trying to decide what to do, Gina rolls over and mumbles something totally incomprehensible, then falls back to sleep with a 'snicket;' my term for the comical, hitched half-snore she often comes out with in her sleep.

I'm now too concerned about next door to drop off again, so I get back up, grab a dressing gown from the hook on the back of the bedroom door and go back downstairs. I slide my feet into my funeral shoes that are still sitting by the door where I quickly kicked them off as we came in earlier. Gina thinks it's hilarious that my shoes are always the first thing to come off whenever I get home, even before I take my coat off.

I edge out through the door, into the darkness. I stop on the front porch, listening for sounds in the cul-de-sac that might account for what I heard, but the silence is settled. The rain that has soaked everything all day has finally stopped, but there's not even a barking dog or a hooting owl to puncture the dark blanket of night.

Prowling around my neighbours' garden in the dead of night isn't something I would normally dream of doing, and it vaguely occurs to me that I must look quite ridiculous in a fluffy dressing gown and four-inch black patent pumps. But that breaking glass sounded so sharp and clear, and there was definitely shouting.

I'm at the back of Bryan and Adie's house and debating whether to call the police anyway, even though I can't see anything out of place anywhere, when I am suddenly startled by a light snapping on in the kitchen, the back door opening, and my neighbour gruffly demanding 'Who's there?'

'Oh! Bryan, it's only me; Ruth. I'm so sorry. I heard the sound of breaking glass, and someone shouting, I just wanted to make sure you were alright.'

Bryan Bostock is fifty-five. He's a construction worker with his own successful company. He is built like a brick shithouse with hands the size of shovels and a neck like a prize bull. He's the kind of guy even the most brazen of burglars would decline to mess with. He'd eat an intruder for breakfast and spit out the bones, but that hasn't stopped me from being concerned about his and Adie's safety in the dead of night.

'Thanks, Ruth. Bloody hell you gave me a fright, though! I just saw a moving shadow out of the corner of my eye from the kitchen. I nearly shit myself! Looks like that security light needs fixing. I'm up with heartburn again,' he adds. 'I think I'm going to have to stop eating curries right before I go to bed. But everything's alright here, Ruth. Whatever it was you heard, it's not around this house. Sound does carry across the night, so don't be too worried. Whatever it was, it was probably miles away. Go back to bed, love.'

'Ok, Bryan, I'll do that, although I doubt if I'll sleep.'

He looks at me thoughtfully. 'Do you want to come in for a cup of tea?'

I think for a few seconds. Actually, it might be good to sit for a short while with someone who's not involved in the whole Rebekah thing.

'That would be really nice, thanks Bryan, if you're sure you don't mind?'

'Not a problem. It takes a while for this medicine to kick in anyway, and I'm sure a cup of tea will help me as well.'

He opens the door wider and I step into his back porch. It smells of dubbin and dog, and I turn to see Creole, Bryan and Adie's ageing German Shepherd, sitting up in his bed, blinking at me. His ears are pricked and his tongue is lolling, and he gets up, stretches, yawns and comes over for a pat.

'Hello, Creole, old thing. You're not much of a guard dog, are you?' I say, as I fondly ruffle his ears.

'He's nigh on bloody useless these days, Ruth. I'm sure the old boy's going deaf. I might have to get him some company, a Jack Russell or something else he can still feel superior to, because we do need a sparky dog that will bark at anything untoward, and Creole's a bit long in the tooth to be woken up by a menacing babe in skyscraper heels and a sky blue bathrobe!' He crosses his eyes and chuckles, and I laugh too.

'It's a dressing gown Bryan, and if you call me a babe again I'll crack that bloody teapot straight over your head.'

Bryan gives me a cheeky grin, pulls out a chair for me, and sets about filling the pot with tea. He and his wife Adie have been the most wonderful neighbours to us, right from the beginning. They moved into the house next door to us a few years ago now, and before the departing removal truck had even turned the corner of the street to leave them on their lonesome, Adie was on the doorstep with an invitation for us to go over for tea and muffins, explaining that she and Bryan were keen to make connections as soon as possible to help them settle into the neighbourhood.

We never even knew the house next door had been for sale, but we didn't really know the previous neighbours. They'd largely kept to themselves. So it was with real delight that we all started getting to know one another quite well from the beginning, and it wasn't long before a firm bond was established.

Adie makes a mean batch of blueberry muffins, and since Gina also loves to cook, they spend a lot of time exchanging recipes, and trying one another's concoctions.

I'm no great shakes as a chef. I can do the basics well enough, but I leave the creative stuff to Gina. She cooks the typical Italian way, with a dash of this, a pinch of that and a handful of the other; instinctively knowing how to make a dish taste amazing without the need to measure anything that goes into it. My baking is so poor, I'm the one you'd come too if you wanted your shoes resoled with what doesn't pass for a Victoria sponge, and I used to regularly overcook the roast chicken until I found a pink plastic pig-shaped timer stuffed into the toe of my Christmas stocking one year.

Gina laughs at me for my lack of creative talent in the kitchen, but she does it with affection. When we want something simple, I do the cooking. When it's time for something a little more interesting, Gina steps in and commandeers the kitchen with a truly terrifying zeal. Chiara and I generally respond by scuttling for the safety of the living room. Gina doesn't appreciate help in the kitchen. It drives her mad.

The Bostocks are solid, salt-of-the-earth people. They mind their own business but their door is always open to us and they're always on hand to help in a jam or a crisis. We've had a few of Bryan's speciality barbecues with them in the summertime, which we fell into the pattern of pretty quickly after they arrived on the scene. Adie typically hosts a Christmas Eve cocktail party too, because it's her birthday, and we're always invited.

Gina bakes them a *Colomba di Pasqua*, a special Italian Easter cake, every year and we often stop for a quick coffee (or a cool glass of wine if it's hot) on a weekend or a summer's evening if we all happen to be working in our gardens at the same time.

So we have our little traditions, neighbourly rituals that enrich what's developed into a really nice, gentle and respectful friendship. Chiara loves Adie and Bryan, and they have watched her on plenty of occasions, including times at short notice when we've been let down by babysitters. Their own kids have grown up and left home, but I think Adie still can't resist a baby or a child. She adores Chiara and never misses a chance to connect with her. We look after Creole for them from time to time too, when they go on holiday and can't take him with them. Each household has a spare key for the other, and we've all got one another's numbers stored in our cell phones.

For all that, we're not in each other's pockets. If we all happen to be busy, weeks can go by when we don't see one another, and I haven't told them any real details about my family issues. They heard about Rebekah's death of course, since it was all over the papers, and they put a heartfelt condolence card through the door after it happened, but that was the extent of their communication about it. They are incredibly respectful people who would never push to know details I don't want them to have.

As I'm sitting here in the dead of night with Bryan, Adie comes downstairs. She heard our voices, and I apologise for waking her up but she just smiles sleepily at me, and mutters something about the menopause messing with her sleep patterns anyway. She asks me very gently how the funeral went, since it was Gina who had picked Chiara up from them while I was in the shower, in a vain attempt to sluice off some of the horror of the day.

Quite unlike my usual self, I suddenly feel the urge to start talking, so I do, and before I know it I'm telling both of them my whole miserable sordid story.

I do say, at intervals, that they can stop me if they don't want to hear any more, but Bryan shakes his head and stays silent, letting me tell it all. Adie is sitting there with a frozen, horrified look on her face, but she doesn't run from the room, or tell me to stop, and I'm finding the whole experience of unloading quite cathartic, like I really *need* to do this. I think they probably understand that it's helpful to me, to offload to someone relatively impartial who doesn't have a vested interest in solving either the case or my family problems, or both. Bryan and Adie just listen, and Bryan pulls the appropriate faces from time to time. Adie seems entirely spellbound and unable to speak. They both let me run my course.

'So we're still none the wiser about who killed her or why,' I conclude, 'and it's starting to get a bit tedious. All we want are answers and, of course, for whoever did it to be hauled off the bloody streets.'

Adie speaks quietly, and she appears to be choosing her words with great care. I'm surprised to find her trying not to cry, and her voice is scratchy, like she's about to lose it altogether.

'I'm so sorry Ruth, for your loss, and for the anguish. We've never talked much about your past, and although you've mentioned that your parents don't approve of Gina, I never knew you had such terrible problems with your family. I'm so sorry they've been so horrible to you. That must make everything *so* much harder to bear!'

She swallows, hard, and I'm astonished at how much my story seems to have affected her.

Bryan thinks for a minute or two and then says; 'Ruth, Adie and I are very fond of you and Gina, and Chiara. We've never known about your family situation, so we've never known how hard all that must have been for you, and for Gina.' He looks at Adie.

'I think I can speak for both of us when I say that we'd never want to press you about anything, or seem like nosy neighbours, but you and Gina are more than just neighbours to us now, after all this time. If either of you were our daughter, we'd be bloody proud to call you such, and if you ever want to see us as some kind of surrogate Mum and Dad, that would be ok. I mean, I know there's not even a full generation difference, but we're probably not *so* far off the age of your parents, or Gina's, and whatever wisdom we might have gained over our lives, well, you're both welcome to it any time, if it would help.'

Adie spoke again, her voice still thick with emotion. 'Yes. We're on the same page with that. And of course Chiara is like a granddaughter to us anyway, since neither Matthew nor Teresa has produced anything for us yet.' She says this about her own grown-up and gone children, then Bryan picks up the thread with a light chuckle and continues;

'But they're only young yet, of course. And even if or when they do have kids of their own, there'll always be enough love to go around, Ruth. Don't you worry about that. We're not the sort of people who could switch our affections, like the ones who call themselves your mum and dad.'

'We'll always be here for you all,' Adie states quietly. She looks a little peculiar, like someone's hit her with a brick, but since I've never seen her only-just awake before, I'm sure it's just that Bryan and I have woken the poor woman up from what was probably a deep slumber. She is too nice to admit it, that's all. Their warm, well-meant words are like a salve to my soul, and I struggle not to cry as I sit there in their quiet kitchen, in the dead of night, sipping my warm tea.

Unused to such kindness, I just look at them both and nod, unable to speak. Adie grabs my hand, squeezes it for a moment, and then lets it go. I'm surprised that she is crying, and I find it ridiculously ironic that people as down-to-earth as she and Bryan can accept me and my little family as if we were their own, and treat us as normal, when my own holier-than-thou flesh and blood can't manage it.

We sit in silence for a few minutes, all with our own quiet thoughts, and clutching our cooling teacups. Then I drain mine and stand up, remembering I've left the front door off the latch, leaving the two people I love most in the whole world vulnerable while they sleep. I hug Bryan and Adie goodnight, and go home, but I don't feel quite ready to go back to bed. The prospect of sitting in the house alone in the dead of night doesn't appeal so I decide, instead, to sit for a while on the front doorstep and watch the stars. I wonder at their wisdom; how much do they see, and what they would tell us about it all if they could?

So many different thoughts are tumbling around in my head. I went to bed calmly enough, after the funeral, after dinner, but I woke up a few hours later with my head like a blender. Something happened to me while I slept. Something changed. My brain somehow kicked into overdrive, and even my mood is different now than it was when I went to bed. I'm feeling introspective, as if being quiet, still and alone is what I need now. I feel a deep need to let the blender run its course, so my thoughts can eventually settle in their own good time, things can sink in fully in their own way, and I can find a place in my head where I can live with the all the rejection, pain and loss that has finally engulfed and submerged me today.

The events of Rebekah's funeral have made it abundantly clear to me that I now have to try and reconcile myself to the loss of my family proper. For too many years now, I've been holding onto the forlorn hope that one day my parents would have some sort of religious or moral epiphany and decide to accept me, my wife and our child, as part of their family.

My father would argue in church that all living beings are part of God's family but, privately, he clearly has a different view. I no longer think it has as much to do with me being lesbian as it does to do with the fact that I just never measured up to the golden girl, Rebekah.

There was always an underlying expectation; never articulated but always there. I sensed it, growing up; the assumption that I would 'mend my errant ways,' learn to conform and eventually become someone significant out in the world, to make up for the fact that I was such a crushing disappointment at home. That was bad enough, but it was made so much worse by the relentless, smothering sense of failure. Even though I never knew exactly what my parents' expectations were, I just knew I'd never meet them. I'd never be worthy of their love or respect. I'm too strong a character to bend to their will, I think, and that was the biggest betrayal of all to them. They couldn't mould me. I was born as my own person, and I have continued to be my own person for my whole life. I've always known who I was, and what I wanted in life, but that has never been good enough for my family.

Who should you be true to – others, or yourself? It's a really important question that many people wrestle with, but it's always been clear to me. I've never been capable of pretending to be someone I'm not, and I wasn't going to make myself sick in trying. Now I'm starting to realise that even if I had gone that far in trying to please them, it still wouldn't have been enough, because where I was concerned, my parents simply weren't capable of having unconditional love for me. They managed it with Rebekah but, for some reason, not with me. And I came along first! So did they *never* love me? Or did they just switch the love they first had from me to Rebekah, when she was born?

Their attitude doesn't make sense to me at all, especially when I think about loving little Chiara the way I do. The fact that she's not my flesh and blood is irrelevant. There's nothing I wouldn't do for her. She's my daughter and I'd fight to the death for her. As such, feeling the way I do, I can't comprehend the way my emotionally impoverished parents think.

But here's the thing; I can't keep asking why. I have to stop all this; driving myself to despair over things I can't influence or change, despite my best efforts. I can't keep doing all this soul-destroying shouting, into a big black hole, and never hearing anything back.

I have to let it go now; all of it. It's their shit, not mine, and I'm realising that everything my well-meaning friends said was right. It *is* my parents' loss, and Rebekah's too. I'm a good person, and I know that. I don't need them to affirm that for me. It would have been lovely to have had their approval and their blessing for the way I've chosen to live my life, and although I'll never have that now from Rebekah of course, I'm realising that it will never come from my parents either, and it's their choice, not mine. I've always left the door open, in the hope that one day they'd walk through it. They never have, and after today I know they never will.

So I have to give up now, and walk away. They've made their choice and now I have to make mine. I can let this eat me up and cast shadows over all I have in my life that is wonderful. Or I can let my parents go, and let their poison wash off me as I keep walking forward with my head held high, and concentrate on what makes me and my beautiful little family happy. I have to shut that door. If I leave it open, I could never stop expecting or hoping, on some level, that one day they might step through it.

Hope is the hardest thing to let go of, when you want so much for something to change, and admitting defeat and walking away is acknowledging the end of all hope. It's gut-wrenching and heartbreaking, but that's what I now have to do. I *have* to close that door, accept that my sister is dead, and accept that my parents may as well be. Rebekah is gone forever, along with any opportunity for reconciliation. My parents have chosen not to be a part of my life either, or to allow me to be part of theirs, so I now have to save myself, choose Chiara and Gina as my one true family, and let that be enough.

Grief takes many forms, and there's no prescribed formula for getting through it. Whoever you are, you feel whatever you feel, and you go through it in your own way. You just have to let it happen and hope that you have enough support around you to stop you from going completely mad in the process of working your way through it. So as I sit here in the quiet shadow of the front porch, safe in the comforting darkness, while I stare at the twinkling stars and a few graceful satellites drifting silently across the sky, as the world turns gently and inexorably on its axis, I decide to let go of all that belongs in the past.

After what feels like an hour, the night chill starts to get the better of me so I stand, step back into the house, and close the front door quietly behind me while the all-seeing stars wink their support. The upstairs landing light snaps on.

'Ruthie? Ruthie, is that you?' Gina stands sleepily at the top of the stairs blinking in the light and looking down at me. She is peering at me slightly, and I remember she'll have taken out her contact lenses. She's as blind as a bat without them.

'Yes darling, it's only me. I heard a noise and I went to investigate, that's all. But don't worry, everything is fine.'

'You were gone for a while. Where did you go?'

'I thought something might be wrong next door, at Bryan and Adie's. I went to take a look, to make sure nothing was amiss over there. But it's all fine. Bryan was up though, with his heartburn, and then Adie got up as well, so we all had a cup of tea together. Then I sat stargazing for a bit. Contemplating my navel. That's why I've been gone a while.'

'Ok, but what kind of noise did you hear, *cara*?'

I explain that I heard the sound of breaking glass and someone shouting, but could find nothing wrong, either in our house or next door. With a typical shrug Gina turns around and shuffles, yawning, back to the bedroom. I follow, switching the light off as I go, and we get back into bed. I put my arms around her and snuggle into her warmth, pushing away my anxiety about what I heard, and concentrating instead on Bryan and Adie's lovely offer of ongoing support and friendship.

As I feel myself start to drift away on a gentle tide of warm comfort, my last thought is the hope that nobody has been hurt by broken glass or someone else's temper. The next thing I know, it's morning.

Chapter Six
- Adie -

When I first found my daughter I wanted to wade right in, with champagne and sparklers, and a hiss and a roar, and tell her she was mine. I had the most overwhelming, irresistible urge to approach her, to declare myself. My heart was singing arias over finally managing to track down the child I'd signed away within two hours and fourteen minutes of giving birth, and missed for more than thirty years thereafter, like a limb torn from my body. But, on the brink of giving into the primeval urge to surge forward and lay claim to my flesh and blood, something stopped me from standing up and being counted. Call it cowardice if you want, but when push came to shove, I bottled it. I couldn't make myself approach her.

It wasn't that I didn't want to meet her, or find out who she was inside and out. The deep longing within me to establish a relationship with her had grown into a physical ache, like the toothache you can always feel, even when it's receded for a bit between the bouts of silent savagery that keep you awake and cringing half the night. Sharp or dull, depending on how it decides to take you, the agony is always there.

But by the time I found the beautiful woman my child had become, she had a lovely life all nicely pulled together, thank you very much and, let's face it, so did I! Nobody left alive in my family knew a single thing about what had happened to me all those years ago when I was fifteen years old, and I've long since lost touch with anyone who may have remembered anything untoward, like me disappearing for six months to 'stay with an aunt' for the duration of my clandestine confinement. Even my best friend Miranda, who I've known since I was in primary school, never knew where I *really* went over the summer holidays in Year 10, or why I was so late in coming back. I told her it was glandular fever, and she never questioned it.

So my baby remains to this very day the secret she started off as, thirty-seven years ago, and revealing it now after all this time? Well, the cost could be colossal. I've worked all my grown-up life to put those early years behind me, make a new life, and have a family of my own; children that were planned, who nobody could take away from me or force me to give up.

The last thing my family needed now was for life as we all know it to come crashing down around our ears. No; I made my choice, long-since, to stay silent and let the matter rest. I've accepted that I'd somehow have to live with my secret for the rest of my life.

I really thought I'd succeeded, too. I've made a happy life with a nice husband and two gorgeous children who have grown up well. Matty and Teresa have both become wonderful, well-functioning independent adults, in spite of what mistakes Bryan and I might have made in the course of raising them. Bryan is a decent enough husband, when he's actually around, and my kids are amazing human beings. We've had a solid, secure family life together, and I always hoped it would be enough.

But I was kidding myself, that the hole left by what I'd had to surrender had been perfectly plugged, because it hadn't. Decades of denial had all been futile. Having never heard a single, solitary detail of what might have happened to my baby in all that time, I finally had to give in to my intense longing to find her. So I set the wheels in motion, telling myself that once I found her I would decide at that point, what to do about telling her or my family. I knew in my heart that it would be enough, initially at least, just to know who and where she was, and whether or not she was happy.

But the records of the adoption had been closed at the outset of proceedings and the agency wouldn't entertain my requests for information about her.

'A deal's a deal,' the pitiless, nonchalant and vaguely insulting clerk had implied. 'You gave up all rights to the child when you gave her away, so tough luck, old tart.'

She hadn't *said* those words aloud, but I'd heard them through her attitude, nonetheless.

I left that building feeling judged and condemned, and wondering how the hell anyone like that could be in a job where sensitivity was so important, in letting someone down.

Determined not to be thwarted by such small-minded prejudice, I hired a private investigator. Two months later, in return for an exorbitant fee, she delivered a small, thin envelope to me containing everything she'd been able to find out. The meagre file held scant detail other than my baby's name, the names of her adoptive family, her marital information, educational history, occupation, and current address. Copies of her birth and marriage certificates were included, along with copies of her various degree transcripts. There was nothing like as much information as I'd hoped for, or believed I'd actually paid for, but it was more than enough to get me started on finding out more about her.

I learned that she had been adopted by a vicar and his wife, and christened Ruth Ann. They'd since gone on to have a child of their own, another daughter, and the family had lived for a time just forty miles from where Bryan and I and our kids were living. If they'd been much closer they could have all gone to the same school!

My beautiful girl had gone on to university, studied history, graduated with a master's degree and was now a lecturer at the same university. She was also completing a PhD on the diversity of modern attitudes to the historical context of marriage. She was settled in a marriage herself, with a female partner, the dress designer Gina Giordano.

That was an extraordinary nugget to find! Most women I know are familiar with the incredibly exclusive Giordano label. Most can't afford to buy even the most basic of beautiful pieces, but it's certainly something they dream about.

The report stated that the couple had a child, a baby girl, to whom Gina had given birth. Ruth was listed as the other legal parent to this child, Chiara Giordano.

So it appeared that Ruth had a pretty decent life mapped out, which raised the critical question for me: would declaring myself to this woman help her in any way, or would it blow her settled existence apart? She was, after all, a complete stranger to me in all but the biological sense. What if she didn't even know she was adopted? If not, what would it do to her, and her family, if she found out? I realised how big a deal this really was; that in stepping forward in my own self-interests I could do all kinds of damage. Since the investigator I'd hired said she couldn't find any evidence to say Ruth had ever been told, I couldn't make myself take the risk.

Furthermore, what if the simple selfishness that propelled me to try to claim a place in her life actually worked and she then decided she wanted to be in my life too? Could I put my husband, son and daughter through all the trauma of finding out that their mother had had a baby at fifteen, given it away to total strangers, zipped her mouth about it, and then gone on to build a big, grown-up life for herself as if butter wouldn't melt in that mouth? What would they say to all that?

Or would I have to keep Ruth under wraps, to protect myself, my family, and quite possibly hers as well? Could I continue to treat her as a secret, once we'd made a meaningful mother-daughter connection? It would mean leading a double life, and expecting her to as well. I've kept my secret all these decades, about a long-lost child, but I'm pretty sure I couldn't carry on lying to my family about something as huge in my life as the *return* of that child!

When my parents forced me to adopt my baby, I went through all kinds of hell. I hated them for it. I hated *myself* for it and in later years, after leaving home and building my own life, I could never really understand why I'd never had the guts to stand up to them. I let them bully me so hard into giving my baby away. It was the 1980's, for Christ's sake, not the 1890's! I had rights. But I was far too young and naive to know what they were, and it's not like the authorities were queuing up to tell me.

All my getting pregnant had amounted to was a simple fumble with a boy I only vaguely fancied, and his half-successful attempt at penetration that didn't even seem all that significant to a nervous virgin. It had happened in briefest of moments, before I even had time to really register what he was doing, around the back of the school hall after a glass of spiked punch at the summer prom. I struggled to believe that something so pathetic could actually result in a pregnancy, but I found out the hard way just how determined sperm could be. By the time I'd gone three months without a period, the inevitable finally hit me. I was shocked and scared to death, and I didn't know what to do.

So I let my parents decide. It wasn't about *shame*, they said, and I did believe that. They weren't ashamed of me. They just thought I could do without everyone in my small village full of small-minded people sniggering at me, pointing fingers and talking behind their hands in the corner shop whenever I walked by. They wanted me to be able to hold my head up, and they didn't want the local boys thinking one mistake made me easy, or untouchable with a bargepole by any from a 'decent' family. Villages are funny places. Tolerance can turn to contempt in the blink of an eye for the exact same things that no one thinks twice about in bigger towns and cities.

I understood what they were trying to do. They wanted more for me than being the butt of everyone's gossip or jokes in a place I had to feel comfortable about calling home. I needed to feel that I always could, and hopefully always *would* call it home, at least to some degree, and I couldn't have done that if I'd been ostracized or ridiculed by the people there.

My parents also wanted me to finish my education, have my full youth, and find my true place in life through establishing what I liked and was good at doing. In their view, being stuck with something forced upon me before other opportunities even had time to present themselves was too life-limiting, and I have to admit they were right.

Had I been eighteen, of course, it would have been a different story. But being still technically a child, I was deemed (correctly) to be too young to raise one, and my parents didn't want to take it on. I'd been a 'surprise' to them myself, arriving a decade and a half after my brother Raymond, as a peri-menopausal baby Mum never expected to have. So by the time I popped up pregnant, my mother was already pushing sixty, and my dad was sixty four. They'd more or less raised their kids, they'd done their bit. How could I have expected them to spend however many more years mopping up the mess I'd made? They might not even have lived long enough for me to have established enough stability to take the child back to live with me.

Although we discussed it, Mum and Dad weren't comfortable with the thought of an abortion, and that was – absolutely – the right decision. I look at Ruth now, and I marvel at her beauty, her life, and all she has to strive and live for. I'm so very, very glad that I didn't get my way on that, at least; that we didn't wipe her existence from the world, because she so enjoys her place in it, and she has so much to offer it. At fifteen years of age, I laboured to give life to her, and of all the things I have so many regrets for in my own life, that could never be one of them.

Anyway, after a great deal of soul searching, I decided I didn't have the right to turn her world upside down. But I wanted to work out a way of still being close to her, and when I saw where she lived, a plan began to form in my head. Once it started, it turned into a juggernaut that simply couldn't be stopped.

When I knocked on the door of the house next to Ruth and Gina's, telling the owners I was interested in buying if they were interested in selling, my heart was in my mouth. I could hardly believe my own cheek. But, as I kept telling myself, we actually did need to move. The kids had more or less left home. They were at university and didn't often come home to stay, even between terms, so we no longer needed as much room.

Our huge house and garden had been perfect for small children who liked to run amok but, after they grew up and became more interested in videogames and i-phones, when it became just Bryan and me again, it all started to feel like simply too much to manage, with a building boom stealing his every waking hour. I was running out of the kind of stamina the house and garden demanded, even with domestic 'help.'

We had outgrown the house in reverse, in a manner of speaking. At twenty, Matty was already working part time and saving for his own home for when he finished uni and started a career, and I reasoned if we sold our big one we could probably help both kids with an invested nest egg that they could each build a solid future with, in just a few years' time. It made a lot more sense than providing for an inheritance they might have to wait decades to get their hands on.

I was fairly sure Matty would use his chunk as a deposit for a home of his own. Where he was the solid, dependable 'plodder-with-a-plan,' Teresa was more impulsive and flighty. I could see her flatting with her uni friends for a good while longer, or backpacking around Asia or something, with her hair tied up in a messy knot and leather bracelets around her wrists and ankles, before she settled into home ownership. But the time would definitely come and, as different as Matty and Teresa were, they had one big thing in common; they would be going their own separate ways from us completely, in no time at all. They wouldn't want their bedrooms again, and what better way to offset the final painful throes of accepting the impending empty nest and rattling around in a ridiculously oversized house, than with a project like redecorating a new and more manageable one? Moving into a gorgeous new house and making it my own felt like just the kind of project I needed.

Somehow, it felt like the right thing to do. My ulterior motive made the rationalizations easy, of course, so I chose the time, turned up unannounced at Ruth's neighbour's front door, and made my best pitch.

It took a great deal of wrangling over price and chattels, but we settled on a deal, and although some of the finer details went a lot more in their favour than ours, I was ready to agree to almost anything under the sun that would enable me to move in next door to my lost, first-born child. I could keep a loving eye on her, even if she never got to know who I really was. That was a price I was willing to pay, forevermore, to be able to see her often and be even just a tiny part of her world as a caring neighbour and hopefully friend. It was either that or nothing, so it wasn't even a choice, really.

Bryan and the kids were astonished when I announced that I'd gone out by myself and bought a new family home. I'd never done something so huge, impulsive or exclusive before, and it took them a while to get their heads around it. The kids protested (predictably) at how much longer it would take them to get to and from uni on the train when they came to stay over.

Only Bryan seemed to take it in his stride. He wasn't happy at all, to begin with. He loved the big house, even though he hardly spent any time in it. But he became philosophical about the move and, after making the obvious point that it would have been fair and reasonable to have been consulted, all he said was;

'Well, alright then, but you'll need to sort the details. I'm too busy right now with this new library build to think about something as big as a house move. Just show me what I need to sign, get our stuff packed up and shifted, and tell me the new address when it's time to move.'

So I put our huge house on the market, priced to sell, and it did within two weeks. The next thing we knew, the packers were in, and we were on the move. They say that moving house is stressful to the point where it's up there with death and divorce, but the greased-wheel simplicity of the whole process convinced me I'd made the right decision. It was like the universe speaking, telling me it was the right thing to do.

And finally I was going to be able to see my long-lost, grown-up child as often as I wanted. I could hardly contain my joy.

Ever since we moved in, I've been content to keep my secret, secure in the knowledge that I've made friends with this lovely woman. I've seen so many wonderful qualities in Ruth, and I couldn't have wished for a lovelier daughter if I'd used every magic spell in the world to create one. She is everything I always hoped she would be, for herself and to the people who love her.

She is so happy with Gina and Chiara. She also has a successful career, a beautiful house and plenty of friends who care about her. Chiara is a delight to watch grow, and Gina is so loveable too. She's the typical Italian diva, and I mean that in the nicest possible way. Her smile and her heart are huge, she is generous and expansive with her affection (and equally so with her vitriol, so it pays not to rile her if you can help it), and she is totally devoted to Chiara and Ruth. A happier, more loving little family you'd be hard pushed to ever find.

But it hasn't all been joyful, as I've just found out in the most devastating way. Tonight, Ruth unexpectedly and uncharacteristically poured her heart out to me and Bryan, and I've learned that that the very people who said they wanted her enough to adopt her have never fully loved or accepted her as their daughter! I feel utterly outraged, and desperately sad, that she has always fought for and failed to find acceptance from them. Try as I do, I just don't understand it. All I can think is that when they managed to have Rebekah; a child of their own, she somehow became more significant to them than Ruth was.

She is a gay woman, and they genuinely and wholeheartedly hate that about her, to the point where they cannot bear the sight or thought of her around them. It is so far beyond strange, I'm struggling to comprehend it. And, while we're talking about strange, it seems fairly clear to me, from tonight's conversation, that Ruth still doesn't even know she was adopted! If they couldn't or wouldn't love her, why have they kept her in the dark about something so important? It doesn't make a blind bit of sense.

Ruth's 'parents' apparently misunderstood her to the point where the only response they were capable of was to treat her with fear and loathing. It's brutal and unfair, but maybe they were such morally bankrupt people they simply didn't know any better. Just because Michael Stenton was a vicar, it didn't necessarily make him a compassionate or understanding man, did it? Sadly, not everyone who undertakes a vocation ticks all the boxes for doing it well. It was clear that he and his wife had no idea how to accept Ruth's sexual status, or the fact that she wasn't their own flesh and blood. When they had their own child, Ruth was pushed out, and when it became clear that her future lay with another woman and not a man, it was more than they could cope with, to have such an 'aberration' for a child.

She wasn't their flesh and blood, but did that somehow give them the right to be mean and exclusive? And secretive? It's pathetic, and inexcusable, and no matter how they might seek to try and justify themselves and their terrible behaviour towards her, I hate them for how they've treated my beautiful girl. Ruth's story, in the random bits and pieces she divulged tonight, was heartbreaking to hear. It was so hard for me to take in, and even harder of course to keep to *myself* how devastating it was, to learn that she had to endure that life because I gave her away!

I trusted the adoption agency when they assured me my baby would go to a loving home, and they let me down. More importantly, they let Ruth down. She was a tiny baby who deserved the very best possible life. That's what was promised, but it wasn't what she got, and I feel responsible. In giving her up, to what I thought would be a wonderful life, I condemned her instead to a loveless childhood, growing up with people who, despite saying they wanted her with all their hearts, didn't even make a proper effort to even understand who she was, let alone accept her.

It's even worse for me to know all that, also knowing that I would do anything, kill anybody I had to, to protect Matty and Teresa from harm. I'd go to any lengths necessary to keep them safe, and I don't know what true committed parent wouldn't. How that monstrous vicar and his mealy-mouthed wife could have thrown an innocent child to the wolves like that is something I'll never understand. I've never met those 'parents' of hers but one day, if everything comes out in the wash as these things are sometimes wont to do, I will make myself known to them, and I'll make sure they feel the full weight of my loathing and disgust.

But I do take comfort that Ruth is so cherished by Gina and adored by little Chiara. It is obviously the kind of loving family she really deserves, and I find it remarkable that she has turned out so well. She's a beautiful person, inside and out, and that is in *spite* of those hideous parents. Anyone with an ounce of insight would be proud to call her their daughter, as Bryan and me both hastened to reassure her tonight, but the hypocritical vicar and his loathing for lesbians? It would be laughable if it wasn't so tragic; if I hadn't seen with my own eyes the pain it has caused for far too long. And all from a man who speaks of God's love of humanity in all its imperfect forms! I always knew the church was full of brutality and hypocrisy. I just never expected it to ever reveal itself to me, or to my first-born child, in such a personally insulting and heartbreaking way.

How emotionally impoverished must someone be, to have a lovely little girl, raise her from a tiny baby for three whole years, then effectively abandon her because she suddenly doesn't fit with their family ideals anymore, about who their kids should be? Didn't they get it, that bringing up a child is not the kind of responsibility you simply walk away from when the going gets tough or something happens that you don't understand?

Fifteen or not, if I'd had the choice, I would have fought tooth and nail to keep Ruth. Its far easier to say in hindsight than it was at the time, but if I could in any way have stuck to my guns, I'm sure we'd have figured it out, as a family.

It's a terrible shame that Rebekah was murdered, and even more of a shame that such a tragedy failed to reunite Ruth with those pathetic parents. I would have liked to go to the funeral today, but an invitation wasn't forthcoming, and it didn't seem polite to impinge. I'd never met Rebekah, and I would have struggled to pay my respects in any case, to one who was so consistently horrible to Ruth, because that was one thing I did know about. She'd told me before, that she couldn't get along with her sister, but I had no idea that things were as bad as they were. That family is deeply divided, far beyond what I ever imagined, and I would have liked to have been at that funeral as a show of support for Ruth. Gina was there too of course; incredibly fearsome, no doubt, in her loyalty. I take comfort from the knowledge that Ruth wasn't isolated or alone at such a terrible event. She had people around her who really care.

Bryan and I enjoyed having little Chiara with us today. It's *always* a pleasure to spend time with that beautiful child. She's my adopted grandchild. That's so incredibly odd, when you think about it, that I adopted out my child and I now have *her* adopted child to cherish from time to time, albeit in secret form.

I hope that one day we can bring everything out into the open. Under whatever circumstances it may happen, it would certainly be traumatic for all of us, but maybe it would be a healing process too. I would love nothing more than to shower Ruth with the motherly love she deserves but has always been denied. While my dream quietly sits in the shadows, I'm not giving up hope that eventually it will come true. Until it does, I will continue to be the best neighbour and friend that darling little family could wish for. They deserve that, and so much more besides.

Chapter Seven
- *Matthew* -

So, Becky Starr wasn't her real name. It doesn't surprise me all that much, with her being so in-your-face about her somewhat unusual sexual preferences, shall we say, but being dragged into the cop shop and held on suspicion of murder is a hell of a way to find out that she's dead, and she wasn't who she said she was. If that's what I get for being obliging in the past, and providing a 'rule-out' DNA swab to help police eliminate me on a different matter, I won't be so keen to help again. Next time they want support from the public, the bastards won't be finding me in the queue. Next time they want anything voluntarily from me they can sing for it.

Since when do voluntary, ruled-out DNA samples get to stay on the fucking grid? That seems wrong to me, holding onto irrelevant information about innocent people. It can lead to all kinds of corruption. You give a swab in good faith and you don't expect to be harassed years later when you *still* haven't done anything wrong. Having sex with a consenting adult isn't a crime, even if it's kinky. Anyone with half a brain knows that.

I certainly didn't murder Becky, or Rebekah as the police are calling her. Sure, we had some fun with her, and I know we should have used condoms with her, as per the agency's policy, but she always asks us not to, and she produced her usual up-to-date certificate to say she was clean as a whistle, herself. So, like good employees ever-mindful of our obligations to provide the best customer service, we gave the Client what the Client wanted.

Becky Starr always wants to be shagged without condoms, so that's what we do, and it's what we did that night. Why would any of us ever have imagined in a million years that she'd end up being strangled just 24 hours later, and our issue, (as it were) would become the major issue? We always knew the agency would go bloody mad if they ever found out about the no-condom routine, because it goes against every principle they've got, and mine too as a rule. But she's a regular; we've done her a dozen times before, we know she's kosher, and the kind of money she pays? At four times the going gig-rate, who's going to turn that down?

The agency gets clients to sign a disclaimer, so even if a condom breaks there's no come-back on the service provider. We could say that one condom broke, I suppose, but four? That's too much of a stretch, and they'll be all over this like a bloody rash, because I doubt very much if we'll be able to keep it quiet from them. In all good conscience, since the worst of crimes has been committed and I don't know that one of the other lads didn't go back there and kill the poor bitch, I'll have to give them up as the 'depositors' of the other sperm, as it were. Bang goes the most lucrative job I've ever had.

Having sex with a client without a condom is reckless, yes. It's a sackable offence and the other lads will be looking to kick my head in for that, because we'll *all* lose our jobs over it, but it's not an actual crime, is it? No, and even if it was, bareback shagging someone is a hell of a long way from being guilty of killing them as well.

Yet here I am, a suspect, and all thanks to providing a voluntary DNA swab years ago after a girl was raped in the back room of a nightclub. I was happy to help the police at the time. I didn't even know her, let alone rape her, and I figured the poor cow deserved a bit of justice, no matter what the circumstances might have been. You hear all the time about girls being raped, and the lawyers for the guys that did it trying to get them off by discrediting those poor girls by implying that they asked for it.

In my book, no means no, no matter how they're dressed, or how much make-up they're wearing, or whatever other shitty excuse those lawyers trot out, to try and get their scumbags off scot-free. If a girl says say no, that should be the end of it, and if it's not, the bastards that press on are as guilty as sin. Throw the bloody book at them.

I know some girls cry rape when there hasn't been one, but somehow it seems to be normal to treat them *all* as if they're lying. Well, they can't all be, can they? The evidence proved the nightclub girl wasn't lying, but I can only imagine what she had to go through to get the bastard convicted.

So yeah, the cops got their man over that nightclub deal, which was great, and the truth is I'd long since forgotten I'd ever given them a swab. Until last week. I didn't even think to ask them, at the time I gave it to them way back when, whether they'd be holding onto it. I guess I just figured they wouldn't, and I'm the sort of bloke who's never planned on getting into any kind of trouble, so that really was the last I even thought about it. It never even occurred to me that it could come back to bite me on the arse like this, but it has, and its proof that however clean you think you've kept your nose, you might end up having to think again.

But honestly, what agency employee would take the time to research the background of any attractive client who paid great money for group sex? It's not our job to dig into anything. We show up, do the client, leave again, and watch the payment fold into our bank accounts. That's the deal, and it's pathetically simple, really. It's why I went for it. We don't even have to think on the job, if you'll pardon the pun. I do enough thinking in my computer-programmer day job, thanks very much.

Working for the agency means I get more sex than I can shake a stick at, without the drama of a relationship that demands more than I'm ready to give. It's perfect, because the clients are always up for the sex, you never get a 'no,' it's usually pretty good, and I've even got my regulars now, like Becky, who keeps re-booking because she knows she'll always get exactly what she asks for. She's the youngest client on the books, so doing her feels as close to normal as anything could, really.

I usually work alone, or occasionally with just one colleague. Requests for gang sex are very rare; only a couple of clients want that. Most just want a decent bang with an orgasm at the end of it, and a cuddle and a cup of tea to follow. Although some are a bit past their sell-by date, so to speak, I've stopped worrying about that. A shag's a shag, and its bloody good money, and some of the older women are as good as the younger ones anyway, and nearly always grateful enough to give me a decent tip on top of the fee. One even paid for me to go on a week's holiday with my mates, and stay in her swanky villa in Spain, with its own swimming pool, stocked-up bar and everything.

Escorting's easy money and if I could keep going like I have been, I could probably pay off my mortgage in a quarter of the time it would normally take me. That was the plan, but somehow I think my gigolo days might be numbered, and soon, because this whole thing feels like it's going to turn into a proper bloody mess, and not just for me.

Becky Starr was troubled, I knew that. We see a lot, on those type of gigs – especially with women who like a lot of attention, if you get my meaning. In my book – and it's only my opinion of course – anyone who gets off on having four men fuck her at once in every available orifice has to have issues with self-respect and other things besides, but there was nothing needy or strange about Becky. She was ultra clean, and tidy too; everything neatly trimmed.

From what I could understand from general conversation, she had a job, normal friends and a normal routine. She was pretty enough, she liked to have fun, and she wasn't overly kinky or off-the-wall or anything. She was a few years older (although still a lot younger than most of our clients), but there were no warning bells, nothing about her that screamed 'run,' and I'm not so overloaded with hormones or greedy for money that I couldn't heed a nutter-warning if one reared its head. But the only thing that did rear its head was my dick, so to speak, and yeah, I followed it. We all did; all in a night's work.

Becky always said that the one night of the month we all went round there was the best night of her month, and she couldn't get enough of us while we were there. Sometimes we'd be there for a couple of hours and she was always a very enthusiastic participant. It was always a lot of fun, shagging Becky. She was a good-time girl, and no mistake.

So yeah, we did it without protection (and never again for me, no matter what), then the cops put DNA samples together, one and one make two, and now I'm a suspect in a fucking murder enquiry.

I can't even begin to imagine what Mum and Dad are going to say. I know they'll be devastated to know I do this, even though it's nowhere near as sleazy as it sounds. Mum will never understand it in a million years. Dad? I think he'll try, but I know they'll both be shocked, and disappointed too, to know what I do in my 'spare time.'

At least I don't live at home anymore, so it's a bit easier to hold off telling them anything until things get a bit clearer. I might not have to say anything at all, yet. As far as my innocence goes, and if the justice system works as it should, it's only a matter of time before everything comes out in the wash, so there's no point in freaking them out over something I'm not guilty of, is there? This could all blow over by morning.

But maybe not, because there *is* a slight problem; I can't very easily prove where I was on the night Becky was murdered. I was on another job, but without blowing the agency's reputable cover right out of the water and hanging a client out to dry, I've got no way of proving it. My mobile phone was switched off, and that looks really bad. Truth was, the battery was flat, and I had to leave it at home on charge while I went to work.

What's worse is the fact that the client I was with that night wouldn't back me up in a month of bloody Sundays, even if I begged her on my hands and knees – and I would, if I thought it would work. Rich (but neglectful) husband, high profile couple? Works her socks off for charities? Nope, old

Christine, she's got too much to lose. She'd deny my existence till the cows come home, and who do you suppose the authorities would be more compelled to believe?

So I'm a bit screwed on that count. I can't produce an alibi for the night Becky Starr was murdered. Or Rebekah Stenton, as she's really called. And that puts me, potentially, quite squarely in the shit. I'm a suspect, a proven associate, there's evidence of me being in the bedroom of her flat and she was murdered in that bedroom.

I can't prove I wasn't there. It's as simple as that. The other lads may be luckier, depending on what (or who) they were doing that night and who could vouch for them, but I can't prove I didn't leave my mobile phone at home on purpose and go round to poor Becky's flat and choke her to death. Why anyone thinks I would want to is something else again, but the cops aren't too bothered about motive, are they? No. While motive might be helpful, all they really want is evidence, and once they've got enough of that, a case can close as fast as a fucking gin-trap.

I want my bloody phone call. Like it or not, I probably do need to phone Dad, because the way these cops have been talking, I might be in need of a decent lawyer and if anyone can find the right one for the job, Dad can. He's going to be one really unhappy camper, and I can't even begin to dwell on what Mum might think. I just have to hope they have faith in the way they raised me. I might be a lot of things, including a paid male slut, but I'm not a murderer. No way. I hope they know that. I can't imagine what it would be like, for my lovely Mum and Dad, to have any doubts about whether I could do something like that.

One thing that might help is the fact that there's other DNA in Becky's flat too, and in Becky herself, from the other lads, one of whom might be her killer. I'd be very surprised if it turned out to be one of them, but in truth how would I know? You can know people for a hell of a lot longer than I've known this lot, and still not know they're completely bloody bat-shit crazy underneath that sociable, friendly demeanour. You only have to hear the neighbours of psychos who stashed victims in the walls of their houses, or buried them in the bloody garden, banging on about how shocked they are about the bloke over the back fence.

'He seemed about as normal as you'd ever expect. Quiet, kept to himself, but always said hello. We never imagined he'd be a serial killer.'

So there are at least three other people in the frame that I know of. But realistically there could have been any number of other people in there. Becky was killed the night *after* we went there, and that might be a bigger fly in the ointment for the cops than they're willing to admit, in tying it to me, but if they have any other leads, they're not saying. They haven't said jack-shit to me actually. I'm waiting to be spoken to, but I want my phone call first and right now they appear to be too busy. After arresting me on suspicion of the murder of Rebekah Stenton (also known as Becky Starr) and reading me my rights, they've more or less just left me to sit here in this grim little holding pen. Everything is grey in here, and I mean *everything*. Walls, floor, ceiling, bed and blankets. Everything bloody grey.

My good arresting officers did initially try a bit of banter when they first brought me in, which I knew better than to engage in. Then they were a bit more direct, asking me what I knew about Becky. I declined to comment. I haven't said jack-shit to them either, and I don't plan to without a lawyer, thanks all the same. Stalemate, my friends.

I wouldn't know what to tell them in any case, because Becky never talked about her personal life. We never ask a client personal questions, and we don't answer any about ourselves. It's agency policy, and it's explained to all clients before they agree to book our services that the ban on sharing personal information is intended to protect both sides from any potential blackmail. It also stops us from getting emotionally involved with them, which would be surprisingly easy if we weren't careful, because some of them are vulnerable in different ways. So we're contractually required to disregard anything they do volunteer that's personal, outside of being duty-bound to report anything relating to real or potential harm of the clients themselves or to any vulnerable people or kids in their care.

I've never had cause to do that. The clients know the drill; it's all about sex, not conversation, and they tend to be home alone, apart from the odd husband who gets off on watching his wife being shagged by a stranger. There's never been kids in a house I've been to. It would be pretty hard to get in the mood to do the job if there were.

I've just been told I can have my phone call, and it's with a real sick feeling in the pit of my stomach that I dial Dad's number. It only rings a couple of times before he picks up. He never strays far from his mobile, in fact Mum's often threatened to take him to the hospital to get it cut away from his ear.

'Dad, it's Matthew. I'm at the cop shop, Dad. I've been charged on suspicion of murder. I haven't done it, Dad, but I think I need a lawyer. Can you sort one?'

There is silence at the other end of the phone. 'Dad?' I prompt. 'Are you there?' I can hear my own voice, it sounds shaky and scared. It doesn't sound much like the normal me at all, but then these are not normal circumstances and if I'm honest I am starting to feel a bit shaky. And I might have good reason to be scared.

Dad clears his throat before answering. 'Yeah, son. I'm here. Say nothing else into the phone, and nothing to a soul down there. I've heard what you've said, and I'm on my way. Sit tight.'

The phone goes dead. I hang it up, and I'm taken back to my cell to wait for Dad, and/or whichever lawyer he manages to get hold of, to come down here and help me sort this out.

Chapter Eight
- Ruth -

It's my own piercing screams that wake me this time, 'No! NO! Stop it!'

I open my eyes to find Gina leaning over me. She looks intensely worried, and she has a tight grip on my hand. I'm sobbing and shaking, my heart is racing, and the fact that I've had a nightmare bad enough to cause those reactions makes them even more acute. I'm scared to death, shaking with fear in fact, and an almost feral panic threatens to swamp me. My face is wet with tears and my pounding heart feels like it will explode at any second and fly right out of my chest. I try to speak, but nothing comes, except for a tiny, pathetic, reed-like wail from somewhere deep inside me.

'*Cara, cara*, it's ok, it's nothing, it's just a bad dream. Shh, *la mia amore*, I've got you. You're ok, you're ok.' Gina has her arms around me now and she is hugging me tight and mumbling soothing words to me quietly in her native tongue. I cling to her while I fight to get my breath back. She rocks me gently and strokes my hair until I've calmed down a bit.

'Oh, my God', I say shakily. 'What the hell was that?'

'I don't know, *cara*. You had a very bad dream, it's all I know. You were tossing and turning, and mumbling to yourself, and breathing like you were running or something, then you started shouting and you woke up. You seemed terrified, like someone was trying to hurt you.'

I sit up in bed. I *am* terrified, and I feel as if someone *was* trying to hurt me, but I don't know who, or why. Gina props a plump pillow behind my head, and holds my hand again and strokes it. Neither of us speaks for a while then Gina says;

'It seemed to be a very bad dream, Ruthie. Can you remember it?'

I shake my head. I'm only remembering the barest bites of the dream; the faraway but still-sharp sound of splintering glass, someone shouting something aggressive, threatening me, but I can't decipher the words, then me shouting, screaming at them to go away. In vain I try to hold onto the fading fragments but they evaporate from my memory and out into the ether like smoke through futile fingers.

Gina leaves the bedroom and returns a few minutes later with a steaming mug of slightly sweetened chamomile tea. 'Here, drink this', she says. 'It will help you feel calmer, *cara.*' She also hands me two painkillers, presumably to help take the edges off whatever she thinks I may be feeling. I wave away the drugs but take the mug with trembling hands, and as I inhale the tea's sweet fragrance I do start to feel a bit calmer. I haven't woken Chiara with my screaming out loud, which is a blessing to us all.

As my breathing slowly returns to normal, I try to remember the last time I had a nightmare. I can't recall when the last one might have been, or ever having had one at all, as brutal as this one felt. I do dream, but I never manage to remember the details, and that never really matters to me. I read somewhere that dreams are the brain's way of dumping the irrelevant minutiae it accumulates in the course of the day. It makes sense to me, because I once had a silly dream where different friends kept phoning me to complain they'd lost five pence. When I gave it some thought, I realised it was after a day where the end-of-month trial balance in the accounts office at a holiday job I had at the time had been 5p short and the staff had been tearing their hair out all day trying to find it!

With the dumping theory making perfect sense to me, I've never worried about what I couldn't remember from a dream, except for the odd occasion where it's felt like a really nice one and I've woken up feeling a bit bereft from having the joy of it disappear too soon. But this feels different. This wasn't a silly or delightful dream. It was a horrible, truly nasty nightmare and rather than wanting to forget it, somehow it feels really important to me to recall the details. It's so frustrating that I can't.

I tell Gina the scant bits of what I can remember, and she reminds me that it sounds like an extension of the same dream I had a few nights ago, after Rebekah's funeral, only then I didn't realise it was a dream. It seemed too acute, too real, to the point where I actually got out of bed, checked our own house and then went prowling around Adie and Bryan's garden in the dead of night to make sure everything was alright!

This nightmare, tonight, was a lot more intense. I didn't wake up wondering what I'd heard. I woke up half-hysterical with terror, knowing I'd had a fierce, full-on sleep experience of being in a scary situation where I was acutely afraid of someone. I just can't quantify the details to make any sense of exactly what malevolence was stalking me as I slept.

I look at the clock, its 4.20am. Gina is still concerned but I know she is dog-tired from a very long day, bless her. I hug her and apologise for having woken her, but she shakes her head. 'It doesn't matter, *cara*. I wanna know you are ok. That was some dream, huh?'

I nod and sip my lovely tea. 'Yeah, it was some dream.'

'Maybe Rebekah's funeral got you rattled,' Gina observes. 'I don't blame you *cara*, but try to think of good thoughts now. Maybe we can book a holiday. Take Chiara somewhere nice? I have friends in *Sicilia* who would love to see us all. Maybe we could have a week away in the sunshine, to put this *miseria* behind us, yes? You would like *Sicilia*. It is beautiful there.'

'Sounds wonderful, my love, but maybe once they've caught Rebekah's killer? Then we can draw a line under *all* of the misery with a lovely holiday, and maybe go for two weeks, not just one, and really unwind.'

Gina shrugs and pulls one of her many little faces, most of which I know very well. This one means 'well okay, if you think that's a better idea than mine.'

The lovely little quirks and bangs that make up my beloved's personality are always fascinating to me. On this shocking night I find that focussing on how comical and sweet she is, instead of what has hurled me so savagely into being wide awake in the wee-small hours of the pre-dawn morning, helps me to regain my equilibrium. I'm sure I won't sleep again tonight, but I can rest alongside Gina, and the rhythm of her slumberous breathing will soothe me as I lie here trying to make sense of a terrifying dream that had me mewling like a kitten with fear.

I finish my tea and snuggle back down in the bed. Gina pulls the covers up under my chin and pats the duvet at either side. She gets back into bed herself, and switches off her bedside light. The room is in darkness again, and she takes hold of my hand and kisses it. I squeeze her hand in return, and for the millionth time I say a silent but heartfelt 'thank you' to my angels for bringing her into my life.

* * * * *

The morning dawns bright, and I'm amazed to find I did manage to sleep a little after the nightmare, but I feel dopey, drained and lethargic. Gina takes one look at me and decides to make me stay at home for the day. 'No work for you today, Ruthie, and that's an order.'

She has that no-nonsense tone to her voice this morning, and whenever I hear it I know better than to push my luck with her. I decide to let her be protective today, since it's clearly what she wants, and I didn't have anything concrete in my diary anyway. There are no lectures today, so it was to be a grading day anyway, and the students' assignments are all online, so I actually can work from home.

I usually enjoy the atmosphere of the university environment and I look forward to going to work, but today I'm happy to let Gina have her way. I have so little energy, I can just about make a pot of coffee and get my laptop set up at the kitchen table, and that's about it. Gina is working from home today too, on colour palettes for her next collection. I commandeer the kitchen table, she takes the one in the dining room, and it's a warmish day, so we leave the back door open to let the air flow through from the garden.

We're both well underway with our work, and it's all going absolutely swimmingly for us both, until the doorbell rings and Gina goes and opens the front door to a delivery man. The draught causes the back door to slam so hard that the top glass panel falls out and shatters all over the floor, and the next thing I know I'm on the floor too, with my back against a cupboard door, shaking and crying and gasping for breath.

Gina runs into the kitchen and sees me. *'Mio dio'*, she mutters, as she kneels beside me, her face full of alarm. 'Ruthie? Are you ok? What the hell is happening with you, *cara*? It was only a slammed door; just a pane of glass, nothing more.'

Fat tears are rolling down my face, and my voice breaks as I say the words. 'I don't know Gina. I don't know what's the matter with me.'

She helps me up off the floor, and back to the chair I just flew off in panic, and she sits opposite me. 'Ok, Ruthie. Time to tell me what's going on.'

I tell her again that I have no idea what happened, or what might be wrong, and she looks at me for a long time. I can see her internal turmoil as she struggles to comprehend my behaviour. I try to reassure her.

'Look, I think I'm just feeling a bit overwhelmed about this whole Rebekah situation, and with the trauma of the funeral and everything. It's a lot to adjust to, all at once. I've never had anyone in my family murdered before! But I'm sure I'll be fine, Gina. We just need to find her killer, and then I'm sure everything will settle down.'

Gina looks doubtful. Concern is written all over her face, but she thinks better of trying to press me any further and goes to clean the broken glass from the back door. She keeps glancing at me as she sweeps everything up, wraps it in newspaper and places it in the bin. Then she gets a measuring tape out of the utility drawer, climbs up on a step-stool, measures the now-paneless window and then sets about cutting out a large piece of cardboard that will fit into the gap.

All the while she works, I am conscious of her glancing over at me, willing me to speak, but I can't. I'm struggling to understand, myself, what just happened. I know that war veterans and victims of other types of trauma can exhibit behaviour like this, when a noise occurs that reminds them of something that happened to them previously. It's PTSD; post-traumatic stress disorder, and I'm familiar with it, having seen it in a couple of students over the years and seen enough TV to know how people are affected by it. But I don't understand why it's affecting *me*. I haven't had a traumatic event. At least, not one that I can remember.

Fed up with being under my wife's watchful eye, I sigh heavily. 'Gina, I'm fine, truly. I just got a big fright, that's all. I was immersed in this paper I'm reading, and I didn't expect such a thing to happen. It sounded like a bomb had gone off in here,' I try to make light of it, but I can see Gina is clearly not mollified by my explanation.

'I don't know, *cara*. Bad dreams and now this, cowering on the floor like a terrified rabbit because of a simple broken window? This is not like you. I have never seen this before with you. Something is wrong.'

I have to admit, it must have been very alarming for her to have come into the room to find me on the floor, as a gibbering, hyperventilating wreck. It *was* only a broken window, after all, a simple accident with a door that caught a draft. My reaction to it *was* extreme; she is right about that.

'I think I'm just very on edge.' I try to put some finality into my tone as I try to shove the incident from my mind and focus on my work. Gina shrugs and silently finishes up with the window, then goes back to her own work. An hour or so later, the doorbell rings again, and once more Gina goes to answer it. Within seconds she is walking into the room, stony-faced, followed by the detectives. They both have faces like a couple of smacked backsides too, and my stomach lurches. I brace myself for what looks like being very bad news.

'We're sorry to bother you at home, Ruth. We went to the university, but they told us you were off today. We have some information we think you should have.' They both look fidgety and uncomfortable, and I invite them to sit. They decline.

'Well, spit it out then,' I say, struggling as usual to find the patience to indulge them, when every encounter we ever have seems to feel like pulling teeth. One of them (I call him Smiley) clears his throat.

'You might recall, at the beginning of the enquiry, we took your DNA to rule you out as a suspect. We also ran your parents' too, as a matter of course, to eliminate them as well. There's a lot of Michael Stenton's DNA in Rebekah's flat, but we gather they had a close relationship, so we're not surprised to see evidence of him being there; fingerprints and the like.'

I'm starting to wonder where this is going, and so is Gina, who is now standing behind them both, with her arms folded. She is tapping the fingers of her right hand on her left upper arm, and she has shifted all her weight to one leg; the very early warning signs of a spectacular eruption, if they can't quickly get to their point.

The female detective (who I've decided to call Giggles) continues 'It's all routine. We always take family DNA first, before we go any further, mostly for elimination purposes but also because a lot of murders are familial, and it's surprising how much evidence a family member can leave at a scene. They don't tend to be as careful. Their emotions usually get the better of them.'

Everything goes quiet for a few slow seconds and nobody speaks. Gina rolls her eyes. I raise my eyebrows at the detectives, and the female one continues, 'However, in the cross-matching process we've just done, we've discovered an anomaly.'

'What kind of anomaly?' Gina demands.

Smiley and Giggles are looking uncomfortable again, and they fidget a bit.

'Ms Stenton, perhaps we can speak privately?'

I sit up straight. 'That won't be necessary. You can say whatever you have to in front of Gina. She's my wife.'

Just get on with it, you idiots, because I have work to do. My wife hates you and she's about to launch a verbal attack on you, the likes of which you've never heard before, and if it comes to that I really hope you don't speak Italian.

'Well, the DNA reports indicate that you and Michael Stenton are not in fact related.'

Crash. Bang. Wallop. I'm suddenly reminded of the sound made when a nice piece of music comes to a tooth-grinding stop, when the needle gets dragged across the vinyl.

Gina and I look at one another in confusion. I find my voice; it sounds reedy and thin, like I'm speaking a great distance from my body. 'Not related? There must be some mistake.'

Smiley and Giggles look anything but happy. They aren't smiling or giggling at all – not that they ever really do lighten up, but they look particularly serious now, even for them.

'Are you sure?' My addled brain struggles to process what they're saying.

'I'm afraid we *are* sure, Ms Stenton. One hundred percent.'

'What – so you're saying that he's not my father? That I'm not his daughter?'

They both nod, slowly, apologetically. 'That would appear to be the case, Ms Stenton, yes.'

Several seconds tick by, and the only sound that any of us can hear is the fridge, doing its usual grumbling, gurgling thing, sounding abnormally loud in the stunned silence, which grows oppressive and heavy around us.

Nobody knows what to say, until Gina gathers herself with a start. 'Is there anything else?' she demands, staccato-like, 'or is that it?'

'No, I'm afraid that's not all,' Smiley says, taking on a slightly hunted stance as he continues, and I'm wondering if the poor man would rather be in the worst room in hell than standing here in front of me right now, when he delivers the second decimating body-blow.

'Michael Stenton has instructed us not to give you any further information about Rebekah's case. I'm sorry.'

'What? But she's my sister! I have a right to know!'

Giggles clears her throat. It seems there is yet more to tell me. 'Ms Stenton, it would appear from DNA analysis that the deceased is not your biological sister.'

As I'm reeling, trying to get my head around it all, she goes on to tell me that they are simply acting on the instructions of the next of kin, which I am – apparently – no longer. She says I'll need to have a conversation with my father about it, whatever the hell that's supposed to imply.

It's clear they are not going to be drawn on anything else. They've dropped their bombs, they've since shut down, and they have no intention of saying anything further. It's as plain as the nose on my face.

As I sit there in shocked silence, Gina gathers herself up.

'You need to leave. Right fucking now.'

Both detectives look like they wish the ground would open and swallow them whole. I know that feeling, and I wouldn't do their job for all the money in the world. So often do they appear to be uncomfortable and out of place. Wanting to catch murderers and make the world a safer place is a great goal to have, but the ways in which they sometimes have to get there? No thanks. I'll stick with giving lectures and grading the occasional essay, thank you very much.

'Get out,' Gina snaps, as they fail to react. Leaving no room for argument, she goes immediately into border-collie mode, shepherding them back toward the front door. She is brisk and barely tolerant, hanging onto the last shreds of her ability to be polite. She ushers them out in record time, and soundly slams the door behind them. I'm on my feet in the same instant, running past her towards the door, and yanking it open, desperate to reach them before they go.

'Wait!'

They turn around and start walking back towards the house. I'm standing in the doorway, Gina is right behind me, and as they get to within two feet of me, I ask the question. 'Does he know you've told me he's not my father, and Rebekah's not my sister?'

'He knows we were coming to tell you. The fact that you've been proved to be no relation is why he no longer wants you involved.'

Without a word, Gina grabs the collar of my shirt, hauls me back inside, and slams the door again in both of the detectives' faces. As their car starts up and pulls away we stand, stock still in the hallway, staring at one another in disbelief.

Chapter Nine
- Adie -

Bryan's been on the phone for a few minutes. I have a niggly feeling it's something he has to go out and deal with, as I've head snippets of his end of the conversation, but it was muffled, so I don't know if it's work, his Mum, or what. But he doesn't sound very pleased. I hope he doesn't have to go out. It's a rare night that he's actually even at home, and it's a *filthy* night; bucketing down, chilly wind, just the kind of night to get cosy in front of the telly, choose a thriller with a decent plot, order in a Chinese takeaway, and make a start on scoffing that lovely box of chocolates I splurged on last week in Waitrose.

No such luck. As soon as Bryan walks into the room I know my embryonic plan for a snuggly sofa night is dashed before it's even fully formed. He is ashen-faced and stunned. He looks like someone's just sucker-punched him hard. Something is seriously wrong.

'What, darling? What is it?'

He comes over and sits opposite me. He takes my hand in both of his, and takes a deep breath. I'm scared, suddenly, because this behaviour is completely out-of-character from the man who always sorts everything. I never have to worry about *anything* when he's around. That was his promise to me on our wedding day, that he would be the unfaltering rock of this whole family, and in nearly twenty-seven years he has never once let any of us down. But somehow, tonight, right here with my little hand encased in his big ones, I feel like that is about to change. I feel like I'm standing on the edge of a precipice and he's not there behind me, to pull me back before I fall headlong into the abyss.

I know that there have been 'things,' over the years; issues, stuff that's gone on with the business and different concerns over finances, and he's been worried a few times, enough to have had the odd sleepless night. He's so often away, too, with work related stuff. He never says much about it, and I don't ask. I know if it was something he thought I should know, he would tell me. He rarely does. In the past, he's always managed to sort out whatever might be a problem before it blindsided him completely or had a negative impact on the family. In truth, I have no idea what he may have shielded us from. But I've never seen him like *this;* lost for words and struggling mightily, to find them. This is a first. To say I'm alarmed is an understatement.

'Bryan, you're really scaring me. What's happened? Is it your Mum, is she okay? I'm meant to be doing her nails for her this week!'

Bryan's beloved Mum had a stroke a couple of years ago. It was very debilitating, and she wasn't expected to survive it, but she did. That lovely lady hung on like the proverbial limpet, clinging to the gnarled, pitted, sea-swept rock of her own life, determined not to let go and leave us. She can't speak anymore, but she still has that sassy spark in her eye that lets you know she's got the joke, or she understands what you've said to her, or she knows exactly what's going on, even when you haven't said a single thing. She's still as sharp as a tack in her own head, apart from having lost her speech, but her body is dramatically declining and it's simply heartbreaking to witness. I love Sylvie Bostock like she's my own mother, and every time the phone rings in the evenings like it did tonight, every time we get a call we're not expecting, my bowels loosen a little, and I think it's someone from the home, to tell us she's gone – a day we know is coming, but are dreading, nonetheless.

Sylvie's eventual end is the one thing Bryan cannot wave his magic wand to prevent, and we all know it. It hangs above our heads like the swinging sword of Damocles, ready to fall and disembowel us all without warning.

He keeps hold of my hand, and shakes it up and down a little between his two big warm ones. He's having trouble speaking and I'm sure it's his mother. My throat fills up and I'm starting to think about what sort of funeral arrangements she might want, when he clears his own throat and shakes his head.

'No, Adie, it's not Mum. It's Matty. He's alright,' he hastens to add when I jerk back involuntarily, like I've been slapped. It's every parent's most visceral nightmare; that something unspeakable and harmful has happened to their child.

'He's not hurt, Adie, but he's in trouble. He's at the police station. They've arrested him on suspicion of murder.'

Bryan gives me a minute to register what he's just said to me, but my mind suddenly feels like its travelling around in a dark oppressive maze, running through, crashing into a dead end, then doubling back and doing the same thing, over and over again, as it tries to fight its way forward to the exit that means understanding. My boy, my Matty? Suspected of *murder*? When? Of whom? Is this some kind of sick, cruel, crank-call joke?

I look at Bryan and I can see he doesn't think so. I can see his confusion and I can feel it on my own face. He sees it, and squeezes my hand a little tighter.

'I think it's just a precaution, Adie. I spoke to the duty sergeant after Matty's call. We should try not to worry too much. A woman he's been seeing for a while has been murdered – strangled – and the police are looking for suspects. Since he's been seeing her, they do have to talk to him, and once they have I'm sure they'll rule him out.'

My bewilderment eases slightly. Of course they'll rule him out! Bryan's right, but it's still a massive shock. Hearing that my son is being held on suspicion of murder is not the kind of thing I ever thought I'd hear, sitting here in my own living room, in the middle of what has been, until now, a mostly unremarkable and ordinary life for this little family.

'Who was murdered, Bryan? I didn't know Matty was seeing anybody. He never said.'

Bryan looks at me, cynically. 'I bet there's a lot he doesn't tell us, if he's anything like I was at that age. He's not living with us anymore, Adie, and he's a grown-up. He doesn't have to tell us anything.' He shrugs his shoulders.

'It probably wasn't serious, that's all. We'd have known if it was. I'm sure he'd have told us about anyone important or special to him, but I don't know who she was. The details I've got so far are a bit sketchy. I guess I'll be given more information at the station. They haven't charged him yet, but I need to get down there.'

Yet. They haven't charged him *yet*. Bryan's words hang in the air between us like a heavy black storm cloud that won't be swept aside with a wave of my hand.

'Matty couldn't do anything like that. He could *never* do something like that,' I say in disbelief. My voice sounds small, and far away even to myself. I'm dazed, trying to make sense of it all. I don't trust my legs to get me up and hold me, but I can't just sit here. I want to go with Bryan. I know he'll try to talk me out of it, with some comment along the lines of a police-station lock-up being no place for a lady, but staying here while he goes is out of the question. I have to go too. I need to see my son. I need to make sure he's alright, that he's coping with this nightmare. I can't even begin to imagine how he must be feeling.

'I'm coming with you,' I finally find the legs to stand, and seeing the look that passes across my husband's face, I quickly head him off at the pass.

'No arguments, Bryan. I need to be there.'

He sees that I'm determined. There's no way he's going to talk me out of this one, and he knows it. As he pulls the car keys off the hook and throws me my green quilted jacket, he says 'Find Trevor Jones' number in my phone and call him. Ask him to meet us down there.'

Trevor Jones is one of Bryan's solicitors. There are several looking after the firm and the family, all with different specialisms, and we call on any one of them when the need arises. Trevor Jones handles criminal matters. He's the guy that was first sent to us a few years ago by the big law firm we use, after one of Bryan's most trusted employees was wrongly accused of stealing the contents of a van belonging to a competitor. It turned out to be a blatant attempt to fit him up for a crime committed by one of that company's own employees. All very complicated and distressing for all concerned, but Trevor Jones successfully proved our employee's innocence, with expertise second-to-none, so he's the obvious guy to call, on a criminal matter like this. He will get to the bottom of everything and we can bring our son home. I'll get Matty to sleep here tonight and I'll make him a cheese-toastie supper, and do him a good breakfast in the morning before he goes off to work.

We're in the car and halfway to town before I manage to speak to Trevor Jones, after trolling my way through the long list in Bryan's phone to find his number. He's at home, and it sounds like he's in the middle of watching something on TV himself, but he agrees to meet us at the station in half an hour, and I click off and stare out into the night. The windscreen wipers beat in time with my thumping heart, sweeping aside the rain as it slashes across the bonnet in jagged, white-on-black blades.

Neither one of us speaks. We are both lost in our own thoughts; mine being driven by denial, and Bryan's undoubtedly more focussed; seeking solutions to getting this matter resolved as quickly and cleanly as he can. We pull into the parking lot next to the police station and make our way inside. I worry vaguely that we haven't paid for our parking, but then I reason that in weather like this, most wardens have better places to be than scuttling around a parking lot in the pouring rain, trying to find the few delinquent drivers who've gone to the movies or dinner without first having paid to park. If it's a numberplate recognition place, we'll just have to deal with a fine if it comes.

Inside the police station (the cop-shop, as Matty's always called it) we are met with a scruffy linoleum-covered floor littered with the scars of old cigarette burns. Stark white walls reflect back the harsh, fluorescent lighting that strips your skin of its colour, and eventually feels like a dead weight crushing your head down into your shoulders. The chairs are plastic, and there is a water dispenser at one end of the room, with just a few plastic cups left in the holder at the side. Even the bin is plastic. This clinical, cold, unwelcoming space conjures up images of torture rooms where the enemy shine bright lights into your face.

I tell myself it's just me, feeling hostile and impatient, and that most people who come in here probably don't give any thought to the ambience, or lack of it. They just come in, and make their complaint or enquiry, or get processed for custody, and move quickly along from this cheerless chamber that serves as 'reception.' It's a far cry, this mean little plastic pocket of space, from any reception I've ever been to in the past.

The sergeant behind the desk takes our names and asks us to wait. Time drags on, and thankfully Trevor Jones arrives. Bryan and I stand to offer our hands and he smiles at us and shakes them, Bryan's first then mine, and he asks Bryan what we know.

'Not much, Trevor. Not yet. We're waiting for someone to talk to us, and hopefully we'll find out more.'

Trevor rolls his shoulders. 'I will ask for disclosure now, and after that I'll go and see Matty. I'll get all that out of the way and hopefully I'll be back out here soon to sit with you while they prepare for Matty's formal interview. Just accept whatever information you might be told in the meantime, and don't ask or answer any questions until I get back, ok?'

He sounds confident and competent, which is reassuring to us both. He strides up to the desk and asks to be taken through to see the officers connected with the apprehension of Matthew Bostock. He hands over a small card, and the sergeant shows him through straight away. The door bangs behind him and we are left again, to sit in silence.

After another twenty minutes, Trevor returns. He pulls up a chair and sits opposite us.

'I've had a word with the officers in charge of this case. I've also seen Matty, briefly, and he's ok. He's had something to eat and drink, and he's comfortable enough in a holding cell on his own, with a blanket and a pillow. I've told him you're here.'

The basics are covered. My grown-up little boy is neither hungry, thirsty nor cold, and he knows we are here for him. I smile at Trevor gratefully. Small details but critical, he knows, to a worried mother.

Trevor continues, 'The police are about to interview him now. I don't know yet if they'll charge him. It will depend on the evidence. If it's solid they will, and on that basis I doubt if I'll be able to get bail for him, but they can't charge him without proper evidence. If it's shaky in any way at all, I'll be insisting they let him go, since they have to have legally sound reasons to detain him without charge and I don't know that there are any, yet. I'll be pushing for the best outcome I can get for him. You can trust me on that.'

An involuntary cry escapes me. My son, in jail overnight? This can't be happening. Trevor's voice is firm. 'Adrienne, try to stay calm if you can. I know it's frightening. But they haven't even formally interviewed him yet and once they have, they have to review what evidence they've got against what he tells them, and from what Matty tells me, it doesn't sound like they've got much, only a tenuous link to the victim, and I'm going to be advising him not to say anything to them at all.'

'It's all circumstantial, you mean?' Bryan asks hopefully.

Trevor smiles ruefully. 'Not exactly. From what I understand, there may be some forensic evidence, but I'm fairly sure it's not enough at this stage for them to charge him with murder. We're about to go into interview now, so it might be a while yet, I'm afraid, before we know the state of play.'

Apparently the police read Matty his rights properly when they arrested him, and made sure he understood them. He did, and he wisely chose to say nothing at all until he had made his permitted phone call (to Bryan) and arranged to have a solicitor present. I've never been more thankful for anything in my entire life.

Bryan speaks up for us both. 'We're not going anywhere, Trevor. We'll be here, even if it takes all night.'

'It won't take all night. I'll see to that. But it's likely to be at least an hour, possibly two, so why don't you go over to the hotel across the road? You can have comfortable seats over there and a decent coffee while you wait. It's got to be better than this miserable fridge of a place, and nobody important over there can hear your conversation who maybe shouldn't. I can call you as soon as it's appropriate for you to come back.'

We reluctantly agree. Trevor again reassures us that he will do everything he can to make sure Matty doesn't spend a minute longer than necessary in the holding cells. I've never felt this powerless or vulnerable, or dependent on someone I barely know from Adam, in my whole adult life before. I know Bryan feels the same, as he takes my hand and squeezes it, and we leave the sterile functionality of the police 'reception' room and head across the street to an infinitely more hospitable hotel.

After locating the restaurant and confirming that we can just order coffee, Bryan steers me to a sofa. We sit down and a waitress comes to take our order. 'Would you like anything to eat?' she asks politely. Bryan looks enquiringly at me, but in spite of us having had no dinner tonight I don't think I could manage a mouthful of anything, so I shake my head, and so does he.

'Just coffee, thanks.'

She smiles and leaves the table. Bryan reaches over and grabs my hand. 'Don't worry. It's probably all just a misunderstanding, and if anyone can sort it out, it's Trevor Jones.'

My thoughts start to settle slightly, as the coffee arrives, and I find myself thinking about the woman who was murdered. We have so few details to go on but nonetheless, regardless of the circumstances, a woman my son was involved with has lost her life. I am sure beyond all doubt that Matty would not have been responsible for that, and my thoughts now turn to how he might be feeling about the woman's death. Did he have strong feelings for her? Is he shocked? Distressed? Grieving? If so, that's bad enough, but to be accused of her murder as well, when he is innocent? Poor darling Matty; he won't be in a good place at all right now, and despite what Trevor Jones might have said about him being ok, he might just be making a bloody good show of not being truly terrified. I say as much to Bryan, who nods miserably.

'All I want is to see him. If they end up keeping him overnight, I need to see him, Bryan. Surely they'd let us do that?'

'I don't know Adie. I don't know what the rules are. We have to wait for Trevor to report back, and it could be hours yet. If it drags on, we can maybe get a room here for the night.'

I nod, thinking that if we do end up being here all night, sleep would be out of the question, but I don't say it. I can't bring myself to say anything at all, and so the conversation peters out. Neither of us knows what to say anymore. Most of what either of us could offer would be hollow platitudes, or unhelpful conjecture. Both of us know the futility of that, and since talking of anything else would feel too inappropriate and ridiculous under such barely believable circumstances, we're left with little to say.

The minutes tick wordlessly by, and out of sheer boredom and awkwardness and the inability to think of what else to do while we wait, we order a second round of coffees. It doesn't occur to Bryan to order decaf, and I'm simply too strung out to correct him on it, so at this rate, sleep will elude me, no matter what the outcome of the night might be.

Just as we are finishing the coffee, into the restaurant walks Trevor Jones. With Matty. In a split-second, I am on my feet and crossing the floor space, and wrapping my arms around my son. I'm weeping and shaking, overcome with relief at seeing him free and able to talk to us. Bryan grabs Matty and hugs him too, in a rare show of fatherly affection. Trevor shakes Bryan's hand again, but he doesn't smile.

'It's a win Bryan, but it's a small one. We're not out of the woods yet. Matty hasn't been charged; he's free to come home for now, as there isn't enough evidence to charge him or apply for an extension on holding him. But the police have made it clear they still regard him as a suspect because of the type of evidence that links him to the victim. You all need to know that he could be re-arrested at any time. I'll leave it to Matty to fill you in on the details, as he sees fit. I'll get going home, if you don't mind. I'll call you first thing tomorrow morning, and we can set up another meeting. Meantime, don't talk to anyone else about this, ok?'

We all nod at Trevor, who is groping in his pocket for his car keys, muttering almost to himself; 'I hope I haven't got a blasted parking ticket. I didn't pay and display!'

It's almost shock-horror comical, that this criminal lawyer didn't pay for his parking either, but I decline to comment. People in glasshouses, and all that, and solicitors are human too. Bryan quickly pays for the coffees and we all head out together, back to the car park.

Ironically for having parked right across the street from the police station, neither of us has been ticketed, so we've all dodged one potential bullet. But, as we pull away, out into the street and on towards home, I have the worst kind of feeling, an almost visceral certainty, that there's a lot more bullets coming our way and we won't be able to dodge them all. If there's one thing I've learned in my lifetime, it's that you have to listen to your gut feelings. You ignore them at your peril, especially when they tell you a storm is coming, the likes of which you've never felt before.

Sadly, it's not long before I'm proved right. Within minutes of getting home, organising a cup of tea and sitting down to go through everything with Matty, the storm unleashes itself upon me, with three profoundly shocking facts that threaten to topple my world on every possible level.

Matty confesses that he is a sex worker and the murdered woman, Becky Starr, was one of his clients. He cannot account for his movements on the night she was murdered; and he found out tonight that her name wasn't Becky Starr. It was Rebekah Stenton; the sister of the woman next door, who Matty has no idea is *his* unknown half-sister, and who *nobody* knows is my daughter.

Chapter Ten
- Gina -

Mio Dio! Those *bastardo* fucking police! I can't believe they just waltzed in here like that, like a couple of crazy *terroristi*, and calmly dropped so many bombshells, right on top of what is already the most foul family wreckage. This is napalm-insane.

I say as much to Ruthie, who just shrugs her shoulders and says it's not their fault, they are just doing their job, it's important information she needed to have, blah, blah. She is right of course, but me? I need to be angry at someone who brings such devastating news, even if it is just doing their damn job.

I wonder how much more misery and devastation is gonna come out of this horrible mess. Damn Rebekah to hell, for dying like that and throwing all kinds of shit at her family. It's one thing, if she wanted to live like a whore, but to die showing it off to the world? Her legacy is chaos and confusion, and so much sadness, I wonder when and where it will end.

I know that Ruthie is reeling. A murdered sister with horrifying and heartbreaking details about her death and her life, a farcical funeral, *umiliazione pubblica* from her family, and now this; a parent who is not a parent (maybe even two? Nothing was said about Cat's-Arse), and a sister who is not a sister, and Ruthie is no longer allowed to know anything about the investigation that matters so much to her. She has had so many doors slammed in her face now, and I can see by her body language that despite her *reazione pragmatico*, and being so gracious about those *bastardo*, slab-faced detectives just doing their fucking jobs, she is struggling to process these revelations.

So Rebekah is not Ruthie's sister after all, huh? I don't know why but I feel more glad about that than maybe I should.

There is a lot more going on here, I think, and we need to make sense of it. Ruthie is devastated at being cut off from the investigation, but part of me thinks that might be a good thing, now. I have worried, about how much she knows of some of the horrible details. No good can come of something that makes a sad situation even worse. Maybe this is good, this block from getting information. Maybe it is time for her to step back and let those slate-faced freaks do their job, and maybe they can somehow start to do it better. It's okay to hope for answers, but maybe it's not okay to want any more of the ugly details, or to be told, over and over, that there are no new leads. Maybe the only new thing Ruthie needs to hear, whenever that may be, is that they found the person who killed Rebekah.

As humans, we are conditioned in life to look for answers. We need to make sense of what goes on around us, always looking for the 'why,' for whatever we can't explain. Chiara went through a phase, a couple of years ago, of asking 'why' to almost everything I asked her or told her. It was exhausting, and it almost drove me *loco*, but it taught me something important, because when I thought about it, I realised that I too wanna know the whys of life. We all do!

The torment of not knowing answers to the questions that are *importanto* can be enough to drive us crazy. It forces us to find our own answers, even if they are wrong, because we have to know the why. We need a reason why something has happened, so we can live with whatever it is. I've done it myself, for things I didn't understand. I've found my own explanations, and maybe they weren't the right ones, but explaining things to myself the best way I could when there were no other answers to find made those situations bearable for me. The alternative was *angoscia* and a destructive preoccupation with things that were never gonna give me any peace.

More than anything else, peace is what Ruthie needs now, but I fear it won't be coming for a while, because there are still too many whys. Too many answers still to be found.

I bring a pot of herbal tea to the coffee table, and pour us a couple of cups. Ruthie is sitting in her favourite chair with a cushion in front of her, almost like a protection against whatever else might come through the door. She is pale and she looks exhausted. It has been quite a day for my darling, with her nightmare and other shocks.

'Are you okay, Ruthie?' I hand her a drink and my reward is a watery smile. She sighs deeply, and looks at me. 'I think so. At least, I think I will be, once I've made some sense of all this.'

'I think you need some answers from your parents, or whoever those people really are, *cara.*'

She nods, slowly. 'Yes, I think so too, and I think the only way to get those answers is to confront both of them.'

'Hey, Ruthie, are you sure? That is a big thing to do, you know? You could be putting yourself in real danger, doing that. You saw what your father was like at the funeral. He behaved like a wild animal. It was his daughter's funeral, and he still couldn't be decent, in spite of that. What might he do, if you confront him?'

'I suppose there's only one way to find out, isn't there?'

Ruthie sounds determined but she looks wiped out. Me, I don't know what to think of the events of the day, but she has a *resoluta* look on her face and I don't know what it means. I'm almost too afraid to ask what she is thinking, but I do.

'I need to see them, Gina. Have it out with them.'

'Ruthie, please. I know why you wanna do it. But think about it carefully. Don't make any rash decisions, *cara*. You don't wanna make things worse.'

Ruthie laughs but it sounds bitter. 'Worse! How the fuck could things be any worse?'

'You could get really hurt, Ruthie. That would be worse.'

But Ruthie shakes her head. 'I'm going to confront them Gina, and I'm going to do it tonight. You can't stop me, so don't even try.'

She gets up and walks away from me. I see that she is going upstairs and I imagine she intends get changed and go see her parents. She is more determined than I have ever seen her, and I *know* I can't stop her. This is something she needs to do. But I can't let her do it alone, so I pick up my car keys and wait for her at the bottom of the stairs. Chiara is having a sleepover at her friend's house tonight, so the timing does seem okay for this. It feels like a kind of gift, that we don't have to worry about her tonight. As much as I don't wanna let Ruthie go over to that house, I will stand beside whatever she wants to do, even if its gonna hurt.

Chapter Eleven
- *Ruth* -

Gina pulls her car up alongside the kerb, kills the engine and switches off the lights. It's hard to make a surreptitious entrance anywhere, in a gleaming purple Porsche Panamera V8 turbo. Actually, its aubergine (with a smattering of hot pink glitter under the lacquer), but I call it *G's Triple P*. Custom ordered, custom painted, it's sexy, sleek and powerful; just like the woman herself.

Thankfully, my parents live in the vicarage of an affluent enough neighbourhood for the car to not look out of place so, as we sit here at the kerb, no neighbours' curtains appear to be twitching. All appears quiet on the Hostile Front.

'Right', I say with conviction. 'Wish me luck.' As I move to get out of the car, Gina grabs my arm.

'I still wish you would let me go in there with you, *cara*. Promise you will call me if it all gets too intense. Just yell out for me. I will be right here, waiting, with the windows down and I can be there in two seconds if you need me. *Buona fortuna,* my darling, and don't take any shit from those two, no matter what.'

Even to my own ears, my voice sounds grim. 'Trust me, I don't intend to.' I grab Gina's hand, kiss it, and then let it go. I take a deep breath and get out of the car. As I walk towards the front door, I can feel the determination settling like a stole around me. For the first time in my whole life with these people, I have the control here. And I intend to use it.

The doorbell seems overly loud as I press it, ringing all across the inside of the vicarage in eardrum-piercing peals. I hear footsteps approaching and I draw myself up with a deep breath.

The door opens and my mother stands there, open-mouthed and speechless at the sight of me. Within a split second, she has gathered her thoughts and is moving to slam the door in my face but before she can, I push it back violently and step over the threshold. Her initial reaction to me was entirely predictable, but instead of making me sad and frustrated as it usually would, it simply makes me furious. It galvanizes me; I will not be leaving here without the answers I've come to find.

'Shut the door on me? I don't think so, *mother*,' I say with a menace I actually do feel. Something has just snapped inside me; I feel it on a physical level, and in that moment I realise I've finally had my fill of these loathsome people. It will suit me very well indeed, if I never have to call them parents again, after tonight.

'Michael!' Mum shouts in panic, and the man who is not my father comes skittering up the hallway, stopping short in disbelief when he sees me. He opens his mouth to speak but before he can get a word out, I'm there first.

'Shut up, Michael. Shut the fuck up, both of you, and listen. You owe me some answers, and I will not be leaving this house until I get them, so try and throw me out if you dare, but it won't work. Hit me if you want, Michael, but I'm warning you, I will hit you straight back, twice as fucking hard. Don't be dumb enough to imagine I don't mean that. You have no idea what I'm capable of.'

My not-father looks livid but quickly realises just how angry I am. He is clearly wrongfooted; distinctly unnerved by my mood. He's never seen me in a state of incandescent rage before, and he opens his mouth and then shuts it again. Clearly, he thinks better of trying to launch any kind of attack on me, either physically or with words. My mother is also silent. She stares at me with a contempt I can feel, but it no longer intimidates me. I'm above it. I am powerful, I am pissed off, and I plan to take no prisoners here.

Even if this mean-spirited, brittle woman is my biological mother, she is no real mother to me. She never was, nor will she ever be. And in a lightning-flash of pure epiphany, I realise that I am finally free. If these miserable, lifelong-lying people ever meant anything to me before, they now no longer do, and there is nothing that will hold me back now, from finding out what I came here to learn. And I no longer care what I have to do to this repulsive pair in the process.

I walk determinedly towards the two of them, and they both back away, down the hallway and into the living room.

'Sit down, both of you,' I say tightly.

They both stand staring, and neither moves.

'I said sit the fuck down!' It comes out as a roar that surprises even me. Jolted by the force of my barely containable rage, they both suddenly sit, ramrod-straight, on an over-stuffed sofa. It's ostentatious, and outrageously ugly, and I hope it's every bit as uncomfortable as it looks. It won't be the only thing that is, tonight.

They look at me warily. They have never seen me ferocious, or in full control before. It's a first for them and they are stunned by the force of my fury.

'Right, Michael, Margaret. Start talking. Who the fuck is my father?'

They both look at me, mouths hanging open. Neither says a word but I can tell they are both completely stunned that I'm here and confronting them, demanding the truth. Or course my not-father already knows I'm not his child, but he doesn't look smug, as I first thought he might. He actually looks quite scared. He knew the detectives were coming to tell me, but I'll bet the last thing he ever expected was for his previously pathetic not-daughter to come barrelling into his house in cold, calculated fury, demanding answers with a real undertone of menace in her voice. This is a first for him. As I look at him, sitting there on his spectacularly horrid sofa, I get the most curious feeling inside myself, of something simply crumbling, and turning to dust.

'Okay, I'll ask you both again. Who the fuck is my real father? Either one of you can activate a brain cell any time you like, and answer my question. And sooner rather than later if you don't mind, because you are truly repugnant people and I don't want to spend one more minute of my life with you. Ever. But trust me, bastards. Even if we have to sit here all fucking night, until this time tomorrow even, I will not be leaving here until I know.'

The silence is thick enough to slice through. Nobody speaks, nobody moves. We are all in suspension, silent and static, while outside the window, oblivious to the angst that threatens to tear apart what's left of these tortured relationships, cars drive by, dogs bark at the night, people switch channels on their TV's, and life goes on all around us. Odd, how in the midst of the most desperate disappointment and soul-destroying revelations, the world just quietly and inexorably continues to turn.

Michael Stenton glances furtively at a phone that sits on a side table next to the sofa.

'Don't make me pull that thing out of its socket, Michael,' I say softly.

Still nobody speaks. I let the silence stretch, knowing that it will eventually become unbearable to both of them and one or the other will feel compelled to speak. I have all the time in the world, to wait.

The minutes tick by. My mother tries to sneer at me, but because I'm now unmoved by it, I just look at her without expression. She sees that her attempt to undermine my confidence has had no effect, and she stops scowling and struggles to force her own face into some kind of neutral expression. She fails. She can't hide the fact that she's frightened.

Suddenly, Michael makes an unexpected move. He lunges for the phone and, in that instant, adrenaline floods through me and I'm around the coffee table and yanking the phone from his grasp. I pull it hard and it comes away from the socket in the wall. I turn, with momentum, and hurl it with all my strength, at the chimney breast, which just happens to have a very large ornate mirror hanging on it. The phone hits the mirror with an almighty, tooth-jangling crash and *everything* shatters, sending splintered shards of jagged mirror-glass and pieces of the plastic phone flying all around the room.

We all flinch hard at the deafening smash. My ears are ringing and, just as that stops, something indefinable literally shifts in my brain. I feel it, like a sliding door, something unlocking, and taking shape. But then, just as quickly, it is gone, and I am forced to refocus.

My 'parents' are now both wide-eyed and shell-shocked. Good. That's exactly where I want them, right now. I notice that my mother's right cheek has started to bleed a little. She must have taken a hit from one of the razor-sharp airborne missiles.

Seeing her bloodied face somehow has the interesting effect of reducing some of my anger, and I'm now feeling myself morphing more towards sarcasm and semi-detachment.

'Whoops!' I say lightly. 'Sorry, guys. Lousy aim, huh? Oh well, seven years bad luck then.' I shrug my shoulders and stare dispassionately at them as they sit there, glowering back in silent, seething fury. 'But it was a pretty horrible mirror anyway, wasn't it? So, no great loss. And as for the poor old phone, well, I guess they're probably still making them.'

Gina comes barrelling into the living room and skids to a halt. I must have left the front door open.

'*Mio dio*, Ruthie! I heard breaking glass. I thought someone was dead!'

'Hello, my darling! It's ok, no-one's dead. At least, not yet. Michael, Margaret, you both know my beautiful wife, Gina?' I turn my attention to Gina who looks warily at the three of us. She's wondering what the hell just happened, and I don't blame her.

'We've just had a little accident with the phone, Gina, that's all. Nothing to be concerned about. Our visit was just getting interesting, actually, so you're here just in time. Pull up a chair. That's if you can meet the monumental challenge of finding one that might be even halfway comfortable. Oh, and just watch out for that broken glass, darling. There's rather a lot of it. Michael and Mags here are just about to tell me who my real father is. Aren't you?' My last two words come out as more of a vicious snarl than I once would never have believed myself capable of.

'Ruthie', Gina says quietly; 'your mother is bleeding.'

'Yes! She is, isn't she?' I say brightly. 'But you might not be my mother, might you, Mags? So bleed away, you old bitch, since you don't want to tell me what I came here to know. Have fun, dripping onto that truly God-awful excuse for a dress! Poor old you. You were never going to win any prizes for style, were you? Even at Rebekah's funeral you somehow managed to look like a binbag. Still, you can't make a silk *anything* out of a sow's shitty arse, or whatever it is they say about terminally ugly things. I really don't remember the finer points of it, sorry, but I'm sure you get my drift.'

I can hear how clipped and brittle my own voice is, like it's pinging off a tightrope. I have a peculiar mix of rage and confidence coursing straight through me, and it feels *wonderful,* to be insulting these terrible people, after decades of swallowing the insults and cruelty from them. I'm fighting back, and I feel so almighty and powerful, like I'm soaring above everything, and I find myself wondering why I never stood up to them before. How pathetic I've been, these long, long years, so desperate for even the most meagre crumbs of affection or acceptance from this emotionally stunted, thoroughly incapable pair!

Gina sighs shortly and shakes her head. She spies a box of tissues on a nearby sideboard, so she pulls one out, reaches across, and hands it to my mother, who snatches it from her without a glance, or a word of thanks, and holds it against her cheek. Polite as ever, it seems.

'You're welcome, Cat's-Arse'! Gina says with a short smile.

Margaret's dismissal of Gina's attempt at kindness makes me feel savage all over again.

'Manners, mother, or not-mother, or whatever the fuck you are,' I bite at her. 'The words you need are 'thank you,' you miserable, shit-for-brains bitch.' I take a step forward towards the sofa where they are both sitting, mutinously silent. They are trying to look angry, but I know they are scared.

'Ruth, you need to calm down, and perhaps you could also temper your foul language in this house,' Michael says quietly. He might be scared and seething, but he sees that the chances of winning any kind of fight with me have exponentially plummeted with the arrival of Gina to even up the odds. He's going for the vibe of being 'reasonable,' now. Well, good luck with *that!*

'Calm down? *Really*, Michael? Temper my fucking language? Thanks for the invitation, bastard-face, but no. You've been lying to me my whole bloody life, you pathetic sack of shit, so why the fuck should I calm down about that, or temper my language, or cut you a scrap of politeness? Especially since you don't have the guts or even the basic human decency to answer my questions.'

'You need to calm down, so that nobody else gets hurt. Your mother is already hurt, and it's your fault.'

'Oh, well *that's* the kind of statement that will calm me down, Michael! And actually it's *your* fault she's hurt, since I warned you politely not to make a move for the phone and you ignored my nice request.'

Gina steps forward. '*Everybody* needs to calm down, including you, *bigotto bastardo vicar*. You don't want us here, and we don't wanna be here in this *casa disgustosa* with you revolting, stinking people. But it is easy to fix, no? You just need to tell Ruthie what she wants to know, and then we will gladly leave. Surely that is simple, even for *imbecilli stupidi* like you?'

'We don't know who your real father was,' my mother mutters, from behind her blood-soaked tissue. 'We *never* knew. We adopted you and it was the worst mistake we ever made. So no, I am not your mother either thank God, and I don't know who was.'

A heavy silence settles over us all again. You could hear a pin drop in here. I can hear my own pulse as the blood rushes through my ears, but strangely I am not distraught. Unexpectedly, laughter bubbles up from deep within me, and I relax, give into it, and let it loose. As I stand here in front of these thoroughly unpleasant people, I am suddenly *roaring* with laughter and relief, with tears rolling down my face. I'm grateful beyond measure, that their miserable genes haven't touched me, that I never have to see either of them ever again, and that it no longer matters whether they love me or not.

Deliberately, I blaspheme, because I know how much it violates Michael's sense of propriety; not that I imagine he will pray for my eternally damned soul. As far as he is concerned that's long gone; drowned in the sea of moral depravity, never to be resurrected. I am the devil's own. He would no more pray for me than he would gouge out his own eyeballs.

'Oh Jesus fucking *Christ* and hellfire! I have never in my whole life been more relieved to hear *anything!* I'm nothing to do with your sickening vomit-cake gene pool! You've *no* idea how happy that makes me feel!'

When my shoulders have stopped shaking with mirth, and I have regained the bulk of my composure, I look at the scowling, furious faces of the two people I once craved love from, and I feel nothing.

The atmosphere in the room has also changed. Curiously, I now no longer hold any malice towards them; there are no feelings at all, and they feel it too, because they both slump back into their silly-looking sofa like the life force has been sucked from their bodies. They look exhausted, sad, diminished. They are suddenly a lot smaller and older, and infinitely more pitiable, than I ever once believed they could look.

'So, when you say you don't know who you adopted me from,' I say quietly, 'how did you get me? And why did you take me in the first place, when you so clearly couldn't love me?'

Michael stares at the wall and says nothing. My mother (who is not my mother) says; 'we did want you, to start with.

And we did love you. We were told we couldn't have a child of our own, but then we did, and Rebekah changed everything.'

'So you had a child of your own, your own flesh and blood, and that meant your adopted child wasn't good enough anymore? Just like that?'

'If you like,' she mutters. 'It's hard to explain.'

'Try,' I say quietly.

'You were so wilful, Ruth. You never did what you were told, you continually embarrassed us, and then you had the gall to go off with *that*,' she gestured rudely towards Gina. 'It was all just too much for us.'

Gina slowly walks around the coffee table, staring at my not-mother with something approaching the worst kind of wonder. '*Mio Dio*, what kind of woman *are* you?' she asks in disbelief.

Margaret Stenton says nothing further. She looks resolutely ahead, in direct defiance, into the middle distance. I see now, more clearly than I ever have, that there is nothing in the world that will ever permit her to acknowledge Gina, or the reality of our relationship. She hasn't the capability to even try to understand, but the knowledge doesn't make me angry. All I feel is pity for her; this sad, pathetic woman, drowning in her own hostility, driven so hard by fear and loathing.

She appears remorseless about my parentage too, and it strikes me for the very first time that I've never seen someone so cold, so devoid of kindness or compassion. The relief is palpable, that I am not of her unfeeling flesh.

'Why don't you know who my parents are?' I demand of Michael. He refuses to look at me, but he does answer.

'We didn't *want* to know. We knew very little about your birth mother and we were told that she didn't want to know any details either, of who you went to. Apparently, she wouldn't even tell anyone who your father *was*, so we wondered if she even knew herself. It didn't seem like she cared about anything. We decided that ongoing contact wasn't appropriate, under those circumstances, so we had the records closed by the agency that handled the adoption.'

I struggle to get my head around the ruthlessness of this. 'So you made wild assumptions about a woman you didn't even know, and cut off any opportunity for me to ever find out about my birth family or gain access to any relevant medical information that might become important. Was that before or after you decided you didn't really want me?'

Michael doesn't answer. He is also now staring into the middle distance, and it is clear that there will be no more information forthcoming from this repulsive reptile of a man. I'm not sure what else there could be for him to tell me, in any case.

He is vile. As I look at him now, I have a peculiar sensation of my flesh actually *crawling*. The hair on the back of my neck is literally standing on end, and a wave of nausea washes over me so strongly that I actually have to bend and vomit hard on the carpet.

The need to say sorry for that does escape me, even though I'm vaguely ashamed to have done it, and I look at Gina, who simply looks sad. A clock on a sideboard ticks quietly, the sound amplified against our collective, stunned silence.

Margaret's face has stopped bleeding, and it is clear that she is also not prepared to offer me any further information. She continues to stare stoically at nothing in particular, while the strong smell of sick starts to fill the air, and the night chill seeps slowly but surely into the house through the still-open front door. All the rage has receded. We are all completely depleted, like a bunch of burst balloons. I have no will to press any further, and all of a sudden I feel like a little girl who needs to run away, even though she doesn't quite know what from.

It's time for us to leave. Silently, Gina extends her hand to me and I take it. As we go, picking our way gingerly across a floor strewn with shattered glass and pieces of plastic phone, I don't look back. I don't shut the front door either. I leave it wide open like a gaping gullet after we step through it and head back out to Gina's car.

She looks across at me and grins. 'Throwing up on their carpet! Nice touch, *cara*.'

She starts up the Porsche, and revs the engine aggressively a few times. Its burbling, powerful V8 sound is somehow comforting, and this time a few curtains do twitch. She deftly spins the car around and the tyres shriek in protest and lacerate the hanging, silent shroud of night. Grinning, she plants her foot and we roar out of the street towards home.

Neither of us speaks for a mile or two, and then she reaches over, pats me on the knee, and says 'You were amazing in there, Ruthie. *Spettacolare*! But how do you feel, *cara*?'

'Like I've run a marathon, or climbed a mountain I never knew I could conquer,' I admit. 'I'm absolutely exhausted, Gina, but I'm very clear in my mind now, about those two. I don't care about them anymore.'

'I know. I could feel it as soon as I came into the room. The atmosphere, you could chop it with a chainsaw, *cara*.'

I smile at her innocent misuse of a typical phrase.

'I can't believe you called her 'Cat's-Arse.' I chuckle to myself, in spite of the awful, devastating confrontation we've just walked away from. 'Why did you call her that?'

'*Cara*, I have *always* thought of her as that! She has the miserable mouth, all pulled in tight like a cat's ass. And anyway, you kinda called her *pig's* ass! I think that's worse.'

The penny drops and I start laughing again. Gina starts laughing too, and the same thing happens that always happens when one of us starts and the other joins in. In less than a minute we are both howling hysterically, letting off some seriously pent-up steam in a perfect pressure-cooker lid-blown moment. The last of the tension finally flies away and I am left with a fantastic feeling of freedom from the shackles that I once believed bound me to such dismal, joyless people.

Gina finally stops laughing and shakes her head. '*Mio Dio*. What assholes! Are they for real?'

I'm wondering the exact same thing; how either of them can live inside such hostile skin. I can't imagine what kind of life it must be, to be filled with the kind of hate I've had flung at me from those two. I'm thankful beyond measure that whatever gene pool I did come from had something better in it than the black bile I just witnessed.

Gina continues, 'I guess Ruthie, at the root of all of this, you are not related to *any* of them, not to your parents or to Rebekah. It must feel strange, to find all that out. I can't imagine how you must be feeling, but whatever it is, it's okay to just feel it, *cara*.'

I give some thought to how I'm feeling, and now that there are a few miles between me and the people I once thought of as my mum and dad, I'm relieved to still be feeling more thankful than sad about the way our lives have blown apart.

I wonder how long the relief will last. I'm sure there will be periods of grieving and adjustment lurking around the corner that will roll by and blind-side me when I least expect it, which is what Gina has just alluded to. But I know from experience that when something horrible happens to you, what matters is how you deal with it. Someone once described it as a huge pile of shit in front of you that's so huge there's no way over, under or round it. You have to go through it to get to the other side, to the point where you know it's behind you for good, and none of it is stuck to you anymore.

Letting myself go through my process of adjustment as best I can, with no expectations or self-imposed time limits around my progress; that is how I will deal with this, and everything will be fine. Maybe I could get some professional support to work through it, and help me to put it behind me. It's happened, I cannot change that, but I *can* change how I feel about it. I'm a survivor. I'm a success, in spite of that pathetic pair of liars who are literally hog-tied by their own bigotry and prejudice, and I'm happy in a way they could never hope to be. I say as much to Gina, who simply smiles and says nothing.

I lean back into the comfort of the luxurious cream leather seat while she navigates us home. Weary beyond belief, I simply nod at her suggestion for picking up a pizza and a couple of bottles of wine before we head for home.

So I'm adopted, and there is apparently no access to the records. I don't accept that. Times have changed, and as an adult I should be able to get access to my real birth records.

I stare out into the starry night and wonder who and where my real parents are, whether they are looking at the stars tonight and wondering about me too. And I wonder what the circumstances were that caused them to give me up.

As the miles fly by, I make a quiet but firm promise to myself. When the dust finally settles on the whole depressing debacle around Rebekah, I will look for the information about my birth family and the circumstances around my adoption, and I won't stop until I find it. On every level imaginable, I need and deserve to know who I really am, and where I came from.

Chapter Twelve
- Adie -

Never in my life before have I had to sit at a table with two of the people I love most in the world and pretend I don't want to fall to my knees and howl like a chained-up dog.

As my breathing goes into suspension, an ice-cold finger of fear slides slowly down my spine and my stomach moves sideways in a sickening lurch. I manage to maintain as neutral an expression as I can, but it doesn't last long. I can feel the last shreds of my self-control slipping, and I don't trust myself to hold back the tears of revulsion and fear. I rise from the table and busy myself at the sink, where I can keep my face out of view from my husband and my son until I can collect myself and drag my dismembered thought process back into some semblance of order.

Matty and Bryan are still talking, but I've tuned out. My head is a jumbled mess of facts, all jostling for position, and I'm struggling to get some clarity.

My son is linked to the murder of Ruth's estranged sister, and he can't prove he didn't do it, so he may be facing prison. And because the woman in question was who she was, this family and the one next door both stand an excellent chance of being blown apart forever, as families, friends, or anything else.

Realising the enormity of what has just blindsided me, I make an excuse to leave the room. I busy myself making up a bed for Matty in his old room, which is now my sewing room. As I work, I find myself unable to stand against the overwhelm. My legs give way and I find myself suddenly sitting on the floor with my brain full of fog and my breath coming in ragged gasps. I know I need to get a hold of myself before I start screaming and somehow forget how to stop. I breathe slowly and deliberately, to get my shaking under control and try to make sense of what this might mean for us all, and my haphazard thoughts come back into coherence.

Calm down, Adie, and look at the facts.

Matty is a sex worker. An 'escort,' to use the polite term, but let's just strip away the niceties here and call it what it is. He's a male prostitute; an older woman's paid plaything. As shocking and revolting as that is, it's something we can deal with later. What's more problematic is that he was involved with someone he has no idea was related to Ruth, and he has no idea that Ruth is related to *him*. He knows Ruth superficially as the next-door neighbour he's had the odd family supper or barbecue with, when he's been around. But, to my knowledge, he never knew she had a sister, and Stenton is a common enough name anyway.

His involvement with Rebekah Stenton, who he knew as Becky Starr, was a business arrangement, for want of a more truthful and less palatable way to describe it. That's all it was. Ruth was adopted into that family so Rebekah was not in fact her biological sister anyway, so the only familial connection is between me, Matty and Ruth, and it's only me that knows the connection.

For now.

I can't predict what kind of unstoppable runaway train might hit the tracks in the coming days and weeks, as more of this mess comes to light. I don't know what impact it will have on us all, but right now I just can't allow my mind to take me to that awful place where nothing will be certain except for the indescribable, hellish upheaval that threatens to engulf these two families and change them forever.

I'm starting to get a handle on what tonight's revelations may mean, in real terms, when I hear an argument flare downstairs between Bryan and Matty. I run back down to find them glaring at one another across the kitchen table.

'What's going on?' I demand.

'Just a difference of opinion, Mum,' Matty says tightly, without even glancing at me. His gaze is still firmly fixed on his father.

'Bryan?' I turn to my husband, who looks like thunder.

'I've told our son to contact the 'client' he was with on the night this Becky Starr, this *other* 'client' of his, was murdered, to see if she will confirm it. But he flatly refuses, Adie. See if *you* can talk some fucking sense into him, because I don't seem to be having much luck.'

Bryan's voice is bitter, his words barely concealing an anger I so rarely see in him, and I flinch at his use of a word he seldom uses. Matty himself doesn't flinch. He just continues to look stonily at his Dad.

I'm confused. 'Matty? Why wouldn't you contact her? If she's the only thing standing between what the police would know is your guilt or your innocence, why wouldn't you want to ask her to vouch for you? I don't understand, darling.'

I'm trying but failing to see what the problem is. Frustratingly, my fogged-up, stunned brain is not managing to make any connections; synapses falling, failing to connect.

As I look at Matty I see his face darken, in a way I've never seen before. Then he looks me straight in the eye with an expression that chills me to the bone.

'For fuck's sake, Mother. Do I have to spell it out? The woman is a client, a person of good standing in the community, with everything to lose. She would never vouch for me in a month of fucking Sundays.'

My own anger flares. 'Don't take that tone with me, young man. Just because you're a grown-up, and you're under pressure, that does not give you the right to speak to me like you just did.'

Expecting contrition, and an apology, I'm truly amazed when neither is forthcoming. Instead Matty heaves a great sigh, glares off into the middle distance, shakes his head and rolls his eyes, like I'm some inconsequential person whose ridiculous opinion he has no care for. His face is contorted into a rage I've never seen in him before. I know he's probably just scared, but this is not acceptable behaviour. We didn't raise him to be like this.'

Bryan gets up out of his chair, heaving a weary sigh of his own. 'Go to bed, Matthew. I think we might all have clearer heads after a night's sleep.'

'I'm not staying here. I'm going home,' Matty mutters, half under his breath.

'What? No! Stay, Matty. Please?' I plead with him. I'm really struggling to make sense of everything. 'It feels wrong, to let you go out into this shocking night all alone. It's pouring cats and dogs out there! Let's have another cup of tea, and talk things through?'

I'm desperate to keep my son safe under our roof, after a very traumatic night, mindful of that terrifying point, early in proceedings, where I wasn't sure he was going to be able to leave the police station at all.

Matty rises from the table with a sneer. 'Tea? You think a cup of tea solves everything, don't you, Mum? Well, newsflash; on this occasion, it just might not. I don't want your fucking tea, and I certainly don't want your fucking sympathy. I also don't want to sleep here tonight, so forget it. I'm leaving.'

He pushes past me violently, shoving me directly, to get me out of his way. Suddenly and unexpectedly off balance, I stagger and fall against a wall I'm glad to bang into. If I were standing in a different place I'd have ended up on the floor, and would my son have cared? It doesn't seem like it.

I'm struggling to take in this hostile, wound-up young man who I barely recognise as my own sweet-natured son. Matty has always been so respectful; spoiled and too-long indulged growing up, yes (which is our fault, of course), but he is usually so patient with people, particularly his parents who he's always gently and good-naturedly mocking as 'marching towards their dotage in fine form.' But he's not respectful tonight. In fact, he reminds me of a hissing cornered cat, spitting and snarling at everything in the way of its path of escape.

Against my motherly instincts and my better judgement, and shocked at the ferocity of the entire exchange, I capitulate, telling Matty he can leave if that's what he really wants to do. I ask Bryan if he'll give him a lift home.

But Bryan's having none of it. 'Nope. Not happening. I'm sorry, Matthew, but I've run around enough after you, tonight. If it's not good enough for you to stay under our roof, apologise to your mother who is only trying to support you, and let us help you work things through, you can bloody-well walk home. I don't care if it's a monsoon out there. And you might be younger than me and a little bit faster, you ungrateful little bastard, but if you ever push your mother like that again I will put you in a fucking coma.'

He is beyond angry, I know that. But I remind him that Matty is under a lot of pressure, he may have the threat of a murder conviction hanging over him, and now is not the time for high horses. I'm trying to cut our son some slack, and I want Bryan to do the same, but tolerance seems to be in short supply for both of my men tonight. I'm not doing too well myself now, for patience. Our jangling nerves have all been stretched to their limits.

'No, Adie. Matty is assuming he won't get any help from his *client*.' He spits the word in distaste, 'but he won't even try to find out. He won't even make the call. I'm not going to indulge anyone who won't try and help himself, even if it is my own son in the middle of this mess.' He looks at Matty, 'We raised you better than that.'

'Better than what? Better than *what*, Dad?' Matty takes a menacing step towards Bryan, and my heart skips a beat. 'Better than shagging willing old bags for a living? Or better than not wanting to spend the night with a couple of judgemental, patronizing old fuckwits like you two?'

'Both,' I say quietly, as my heart starts to truly hurt. 'We raised you better than both of those things. We raised you to have respect, for other people and for *yourself* Matty, but sadly I don't see much evidence of either, right now. And if you were comfortable with the way you live, you wouldn't be behaving like this, taking your frustrations out on us. I know you're scared. I am too, but we're your parents and we love you, and we're trying to understand this mess and help you find a way through it.'

Tears prick against my eyelids as I plough on. 'I'm trying to tell myself that this vile behaviour isn't personal, Matty, that you're just in a very difficult place and reacting out of worry and fear.'

'Tell yourself whatever the fuck you like. I'm going,' Matty mutters, and moves to get past his father. Bryan steps in front of him and grabs him by the shoulders, presumably to reach him, to make a touch-connection that may make all the difference to how we go forward from here, but it doesn't work. Instead of stopping and thinking twice, as we would normally expect our son to do, Matty swings his right arm up, super-fast, and hits Bryan squarely in the face with his fist. I hear a short, sharp crack, and at the same instant Bryan's nose bursts and blood sprays across the lower half of his face, and starts dripping onto the kitchen floor. He staggers back but regains his balance. His face is a bloodied mess.

Matty stops in his tracks, breathing hard. Bryan doesn't move and neither do I. We are literally frozen in horror at what's just happened. From some dark corner of my numbed and wounded mind, I pray for a shocked apology and contrition from Matty, but again nothing comes. Instead, our son pushes past his father and marches out of the room and down the hall to the front door. He yanks it open, strides through it, and doesn't even bother to close it behind him. With its lashing rain and whipping wind, the night closes in and claims him as he vanishes from view.

I rush to Bryan who is now at the kitchen sink, allowing his nose to drip slowly into it. Each drop hits the stainless steel with a light 'plunk' and a tiny splash. For the second time tonight, I'm a shaking, shivering mess of shredded nerves and disbelief. I get a packet of peas from the freezer and guide Bryan to a chair, tilting his head back and placing the peas-pack across the middle of his face. After feeling along the bridge of his nose and deciding there is no major damage done, he decides he doesn't want to go to the hospital.

'I've had a brok-ed doze before Adie. It's doe big deal. Be alright by bordig.'

I'm not reassured. It's all I can do not to cry. Bryan feels for my hand, takes it and squeezes it gently, like he always does when I'm troubled. I squeeze back, knowing he needs comfort too. He will be as shocked as I am. He just tends to hide it better.

After twenty minutes or so, and a stretched-out silence as we both contemplate the events of the evening, the bleeding stops and I help him to a more comfortable armchair in the living room. I hand him a glass of water and two paracetamol for the pain which I know will otherwise plague him all night long. Then I clean his blood off the kitchen floor.

Neither of us speaks. We are spent and silent. It's been a long night of frustration and fear, silence and shouting, with some truly heartbreaking revelations at the end of it, the likes of which I never thought I'd ever see or hear, and certainly not under my own roof, from within my own family.

It's almost midnight. I remember the front door is open, and I go to it. I'm too late to stop the moths from coming in, and they swirl in a frenzy around the lamp on the hallway table. I step outside, and go to the gate, looking up and down the road to see if there is any sign of Matty, hoping he's seen sense, and found his way back. I'm hoping he's thought better of storming off in the torrential rain, and is coming back to apologise to his father, whom he must know he has hurt. But there is no sign of anyone in the street and nearly all of the houses are in darkness. Most people have gone to bed, including Ruth and Gina. Maybe we should as well, but even if we do, I doubt we'll get much sleep.

Through the rain, I can see something lying on the footpath, near to the kerb, illuminated by the streetlamp overhead. Curious, I go to see what it is, and to my surprise it's Matty's mobile phone. It has a silly blue and yellow Minions cover, and I'd recognise it anywhere. Confused, I bend down to pick it up. As I stand there in the downpour, getting slowly but surely saturated, I can hardly believe what I have in my hand.

I have my son's smashed up mobile phone, and not from an accidental drop. This phone has been stomped on with considerable force, enough to shatter the screen to the point where half of the glass has come out of it. What's left is a jagged mosaic of more than a hundred tiny shards, and it has been thrown against a lamp-post with such force that bits of its splintered, cracked cover are embedded in the wood.

With a heavy heart I go back to the house, close the front door and bolt it, knowing full-well that if my son came knocking at whatever time of night it might be, I would hear it and gladly unlock it, regardless of what's happened. Despite the unhappy events, I'm sure Bryan feels the same. But I don't think Matty will be back tonight. I just hope he makes it safely home. I can't call him to make sure, because he has no landline and his mobile phone is a smashed-up wreck in my hand.

The best I can do is call his work in the morning to make sure he got there alright. Even if he won't speak to me, I just want to know he is safe, my poor frightened, lost little boy, facing all kinds of turmoil he has no idea how to navigate, but refusing all offers of help.

Without a word, I show his phone to Bryan who looks at it and simply closes his eyes and shakes his head. I suggest bed, and he nods. He looks sad, my poor, shell-shocked husband, like he's lost something really important and doesn't know how to get it back.

We go upstairs, get organised for bed, and as I turn out the light, knowing there won't be much sleep for either of us, I find myself wondering just how much was really going on with our son, and why we somehow managed to miss so much of it. Bryan speaks into the darkness, in a low voice;

'I don't know who that was tonight, Adie, but it wasn't our Matty. And that dead woman, it's Ruth's sister, isn't it? How the hell do we deal with this?'

I don't know how to answer so I take hold of his hand and squeeze it slightly.

'Things might seem less traumatic in the morning, Bryan. Let's try to sleep, if we can, or at least get a little bit of rest. Let that paracetamol take the edge off the pain in your face, and we'll see how things look in the morning.'

He turns over, away from me, into his customary sleeping position. I turn away from him, into my own, but sleep doesn't come, as I know it won't.

Earlier this evening, I thought to myself; *'my son needs an alibi, and it would be easy enough for me to provide him with one. I could simply say he was with me, that night. It's against the law, yes, but it's what any mother would do to protect her child. There's plenty that have done it, plenty more who will, and they'll go on doing it for time immemorial. And it's what I want to do, because I know Matty is innocent.'*

That's what I thought, before. Now, after the rage and the violence I saw and felt in my son tonight, I'm utterly horrified to find myself thinking a little differently. Now, I'm just *hoping* he is innocent. The one question that keeps coming back, that I cannot keep pushing away despite my best efforts, is this: if Matty could push me like he did, and if he's capable of such a vicious and unwarranted attack on his own father, living in sleazy circles and having sex with dried-up old women who have to pay to get themselves serviced, and getting enraged enough to smash his own precious thousand-pound i-phone into a million pieces, *what else is he capable of?*

I know he's scared, but the young man I saw tonight bore very little resemblance to my loving son. Is fear enough to cause such a radical change in behaviour? It was shocking in the extreme. And where did that fear really come from? Was it from the prospect of being charged with something he didn't do? Or was it the fear of being caught because he *had* done it? Incredibly, as much as I want to believe that my son could never do what he's suspected of, the man I witnessed tonight has only managed to convince me of one thing; that I don't know him like I always thought I did. He himself has given me reason to doubt him, and there's no worse feeling in the world than this.

And there's one other thing. If he's guilty, I'd still want to protect him; of course I would. I'd still want to lie for him if I had to. But now; how could I, if doing so would deny my first-born daughter the justice *she* deserves and the right *she* has to be at peace with the death of her own estranged but much-loved sister? How could I stand in the way of justice? How could deny her the ability to move on because that justice hadn't been served? How could I leave her with the terrible torment of never knowing who killed Rebekah?

Chapter Thirteen
- Matthew -

I'm blazing. I can't remember the last time I was angry enough to punch someone. Fuck Mum and Dad and their pathetic pots of tea. Do they really think a cup of tea's a game changer when I might be going down for bloody murder? What planet are they on?

It's incredible, how fast things can change. Earlier tonight, after the cops let me go, I was more relieved to see my parents in that hotel than I've ever been to see anyone in my entire life. When Mum insisted I go back to theirs for the night I didn't even put up a flicker of a fight, because not having to spend the night at home on my own was a big relief. I felt protected by my parents in exactly the way I needed to feel, like I haven't felt for a long time. I felt that I just might get through all this, with their support. It's unbelievable that within one short hour of that, I've ended up feeling like they've thrown me to the fucking lions.

I know I had to tell them everything. Trevor Jones made it crystal clear that I'm still stuck deep in the woods, and if the other lads' alibis check out, the cops will be battering on my door again in quick-time, and no doubt hauling me off in handcuffs. I need to make sure I'm completely and totally honest with *everyone*, including my scandalized parents. I can't conceal anything, even the most minor detail that could come back somehow, to work against me later.

I haven't committed the crime, so if I'm honest about everything I have and haven't done, and I put it all out there for everyone to see or hear, there's nothing to trip myself up on, is there? I hope I'm not just being naïve, in thinking that justice will prevail. A lot of people do go to prison for stuff they haven't done, just because they couldn't prove their innocence. I know the system hinges on reasonable doubt, but somehow I don't quite trust it as well as we're all supposed to.

So in spite of how awful it must have been for Mum and Dad to hear, I took Trevor Jones' advice and told them the whole truth. Everything, all of it. Besides, if it really is all going to come out anyway, I'd rather they heard it from me than a sordid, sleazy story penned by some third-rate, would-be journalist, in the kind of newspaper you wouldn't normally wipe your arse with, that never lets the truth get in the way of whatever they want to write.

Dad's fronted up with a damn good lawyer, a much better one than I could have found on my own, I reckon, so I figured I needed to be straight with them early. I owed them that. But the look on Mum's face was pretty hard to stomach. She was revolted by what I told her, and she couldn't hide it. She looked like someone had hit her with something heavy; shocked, dazed, and actually fearful, although I don't know why she'd be scared. I think she just wasn't expecting to hear what she heard, about her lovely little Matthew, light of her life, shagging sex-starved old bitches for money. I guess when you collapse completely off your pedestal, the people who've put you on it are always going to feel cheated and disappointed with you for not managing to somehow keep yourself there.

But she looked like a bloody bomb had gone off right in front of her, and when she asked me if I was having sex with women who are older than she was, I was honest with her. I did expect her to be unhappy about it, of course, but the level of disgust and confusion I saw tonight in both of their faces, hers and Dad's, well it really pissed me off, and it proved that they don't understand a fucking thing about my life, or how I choose to live it.

They don't have the right to judge what they don't understand, and they didn't even give me chance to explain, so where exactly was that conversation going to go next? Mum couldn't speak at all, she even left the room so she didn't have to look at me, and Dad was just ignoring the whole sex-work thing and banging on about sorting out my fucking alibi.

He was really starting to get on my wick, repeating himself, refusing to listen when I told him it was futile trying to get this particular client to talk and get me off the hook, and he just wouldn't give up trying to make his point, even though I'd long since got it. He was like a dog with a trouser leg, then when he tried to stop me from leaving, that was like a red rag to a bloody bull.

I probably shouldn't have hit him, but he asked for it, grabbing me like he did when I was trying to fucking leave, but they'd both wound me up so much, I just lashed out. It's his own fault. He should have left well alone.

I really wish I hadn't gone there now. I should have said no, manned-up and just gone home to my own bed, where the space is my own, where there's nobody to disappoint, and I don't have to answer to anyone. That would have upset Mum and Dad, sure, but despite what Trevor Jones might think, maybe it would have been better to be seen as secretive and bloody ungrateful than to tell the truth and be judged for it. They're my parents, for God's sake, they're supposed to be supportive, but they clearly don't understand my life, or what I want.

It's alright for Dad. He's been successful with his business since before I was even born. He's always had the Midas touch; everything he looked at turned to success for him. We never wanted for anything, growing up. Some might say we were spoiled rotten, me and Teresa, and I guess that's how it might look from the outside looking in.

But then, from out of nowhere, we were suddenly just left to get on with it, to go out into the world to make our own way. We got a small nest-egg when they sold the big house, but it was barely enough to use as a deposit on my little place. I thought we might have got a bit more support than that, but once we'd graduated from uni Dad thought his work was done and he stopped bankrolling anything at all. We didn't even get an allowance. No financial bridge until we started earning. Nothing, and he'll never know how hard that was. I had to sell my scooter, just to keep going. He thought he was doing us a favour trying to make us independent, arguing that we didn't need support anymore, but he was wrong, and the one time I tried to talk to him about it, he accused me of being lazy and ungrateful!

He just doesn't get it. He doesn't know how hard it is to take, every night, going back to my poky little place after living the life of Riley in his and Mum's big posh one, and how hard I've had to fight just to keep it.

Dad's never had to struggle for anything much, even in the early days. The lucky bastard's *always* had that golden touch, right from the minute he was born. Even Gran always called him a 'very lucky boy.' He doesn't have the slightest idea how hard it is to actually make a decent life for yourself and keep up with your mortgage while you're scraping by on a graduate wage, with the big expectations from the family that have bankrolled your bloody education. They somehow seem to think that means you should have that high-flying career already, or that big mansion or that fucking flash car by now, just because you've got half a brain. They expect you to lurch along on a pittance, somehow pay off your student loan at the same time as trying to keep up with your mortgage, and try and imagine ever being able to aim for something better than the miniscule two-up-two-down, swing-a-cat-and-still-overpriced place you did manage to get. Oh, for a magic fucking wand.

I realise I'm just feeding my own anger, thinking like this, and I take a few deep breaths, to get myself into some semblance of calm. I do need to make the phone call they were pushing me to make, but I couldn't bring myself to do it with them listening, because I think I know how it'll go, and I don't want them to see or hear me humiliated like that. When I'm told to take a hike, I want to hear that on my own terms, without Mum wringing her hands, or Dad roaring his head off in the background.

I'm standing under the big chestnut tree off to one side of the front garden, trying to shelter at least a bit from the pouring rain. I'm hoping it will stop, or even just lessen a little bit, before I walk to the bus stop. It's a fair hike, and I'll be like a bloody drowned rat by the time I get to it, in this. But so far it doesn't seem to want to stop, and I figure if I have to stand here for a while yet I may as well make the call I need to. It's already pretty late.

As I scroll through my phone, to find the number I need, my hands are shaking. Even as I let the number go through and wait for it to connect, I know I'm on a fool's fucking errand. She's not going to want to know. But I have to try, so I can say I did, and you never know, do you? Maybe I'll get lucky after all. Hope springs eternal, as the saying goes.

The phone rings six times before she answers it, and it's the longest six rings I've ever waited to have answered, in my whole bloody life.

'Hello?'

'Christine, I'm really sorry to phone you so late, but I need to speak to you. Can you talk?'

'Who is this?'

'It's Matthew.'

'Matthew who? I don't know any Matthew, unless you're the travel agent? Why are you ringing me so late?'

My mind goes blank for a few seconds, then I remember that Christine knows me as Wayne.

'Sorry, Christine, I mean it's Wayne. From the agency?'

There is silence for a few seconds, then she speaks quietly into the phone. 'Why are you calling me? How did you get my number? The agency aren't supposed to let you have my number.'

'You gave it to me yourself Christine, a few months ago, after you need to change your time with me at short notice and you wanted me to confirm privately when I was on my way.'

She doesn't speak for a few heartbeats, then she says 'That doesn't mean it was okay for you to keep it, or use it to call me without permission. It's late, and I'm not alone in the house. What do you want?'

'Christine it's about the night I was round at your house last month. I need a really big favour from you.'

'*You* need a favour from *me*? What kind of favour?' The voice becomes wary, and decidedly unfriendly. My heart sinks, but I plough on.

'I'm in trouble, Christine. Someone was killed that night, and I'm under suspicion. I didn't do it. I was with you that night, before and way past the time the murder took place, but I need you to tell the police that; what time I got to you, and what time I left.'

My voice sounds desperate. Maybe this woman is my last hope, but she's always been really nice to me and if she comes through for me on this, I'll gladly do her for a year for free, on my own time, as many times as she wants.

'Are you *joking*?' Her voice is openly hostile now.

'No, Christine, I'm not joking. I'm in real trouble and you're the only person who can help me prove I wasn't there.'

There is an incredulous silence at the end of the phone. I close my eyes and pray she'll say yes, but deep down I know it's not going to happen. I expect her to say no, apologetically and politely, and end the call. But that doesn't happen either.

The silence grows. 'Christine?' I ask tentatively. I feel like I'm teetering on the edge of a big black hole, and I've never felt so small in my life. 'Christine, are you still there?'

She clears her throat. 'I will do no such thing. How dare you call me at home, this late at night, asking for something like that? How *dare* you?'

'Please, Christine, you're my only hope.'

I can hear her breathing into the phone. Anxiety gnaws ever-increasing craters in my bowels. They threaten to collapse completely, and I've never prayed for anything as hard in my life, as I'm praying for her help now.

And then she takes a deep breath, takes aim, and lets me have both fucking barrels.

'Now you listen to me, you little shit. You're a low-class piece of trash, and I owe you nothing, do you hear me? Nothing! And you've just outlived your usefulness. You and your fucking agency can consider yourselves fired. Delete my number right now, and don't call me again. Ever.'

I'm reeling from her hostility, which I didn't expect at all. I know I should just apologise for bothering her and hang up the phone but desperation wins over pride and, so help me God, I actually resort to begging.

'Christine; don't hang up. Please. Please help me. I gave you good service' As I say those last anguished words, I'm acutely aware that I sound like a whining, frightened, needy child, and I know I've just signed the equivalent of my own and the agency's death warrants.

'And I gave you good money,' she hisses into the phone, like a spitting viper, 'for an *average* service. You mean nothing to me, and I'll be damned if I'll hang my whole life out to dry for a jumped-up, arrogant, two-bit whore like you. Fuck off and don't call again. Leave me alone or you'll be going down for murder whether you did it or not. I shall see to it.'

The phone goes dead, and I find myself staring at it, open-mouthed. Why did she have to be so fucking nasty? And what's with the threat at the end of that, to fit me up if I implicated her? That takes things to a whole new level. I know she's well-connected, and that's why discretion always had to be over the top, but threatening to *frame* me? *Is that what she just did?*

Why did I never see how selfish that wizened old bitch really is? It's one thing to say no, she won't admit I was with her on the night Becky Starr was strangled to death. It's quite another to hurl horrible, undeserved insults at me and threaten me like that. It's quite another *again*, to hang me out to dry, in the interests of her own self-protection.

I try to digest what she's said to me, and grasp the implications of the conversation, and I realise how naïve I've been in even daring to hope that any client might have a soft spot for me. They all tell me how great I am, how they can't wait to book me again, how I'm the best, all that shit, and that's all it is! It's shit, and they don't mean a fucking word of it. I mean nothing to these people at all. They are all looking out for number one. It's why they insist on satisfaction, even if it costs them the earth. They tip big because they just want more of the same, for *themselves*. They don't give a shit about who's giving it to them, really.

So that was a pedestal I put *myself* on, only to be kicked off it quick-style by someone who never thought I was as good as I thought I was myself. Lesson fucking learned.

My heartbeat is all irregular, and as I stand here in the pouring rain, with my dignity and hopes ripped to shreds, I try to ignore the nagging little voice in my head that gently reminds me I was willing to do the same to Christine; hang *her* out to dry, to protect myself. But I have to acknowledge, as my own future takes an abrupt turn for the bleaker, that it's just incredible what people will do, what they're capable of, when their backs are against the wall. Under enough pressure, charming, affable people can turn into raging monsters, and some will throw anyone and everyone under the nearest bus if they have to, to protect themselves. Christine is no exception. But neither am I.

My rage returns with full force, as I realise just how close I may just be now, to going down for a murder I didn't commit.

A roar of frustration rolls up from within, and I throw my phone to the ground and stomp it with my heel, not just once but three or four times. Then I pick it up and hurl it hard against the lamp post, where it shatters and falls to the ground. I don't even stop to look at it, after giving it a last kick for good measure. I walk away from the family home, wondering how long it might be before I see it again.

My mind is crowded with questions as I walk towards the bus stop. The rain is relentless, and has been for hours. Drains are blocking up, there's puddles all over the road being fed from the gutters, and the bus stop is awash with rain. It's a hell of a night on all levels.

Will the cops be picking me up again after they've spoken to the other lads? Do they all have alibis that will leave me, and only me, squarely in the fucking frame? Will Dad still want to meet with me and the lawyer in the days to come?

Will Mum get over thinking her son is the scum of the earth and violent to boot, after I shoved her tonight and she nearly fell over? Will the agency even let me walk through its doors again? Will any of my clients still want me on an ad-hoc basis if I've been suspected of murdering a woman in her own bed?

For the first time, thanks to one of our clients having the terrible misfortune to get herself strangled, I'm beginning to realise the implications of the way I've chosen to live. The truth is, I've never thought being a sex-worker was all that bad. I know that a lot of people find it morally distasteful, and I know that most men couldn't imagine how I could even get it up for an old woman, let alone use it. I never once thought about it in the context of how I'd feel if someone my age was shagging my mother or my Gran.

We tend to live life in a bubble, don't we? We have our own little universe in which we function, and most of the time we don't give much thought to what goes on outside of it, until it directly affects us. Like terrorist acts in Syria, it's largely meaningless, unless we have a loved one there. A bomb going off at home, well, it's so much closer, and with six degrees of separation, it's a lot more likely that we'll know someone who knows someone, who knows someone involved.

It's all part of the agency customer service training actually; 'people's worlds.' We're told about a fictitious Mrs Johnson, and what goes on in Mrs Johnson's world, as being distinct for her and nobody else. We have to appreciate her world, even if we stop short of delving into the guts of what makes it work. In Mrs Johnson's world, she wants everything to work well, to happen when it should. There are certain things that should not happen at all (like not using a condom, or being phoned at home late at night by a renegade worker on a private mission of favour), and we have to be mindful of her world when we enter it. We have to respect Mrs Johnson's own little bubble of functioning, and we have to do our bit to ensure it stays the way she wants it.

Until now, my work has never had an impact on anyone else. All things being equal, if poor Becky hadn't died, it would all be business as usual. I would still be happy in Matthew Bostock's world, where everything is rosy, I'm doing exactly as I please, I'm not hurting anyone, and what nobody else knows can't affect them. But as I'm discovering, what they do know can, and as it stands I've broken my mother's heart and probably my father nose. I've ruined my contract with the agency and jeopardized the most lucrative job I'm ever likely to get, at least until my real career takes off, which it probably never will if I go down for murder, and I've fucked up my friendships with my colleagues, along with their lucrative lines of work. For doing what I want, in my own little Matthew's world, that's all starting to feel like too big a price to pay.

If the events of the past few hours have shown me anything, it's that we can control our own little worlds to a great extent, but it's not so easy to control the impact on them from outside influences. And it's pretty much impossible to control some of those outside influences at all. To say I've been kicked out of my bubble feels like the understatement of the century, and just how far the trajectory will take me depends on my ability to prove where I was on the night Becky Starr was murdered. Right now, if anything looks impossible, that does.

Have a cup of tea in the bosom of my family and everything will be alright? Well, somehow, I don't think so, not after tonight. After tonight, I have a strong feeling that for however many years to come, whenever I look behind me, all I'm going to see is a bunch of broken bridges – all on fire and falling away. Burning bridges, with no way back to the place I was before.

Chapter Fourteen
- Ruth -

The cellar light isn't working, so I'm running down the steps in the pitch black, and I can't even see them, and I don't remember how many there are, so I hope I don't stumble or fall before I get to the bottom. Luckily, the door wasn't locked so I'm able to get in. It feels like such a long way down in the dark, and I still don't know what I'm going to find when I get to the bottom but she is screaming and she is frightened and calling for me, and all I know is I have to find her. There's nowhere else to go from here. If she's down here, I'll find her.

I'm at the bottom now and blinking, trying to see through the dark. The little window in the top of the cellar door is useless for letting in light. I don't even know why it's there. Remembering there's an air vent along the far wall, I grope around to find it and I manage to pull its grubby cover off with a yank. It comes away easily, in a puff of old dust, and lets in just enough murky light to lift the gloom but its barely enough to make out a few random shapes. It's so long since I was down here, I don't remember what there is. I do know there's no door down here to anywhere else. The only door is the one I've just come through, at the top of the steps. She's down here; I know she is.

It's so hard to see! There's just walls, and no way out. She has to be here but I can't hear her now. Up in my bedroom, I could hear her screaming but everything's gone so quiet, it's terrifying. What's happened? Is she dead? If she's dead, how will I bear it? How will I tell Mum and Dad? Please God, if you're out there, don't let Rebekah be dead. I promise to be good, and not make anyone mad anymore, I just don't want my sister to be dead. Please? We're going to school camp in two weeks, and we've both been looking forward to it for ages.

It's all dark shapes down here, like boxes or trunks and broken bits of furniture, and I do know there are some wine racks against the walls, all well-stocked for parties and presents and stuff. Maybe I could use a bottle of wine to hit someone with, but as soon as I think that, I know it won't work. I know I can't fight anyone. I'm just too small. The only thing I can do is hide and hope I'm wrong, and that Rebekah's not here, and wherever she is, she's ok.

As I stand here in this horrible place, the one that gives me nightmares, the one I never come into because its full of dust and mice and big spiders, I'm suddenly aware that even though I can't see anything, I can smell and hear things that shouldn't be here. I can smell sweat, male sweat, like I've smelled when I've got on the school bus and it's been full of boys, and I can hear breathing. I'm not alone down here! I call Rebekah's name, feebly, in my fear. There is no answer but I hear a sniff, a quick gasp for breath. It's so slight, but I'm sure it's what I hear. I take a step forward in the dark, towards something low on the floor, an unfamiliar rounded shape, and I trip over something metal. It clunks, and I jump out of my skin, but I bend to pick it up. It's a torch! A tiny little pocket torch, just like the ones Rebekah and I both got in our Christmas stockings last year. I can't believe I've been lucky enough to find this. God really is there, and he's really helping me like I asked him to.

With shaking fingers I switch the little torch on. Its light is feeble but it's enough. Enough to see what I'm expecting - my frightened sister, except there's a lot more than that, and none of it is what I expect to see at all. There's only a split second between imagining putting my arms around her and telling her not to be frightened, and leading her out of the cellar, with the help of the little torch, and the reality of what's in front of me. But reality wins and my thoughts of protecting my little sister, so naive and innocent, are dashed forever in less than the time it takes to piece together what's happening to her.

Right in front of me, there on the filthy floor, is my father. He is on his knees. He has Rebekah pinned beneath him, on her stomach with her face in the dirt, and he has his hand over her mouth. Her face is filthy and streaked with tears. Her skirt is hitched up, her knickers are around her ankles, and his trousers are undone. Even to my small, uninitiated mind, I know what is happening, and I'm sure I scream as I drop the torch, and the next thing I know he is on his feet and pinning me by my throat to the door of the wardrobe I always hoped would take us into Narnia.

We never made it though, because we needed to have a fur coat in there to go behind, for the magic passage, and there was no fur coat. Narnia was only ever a dream. All this has ever been, is a big old wardrobe with a big split in the side panel and rusty hinges.

But he pins me against it. Then he lets go of my throat until my head comes forward and then he grabs me again and smashes my head into the mirror. Glass splinters and flies in all directions, I can hear it hitting the floor in tinkles. I can hear Rebekah crying, and I can feel something warm at the back of my head. I think it must be blood. I've cut my head, but I don't know how bad it is.

He is really, really angry. He is shouting and swearing, and spitting in my face as he screams for me to forget what I just saw or else he will kill us both; me and Rebekah. Suddenly everything seems clearer and I can see a bit more than I could before, and I make out Rebekah's shape. I jam my knee into my father's balls like they told us to do at school if someone was attacking us, and I feel my knee connect with the softness between his legs. Its squishy and revolting, but I can't keep thinking about that because I have to get Rebekah out of the cellar before he does kill us both.

As he doubles over, howling, I grab hold of Rebekah and drag her towards the cellar steps. She stumbles because she hasn't pulled her knickers up, so she kicks them off instead and we run for the stairs that I can just make out in the gloom. We tear up them and out into the upstairs hallway. I slam the door shut behind us and lock it with the key that's still in it. He starts to climb the stairs. He is raging and swearing, hammering and kicking at the door, demanding that we open it.

Can he break it down? I thought that only happened in movies. I've seen our neighbour trying to break a door down after he locked himself out and left a gas ring on, but it didn't work. He kept kicking it and bashing at it, but it wouldn't break, so he went and got an axe and the only way he got it open was to chop it down, and it took ages, and it made a lot of noise and a terrible mess.

So we might be ok. Dad might not want to do all that, and I don't think we have an axe anyway. If we do, I hope it's not in the cellar. I wish Mum was home, but she might not finish work for ages yet. It's different every day.

He yells again and then I hear the window break in the top of the cellar door. It's such a loud noise, like a big shop window breaking, not just a tiny cellar door window, and I can feel bits of glass flying around me again, and I can hear it plink as it hits the floor. He really is going to break the door down! He's telling us he's going to punish us for running away and locking him in, and he kicks at the door, and kicks and kicks.

He's yelling that I'm bad for locking him in. I'm trying really hard not to cry. I'm such a baby really, not like Wonder Woman, who just kicks people in the face and stops bullets with those wrist things she wears. Nobody can get her. But he's going to get me. He'll get Rebekah too. He won't give up. He's too mad now.

With a crash, the door gives way and suddenly he is running towards us. I know I'm not nice for wanting him to fall and break his neck but that's what I hope for. It doesn't happen, we're not lucky. He grabs me by my hair and pulls me back. We both land on the floor on our backs, with me on top of him, and I struggle to get away but he has his arms around me now, and he rolls me over onto my stomach and then he's lying on top of me. I don't know where Rebekah has gone, but then I see her. She has got the rolling pin from the kitchen, and is holding it above her head. I look up at that, *and Dad sees me doing it and he looks too. All the fight goes out of him and he rolls off me. I get up, shaking. Rebekah doesn't move. She is still holding the rolling pin over her head like she wants to smash it on Dad.*

The sound of the key in the front door changes everything. My mother walks into the hallway and in one big glance she sees us and figures out what's happened. I start to cry, and Rebekah does too but she runs upstairs to her bedroom and slams the door. I want to run away too, but the horror of what I saw being done to her in the cellar, and the furious look on my mother's face, freezes me in place. Even though I want to run, my legs won't move.

She shoves me hard, and tells me to go to my room. She doesn't try to soothe or comfort me. She banishes me, like I've done something wrong, and she looks at my father. As I'm running again, up the stairs, I can hear her talking to him. I don't know what she is saying, but something inside me is telling me it's better I don't know.

Chapter Fifteen
- Gina -

A piercing scream wakes me from deeply sleeping. It is Ruthie again, with another nightmare, but she is screaming and screaming, and flailing about in the bed as if someone has hold of her and she is trying to get away.

I snap the bedside light on and she is still asleep and still screaming and yelling 'get away from me, leave me alone, you're hurting me.' Her voice is high-pitched and she sounds like a frightened, anguished child in terrible pain.

I grab her by the shoulders and shake her awake. She is crying hard and mewling like a frightened *cucciolo* in need of its mother, and she trembles like a leaf in the wind. She looks at me but she is not focussed. It is not me she sees but someone else, because she is still locked in the nightmare, and she pushes me so violently that I fall out of the bed. As I fall I grab hold of the top sheet on the bed but it doesn't stop me from tumbling and my forehead head hits the corner of the nightstand. As I get up to go back to her I can feel my own blood as it drips, slow and thick, down into my right eye. I'm scared myself, at this crazy point.

'Ruthie' I yell, right into her face, hoping I don't have to slap her to wake her, and she suddenly snaps awake. My voice has made it through. At the same moment Chiara comes running into the room with wide eyes.

'*Mummia*,' she cries. 'What's happening? Why is Mummia Ruth screaming? You have blood on your face, *Mummia*.' Her voice is afraid now, and she is crying. So my daughter is shaking and crying and Ruthie is shaking and crying, and for a second I don't know who needs my attention the most, right at this *momento orribile*.

I hold out my arms to Chiara. She comes to me reluctantly and I gather her into my arms and kiss her, keeping my bleeding head away from her the best way I can, and I stroke her hair to calm her, but I don't take my eyes off Ruthie as she slowly starts to focus. She looks at me with the blood on my face, and she looks at our frightened daughter, and the look in her eyes is something I've never seen before. Her eyes are just empty, like there is nothing but horror in her head. It's the kind of gaze you see from someone with no soul. It is *desolato*, as black as the night, like the worst kind of shock has sank its claws into her and will not let her go.

'Stay there, Ruthie. I will take Chiara back to bed and I will be right back. Stay right there, *cara*.'

I hurry Chiara back to her bed, wiping my bloodied face with the sleeve of my pyjama top as we go, and I reassure her that Mummia Ruth just had a bad dream and the cut on my head is tiny and everything will be okay. I sing the first verse of her favourite lullaby to her quietly and I tuck Craney in beside her. As soon as she is calm she goes all sleepy again so I leave her to drift away and I run back to Ruthie, who is sitting up in bed. She is still shaking and weeping, and her mouth is open in a silent scream. When I move to touch her she flinches, as if I have hit her and am trying to do it again.

'Ruthie', I say softly. 'Ruthie, it's me, Gina. I'm here. You are safe, *cara*. It's okay, nobody can hurt you now. I'm right here.' I don't touch her, but I sit close so she can feel that I am here. She says nothing. She doesn't even acknowledge that I have spoken. She just sits there, staring into the distance, and I can see that whatever this dream was, it was the worst one yet, and she is so traumatized by it that I don't know what to do or say, to make it better.

So I say nothing, and I reach for a tissue to wipe my eye and stem the blood from my head that still seeps slowly down my face, and after a long time her shaking stops.

It seems stupid to offer her tea. She looks like she needs something a lot stronger than that, but I hesitate to offer it. I don't wanna leave her alone again. It was bad enough leaving her just to take Chiara away. I wanna find out what the fuck this dream was about. She needs to tell me.

After a time she turns to me and she says the words I will never forget, words that make me feel so sick I could fall to the ground and weep too.

'I remember,' she says, in a low shaky voice.' I remember it now; all of it. When I was little. The cellar. Rebekah. He raped her in the cellar.'

She says nothing further, she is still shaking, so I do not press her for more. This is something she needs to say in her own way, and in her own time. But I am wondering who would rape her little sister in a cellar. I wonder when, and who, and why, and how she even came to be there. I think of a frightened child in a cellar, with the *inevitabile* coming, and something inside me breaks.

Eventually, Ruthie takes a deep breath. She starts talking softly, gently, almost to herself, like she is alone. I take hold of her hand and say nothing. I know it may not matter to her that anyone is here with her right now, that she is not all alone, but it matters to me. I do not want her to say all this to nobody. She doesn't shake my hand away, so that is a good sign. Her tears are still falling but it is silent weeping now.

'I was nine. It was two weeks before term broke up. Mum was at work. He was angry with me for wanting his attention. He'd been ignoring me for weeks, but he was spending a lot of time with Rebekah. I think I remember why we weren't at school. We had chicken pox. We both had it at the same time, it was the only time we were ever off school together in term time.

'I was in my room, and he called to Rebekah. I went too, because I thought if they were doing something nice I could be part of it for once but he screamed at me to go back to my room, so I did. I was really upset, so I started reading a book, to take my mind off it.'

The horror dawns on me, that she is talking about her father; the man who is not her father, in fact. Amidst the *miseria* of what she is saying, I feel such relief that he is not her father. He is the worst kind of monster, a total freak of humanity, but at least she is not of his blood. I am hoping he did not rape her too. That way, there is no *violazione* on her, to process too, as well as what she saw happening to Rebekah. That is more than enough to deal with by itself.

I pull Ruthie towards me and I gather her into my arms. Neither of us speaks but I rock her gently, to comfort her, because I know that her head is in turmoil.

After a time, I don't know how long, Ruthie clears her throat, and takes another deep breath. She says, in a small and wobbly voice;

'I must've blocked it all out. I remember it now, as clear as day, what happened. I heard her screaming my name, so I went to look for her. Dad had her down in the cellar, in the dark, with his hand over her mouth to keep her quiet. He must have been hoping I'd give up and go away. The light didn't work. He must've been *counting* on me giving up and going away.'

She is speaking in a whisper, almost distractedly, as if to herself. 'But I tripped over his torch and I discovered them. I saw what he was doing.'

She is shaking. Her eyes are full of agony, and suddenly they go wide and she is staring at me. 'Mum knew. Oh, God! She knew, Gina! They sat me down and ordered me to forget what I'd seen, never to speak of it, never to think about it. They told me that if I ever told anyone they would kill us both and bury us down in that cellar, under the dirt floor.'

She goes on to tell me what else the parents said, the threats they made. Those two little girls, Rebekah and Ruthie; they were terrified out of their minds, and I can hardly believe that a father did such a terrible thing to his child. But that is not the worst thing, is it? What kind of mother lets him? *Che tipo di madre permetterebbe a sua figlia di essere così violato?* She was a monster, to allow that, then to help *il bastardo depravato* cover it up. She was not human. Neither was he. My head feels like it is going to explode.

Ruthie turns to me. 'I don't think I'll go back to sleep tonight, Gina. But you should. It's the middle of the night.'

'What? Are you kidding? How could I sleep, after what you just told me?' I am *incredulo* that even as Ruthie is traumatized, she is still thinking of me. 'Don't be ridiculous, *cara*. I would find it easier to fly to the moon than to go back to sleep right now.'

'I'm sorry.'

'Hey! Don't ever be sorry. Not *ever*, okay? It's alright, and I mean it. I really do, and you should know that about me by now. I am going nowhere, *cara*, especially not back to sleep.'

I ask her if she wants a cup of hot *chioccolato* with a shot of amaretto in it, and she thinks for a moment then nods. I am glad about that, because it is something real that I can do for her, and it will warm her. She is shivering with the shock of this terrible memory, and as I make the drink, I am shaking also, and I wonder if that was the only time Rebekah was *violata* by that man, or whether this is only the start of a lot more for Ruthie to remember, of this horrible, unspeakable thing. I am blinking back tears myself, now.

Her mother knew about it and as that thought comes back into my head, a light comes on inside me, and I suddenly feel there is something there for me to focus on, but I don't know what it is. I try to make sense of this feeling I have, deep down in my guts, like a pull, like there is a link I need to find. I feel I am on the edge of something that is just ahead of my vision, something I can't see or hear that is out there, that I need to track down and understand. It's like there is a hook I can't see but I know is there, hanging just out of my reach, but if I can grab it, I can make sense of something that is so far hiding itself from me.

If that *bastardo* was abusing Rebekah, is that why she was so hostile to Ruthie? It doesn't make sense, at least not yet. Ruthie tried to save her! Surely she would have remembered that? But as I take the drinks through to the bedroom and hand one to my still-shivering darling, I feel that we will need to have another conversation about Rebekah very soon. I feel somehow that there is something more to all of this, something that will link all the ugly pieces of this unspeakable family puzzle together. I pray for it not to be so, but something inside me knows better.

Chapter Sixteen
- Ruth -

I've been tormented to the point of struggling not to scream, all morning, by the memory that has resurfaced, that Rebekah was sexually abused by our father. Then I remember; he is *her* father. He isn't mine. In the last hour, I've finally managed to stop shaking, but my whole body has this terrible, scraped-out feeling, like nothing is real, nothing in my life is certain, except for one thing. The image I now have, of him abusing her in our cellar, and her anguished face, these things will plague me now, forevermore. I'm not exactly sure why it has come back to me now. I had the dreams, the auditory hallucinations of breaking glass, and I wasn't sure what it meant, only that it unsettled me beyond description.

Gina thinks the funeral was the catalyst, the row at the gravesite and the threats my father made. She's probably right, because that is when it all started; the first night, right after the funeral. Then when the glass broke in the back door as it slammed in a draught, it traumatized me too. But when I think back now, to the altercation at my parents' house, when I smashed the big mirror above the fireplace. I remember feeling a very strange sensation, in my head, when that happened. I also clearly remember pushing it to one side, because there was still so much more to be said at that point, and I needed to concentrate on saying it because I wanted and needed that conversation to be the last we ever had as a 'family.'

But now, I think I understand; that the smashing mirror triggered something that had been buried for a long time, and maybe would have stayed that way for my whole life if certain events hadn't occurred that dragged it back to my consciousness. The resonance, that sensation of something 'shifting' and wanting to move into a different place in my head; I now believe that was my memory returning. The memory of being in a dark cellar, scared out of my wits, trying to find my screaming sister, and finally understanding why she was so frightened. The memory of my father, on his filthy knees on the filthy cellar floor, raping a trapped and terrified six-year-old girl.

Him shouting and shaking his fist at the gravesite, that was the beginning of the reawakening.

I have to go to the police with what I know. I have no idea if it will be of any help, but it might account for why Rebekah had certain sexual proclivities. It might answer some important questions about why she was the way she was, and who knows whether that will help or not? I'm no psychologist, but even I know there might be an important connection. But I need to tell the authorities, because if I don't, it means I've let her down again.

And I'm wondering if the reason she hated me was because I let her down before. Because I forgot what happened, or had it forced it out of my mind by the parents I was truly terrified of, for fear of being killed if I ever let it take hold in my mind to the point where I might have spoken out.

Maybe she thought I didn't care about it. I don't know why she never challenged me about it. If she could have helped me to remember what happened, all those years ago, I could have helped *her* so much. And the questions keep coming. Was it shame that stopped her? And what I remembered – was that the first time? Were there more times? Was it a one-time, random thing I witnessed that day? Or was it systematic, a regular occurrence? Will I ever really know? Do I *want* to? What would it do to my psyche, if I found out it was a regular thing? And what would it change for my poor dead sister?

The doorbell rings, catapulting me straight out of my wretched state of mind, and I remember that Gina is out. She's gone to collect some more fabulous fabrics from the warehouse, after they called to say that her long-awaited shipment had finally arrived from Italy. She didn't want to leave me by myself, as she is still very worried about me, but I managed to convince her that I'm fine, and she needs to do this. She took off, all floaty and excited, and it was so nice to know a happy event was happening for a change. Her eyes were all sparkly, like bright new diamonds, at the prospect of having some sexy new swatches to work with. I couldn't help but giggle at her joy. Trying to separate Gina from glorious fabric is like trying to keep a grizzly bear from its brand-new cub. Things can turn ugly if you get in the way.

As I head to the front door, I wonder what fresh misery might be lying behind it this time, since the plague of bad news has felt relentless, but I'm pleasantly surprised to find Adie standing on the doorstep. I smile at her in real delight. It's been a few days since I've seen her, and a random visit from a lovely friend is exactly what I need right now, to take my mind off everything else that's been dragging me down.

But she doesn't look happy. In fact she looks downright miserable and I am immediately concerned. She appears to have the weight of the world on her shoulders, like she's desperate to unburden herself, and it's unexpected to say the least, because this kind of thing doesn't happen with us. For all the strength of our friendship, we don't confide much in one another about our personal problems. I did offload everything to her and Bryan, not long back, but I didn't think that would have put us on a footing where Adie would want to do the same.

It isn't that I wouldn't want to help. It's just that typically, neither of us is a doorstep crier, and I don't really know the intricacies of her family; only that he husband is away a lot with his work. Since she's never given me any reason to doubt it, I've always just assumed that this normally sunny lady is happy in her skin, but today she looks anything but. I vaguely remember hearing Bryan drive off in a hurry about an hour ago. Maybe they've had a row.

'Come in, Adie. I'll put the kettle on. Not sure if we have any biscuits, but I'll see what I can find.'

Grateful for the diversion away from my own tormented thoughts, I bustle about making tea, locate some dusty digestives at the back of the virtually empty treat-cupboard, and shake them onto a plate. I note that Adie is not herself at all. She is atypically quiet and distracted, looking everywhere but straight at me, and her brow is creased in furrows, like she's not quite sure of why she's even here. Maybe there's something in the water that's causing us *all* to behave a bit like zombies right now.

I silently hand her a mug of tea and motion to the kitchen table for her to sit. As she lowers herself into her chair, I offer her a biscuit, and all of a sudden she starts to cry, in earnest. I'm horrified. I've never seen her cry like this before, and I haven't a clue how to react. While my first instinct is always to give crying people a big warm hug, I've learned through long experience that it's not always what they want. I

It dismays me a bit that in spite of the years we've lived alongside one another I still don't know if Adie is a comfort-hugger or not. I shelve the urge to try, and attempt to lighten the mood by remarking that as dusty, battered biscuits go, the digestives probably really are bad enough to make someone burst into tears.

She doesn't smile. Feeling slightly lost, I gently touch her arm.

'Adie, what's happened? Tell me.'

It takes her a while to compose herself and I give her an extra moment while I go and fetch her a box of tissues from the coffee table in the living room. She blots her eyes, takes a deep breath and looks miserably at me.

'Ruth, I don't know how to tell you this, but there's something you need to know, before you find out from anywhere else. I'm still trying to figure out how to make sense of it all myself, and so is Bryan, but our son Matthew was arrested for a second time this morning. The police are holding him for questioning – about your sister's murder.'

I stare at her in disbelief, and I can see by her face, she is full of anguish.

Arrested for the <u>second</u> time? He's already been arrested once, over it?

This isn't a joke. It's a shockingly real truth. The sound of my own blood rushes through my ears like a muffled, faraway jungle drum and my mind casts around, half blindly, for any kind of hook that will stop it from careering completely out of control while I try to process what Adie has just said. Her son Matthew, and my sister?

I don't know Matthew Bostock well at all. Even when I first met him, he didn't live at home. He was away at university most of the time, and then he bought a small house, or a flat, from what I can remember. That's all I know about him; vague sightings across the back fence, a brief nod to one another at the odd summer barbecue as he hung out at the other end of the garden on his mobile phone. He handed me a drink once at a party next door but it was a fleeting gesture; a young man just doing what his parents asked him to do for one of their friends. Truth be told, I probably wouldn't know him if I fell over him in the street, these days.

'No, Adie, there must be some mistake. Isn't Matthew in his early twenties? Rebekah is nearly thirty-five, or at least she was; sorry, I'm still struggling to believe she's gone. But she wouldn't have gone out with someone so much younger, surely?'

Adie shakes her head.

'Matthew is twenty-three, Ruth. And they weren't boyfriend and girlfriend.' She is clearly wanting to say more but appears to be struggling to form the words.

'Adie, please, just tell me what you know.'

She draws a deep, shaky breath, closes her eyes for a heartbeat before looking at me squarely, and ploughs on.

'Okay. Here goes. Ruth, I swear to God, and you must believe me, I didn't know. But Matthew is a sex worker. Rebekah was one of his clients. I'm so sorry to be the one to tell you, but it's the truth. He and three colleagues – other sex workers – were all at her house the night before she was murdered. It was a group thing. There was a lot of DNA at the scene, as you can probably imagine, and some of it was Matthew's.'

She takes another deep, shaky breath. 'I wanted you to hear it from me, Ruth, because although he didn't kill her, he can't produce evidence of where he actually was on the night she was killed. So it looks like he may be charged, because at this stage there don't appear to be any other leads. If he is charged, I'm sure it will be all over the news, like the murder was itself.'

'What kind of DNA are we talking about, here?' I demand. Adie looks desperately uncomfortable, and doesn't meet my eyes.

'Sperm? That's what we're talking about, right?'

She nods miserably.

I'm trying to comprehend the implications of what she's said, but my rational head-voice is saying, *hang on a minute, I don't know much about this kind of thing, but aren't sex workers supposed to use condoms?*

Adie somehow, inexplicably, sees my confusion as a reason to keep rattling on. I really wish she wasn't here, telling me things I don't want to hear. For the love of God, is there not already enough going on in my hitherto stable world without this, on top of it all?

'I know it must be a massive shock, and please forgive me for coming in here and dropping it on you like this. But I'm so aware that the news about Matthew could break at any minute. It's likely to be all over the media, there may well be reporters phoning or turning up on both of our doorsteps, and I couldn't bear the thought of you hearing it like that. Something this awful that links us? It had to come from me.'

Adie's misery is palpable. None of this is her fault, I know that. It must have taken so much courage for her to come over here and tell me something so shameful to her and horrifying to us both. She is clearly struggling to comprehend it, herself.

I'm slowly managing to get to grips with what she's just told me, which kind of answers the questions about the amount of DNA present in and around Rebekah, even if it is completely outrageous and unethical. It also corroborates a nosy neighbour's statement to the police, about a group of people who regularly visited Rebakah at home. The confusion starts to clear a little, only to be rapidly replaced by the worst sadness I think I've ever felt.

'Okay, so that's it then. That's the answer about so much DNA. But aren't sex workers supposed to use protection, Adie? Isn't that the cardinal rule for prostitutes and... and... whatever the men are called? Why did that not happen? I don't understand.' My voice sounds small, childish, like I've regressed in my confusion to being a child again.

'Male escorts. That's what they're called, apparently, and I don't understand either, Ruth. I only know what Matthew told me; that Rebekah asked them not to use any protection. According to him, they visited her quite regularly, and it was always the same request. No condoms.'

My mind threatens, once again, to spin away from my ability to control it. Rebekah asked them not to use condoms? Four different male prostitutes? And every time they went there? Why the hell would she do that? It doesn't make any sense. My sister hated sex, at least that's what I thought, and yet she had regular visits from *groups* of sex *workers* and she asked them to *not* use condoms. Did she want to get pregnant? Did she just think of herself as worthless? Was she on some kind of death-wish? *What?* I just don't get it. I'm seriously floundering. I'm actually starting to feel like I'm drowning.

I'm also feeling Adie's humiliation and pain as if it were my own. The connection I have with her, right here in this moment, as we both bob frantically in a chopped-up sea of confusion and disbelief, is inexplicable. I feel like I want to bury my head in her chest and scream while she holds me. It is an extraordinary impulse, but of course I don't give into it, because she clearly has enough to deal with already. That kind of reaction from me to what she has told me would be wholly inappropriate, and just beyond weird for her, I'm sure. In any case, it's more likely she's expecting me to slap her, or scream at her, or both.

'I don't know what to say,' I manage eventually, staring at the floor.

'I know, darling. I don't expect you to say anything at all. But I do want you to believe me when I say I had no idea Matthew was a sex worker, and I really don't think he killed Rebekah.'

'You don't *think* he did? He's your son. Why aren't you saying you *know* he didn't?' I've picked up on semantics, and I'm chiding myself for being childish and churlish, when she bursts into tears again, and drops another bomb.

'Because I'm not a hundred percent sure. Not anymore.' I find myself staring at her in shock and disbelief. She shakes her head and continues;

'The night before last, when he was first arrested, he was released without charge and we brought him back here. He was meant to be staying the night with us but there was a really ugly fight, and he lashed out, said some really unkind and hurtful things to us both, and he punched Bryan and broke his nose.

'He was so angry, I felt like I didn't know him, Ruth. I was terrified of my own child. He made such a mess of his father. There was blood everywhere, and he was absolutely vile to me, shoving me, saying things I had no idea he was capable of even thinking, let alone ever actually saying to his own mother, and then he stormed out. I found his phone in the street outside the house, smashed to smithereens. Not just dropped. Literally smashed to pieces. It's in a thousand pieces. It took some violence, to reduce it to that.' She is crying again in earnest now.

'I'm not sure what he's capable of, anymore,' she sobbed. 'I really don't think its murder, but I can't honestly say anymore, and I hate myself more than you could ever know, for even *thinking* that about my own flesh and blood. It feels like the worst kind of betrayal of him, even to think it, and saying it is a million times worse, but I have. I've said it.'

Her shoulders are shaking as she weeps, quietly now, into an already sodden tissue. The clock in the dining room ticks gently, as we both sit in silence for a couple of minutes, each with our own agonized thoughts, and then Adie says, in a tiny voice;

'He told us he was with another client on the night Rebekah was murdered, the night after they were all there with her, but the woman won't vouch for him. She's some prominent person in the local community, at least that's what he says. I want so much to believe him. With all my heart and soul, I want to believe him, Ruth. I want to think he's just reactive and scared, and acting out, but after everything I've seen and heard since his arrest, I just can't say for certain that he's telling the truth about that or anything else. And that just breaks my heart.'

Jesus! The napalm just keeps coming, doesn't it? When do I get to have a day free from earth-shattering news that continues to eat me alive and drive me to the brink of the abyss? Will this freakish nightmare that passes for a life lately ever come to an end?

I'm grappling with the maddest melange of emotions. Anger, confusion, disbelief, disgust, and I suddenly realise how mentally exhausted I really am, from everything I've had to take on board, and try to assimilate, in the past couple of weeks. I'm reduced to simply saying the first thing that comes into my head, without my usual thought about how it might sound to someone else.

'So you've known for two days now that he's suspected of killing my sister, and you only come here now, to tell me?'

'It looked like it had blown over, Ruth. Matthew is so adamant he has an alibi, just not one that would vouch for him. We thought that would change, if it were true. We thought the police would have seen to that somehow, talked the woman round, or something, and he'd be in the clear, but that hasn't happened. Apparently she is denying even knowing him or being involved with his agency, and I don't know what that means for any of us. Ruth, I'm so sorry.'

I want to be angry with Adie, for holding back such devastating news, but I cannot find it within myself. Maybe

I'm just exhausted from jumping the ceaseless mental hurdles. Maybe I just can't face any further conflict. But it's not just that. I feel Adie's pain as if it were my own, and ultimately my urge to comfort her overrides everything else and I reach out to her. She comes into my embrace, and hugs me hard, and there is so much emotion in that hug, from both of us, it's like a real connection. Like coming home to something you never knew how much you'd missed.

The hug lasts a long time, but eventually we both let go. She looks at me like she has a million words to say, but cannot get them out. I don't press her further, because I literally can't face hearing anything more. I'm officially on overload. Instead, I prompt her to go, by standing up as I speak.

'Thanks for letting me know, Adie. I still don't know what to say or how to feel about it all. I think I probably need some time for it to settle in my head. Can we talk again later?'

She nods, and gets up to go. At the door she turns to me, reaches up, and gently pushes a lock of my hair back that has fallen across my eyes. It's the kind of gesture a loving mother would make, and I can only wonder at how truly torn she must be, as a deeply dedicated mum to her two children, to be in a place where she actually doubts one of them, over the most heinous of human crimes committed.

'I'm truly sorry, Ruth. I wish I could fix this, make it all go away. But I think we have to wait it out for a bit, see what develops, and hopefully Matthew will be exonerated, the real killer will be found, and we can all get on with trying to repair our lives as best we can. Please come over whenever you feel ready, and don't worry if you don't. Or I can come back here. Just say the word, whatever you want or need. This has all knocked me for six as well, and I'm struggling very hard to come to terms with how Matty has been living his life, so I have to get my own head together, but I couldn't leave you out of the loop. You had to know, and also know that I'm here for you, whatever you need.'

Having run out of words to offer, I simply nod numbly, at Adie. As I open the front door to let her out, she hugs me again, briefly this time, and in the next instant she is gone, scurrying across the front lawn, head down, back to her own house. God alone knows what she is going through, but it's up to her to process it. I already have more than enough shit of my own to deal with, and I'm conscious that, to add to it all, we may soon be under siege right here in our own home, if Matthew Bostock is charged with Rebekah's murder. The news will break, and the media vultures will descend here like flies on a fresh pile of pig shit.

I wonder briefly whether or not to call Gina, to get her come home early, but I decide against it. My lovely wife deserves to enjoy her time at the warehouse without having to worry about me for once. I want her to fully enjoy her time with Chiara too, when she picks her up from school, without having to feel she has to rush back home. Sometimes the pair go for ice-cream on their way home. I hope they do that today. God knows any joy will be short-lived, if what Adie says might happen actually does. If Matthew Bostock is charged with killing my sister, relationships could become more than just a little strained in this nice neighbourhood, and not just for the Bostocks themselves.

Randomly, and ridiculously, an image flashes into my mind of digging a tunnel underneath the back fence so that Adie and I will still be able to see one another away from prying eyes. My need to stay connected to her is as strong and unexplainable as it is inappropriate, at such an emotionally charged time for us all.

I push away the image and deny it room to grow. If the worst of storms does decide to break, unleashing hell around our heads, we'll each need to stay in our own familial foxholes until the worst is over. As much as I feel for poor Adie, I have to leave her to it, at least for now. I've got bigger fish to fry. I need to work out how to tell the police what I know without turning into a basket case as I'm doing it. But then again, does it really matter, if I seem like a basket case? I *am* a bloody basket case. Maybe I can do without trying to find the effort to hide the fact.

Chapter Seventeen
- Adie -

So the other men with Matty who went to Rebekah's house the night before she was murdered apparently all have cast-iron alibis. Matty is the only one who doesn't. The police picked him up again first thing, as he was leaving home for work, and they let Bryan know from the station. From what I can gather, he has been re-arrested and is likely to be formally charged on suspicion of murder, and I'm not sure what happens from there, but if what Trevor Jones said two days ago was anything to go by, it doesn't look like they'll grant him bail.

So my boy is banged up.

I don't know how to feel, about any of this. It's all completely foreign territory to me. Forty-eight hours ago, if anyone had suggested to me that my own son might be capable of murder, I wouldn't have believed it in a million years. I'd have slapped their face for saying it. Today, as I sit here at my kitchen table, half-stupefied with fear, and drowning in my own dread, I cannot say for certain they'd be wrong.

A full day and night went by after the fight here, without a single word from our son. Matty never called once, after his vicious attack, to ask how his Dad was after being punched in the face so hard it broke his nose. He didn't call to enquire how his mother was, after breaking her heart, sneering at her torment and confusion, pushing her into a wall, and then leaving her in tears.

I've always thought of Matty as more of a pacifist than an antagonist. He's, not shy of confrontation if the situation warrants, but he's too good natured to be capable of any real violence. He even voluntarily gave a DNA sample to the police a few years ago after a nightclub rape, because he wanted them to find the man who did it. He wanted the poor girl involved to have her day in court. That is the son we raised.

The man who stood here ranting and raging in our house two nights ago, throwing punches and snarling like a cornered dog, and who has ignored us since, other than to get the police to advise Bryan that he was being taken back into custody; he is someone I don't recognise. How do I reach out and make a meaningful connection with this violent virtual stranger, and does he even want me to? For the first time in my own son's life, I don't know how to reach him.

What I do know is that I now have to have a very difficult series of conversations without delay, starting with my husband. He is on his way home from work, after calling me to tell me about Matty and I ordered him to come home right away, for what was about to be perhaps the biggest conversation of our lives. He agreed without question, electing to wait until he got here to ask me anything, which I'm grateful for, because it gives me time to fully prepare myself. Bless him, even with a broken nose and two vaguely black-ringed eyes, and despite being torn apart with disappointment and despair over how Matty has chosen to behave towards him, Bryan's first instinct was to go rushing down to the police station to meet with Trevor Jones, to find out what arrangements can be made for our son.

Bryan's fundamentally a good man, for all he's distracted and hardly ever at home, and I don't know how he'll take the news, but I have to tell him about Ruth, and he will hopefully help me decide whether or not to tell her about her parentage as well. I think she needs to know that too, especially now since it looks like Matty will be charged, but my head won't go there just yet.

As Bryan's tyres crunch their way up the gravel drive, I put the kettle on. The tea-making ritual is quite farcical really in the face of impending doom, and I can understand why Matty curled his lip at it, but there's no denying that a hot cup of tea usually does seem to help in times of crisis. At best, a teacup will give Bryan something to focus on instead of my face while he takes in what I have to tell him. At worst, it's something he can throw at me.

It's horrible, when you know you're about to break someone's heart by revealing that you've kept the biggest secret of your whole life from them for more than twenty-five years; that you've kept a colossal part of yourself hidden from them for all the time they've known you, and that you've manipulated their lives as well as your own, for reasons you've never been honest about. Bryan just thinks I wanted this house because of the price and the location. He's about to learn that the foundation on which our whole lives have been carefully constructed has a fundamental weakness at its core, a series of secrets, lies and omissions, and the whole lot may be about to come tumbling down around us.

The tension around this conversation yet to be started is huge, and I suddenly start to cry. As Bryan comes into the kitchen and sees me sitting there with tears spilling down my face, he immediately thinks it's because of Matty.

'Oh, come on, Adie! I'm still sure it's all just a stupid misunderstanding! They have to get to the bottom of this, and they will. They just have procedures to follow, that's all, and we have to sit tight until they sort it. So will Matty, and he can, love. He's a big boy.'

Bryan puts his arm around me and gives me a squeeze and then sits at the table. I hand him a cup of tea, just the way he likes it. His smile is full of tension and worry but he gives being cheerful his very best shot.

'Now, what's this momentous conversation we need to have?'

I'm crying really hard now, and he suddenly sees that it's no time for even a forced kind of jollity. He sees that things are about to become serious, and he settles into his chair and leans forward, his face full of worry and concern.

'What is it? What's happened? Adie? Whatever it is, it'll be okay. I promise. There's nothing we can't deal with. You know you can tell me anything.'

I look away, miserably, unable to look him in the eye as I take the deepest of breaths and draw up the words I've had buried inside me for well over half of my life.

'I had a baby when I was fifteen, Bryan. A little girl. I gave her up for adoption.'

Silence hangs heavy for eight or nine heartbeats, then Bryan lets a long breath out through his teeth. He doesn't say anything for several minutes, and I don't know how to proceed, so I just sit there crying into my tea, and giving him time to assimilate his thoughts. I still can't bring myself to look at his face.

He hasn't exploded, he hasn't thrown his cup at me. So far so good. Maybe.

'You had a baby at fifteen. You gave her up for adoption.'

'Yes. My parents decided that,' I said, almost defensively. 'I wasn't in a position to fight them.'

'My God, Adie. Why did you never tell me?'

'I was ashamed, at first. I thought you'd think I'd been a slut, or something. I wanted to tell you, when we first met, but I was too afraid. I tried to work up the courage to tell you just before we got married, because that would have given you an out if you'd wanted one. You deserved the truth, and a get-out option as well, but I just couldn't bring myself to start the conversation. I was so in love with you, Bryan, and I didn't want to lose you. I couldn't face that, so I kept putting it off, and putting it off, and the longer I left it, the harder it got, so I ended up not telling you at all. Somehow it just seemed easier, especially after our children came. I've been such a coward.'

I go on to fill in the gaps, about how I'd fallen pregnant out of naivety, and how my parents wanted me to have a decent chance to make a good life, so I went along with their wishes.

Unburdening myself somehow feels less terrible than I thought it would. The words are out here now; real, in both our heads and our lives, and we will make of it what we will. Whatever happens now, I no longer have to hide my biggest, saddest, longest-standing secret from the one person I love more than anyone else in the world. Whatever Bryan says or does, or doesn't say or do from now on, whatever he thinks of me, at least it is out in the open. No more hiding. No more secrets and lies, at least not from me.

Finally I have the courage to look at him, and as I do so I brace myself for his outrage. Instead I'm surprised to find sadness and compassion, but I know I still have a very long run at the gauntlet yet, before I can say with any certainty that we will recover from this. He doesn't know the rest of it yet.

'Do you know who she is, your daughter? Are you in contact with her?'

I nod, reluctantly. I don't want to tell him. But I have to. 'Yes, Bryan. I know who she is, I've known for some time now. I'm in contact with her, but we're just friends. She doesn't know I'm her mother, in fact I don't think she even knows she's adopted.'

'You could have told me, Adie. In fact, you *should* have. I wouldn't have judged you. You were fifteen, and they were different times back then. I would have understood.'

I look at him again, my lovely bear, and I'm so grateful for the time I've had with him. If it all falls apart after today, at least I've had all that.

'Would you have understood, Bryan? Really?'

'I'd have tried,' he admits. 'I was a lot younger then too, and I might not have taken it brilliantly, but I like to think I'd have tried to understand.'

And he would. I know that he would, and for the first time in all our years I can finally see how monumentally stupid I've been, in thinking he might not have supported me. Of course he would have. He's too good a man to have done anything else.

He goes quiet for a minute or two, staring out behind me through the French doors and into the rear garden.

I'm gearing up for the rest of my confession when he speaks again. 'So Matty and Teresa have a half-sister they don't know about.'

'Yes.'

'And this half-sister would be, what, thirty-six or so years old?'

'Yes, she's thirty-seven. She's married with a child, a daughter of her own.'

'So you're a grandmother already.'

'Yes. In a manner of speaking.'

Bryan can see I am still jumpy, miserable and agitated. He looks narrowly at me then says, 'Why do I get the feeling there's more? Like, why are you telling me this now, Adie? Why now, of all times, when our son is in such serious bother? Forgive me for wondering, but as big as this revelation is, I'm not sure how anything else right now is more important than Matty maybe facing a murder trial. Your timing is a bit strange, if you don't mind my saying so.'

I look at him, trying to find the words to press on. He looks at me hard.

'Adie, does this confession of yours have something to do with Matty's predicament?'

And, finally, there it is – a way across that bridge from here to I-don't-know-where. When I say the words, there will be no going back, no undoing of what's been said and done. I only hope, having been invited onto the bridge, that it will provide me with a safe landing, that my marriage will be strong enough to survive, that I won't be simply hurled into the harbour to take my chances with a churning, turning tide.

'Yes it does, Bryan. Because my daughter is Ruth Stenton; our next-door neighbour, and Rebekah Stenton, the woman he's accused of killing, was her sister.'

Without a word or a glance in my direction, Bryan abruptly gets up from the table, and walks out of the room. I hear him leave the house, get into his car and drive away, and I know he's just putting some distance between us to give himself time to process what I've just told him. I sit here in the burgeoning silence, heading off the self-indulgent urge to start feeling sorry for myself. Instead, I force myself to focus on how Bryan must be feeling, how my children are going to feel, and whether we'll all recover as a family if the worst happens; if my entire family (including Ruth) disowns me, and Matty ends up going to jail.

I'm still sitting there, an hour later, when Bryan returns. He slams the front door and stomps down the hallway.

Here it comes.

Without any preamble, he launches his attack.

'So let me guess. You tracked down your daughter, and you bought this ridiculously over-priced house next door to her so you could be close to her, but none of us – including *her* – ever had the slightest idea what you were up to. You did all this behind our backs. Tell me, Adie, if Matty hadn't been involved with Rebekah Stenton, would you *ever* have told me about Ruth? Would you *ever* have told our children they have a half-sister they don't know about? Are you planning on telling Ruth? Or are we all just expected to carry on being the unwitting puppets in your private show, moved around on whatever stage you've chosen for us all, just so you could have what you wanted?'

Bryan is blazing. I don't blame him. They are all fair questions, but I don't know how to answer them, and that seems to make him worse.

'My God, Adie. You're a piece of work. A teenage baby I can accept. You were young, probably scared and confused, and your parents stepped in and took your choice away. I get it, and I'm sorry it happened to you, and I wish I'd known, so I could have helped you deal with it, because clearly you never did, did you? You tracked her down and moved next door to her like some kind of secret stalker, and your family; me, Matty and Teresa, we all just got dragged along for the bloody ride.'

I will not fight with him. Bryan rarely wants to fight. He hates arguing as much as I do so we've always managed to have *discussions* about things, civilized disagreements, rather than outright fights.

But this is different. I need to let him rant. He fully deserves his platform because I have wronged him – and our kids, in the worst possible way, for the longest time, and he needs to say how he feels about that, even if it means hurling insults at me and shouting and saying things he maybe doesn't mean. I have to accept what he throws at me for however long it takes until the dust settles. Only when the dust settles will we be able to see what can or can't be put back together from whatever rubble might remain. After the hand grenade I've just thrown into the middle of this family, there might not be anything to salvage at all. I'm too overwrought to even hope.

But as suddenly as it boiled over, Bryan's anger is gone. He slumps into a chair and looks at me levelly.

'Adie, I'm trying to understand.'

'I know you are. I want to *help* you understand. Tell me what more I can say. There are no excuses for what I've done, with this house, with befriending Ruth. I was just a coward, that's all it came down to. There have been so many times I wanted to tell you everything, even as we were moving in here. I wanted to. I really did, but I just couldn't. I couldn't face losing you.'

He shakes his head. 'Why do you think you'd have lost me by telling me the truth, Adie? Do you think that the truth would somehow be more destructive to our marriage than all these decades of bloody lies?'

'Mistakes are one thing. A lifetime of lies to cover them up, well, that's a whole different ballgame. Put yourself in my shoes. Would you appreciate being lied to for more than a quarter of a century, about something as important as this? Do you not think I deserved to know the truth about why we moved here? Have I not let you have everything you ever wanted? Did I not say yes, let's move, if it means that much to you? Could you not have respected me enough to be honest about why?'

His voice is calmer now, but he is clearly still desperately upset and I just have to let it run its course. So many questions, and he deserves answers to every last one. I just don't know quite how to answer such a barrage. All I can say is that it was never about disrespect, only fear. It's a completely inadequate defence, but it's all I can offer.

'Are you going to tell Ruth?'

'I don't know, Bryan. I want to. I've *always* wanted to, but I don't know if she even knows she's adopted, and if she doesn't, how can I drop a bombshell like that on her?'

'What, the way you've just dropped it on me, you mean? And let's not forget about our own kids – you know, the ones we have *together*? What about them? They deserve to know, Adie. It'll be something of a bombshell for them too, and do you think Matty really needs that right now, on top of facing going to trial for something he hasn't done?'

'Matty might be guilty, Bryan. Have you thought about that?' My heart is in my mouth as I say the words.

He looks at me, incredulous. 'What? You can't possibly think that! How the fuck can you think that, Adie?'

'I don't want to think that,' I wail, helplessly. 'But after what I saw and heard in here the other night, I have to consider the possibility, and I think you do too.'

Bryan's face closes down. He stares at me, lost for what to say.

'Bryan, there's so much we don't know about him. It hurts like hell to say it but right now, after how he behaved towards us, attacking us like he did, finding out how he makes his living, I feel I don't know Matty at all, or what he might be capable of.'

Bryan slowly gets up from the table, and once more heads out through the door. He turns back towards me and shakes his head. 'You're saying you don't know your own son?'

'You said the same thing yourself the other night in bed, if you remember,' I remind him gently.

Bryan shakes his head again, waving away my reminder. 'Well, okay, Adie. Maybe you don't know your son, but I have to say, right here, right now, deep down I do know who Matthew is. I've *always* known who he is. I thought I knew who you were too.'

As he turns to walk away, I offer a parting shot. 'So if I'm not the person you thought I was, how can you be so sure Matthew's the person you think *he* is?'

My answer is a soundly slammed door and a resounding silence to follow. Bryan has left again, but this time I'm not so sure when he'll be back.

Chapter Eighteen
- *Ruth* -

Giggles and Smiley are staring at me as if I've got two heads. Smiley asks if I'm prepared to see a psychologist; one of their choosing, who can talk me through the memory that's come back to haunt me, and see if there are any others. They said something about professional verification of repressed memories. I told them of course; if it will help in any way, I'll be happy to talk to someone. In any case, a professional will no doubt help me to manage my jumbled, screwed-up thoughts about everything. It's not fair to expect poor Gina to keep trying to help me make sense of it all. As amazing as she is, there are some things that are best left to professionals who know how to navigate such uncharted, delicate and difficult waters. Leaving something like that to the layman can do more harm than good, and I think there's already been more than enough harm done.

'My father, or should I say the bastard who is not in fact my father, would deny everything I've told you, if you were to ask him. Pure and simple. He would tell you that I'm the mad one, the crazy one, making up stories, clutching at straws.'

I tell them about my visit to the vicarage, how I broke their precious mirror and destroyed their landline phone. They may as well have the facts from me about what I did, rather than solely from my not-father. They are clearly unimpressed about me taking matters into my own hands. They retreat to a corner of the room and talk quietly among themselves for a few minutes, then they ask me to wait in the reception area for a while. It's not long before they call me back in.

'You'll probably be aware that we seized a number of things from Rebekah's flat, Ms Stenton, including her mobile phone, and her computer. Could you tell us please, if this makes any sense to you? It looks like some kind of poem. We had no idea who it was directed at, and it didn't make any sense to us. There were a lot of poems, mostly quite dark, and we didn't know what any of them meant. But given what you've just told us, we'd now like to know if this is meaningful to you in any way.'

Giggles hands me an A4 sized piece of paper. I don't even get to the end of reading what's on it before I am sobbing my heart out and struggling to speak, or even to breathe.

'Never' A Leaf Nor A Life

I can never speak the words. They will never come.
Who betrayed me? A better question would be 'who didn't?'
You never spoke of it, never asked me to speak of it.
Long, long years of silence and ignorance, pretending.
'Nothing happened.'
Living life as if we were normal.
But you were never normal, were you?
Lucky you. There but for the grace of God you went.
Your non-normal just was. Mine was forced upon me.
No choice. I never had a choice.
Why did you never ask? Pretending it never mattered.
And just so you know, it didn't end. I was never free.
Never normal. Disgusting to myself, always.
An ugly, barren, lifeless tree. Never, never free.
I wish you'd cared enough to ask, but you never did.
Not once.
It would all have been so different if you had asked,
even once.
But now we have nothing. I am nothing. There is nothing.
And you are as dead to me as I am to myself.

They don't need me to tell them it's significant. They can see it in my face. They can read it in my body language. They can hear it in my anguished tears. They had no idea, before what I've just told them, that this was directed to me. But they do now.

Rebekah thought I knew; that I'd remembered. Just as I suspected, she thought I'd just chosen not to speak of it. She never understood that I'd forgotten; had it forced into repression, in abject fear for my life. She thought I knew, and didn't care.

I was her big sister. She needed me to protect her and I didn't. I was the one person who could have saved her, and I didn't. Right until the last. Right until her two final phone calls that I didn't pick up or return.

No wonder she hated me.

Her poem spoke of betrayal. The detectives said that there were a lot of poems, most with betrayal as their theme, but none of the others were as tangible as this one. I'd still like to read them though, and I told them that. They only said they'd see what they could do. I'm not family, despite what adoption records attest to, and while I could legally fight that, how long would it take, and where would the energy come from? Right now, as I sit here in the worst kind of anguish, I don't have the energy to claim *anything*.

How did I not know it was happening? Was he that clever? Was she that terrified? Was my mother so monstrously accepting or complacent, that it all went on under our family's roof for all the time she lived there, and beyond? Or did all or some of it take place somewhere else until she moved out? And then what? *In her flat?*

I excuse myself abruptly and bolt for the bathroom, where I crash into the first vacant toilet and violently vomit up everything I have in my stomach, until there is nothing left. Deep inside me, something is screaming.

I go back to the detectives who are looking at me sympathetically now. Smiley clears his throat, and speaks with his usual slowness, with the kind of voice that makes you wish you were somewhere else, watching paint dry.

'Your relationship with your parents is very difficult. Was Rebekah's too? Do you think either of them would have had any reason to actively hurt her?'

I shake my head emphatically. 'You mean aside from raping her as a child, and torturing her in God knows how many other horrible ways in the years after that? No. Absolutely not. As far as I could ever tell, they adore her.' *Or at least, they did. Past tense, remember?*

'It does seem that my father's approach to loving her was rather unorthodox though, doesn't it? Not to mention utterly unforgiveable, disgusting and vile? Oh, and illegal too. Let's not forget about that.'

My voice is quiet, and I can hardly believe the conversation. As if violating Rebekah *wasn't* hurting her? I know they are only asking, in their own ham-fisted way, about whether either of my parents could have killed her. These two will never win any prizes for eloquence, and their sensitivity genes are a long way shy of where they should be, even though they're doing their best. I guess it's up to me, to interpret what they're *really* asking.

I recall that Michael had told them he'd called Rebekah to invite her to dinner at home. That was no surprise. Dining together was something they did fairly often, as I understand it. I'm battling to try to understand the warped complexity of their relationship, but my head doesn't want to go there. Rebekah's poem was full of anguish about incestuous abuse, and betrayal, yet they all appeared to enjoy a familial closeness I'd always envied and been excluded from. I'm struggling to make sense of it all, and I tell that to Smiley and Giggles, who don't appear to be at all surprised.

'It certainly looks like it was a complicated relationship,' is all Smiley will offer, before they both walk me to the front door of the station and tell me they'll be in touch.

Chapter Nineteen
- *Matthew* -

Well, then. This is probably just about the end of my life, as I've always known it. 'All change,' cries the conductor, as I'm roundly kicked off the bus and straight under its fucking wheels.

Not only have I been arrested for a murder I didn't commit; I've lost my job at the agency as well, and they're talking about legal action. Breach of fucking contract. They have proof I had unprotected sex with a client, and they want to throw the book at me too. They're 'consulting with their legal representatives,' and there's no rocket science involved in figuring out what *that* means for me, especially when you add it to that the fact that the other three lads can all account for their whereabouts the night Becky Starr was murdered. They've lost their jobs too, and they're all under the same threat of legal action, but at least they all have solid alibis, one of which is a client who actually doesn't mind providing corroboration for the bloke in question. I should be so fucking lucky, but that self-serving old coward Christine seems to be happy to hang me out in the wind and, if Becky's killer isn't found quick-smart, it's only a matter of time before the media feeding frenzy starts around me and my family.

But finding the real Stenton Strangler doesn't look like happening any time soon because apparently the cops have no other leads; at least none that they're sharing. I'm it. Squarely, nicely, and neatly in the frame. And of course they want this all sewn up, don't they, and sooner rather than later, so that people can feel safe in their beds at night. And let's not forget about the prospect of possible promotions that can come after a job well done. I know I've seen my fair share of corrupt-copper films, but I'm not so stupid as to think it doesn't happen in the real world too.

I also have three people very keen to kick my head in. The other lads I was working with at Becky's are bloody fuming at having their own jobs ripped away, but to be fair, they did all sign up for a deal that bucked the system, just like I did. We all just thought we'd never get caught, and under normal circumstances, such as a client *not* going and getting herself murdered before our deposits had had time to clear, if you will, we'd have got away with it like we always did. Complacent, cocky bastards we *all* were, arrogant as fuck, and we're all paying the bloody price. I'm just the scapegoat that gets to carry the can while the others waltz off into a scot-free sunset, albeit without their lovely lucrative lines of work.

Getting smacked over is the least of my worries to be honest, even if by some lucky chance I do end up back on the bloody streets, but losing such an easy income is really going to hurt. I had a full book for weeks to come and I had the finances all planned out around it. I suppose I'll have to rethink a few of those goals that seemed achievable just a week ago but now look like pie in the sodding sky, even if I *don't* get locked up and lose everything. Funny how quickly the landscape of your life can change.

They took me back into custody this morning. My solicitor, Trevor Jones, is a good bloke. If anyone can sort this out, it's him. Dad came down here with him, apparently, but left soon after. He clearly doesn't want to clap eyes on me today, and who can blame him? I know I broke his nose the other night, I felt the crack under my knuckles as they connected with his face. I saw the shock in his eyes, but I just blanked it out. The poor bastard's probably got a face like a purple pumpkin, thanks to me, and Christ alone knows what Mum thinks. I'm telling myself that Dad just doesn't want me to see his face and feel bad about it, but I'm not convincing myself. The real truth is that he doesn't want to look at his violent, whoring son. I wonder if and when he will. He might be wondering the same thing.

After they brought me back in, I told the cops about Christine anyway, and being at her house shagging her brains out, on the night of Becky Starr's murder. I figured if I'm going down, I may as well at least try to take that dried-up bitch down with me. She told me she owed me nothing, so I figured I didn't owe her anything either. She seemed keen enough to shove me under the bus, so if I'm going under, maybe she will too, for perverting the course of justice or something. *That'd be a nice bit of tit for fucking tat, wouldn't it, you old slag?*

The cops still haven't formally charged me, but they've been asking some interesting questions, like what I was wearing on the night of Becky's murder, the precise times I arrived at and left Christine's house, what route I took, and so-on. They want the jeans and jacket I had on, for forensic analysis, and Trevor Jones said it was an appropriate request, so I told them they could go to my place, and I gave them the keys.

It's the last I've heard so far, but I'm sure they'll be doing a thorough search of the place while they're there. Not that they'll find anything important. It's just a regular bachelor pad, no dead bodies stashed in the wardrobe, or even handcuffs in the bedside drawer. When I'm not at work, in one job or on another, so to speak, I'm just a regular average bloke. I don't do my washing up as often as I should, and the bed sheets probably wanted washing three weeks ago, but other than that, there's nothing in that house that could separate me from any other single bloke my age who lives alone and is never home much anyway. There's nothing weird, unusual or remarkable about Matty Bostock, Your Honour, apart from the fact that he's a prostitute, and by all accounts, he doesn't even give a decent shag.

The cops still haven't charged me, and they won't until they can verify things with Christine one way or the other, not that she'll give them anything, I'm sure. They said they'd try to keep her out of it if she 'fessed up, mumbling something about preserving her anonymity for the sake of the public interest, since her old man is a prominent man-about-the-town and certain significant public benefits might be lost if he were to become the subject of a scandal; even one that wasn't his fault. Police corruption at its finest; outside of holding innocent people's DNA on file, that is.

It's a glimmer of hope, but I don't know how bright it really is. Maybe the old bag still won't talk, even with all that lovely protection dangled in front of her.

The cops told me off for withholding important information that could have helped my case, but like I told them, I didn't kill anyone so I thought – naively it seems – that justice would prevail and I'd be found as what I am; innocent. I didn't see the need to incriminate anyone else, in the beginning. It's a lesson and a half, finding out that the wheels of right and wrong don't always turn in the direction they're supposed to. The real truth of the matter, whether we like it or not, is that innocent people do go down, and sometimes they stay down, because the shit-cart commonly called justice can't quite go the full distance once its wheels have started falling off.

One of the desk staff has just been down to deliver me a message from my Mum. Apparently, she called to say she loves me. The desk clerk seems to think that's quite funny, if her smirk was anything to go by. Maybe nobody loves *her*. With a face like an unpeeled potato and a body like a full *sack* of the damn things, with God knows what sprouting God knows where, it's quite hard to tell what she does have going for her. Maybe not very much at all, so perhaps it makes her feel better, a little bit superior, to smirk her way through the missive.

I'm wondering if there's any CCTV anywhere that can put me en route to Christine's or on my way home after, that could provide the all-important alibi. If the bitch won't talk, maybe they can clear things up by pinpointing with some camera evidence where I was at the time Becky Starr was being strangled. Trevor Jones said he'd already asked them about that, and the fact that I got a bus to her place from town and back. Surely to God there's some video evidence *somewhere*, but I haven't heard anything about it, one way or the other.

Trevor was also going to talk to them about whether the agency had confirmed the booking I had with Christine, since it's fair to expect them to do the right thing and confirm it. Even if it hurts them to do so, allowing an innocent man go to jail might hurt them more. Their days might be numbered, either way.

The detectives want to have another chat. I'm requested politely to go with them to the interview room – like I have a choice. As I sit down, they look at me with the same kind of curiosity they'd show to a rat with two heads. One of them clears his throat, in that irritating way he has.

'There's been another development.' I wait for him to elaborate. He doesn't. It's like pulling fingernails out.

'Yeah? Is it helpful?' I prompt, through gritted teeth.

He pulls a face. 'Not really, as far as we can tell. But it is intriguing. Perhaps you'd like to clear up a question we've got about DNA.' The silence stretches out again. I'm getting pretty tired of this prick, who doesn't seem to be at all capable of stringing much more than one three-word sentence together in any attempt at communication. His wedding finger has a ring on it. I bet he's a laugh a minute to live with. Sign up at the registry office for a lifetime of scintillating conversation. Not.

'Well? If you actually ask me the question?'

He looks at me again, and the next question out of his mouth throws me into a state of utter confusion on a level I never knew existed.

'The DNA database threw us an interesting cross-match. There would appear to be a partial match between you and the dead girl's sister, Ruth Stenton. What can you tell us about that, Mr Bostock?'

Chapter Twenty
- Adie -

There's white noise hissing in my head, and my legs won't hold me up. I've just had a phone call from Trevor Jones. It seems that a DNA link has been established between two cross-matched samples – Matty's and Ruth's. Of course it has. They cross-check everything in a murder investigation. Of course they do. Isn't it their job to leave no stone unturned? Why would I have imagined that any one of us could have escaped this?

So the game is well and truly up. Any chance I might have had of keeping the truth from coming out has literally exploded off the pages of a DNA report, and flown straight out of a science-block window. Scientific evidence doesn't lie. The analysts can't get this sort of thing wrong and everybody knows it.

Again, it's not appropriate for my poor daughter to have to hear this from the police. The confusion and bewilderment that would cause is the one thing I can protect her from in the middle of this whole shit-storm. She deserves to know the truth. She always has, but I've always been too much of a coward to give it to her. But this, now? This development means that she needs to hear it from me, and without delay.

I wish Bryan were here. He still hasn't come home, and I would have loved his support with having to throw yet another fireball at poor Ruth. If he could have been here with me as I told her everything, maybe it would have been easier for her too. Bryan's good at saying the right things when it's most important. I'm going to make a mess of this, I just know it. How can I not? And I don't even want to think about the impact it's going to have on Matty and Teresa. Will I have a marriage, a family, or even a friend left in the world, after today?

I call Bryan's mobile but it goes straight to voicemail and I don't know what to say, other than to tell him that the cat is about to come out of the bag, and ask him to come home. Rather than go over to Ruth's, I'm going to ask her to come here. I'll feel safer in my own environment, telling her what I must, and she can be the one to storm out, as opposed to me being the one that gets thrown out of her house. Cowardly, but that's who I am, isn't it? A big fat coward, hell-bent on self-preservation, only coming clean when there's no alternative. Right now, I hate myself. However much everyone else is going to hate me at the end of all this, it will be nothing compared to how much I hate myself.

Ruth seems glad to hear my voice, when I call and ask her if she wouldn't mind popping over for a minute.

'I'll be right there,' she murmurs into the phone as I instruct her to come to the back door. As she is on her way over, a chill runs the full length of my spine. It's one of those sensations you get when you know that after an unexpected and acutely uncomfortable seismic truth comes out, nothing in your life will ever feel the same again.

I brace myself as she knocks and walks straight in. Our kitchen is large but quite cosy, and I've worked hard to make it that way. The big, battered oak dining table and six scruffy chairs we've had since we first got married sit squarely in the middle of the room. If this old furniture could talk it would tell a great many stories about my family's life.

The usual array of appliances grace the sides of the room, including the big, enamelled gas range we had installed last year. It's identical to Gina's. I finally gave in and splurged on it, having coveted hers for far too long. It was incredibly expensive, but worth every penny. The kitchen cabinetry is a rich, mid-grain oak and there are hanging racks and shelves crammed full, everywhere you look. People often say the room has a big personality, it feels inviting and cosy, in spite of its size. This is the best room in the house. This is where I will tell Ruth everything.

She comes in looking pale and drawn. There are dark circles under her eyes, like she hasn't slept, and her shoulders are slumped a little, like she is carrying the weight of the world on them. But she gives me a warm and surprisingly strong hug, and I invite her to sit at the table, while I brew a pot of tea.

'What's up?' she asks. She's assuming I need help with something, I guess, since I've never 'summoned' her like this before. Once I've got the tea and the cups on the table, I sit opposite her. I feel like I'm drowning in anguish. I try to deflect a little of it by asking her how she is.

She looks like she is fighting not to cry herself, with the weight of everything, and my heart breaks just that little bit more. 'Well, Adie, it's been quite a rollercoaster, this past couple of days.'

She goes on to explain that she was told by the detectives that she wasn't her father's biological child. She wasn't Rebekah's real sister either, because her mother wasn't even really her mother. She describes how Michael Stenton has used that as leverage to ensure she is excluded from receiving any further information about Rebekah's case. The family, the one she's not part of in *any* shape or form, have completely closed ranks against her. I am speechless. The way forward has literally been put into my hands; not that it will make things any easier.

Then she tells me about going to confront her parents, and about the dreams she's been having, including the first one, the one that caused her to be sitting at our kitchen table in the middle of the night just a few days ago, when she told us the devastating story of her upbringing. She describes the link between the dreams and the reality of what she has now remembered happened to her sister when they were little girls.

She starts to cry in earnest, when she tells me about the discovery of the poetry found on Rebekah's computer, and what it alludes to. My head struggles to comprehend the magnitude of all this on her life, as I reach for the box of tissues on the sideboard behind me and hand it to her. I'm fighting back the tears too, and I ask the question – the one I never in my entire life I ever expected to have to ask of any of my children.

'Did he abuse you too?'

She shakes her head, and the relief that floods my body is like a religious experience, every nerve tingling in gratitude for the one great mercy in this whole, ridiculous and scarcely believable abomination.

'No. He never touched me. According to Rebekah, I was never 'normal' enough for him to want to try. He must have known who I was, even before I knew myself. I guess that's why he started hating me.'

Ruth goes on to describe how Rebekah must have thought she'd simply chosen not to speak of what she knew, or to encourage her sister to talk about it either. 'She must've thought I was such a bitch, not to even try and get her to talk about it. She's gone to her grave believing I didn't care, didn't think it was important enough to acknowledge, when the truth of it was that I had simply repressed it, in fear for our lives. He told me he would kill us both if I ever talked about it.'

'You were a child, Ruth. Your mind did what it had to do, to protect you. It's the all-important guard against madness, against torment and destruction. You had to grow up and survive, to make your way in the world. The fact that you repressed that memory – that's what protected you.'

She nods. 'I know, Adie, and I can't describe the euphoria I felt, when I walked out of their house, knowing I wasn't their biological child. But the confrontation at their house, when I smashed their big mirror, that must have unlocked everything. Then when I pieced everything together, and my memory came back, I think the only thing that stopped me from spinning over the edge was that knowledge; that I was nothing to do with them. I've had to hold on hard, to that.'

'Yes, and I'm glad that's the reality for you; that you're not connected to them. That's protecting you too, Ruth.'

She nods, almost abstractedly, and looks at me sadly. 'But I still don't know how to feel about your son being a suspect in Rebekah's murder. If he's guilty, I don't know what that will mean for our friendship.'

At least she is honest. But what I'm about to tell her isn't going to make things any easier, is it?

'I know. I don't expect he will be found guilty though, Ruth. In my heart of hearts I really *don't* believe he is capable of something like that. I'm all at sea with my thinking. Part of it is haywire hormones, because I'm horribly menopausal, but a lot of is more basic. It's fear, and the worst kind of confusion about everything. You wouldn't believe what I've got going on in my *own* head, right now.'

But you're about to know, and believe me I would give everything I have, in the entire world, to avoid the things I have to tell you.

Ruth does need to have the full time and space she needs, to say how she is feeling, but there is an underlying need to shift the conversation along so I try a subtle first approach. I choose my words as carefully as I can, in the lead-up to what has to be said after that.

'But, all that aside for the moment, how does it leave you feeling about your parentage? You must have so many questions. Do you want to know who your real Mum and Dad are, and why they gave you up?' I wait with bated breath for the answer. But she shakes her head, as if it's the last thing she wants on her mind at the moment. Even though I'm gutted with the reaction, I can't say I blame her one bit.

'I can't even think about that right now, Adie. It's something that will have to wait, at least until Rebekah's killer has been found and brought to justice.'

I take a deep breath and look her squarely in the eye. *Here goes nothing. And everything.*

'Ruth, it can't wait. It's why I've asked you over here. I know who your parents are. I know who your mother is.' I say it as gently as I can, and I can hardly bear the look of confusion that floods her face. She is grappling to make sense of a statement she probably never expected to hear, at least not from her next-door neighbour and friend. Her voice, when it comes, seems like it is tiny, and far away.

'What? You know my real mother? How would you know that? Did you know I was adopted?'

I nod dumbly. I cannot take my eyes from her face. Her frown deepens as she tries to assemble her scattered thoughts. 'How would you know I was adopted? I only found out myself a couple of days ago. Have the police been talking to you? Why would they tell *you* that, about me?'

They are all legitimate questions, and I wish with all my heart that I could put her out of her misery. The knowledge that all I'm going to do is add to it drags me to the depths of sorrow and despair. I feel utterly wretched.

Out of the corner of my eye, I see a shape moving in the hallway, and I feel a sharp stab of relief, mixed with trepidation. Bryan is home! I didn't hear him come in. He has been listening but I don't know how much he's heard. I don't know if he will support me or not. Ruth is staring at me, and I can see how her mind is trying to piece everything together. My eyes can't be torn away from hers.

'I know who your real mother is, because it's me. I'm so sorry, Ruth. I never wanted you to know.'

I speak the words as softly as I possibly can. But even to my own ears, it sounds unacceptably pathetic. Ruth stares at me, clearly struggling to comprehend what she is hearing. My heart feels like it is being torn apart.

'What? *You're* my mother? My real *mother*?' Her voice is incredulous. I nod at her, and I can't stop the tears from falling now. She looks at me like she's never seen me before, like I'm a complete stranger. Bryan comes quietly into the kitchen and stands behind my chair. He doesn't say a word, and he doesn't touch me. God, how I wish he would, but at least he is here, and he is standing behind me, indicating at least a degree of solidarity. I am profoundly grateful.

Ruth shakes her head. 'If this is some kind of a joke, it's in pretty poor taste.'

Neither I nor Bryan speaks. Ruth looks up at him. 'Oh my God. It's not a joke, is it? It's true, isn't it?'

Bryan clears his throat. 'Yes, Ruth, it is. Adie had you at fifteen and she wasn't allowed to keep you. Her parents forced her to adopt you out. It wasn't what she wanted, but she had no choice. She didn't have any rights in that regard. She was still a child herself, in the eyes of the law.'

Ruth's eyes swivel back to me. 'You said, just now, that you never wanted me to know. Why wouldn't you want me to know?'

I let out the breath I didn't even realise I'd been holding. It comes out in a jagged rasp. 'I couldn't tell you, Ruth. You didn't even know you were adopted! How could I have destroyed the world you thought you knew? It felt so selfish, to want to do that. Before I knew what monsters your parents were, I thought you had a normal upbringing, with people who loved you, and who you loved in return. It's what I wanted for you, what I hoped for, when I gave you up.'

'How long have you known for?' her voice has a harder edge to it now. She sounds less confused, and a little hostile, which isn't surprising. How could I have expected anything else? How could I even *deserve* anything else? Did I really think she was just going to fall into my arms and we'd all live happily ever after?

'I found out a few years ago. Just before we moved here.' I want to hang my head with the shame of how it all looks and sounds.

'And is that *why* you moved here? Why you bought this house?' I nod, unable to speak. There is a hardness now, to Ruth's gaze. I don't know which is worse to witness, the heartbreaking confusion in her eyes or the quiet rage that's replaced it. She looks angrily at Bryan. 'Did you know about this? When you gave me all that spiel the other night about your willingness to be my surrogate parents, did you know about this?'

Bryan steps from behind me and pulls out a chair and sits heavily at the table between me and Ruth. He sighs deeply.

'No, I didn't. Adie wanted to be close to you Ruth, as close as she could be, without disrupting your life. She thought you were from a happy home. That's why she never told you. She would never want to cause disruption in what she assumed to be a happy family. When I told you I'd have been proud to call you my daughter, I didn't know Adie was your mother but, for what it's worth, I still stand by what I said, and I always will.'

I look at him gratefully, but he doesn't look back at me. I guess that's still a little too much to expect, under the circumstances. Two of the people I love most in the entire world feel completely betrayed by me. I try to force back the peculiar hollowness in my gut, a feeling of being completely disembowelled, and I struggle to try and explain.

'When I finally tracked you down, I could see that your life seemed very settled, that you were successful. I had no idea your home life with your adoptive parents had been so horribly unhappy. And I had no idea if you'd even been told you were adopted! It wouldn't have been fair of me to have dropped that kind of bombshell on you. It wasn't my place.'

'So you just moved in here beside me and Gina, and inveigled your way into our family, all the while knowing I was your illegitimate child?' The cold fury on Ruth's face makes me cringe. She looks hard at Bryan again. 'And exactly when *did* you learn about this?' She bites the words out.

He looks desperately uncomfortable. He knows there's nothing to be said here that can make any of this less brutal.

'I found out this morning.' Ruth's face drains of all its colour. She lets this sink in for a moment, and the only sound any of us can hear, apart from our own mismatched breathing, is the ticking clock on the kitchen wall. It's a funny little clock, blue resin with cartoon ginger cats all around the edges. I don't even remember where or when we got it. It's been in the family for as long as I can recall.

Ruth's eyes are now glittering with fury. 'Oh, right. I see. So you never told your husband either, Adie, until now! So I guess that means your kids don't know they've got a half-sister who they've been living next door to for several fucking years?'

It seems churlish to point out that the kids don't live here, and never really have full time, so I don't. I shake my head miserably instead. I have no idea what to say.

'So I've been, what? Your dirty little secret, all these years? Something you couldn't tell you family about? Something you couldn't tell *me* about?'

'I've tried to explain, Ruth. I didn't want to create problems for you. Even when I realised how mean and monstrous your parents were towards you, how could I have added to your misery by telling you? What right did I have, to tell you they weren't even your real parents? It wasn't my place. Can't you see that?'

Ruth shook her head. Clearly she couldn't answer my questions. 'So, why now? After thirty-seven years of secrecy, subterfuge and self-servitude, why is it important that your husband had to find out today – and that *I* had to find out today? Why *today?*'

I gird my loins and take a deep breath. 'Because Matty has been rearrested this morning and he is being charged with Rebekah's murder. And a partial DNA cross-match between you and him has come to light, and I wanted you to hear the full and accurate explanation from me, not a confusing one from the police that would have created more questions than it could possibly have answered.'

Ruth laughs harshly. The sound is like nails being dragged across a blackboard. It sets my teeth on edge.

'Well, that's big of you, Adie. So in other words, if this hadn't happened, you wouldn't have told me at all? If you hadn't suddenly found your back against the wall, with all your lies about to be exposed, would you have told *anyone*? Or would I just have remained your shameful secret love child that nobody would ever need to know about?'

'It wasn't like that. I did what I thought was best for you.'

She pushes aside my repeated attempt at explanation with a contemptuous wave of her hand. I recognise the gesture as one of my own.

'Right! So it actually *isn't* all about you then? It's all about *me*? So, let me get this straight. You're my mother, which makes your son – the man who may have murdered my sister – my half-brother! How perfectly fucking fabulous. Here I was, patting myself on the back, thinking I'd done so well in escaping the abject horror of the family I was condemned to, only to suddenly find myself hurled into the middle of another one, which may in fact be even worse. Could my life be any more messed up? You know what, Adie? You couldn't even *make* this up! If it wasn't so fucking freakish, and nauseating, it could almost pass for a TV sitcom.'

Ruth stands abruptly, kicks back her chair, which falls over behind her with a loud clatter, and she storms out through the back door. I move to go after her but Bryan stops me.

'Let her go. There's no point in going after her. You've done enough damage for one day, don't you think?' He looks at me scathingly. The contempt in his eyes is soul destroying. 'And if you think I'm going to be the one to tell our children about all this, you can think again. You can carry on cleaning up your own mess. I have to be somewhere. And before you ask, I don't know. Anywhere. Anywhere but *here*.'

He also rises and leaves the table. Within seconds, the front door has slammed shut, he is gone *again*, and here it is. My world is spectacularly exploding, and I know that it is far from over yet. There are many more shockwaves to come and as I sit here, with only the little ticking-cat clock for company, and with my kitchen now feeling like the most hostile place on earth, I've never felt more bereft in all my life.

* * * * *

I'm not sure how long I've been sitting here, staring at the wall, when there is a loud, insistent banging on the front door. It sounds like police about to conduct a raid. Confused, I open the door and my heart immediately sinks like a stone. It's Gina and she is trembling with rage. She is a fearsome sight, with her wild, angry eyes and her anger hissing and crackling like a force field around her. I open my mouth to speak but she holds up her hand and barges past me and into the hall. She turns to face me, and the force of her fury is palpable. I feel she is about to raise her fist and knock me out.

'What I have to say will not take long, *A'dienne.*' She never calls me Adie. It's always Adrienne, and she always pronounces it in the most beautiful way. Gina says *A'dienne*, with the inflection on the second syllable. I've always thought that sounded quite magical and special. Today though, all it does is make me want to weep.

This woman's temper is legendary. I've heard many stories about it from Ruth, usually with Gina grinning and looking slightly sheepish alongside her, as various tales of her argumentative Italian passion come out. They're usually quite funny to hear about. I just never thought I'd ever be unfortunate enough to have her anger unleashed upon me.

But here it comes.

She draws herself up to her full height, which isn't much. She must be all of five feet two in high heels, but she could be seven feet tall and twenty-five stone right now. I've never been this intimidated by anyone, ever.

'You are a piece of work!' She holds up her forefinger close to my face. 'It is one thing. *One* thing, to go looking for the child you gave away. It is quite another to find that child in the way you did, and lie to her for this long. It is *inaccettabile, A'dienne*, what you have done to Ruthie. What did you think, huh? That you could fix all this by saying, 'oh come to mama, poor child!'? *Mio Dio*, woman! *Tu donna egoista! Non ti interessata a nessuno tranne te stessa*! Do you have any idea of what you have done? *Do you?*'

She is shouting at me, very loud and fast, and I know better than to say anything at all. Her words are staccato-like and they feel like physical blows, like whacks on my skull with a stiletto heel. The only way I can get through this onslaught is to do what I want to do anyway – hang my head in abject shame.

'We trusted you! We thought you were our friend, and all the while you had another motive! *È contorto, A'dienne! È contorto!* It is twisted! You are a sick, *patetita* woman! *Onestà*, who owns up finally, but only because you think you have no fucking choice. *La tua onestà è troppo tardi!* Well we don' trust you anymore, and we don' wan' you in our lives. So stay away from us! You hear me, *sì*? Stay away from my family! Put your *casa* on the fucking market and move away, because we were here first and we don' want you next to us anymore. *Mi disgusti*! *Non posso sopportare di guardarti, donna egoista.*'

Her rage has caused her to lose some of her articulation. My heart is breaking. I love Gina, almost as much as I love Ruth. To see her this angry, this hostile towards me, is as much as I can humanly bear. And as for little Chiara; my granddaughter, well, the thought of never seeing her again is a physical pain in my chest. I'm shaking now, with the implications of this, of never seeing Ruth ever again, never being a part of their family, even in the smallest of ways.

I'm crying now, big fat, silent tears, sliding down my cheeks, falling off my chin and staining my top. Gina's shoulders slump. The heat of her fire is burning away, but she is still angry and contemptuous. Nobody's eyes will ever tell you more than Gina's will. She despises me. I don't know which is worse – her anger, or the derision in her face.

'*Onestà troppo tardi, A'dienne.* No trust, no fucking friendship.'

She turns towards the front door, yanks it open, it and stomps away without saying another word, or looking back. As thoroughly castigated and stripped bare as I'm feeling, I'm also profoundly grateful that Ruth has such a fierce advocate. Gina is intense, ferocious and possibly even dangerous when it comes to protecting those she loves. She would stop at nothing to protect her wife and child. I could imagine all five feet-two of her tearing someone apart with her bare hands if that were her only option. I've never been more thankful that Ruth, in the midst of all this misery, has such a staunch and unwavering ally. I just never thought, until now, that I'd be the one she'd like to tear apart.

I sit down heavily at the foot of the stairs, while I try to get some kind of equilibrium back. Gina's rant has left me shaking like a leaf in the wind. *Jesus, that was some force!*

She is right, of course, to feel the way she does. Someone has wounded her mate, and she has come out swinging in defence, like any mate would. But am I really so wrong? Could I have handled this any better? How could I possibly have told Ruth, at any time before now, that she was my biological daughter? Until just a few days ago, she didn't even know she was adopted. It baffles me completely, that the Stentons never told her. Were they so ashamed of having made such a huge 'mistake' in adopting her that they could never admit it? Imagine if they'd been kind enough to tell her, years ago! It could have set her free! It could have changed the course of her whole life!

The longer all these secrets stay buried, the harder they become to tell. Then, when you realise the hurt they're likely to cause when they finally do come out, and partly *because* of the time it took, and when the lies or omissions that helped to keep them covered are finally exposed as well, it stops you from going there. You don't want to go there, because all you've ever wanted to do was love and protect your family, and you'd do anything to stop them from being devastated.

But what happens when you can't? What happens when you did the very best you could do, but outside forces converged to blow your shields wide open?

While I still imagined that Ruth's home life had been everything I'd dreamed of when I gave her up to it, all those years ago, I would gladly have stayed in my own tormented longing before *ever* exposing her to the reality of her parentage and risking the kind of trauma she didn't deserve.

Another bald fact is that someone other than my son has murdered Rebekah Stenton. Despite how I feel about the last time he was here, and despite what I said to Bryan, I am absolutely sure deep down in my heart that my boy did not do what he's suspected of. He might be a lot of things, and I'm sadder than I ever thought possible, about some of the choices he's made, but they don't make him a killer. This is the boy that mended a broken bird! It's the man who gives voluntary DNA samples to help the police get justice for a girl he doesn't even know. It's the man who lies on the floor, whenever he comes home, and cuddles Creole until the poor old dog can't stand it a minute longer. He gives his sister his coat on the way home from Sunday lunch at the pub, when she's been daft enough to go out on a cold winter's day with nothing but a silly scrap of a lace cardigan over her equally inappropriate summer dress.

Matty. And Teresa. I have to have difficult conversations with them too. My mobile phone buzzes on the kitchen table. It's a text from Bryan, and just when I was starting to think it wasn't possible at all for my heart to sink still further, it somehow does.

Police have told Matty about the DNA connection to Ruth. He's asking questions. I've got Trevor Jones to tell him everything.

My head reels yet again. That is so brutal, and so unfair! Did I not deserve the chance to tell my own son about Ruth? He should have heard that news from me, not from his bloody solicitor! What was Bryan thinking, in allowing that to happen? My God, poor Matty!

At this point, whether or not he hates me is a lot less important than the fact that he is hopelessly lost and confused, left alone in a small, claustrophobic cell, to somehow try and make sense of things with nobody to question, and no support. Frantically I scrabble to call the station, and when they answer I ask if I can speak to Matty, knowing that at the answer is likely to be no, but needing to do whatever I can to connect with my son.

I'm told that he is with his solicitor. So that's it then. My chance is gone, to get in first, or at least get Jones to hold off until I could get to speak to Matty myself. I leave a message, to tell Matty that I will see him as soon as I can, to explain and answer whatever questions he might have, and that I love him with all my heart. I hope it's enough to help mitigate the shock, at least a little.

Chapter Twenty-one
- Gina -

Mio Dio! *When?* When will the earthquakes stop coming? When will we have some fucking peace? The minute this is over, the very *second* they find out who killed Rebekah, I am taking Ruthie to *Sicilia* for a whole month. And anyone who has an objection can go hang.

As for *A'dienne,* well. What can I say? Ruthie is in pieces. She is more angry and upset than I have ever seen her. I can't blame her one bit, because it has been shock, after shock, after shock, and I don't know how much more she can take. *Questo è intollerabile.*

Even though I knew it was not the best idea I ever had, to go next door in a temper, I was past caring. I am past letting my wife take these punches from people who have no idea of the impact on her. *A'dienne* looked at me like *un cane sgridato,* a scolded dog. She didn't even try to defend herself, but how could she? How can anybody defend what she has done? All those lies. All that *inganno.* Such deceit.

I don't feel so hostile to the dead Rebekah anymore, now that I know where her fucked-up head was. I'm no *psicologa*, but I know a few things about abuse. I know it makes you hate yourself. When I was raped, I thought it was my fault. I thought I should have seen it coming and stopped it, or not put myself where it could happen, and I thought I was as worthless as *he* thought I was; Pietro, my brother's friend.

I, too, told no one what happened to me. It was my shame. It was only love that changed it all for me. Ruthie was the *catalizzatrice* who turned it around. She, I could tell, because she loved me and that made it possible to speak of it, and Ruthie just loved me all the way back to myself. And my baby, the light of my life, is the gift, the silver lining. It is *non importante* that she was born from rape. I could not give her up. I would die first. Ruthie and Chiara, they are my silver linings. They are the needle and thread that pulled my life back together.

What silver lining did Rebekah have? She had nothing to love, and nobody to love her all the way back to herself. All she had were those fucked-up freaks for parents. She hated herself, and she hated everyone who was happy. The poems on her computer implied that she would sit down and have dinner with her parents every week or so, but her father was still screwing her? How *depravata* is that, for Christ's sake? How much torment did Rebekah have to manage? Was the group sex thing, having all those men all over her, all at once, was that her silver lining? Was that something she felt she could control? Did it give her pleasure, or relief from *lo strazio*? Or was it just another kind of self-hatred? The poor dead bitch seemed to be eaten alive by depravity and betrayal. No wonder she was such a fucking train wreck.

I wanna understand. She is dead, and in one way I am glad, but not for the same reasons as before. I am glad now because she is no longer *in tormento*. She deserves to be at peace. I never thought I would get to the point of saying that, but there we go. Things happen. Your ideas change. As much as I hated her, I now only wish her peace. No woman should have to live her life that way.

The doorbell rings. It is, of course, *la polizia*. Noone else seems to come here anymore but them.

Ruthie gets to it first, and I expect her to show them into the living room. I am sick of these people, I am *agitato*, that they keep showing up here with no warning, to throw another bomb at us. They never come with anything good. Layer upon layer of bombing. How much more can we take?

Ruthie keeps them on the doorstep this time, and I don't blame her for that, either. I wait behind the door, and I listen to the conversation, and I brace myself for the next announcement, but when it comes, *io non sono preparato*. There is no way in a million years that I could have been prepared at *all,* for what they have come to say.

Chapter Twenty-two
- Ruth -

I'm officially losing the plot, now. I really have had a complete gutsful of everything, and everyone. Smiley and Giggles, the two detectives, have showed up once *again* unannounced and this time the mere sight of them sends my temper flying over the edge of a cliff and into freefall. I no longer have the energy, or even the will, to be polite to them.

'Well, what a fucking surprise. Hello, yet again. You just can't stay away, can you, even on a Sunday night, when people should be able to fairly expect a bit of bloody peace? Is that too much to ask? When do we get a break, here? Should I just make up a couple of beds for you, in the spare room?'

They stare at me impassively. I'm not usually sarcastic with them, but they seem to take that in their stride, like they take everything else. It occurs to me that it might be interesting to see what they're like with their families, or out at the pub with their mates. Surely, they must be capable of smiling, at some stage in their lives? God forbid, to have to take oneself so seriously that the only feasible facial expression is a grimness worse than granite.

I'm not inviting them in. Not tonight. I make it obvious too, by stepping out onto the doorstep with them and pulling the door closed behind me. They don't demur at all. Instead, they speak quietly, and very respectfully actually, but I can hardly believe what they are saying. On one level, it all makes perfect sense. On the other, my mind is failing miserably at accepting it. But, contrary to my first thought, they're not lying or messing with my head.

They have just told me the news I've been praying for, for weeks now; that they have found Rebekah's killer.

The sound of white noise, the feeling of suspension from reality; they are familiar feelings to me now, so when they tell me that Matthew Bostock is being released without charge or further investigation, because they have a full confession from Michael Stenton, I'm pretty sure that whatever they tell me after that couldn't tilt my world any further off its axis.

But I'm wrong, and although the fact that Michael is Rebekah's killer is almost a moot point for me after everything else that's come to light, what *does* send everything significantly more off kilter is how they came to know that.

It seems that Margaret Stenton herself blew the whistle. After the detectives went to the vicarage to confront Michael with the information they had, that alluded to the crime of incest, they asked some very uncomfortable questions. He wasn't at home when they called, but they grilled Margaret pretty hard and they mentioned, just casually in passing as they were leaving, that someone who is found to have aided or contributed to the commission or concealment of a heinous crime against a person (one of the worst in the book, in fact) is classed as an accessory; complicit, in the eyes of the law. And they can go to prison too.

Within twenty-four hours, Margaret had weighed up her options, and was down at the station, spilling her guts, telling everything she knew in exchange for leniency. She couldn't hide the fact that she'd known all along about her husband's abuse of their daughter, but she trotted out the excuse that he'd told her he'd kill her if she ever told a living soul. She said she'd been afraid. Nobody in authority believed a word of it, of course, because she was so very clearly just as big a monster as Michael himself. But, in exchange for her information, they offered her a slightly easier ride in court. She also said that she didn't know Michael had killed Rebekah. She was sticking to that, and it was no easy thing to prove that she was lying about it.

The detectives had gone to the vicarage with the hope that they could arrest Michael on suspicion of familial sexual abuse. The last thing they ever expected, off the back of that, was to stumble across the fact that the depraved bastard had gone on to kill his daughter.

They picked him up at the church earlier today, in the middle of Sunday sermon, as Margaret hoped they would. As it turned out, protecting herself was only part of what she wanted. Once her conscience had showed itself (albeit thirty years too late), and she'd made the decision to throw her husband into the snake pit where he belonged (and arguably came from in the first place), she wanted him to feel the full force of the humiliation he deserved.

'Maybe I'll still go to jail,' she'd said with a resigned shrug, 'but at least it won't be for as long as him.'

When the worm had turned, it had certainly turned full circle.

Faced with the knowledge that it had been his wife who'd ultimately flung him into the fire, and knowing that he had no real resources to prove that she was lying, Father Michael Stenton decided he didn't have the sturdiness of character to keep trying to lie his way out. He bowed to the inevitable and gave them a full confession. To all of it.

I blink, half stupidly, at Giggles and Smiley, and I say the first thing that comes to mind. 'I don't know what to say, or even how to feel. Heartbroken? Incredulous? Relieved? I'm sorry, but I have absolutely no idea how to respond to any of that.'

They both nod, sombrely. 'That's understandable,' they both say, in unison. Then, of all the craziest and most unlikely things to happen ever, in the world, they both laugh. Admittedly it is only a half-laugh, and it's a very short-lived thing. But, for a brief couple of seconds, I actually see them smile, and I actually hear them laugh.

Well, what do you know? They're human, after all.

In his confession, Michael had admitted to losing his temper with Rebekah on the night he'd throttled her. He wanted everyone to understand that he hadn't gone to her flat that night with the *intention* of strangling her. She'd called him, and he'd believed her to be drunk, but he wasn't sure. When she'd told him she was tired of living with the terrible, stultifying secret of ongoing coercion, control and unwanted sexual interference, and wanted to come clean, he'd gone to her flat to try and talk some sense into her. He wanted to impress upon her, or so he *said*, that nothing good would come of bringing everything out into the open. Lives and livelihoods would be destroyed, and he doubted if she would feel any better at the end of it. He wanted to convince her that she wouldn't.

But his visit hadn't gone according to plan. Rebekah *had* been drunk that night, and she was ranting. Nothing he could do or say would sway her from her conviction. When she'd told him that she'd already rung me, she was calling his bluff, and taunting him. She told him he'd have to wait and see whether she'd already spilled the beans to me in her messages; whether the horrifying secret was already out of the bag.

Michael had found that intolerable. His own daughter was mocking him, and when she'd told him his life was about to be blown apart, and it didn't matter to her because hers was already worth nothing so she had nothing to lose, he saw red and lunged at her. She'd fallen backwards, onto the bed, and he'd hurled himself on top of her. Conveniently, he somehow managed to lose his memory at that point, and 'the next thing he knew' she was dead on the bed beneath him.

'Memory lapses' are very common, according to the detectives, where confessors 'forget' a few of the finer details of their crimes. It makes them think – quite wrongly, as it happens – that they can escape a harsher penalty by pleading a bit of amnesia. Some lay it on a bit thick and find their 'inability to remember' being examined by a psychiatrist, who occasionally deems them to be certifiable – oops – and that's a whole different kettle of fish. It was clearly spelled out to Michael, that he could end up being detained indefinitely in a secure psychiatric unit under certain terms of the Mental Health Act, but he is (at least so far) sticking to his guns in saying he doesn't remember the actual act of throttling the life out of his daughter.

I laugh a little, now, but it's mostly out of incredulity I think. 'A psych report will be done though, right?'

Giggles nods. 'It will, as a matter of course. We're not experts, so we have no way of predicting what might come out of that, but I don't think there's many would argue that he's a very twisted man. The report should be illuminating, to say the least.'

They both turn to go, and I walk them up the path to the front gate.

'Thank you,' I mumble. 'At least now we have a result. I'm grateful for all your work, and all your support. I know it's been a challenging case.'

Smiley sighs deeply, and grins ruefully. Well, it's a half-grin; more of a grimace actually but, as the best he might ever manage, I'll take it. He shakes my hand. 'They're all challenging cases, the homicides. Always a lot of red herrings and wasted time. This one's been more straightforward than you might think, in fact, compared with some of what we have to deal with. I'm sorry it's been so hard for *you*, all this. It hasn't made for easy sleep, has it? But at least now, maybe you can.'

'What *will* happen to Margaret?'

'Well, despite the fact that she's a monster in her own right, she may be as much of a victim as she is an accomplice. We think there are some deep-seated psych issues there too. She'll also be evaluated, and whatever penalty she incurs will be reflective of what's in the report. It's too soon to predict her fate just yet.'

As they get into their car to drive away, a taxi pulls up outside Adie and Bryan's, and it looks like their son Matthew that gets out of it. He looks over at me, as I stand here in my doorway. It's laughable on one hand, and vaguely disgusting on the other, that the detectives drove here at roughly the same time as he was being released from custody in the same building, and yet he had to get a bloody taxi to the house next door! The miserable bastards could've given him a lift, couldn't they? Just another example of a world gone bonkers, I suppose, where nobody seems capable of thinking about anyone else but themselves. I wonder if he even got an apology. I don't suppose he did. The authorities hate being wrong, and they don't make a habit of admitting it when they are.

Matthew seems unsure whether to acknowledge me or not, so I break the ice and nod and smile at him gently. He gives me a half-smile back, with his teeth holding down his bottom lip. It's plain that this young man has a lot still ahead of him, but at least it's not a murder charge.

I'm pleased for Adie and Bryan, that their boy is not a killer. I'm glad Margaret did the decent thing, even if was only to save her own skin. She saved a young man from prison too, and maybe – just maybe – that will mitigate the hell she will have to go through, in the coming days and weeks.

There's a small part of me that kind of hopes she doesn't go to prison, and I'm surprised by that. She *is* a monster, there are no two ways about that, but maybe Smiley is right. Maybe she *is* a victim too. I know nothing like I thought I knew, about my family, so how can I say for certain that she is beyond redemption or deserves to rot in hell? Maybe Michael was horrible to her too, behind the bedroom door, or whatever passed for privacy in that hellhole of a house.

Gina is in the kitchen, and to my surprise, she is opening a bottle of bubbly. She looks up, and grins at the surprise on my face.

'Ruthie, forgive me my darling, but I was listening at the door. *Questa e una celebrazione!* We need to drink to tomorrow being fresh, and the next phase of our lives. I insist that you see this as a good thing. Yes, there are things to mourn, *cara*, but we can do that later, and we will. Tonight, we celebrate the end of a nightmare. Tonight, we look forward to tomorrow.'

I see her logic, and I feel her overwhelming desire to move us forward. Gina is a border collie of the highest order. She shepherds people, and she is shepherding me towards acceptance and a measure of peace. While I don't always agree with her timing or her methods, her unfailing optimistic spirit always lifts me to a better place if I let it, and I choose to do that now. I'm happy to let her have this moment, because I know what a relief it is for her too, all this abruptly settling dust.

The tornado has passed. Whatever happens now, we can face it with the strength we know we have, which is far greater than I could have imagined, just a few weeks ago. It *has* been a nightmare, and we do have to put it behind us, and although I suspect the peace we are craving will be a while in coming, with so many questions still to be answered, this is as good a time as any, to make a start.

I accept the glass of bubbles and I lift it to meet hers. She grins and winks at me. '*Saluti, cara!* Here's to *domani* being better!'

'Cheers, my darling. And thank you, so much, for being my rock. I couldn't have got through this without you.'

Gina shakes her head. 'It still isn't over, Ruthie. The worst of it is, yes, but there is still *lavoro incompleto* with A'dienne, for one thing. How will you deal with that?'

She is right. There *is* unfinished business with Adie – lots of it – and at this stage I'm not at all sure how I want to deal with it.

I shrug and look at her, contemplatively. 'What would you do? How would *you* deal with it, Gina?'

She shrugs at me. 'I don't know. I think I would take some time, to think it over and work out how I feel, after the shock of everything else has passed. There's big danger in acting too quickly. You don't want to set any bridges on fire, *cara*. But it's not okay, what she did. And for you, it *is* okay to feel whatever you need to feel around that, I think.'

Learning that Adie was my biological mother was almost as big a shock as finding out that my sister had been murdered. I don't know how to feel about her, or the fact that I have a half-sister and a half-brother. I don't know how to feel about the fact that she lied through her teeth; not just to me but to her entire family, for all of their lives together.

I don't know how to feel about my not-father murdering my not-sister in a fit of red-hot rage. Michael Stenton always had a temper, but never in a million years did I ever think he could do something like that. I suppose that when the chips are down, and you're at risk of your very worst secrets being exposed; the kind that will literally destroy your life on every level, you *will* fight like a rabid dog to stop it from happening.

But thou shalt not kill, right, 'Father'? You were no father to me, or to Rebekah. You were no Father to your congregation, standing before them every Sunday in your hypocritical glory, preaching good behaviour to keep your flock from straying. What must they think of you now? What does your 'word of God' mean to them now? How sick to their stomachs are they now, and how are they managing to square away what you did to your own child? It wasn't just murder, was it? It was so much worse than 'just' that.

I drain my drink and a sudden wave of exhaustion hits me. The glass of bubbly has gone straight to my head, and all of a sudden, I feel driven by a deep need for sleep – preferably the kind that keeps me comatose for at least twenty-four hours.

Gina sees me stifle a yawn, and she drains her glass too. 'Okay, Ruthie, time for bed. Maybe tonight, like the detective says, you can get a good night's sleep.'

With so many still unanswered questions, I'm not sure how good it will be, but it's getting harder to stay upright. I do need to go to bed, or lie down at least, so I rinse our glasses and put the bottle back the fridge. We turn the downstairs lights out and head upstairs, and I quietly check in on Chaira. She is sound asleep, with her dark hair splayed out across her pillow. I'm so deeply grateful, for her existence, and for the fact that the horror of the past few weeks hasn't touched her. She is innocent and pure, and beautiful and sweet. I kiss her gently on the forehead, and go to bed. A night of good sleep, in the arms of my wonderful wife, is exactly what I need right now.

Chapter Twenty-three
- *Matthew* -

I don't know if there's a knife, or a fork, or a dinner plate big enough for the humble pie I'm about to eat. I was allowed to use the phone at the nick when they let me go, and I just wanted to tell Mum and Dad I'd been released before I headed home to tidy my place up after the cops trashed it, but Mum told me to come here instead. Trevor Jones had already contacted her, to tell her he'd organised me a taxi, so they already knew I was getting out but she appreciated me letting her know.

She's cooked a Sunday dinner, and she wanted me to come over to eat with her and Dad, and I liked the sound of that. The food they serve up at the cop shop isn't what you'd call nutritious or inspiring. A spoonful of cheap-brand baked beans, a dollop of grey and tasteless mashed potato, and a couple of mushy, mass-produced pork sausages, if you're lucky.

So here I am, on the doorstep, waiting to walk back into the place I stormed out of in such a blind fury not so long ago. I'm nervous. Facing Mum and Dad is going to be the hardest thing, after everything that's happened. Emotions are still running pretty high for all of us, but they're my parents and we all love each other. I want us to still have that, at the end of whatever discussion has to happen tonight.

But there's a lot to talk about, from all sides, isn't there? I'm not under any illusions about how difficult the conversation might end up being, once we start touching on the more unpalatable elements of what's gone on. It was weird just now, seeing Ruth Stenton; the woman next door. Apparently, she's my half-sister. She's just lost her own sister, who wasn't really her sister, and her parents who weren't really her parents are both going to jail. Her mother isn't her mother, but apparently mine is! Since my own head is still a scrambled mess, I can't even imagine what must be going on hers, but she did acknowledge me when I got out of the taxi, so that's something, and I guess the whole family needs to feel differently about her now. I don't know what that even really means for us all, but there's a lot to explain, and not just on my side of the chessboard. Mum has a few small things to fess up about too, I think.

Dad's made a point of being here, and that counts for a lot. So I brace myself as I ring the doorbell.

The door opens so quickly, I know Mum's been standing right behind it, waiting. She's crying; she's pleased to see me, and I feel like a lost little boy who's found his way home. I throw myself at her, and let her hug me. Her arms are around me in an instant, because all of a sudden I'm crying too, and I don't know if it's from relief or shame, or sadness, or some strange combo of all three and more besides. But we stand here, in the hallway, with our arms wrapped around each other like we're trying to hold together in the worst of storms.

I let go first. Mum sniffs hard, and puts an arm around me, and leads me into the kitchen. I can smell roasting chicken and it's the best smell in the world. Dad is sitting at the kitchen table, and he looks up as I come into the room. He smiles, but only a little, like he doesn't know what to expect. I'm still crying, and he sees that, and he stands and comes and wraps his arms around me too, and all of a sudden I believe – I really do – that things will be okay.

I decide to get in first. 'Dad, I'm sorry I hit you. That was wrong, and horrible, and there's no excuse for it. I promise, on my life, that I'll never raise a hand to you again. Forgive me, please?'

'Matty, there's nothing to forgive. It was a terrible time, and feelings were running high. I get it. All I will say is if you ever *do* hit me again, I'll drop you faster than a twenty-pound sack of spuds. Agreed?'

I smile, and nod at him, because while he's trying to make light of what happened, I know that he could and *would* knock me out with one punch. I won't get away with snotting him a second time, and it's okay for him to make the point.

'Mum, I was horrible to you too. I hope you know that I'll regret the things I said to you in here, for the rest of my life.'

Mum cocks her head on one side and looks at me. Then she shrugs, lightly.

'Well, people do all kinds of out-of-character things when they're scared. I do know that. You were afraid, Matty. We all were that night, but you were, most of all. It's fine, darling. Really, it is.' Her voice is so quiet I can hardly hear it, but her words are like balm to my battered soul.

I sit down, opposite Dad. He's got his elbows on the table, and he looks tired. One of his eyes is still slightly puffy, and dark underneath, from when I broke his nose. He gets up, goes to the fridge, and brings back a couple of beers. As he hands me one, he asks about the escort agency.

'Oh, they'll survive I think, Dad. They've already issued a media statement, to say we've all been dismissed from our positions, and they're considering legal action. Yarda, yarda. Standard stuff.'

'Are they going to take you to court?'

I shrug. 'I'm not sure. I haven't heard, one way or the other, yet. I think they're still deciding.'

'Might not be worth it to them, son. It's not like they can sue you for millions, is it? They'd only do it as a statement of intolerance. But if you do get dragged into court, and a hefty fine gets slapped on you, I can cover it, and we can figure out a way for you to pay me back when you can. So don't be too anxious about that. Don't lose any sleep over it. We'll sort it.'

He's right. The agency can't do too much to me, except sue me for breach of contract. It's not like they can put me in jail for that. What I did was reckless but it wasn't a crime. A fine would be the worst of it, and it's good to know that I can get it covered. Mum and Dad are amazing. No matter what's happened, they're here for me. Right now, after the way I've behaved towards them, that means everything. It's the last thing I really deserve, and I know it. I'm humble, in a way I've never felt before.

Mum silently hands me a small, blue gift-wrapped box, with a silver bow on it. It's a new i-phone.

'Your sim card is taped to the back of it. The other phone was a write-off, so we decided to get you a new one. You can sort everything out on it yourself, when you want to. But it's there, and charged and ready to go. The old one's here if you still want that too.'

This is a big gesture, from them. It's a bloody expensive phone, but I guess Dad has probably put it through the business. I can't find the words to say how grateful I am. I just have to hope they know.

'Thanks, Mum, Dad. The first thing I'll do is delete a few numbers I'm not going to need anymore.'

Mum nods gently. 'I'm glad about that. Maybe you can close the door on that part of your life, now.'

I know that's what she wants. And I also know she probably wants to talk about it, but I'm not ready for that yet. If the day does come, when I can sit and look my mother in the eye and talk in any detail about the job I had, shagging women decades older than her, it isn't this one. I move to a different, less sticky subject.

'I'm thinking about a fresh start in lots of directions, Mum. I've applied for a new job, actually. It's doing the same kind of work, but it's with a bigger company, so there's more opportunity for progression and maybe diversifying my skills a bit. I have an interview next week.'

I'm just glad I'm not locked up, and can actually attend the interview. The pay's only a little better; still only a graduate wage, but it won't take as long to move up and start earning more. I hope I get the job. A new start might help me draw a line under the stuff I need to put behind me.

Dad pipes up; 'well, that is good news! Good luck, son. I hope you get the job. Could be the start of a real career trajectory.'

Mum looks at me, and her eyes are huge, and so full of love and concern, it makes me catch my breath. 'Do you want to talk about Rebekah, Matty? It must've been a huge shock, hearing what happened.'

'It was, Mum. I'm not ready to talk about what I was doing, in her flat. I think you already know enough, and all I can say about it, to put any more meat on the bones, is that I had a lot of time to think, while I was locked up, and I'm happy to be done with that part of my life. But, as for Rebekah? Well, I knew her as Becky Starr, and she was a client; nothing more than that. I was shocked and sad, to hear that she'd been strangled. Nobody deserves to die like that. I was terrified too, to be accused of doing it.

'But what concerns me more is the links, Mum. Who belongs to who, and all that? Ruth is your daughter; my half-sister, and yet she was no relation to Becky. I'm glad about that, for obvious reasons, but it's all been a bit of a shock.'

Mum nods, and looks sad. She seems to be at a loss for how to start explaining, but she needs to, for me. She needs to try, at least. How everything came out is the kind of thing you really only dream up in your sleep, in weird nightmares that make you wonder what the fuck is going on in your head that you don't even know about, until you go to sleep and it all starts crowding in. I need to get my head straight, and whether she gets it or not, that has to start with her.

'Why did you never tell us, Mum? About Ruth? And why did you never tell *her?*'

'I was ashamed, Matty. The longer I kept the secret, the harder it became to tell, but I couldn't get her out of my head. After you and Teresa started spending more time away from home, the urge to find her became so strong, I stopped being able to ignore it. Some weird reaction to the empty nest syndrome, maybe? Ricocheting hormones, perhaps? I'm not sure what it was, but it started to overwhelm me. I hired a PI to find her, and when I got the information, it became clear that she didn't know she'd been adopted. I couldn't be the one to tell her something so profound, so I did the next best thing. It was wrong, but I just didn't know what else to do.'

'Well, I guess I can see why you couldn't tell her. But we deserved to know, didn't we? Me and Teresa? And Dad too? He didn't know either, did he? You lied to us all, Mum. In doing that, you've implied that we couldn't be trusted with the secret. We would have kept it to ourselves to keep protecting Ruth, if you'd asked us to, but you didn't even give us a chance, did you? You kept us all in the dark. What was that, a power thing?'

'It was a shame thing, Matty. I was ashamed of my past, and as time went on, I grew more and more ashamed of the fact that I couldn't find the courage to tell the people I love the most, what I'd done. In actual fact, if you really want the truth, I feel *crippled* by shame. I always have. I've just somehow managed to find a way to live with it.' She shrugs, and starts to cry again.

My heart hurts for her. The anguish in her face is almost unbearable, but I can't reach out to her. I don't know why, but there it is, and I guess it's just another 'blunting effect' of all that's happened to us all. I feel for my poor broken mum, but I'm disappointed and angry with her too. It's a bizarre and uncomfortable combination of emotions that stops me from even *finding* the urge to hug her, let alone acting on it. There's a great big fuck-off wall in front of me, and I know I've put it there myself. I don't know how I've done it, and I *hate* that I've done it, but I can't pretend it's not there.

Mum was just a kid herself when she had Ruth. I get it; that her parents made her give her up. But it wasn't the dark ages, anymore, was it? It wasn't what you'd call respectable, being pregnant at fifteen, and I guess there must've still been a lot of stigma around it, but would it have been so hard to have told Dad, when she first got together with him?

Mum says she was afraid he'd have though she was a slag. She loved him, so she kept it all to herself. That must've been hard, but I'm not sure I'm ready yet, to cut her that much slack.

It was a pretty big thing to not be honest about. Its family. It's flesh and blood family, and what's more important than that?

'I'm trying to understand, Mum. I saw Ruth briefly, just outside, but I'd really like to talk to her if that would be okay? I'd like to give her my condolences about Becky – I mean Rebekah – and I want to make a connection with her, even just a small one.'

Mum shakes her head and pulls her bottom lip out with her thumb and forefinger. It's what she does when she's deep in thought, or nervous. 'I'm not sure now would be the best time, Matty. Ruth is still struggling to come to terms with a lot of what's happened in her life, including dealing with some very distressing repressed memories that have come back to her.'

'Yeah, I know what they are. The cops told me, when they were explaining why I was being released without charge. It's pretty horrible stuff, Rebekah being killed by her own father, on top of everything else he did to her. I guess now's *not* the right time to approach Ruth, but it's something I want to do in the future; reach out to her, you know?'

'I know, and I think its lovely that you do. Just let the dust settle a bit, and maybe drop her a note, to ask if she'd like to talk to you. Let her decide, if and when.'

Mum's right. She's being sensible about it. I just want to go over there *now*, and try and make that poor woman – my half-sister – feel better in whatever way I can, about the shit that's upended her life. It's probably just insensitive, and if I'm honest, I probably want to do it more for myself than for her, and that's not right, is it?

Mum dishes up an amazing roast dinner, and it's gorgeous; a simple roast chook with all the trimmings. That, and the apple pie and ice cream that follow feels like the best food I've ever eaten. We all tuck in without saying much. At the end I offer to do the washing up, and Mum shakes her head. I drain the last of my beer and put the bottle back on the table.

'I need to get home, then. There's quite a mess to clean up, apparently. The cops turned the place over, looking for evidence or whatever, and I don't imagine for a second they'd have put everything back nicely where they found it.'

'Do you need help?' Mum is as mumsy as ever, with her little boy, but this time it doesn't irritate me.

'Nah. It won't take long, but I want to get it over with. I want to wake up tomorrow in a clean, tidy place, without having to face any more chaos.'

She grins, gently. 'Well, that makes sense.'

Dad gets up from the table. 'I'll run you home. We can stop on the way and get you a few groceries. I imagine your milk might be off and your bread might be mouldy, for a start? A quick stop at Sainsbury's would help, I imagine?'

I grin at him. Ever the practical one. 'Yeah, that would be great, Dad, thanks.' Mum hands me a plastic dish with a lid on it. It's another roast dinner for me to heat up tomorrow night.

There's a little Sainsbury's, a few streets away, so we pop in and I grab a few things. Then Dad drops me off, and I'm finally alone, and looking at the mess the cops have left. To be fair, it's not as bad as I expected. There's a few drawers pulled open, with clothes and other things spilling out of them, and the kitchen cupboards are all open, with some stuff lying on the floor where they pulled it out. I have no idea what they were looking for, but I know there was nothing here that would have given them cause for concern.

It takes me just twenty minutes to restore the place to what it should be, and I take a good long hot shower, grab one of the beers Dad bought, and go to sit on the sofa. I don't put the telly or the radio on. I need a bit of quiet, right now, so I sort my new phone out, and then get a few of my scrambled thoughts in order.

Christine's phone number is the first one I delete. Then the agency. Then, the numbers of every colleague I know there. I read a few of my text messages from different friends, and I delete the ones that are mean and nasty; from people who clearly aren't the friends I thought they were. Some have been supportive, and those are the only people I'm interested in staying in touch with anymore.

It amazes me, how quick people are to judge. Helpful little missives like *'I'm so disappointed in you,' 'I had no idea you could do something like this,' 'slag,'* and so-on. From so-called friends. Well, I might not be on their list of favourite people anymore, but they're certainly not on mine. With friends like that, who the fuck needs enemies?

I've heard it said a lot, in the past, that when your boat starts to sink you find out who'll throw you a lifeline, and who'll just leave you to drown. They also say that the ones in either camp are never the ones you'd expect. As I sit here tonight, with my heart in a hundred pieces, I know just how true that is.

The phone rings, and I jump. It's Teresa, my sister. I'm not sure how much she knows, other than what Mum's told her about all this, so I'm cautious, as I answer, but she's overjoyed that I'm home, uncharged, and in one piece – on the outside at least.

'Oh, God! Matty! I've been so worried! I'm still in Aussie and I plan to be for months yet, but I would have come home if you'd needed me, you know, if things had got any worse. Mum just rang to tell me you're off the hook. I can't tell you how glad I am, about it!'

'At least it means you can stay in Surfers, or wherever you are.'

She giggles. 'Yes, there's that, but honestly, Matty, my heart has been in my mouth. I was tempted to come home anyway, with everything, but I'm more relieved that you're okay, than anything else.'

'I know. I was only teasing. How's it going? Please tell me something happy. I've been in a shitty situation. It would be good to hear some nice news.'

Teresa giggles again. 'Well, its lovely and warm and sunny out here. We're spending a lot of time at the beach, and I've learned to scuba dive! I've had some fun, hugging giant turtles, of all mad things! Oh, and I've met someone! His name is Ross, and he's from Sydney.'

'Is it love?'

She pauses for a beat or two, before answering. Her voice becomes soft. 'You know, Matty, I think it might be. He's very special. I'm going to try to convince him to come home with me for a while, at the end of this trip. If we're still together, that is, but I do think we might be. I hope so, anyway.'

I feel a big swell of love for my little sister. 'I hope so too, Tezzie. You deserve to be happy. Enjoy your trip, keep having fun, and don't worry about me. I'm fine. Keep in touch, send me a postcard, and I'll see you when you get back, whether you're 'Rossed' up or alone.'

Teresa goes quiet again. 'It sounds like there's a lot to talk about, when I do get back, Matty. Mum's filled me in on the whole half-sister thing, too, and I don't know what to think about any of it. I'm pretty pissed off with her, if I'm honest. How could she keep a secret like that from us, for our whole lives? And as for moving next door to Ruth and Gina like that... it's like *stalking,* don't you think? Kinda creepy? No wonder Ruth is so pissed off with her too. I haven't a clue how I'd feel, in her shoes.'

'Yeah, it is pretty bizarre, I'll give you that. I don't know what to think either, sis, but look... as far as you're concerned, all of it can wait. Honestly? You really are in the best place, ten thousand miles away from all this shit.'

As I say the words, I realise with a jolt that my parents didn't exchange a single word while I was at their house tonight. I decide against staying anything about that to Teresa. How will it help anything, to start speculating on what might be adrift in our parents' marriage? She doesn't need that, to worry about.

'By the time you get back here the dust will have settled, Tez, and it will all be easier to talk about. Just have a good time, okay? Don't get too hung up on what's happening at this end. It will all still be here when you get back, you know, the facts of everything.'

She laughs, openly this time, and says goodbye. Before she rings off, she tells me she loves me, and I tell her I love her too.

In that moment, while I'm sitting here alone, with far too much to think about, family love feels like everything. I just hope that for all of us, it's going to be enough, to get us through all this upheaval.

Chapter Twenty-four
- *Adie* -

After waving Matty off, with Bryan, I notice the downstairs lights go out at Ruth and Gina's, They must be going to bed.

Matty being here tonight, even just for a couple of hours, diffused a lot of the angst that's been hovering around the edges for me and Bryan since events have come to light. He is finding it impossible to talk to me about anything at all, let alone the room full of elephants that's sucking up the oxygen and leaving us both breathless with despair. As the hours and days pass, instead of finding a way to come to terms with everything, my husband seems to be growing ever-more upset. He's sleeping in the main guest bedroom now, and he has moved all of his stuff into it, from his bedside cabinet, wardrobe and drawers.

I was glad, tonight, when Matty said he wanted to go home. If he'd wanted to stay, it would have made things tricky, because the new sleeping arrangements are fairly obvious to anyone staying here, and having to explain all that to him would have been upsetting for us all. Matty's predicament might mostly be resolved, but everything else still feels so fearfully fragile, like cobwebs quivering in the wind.

The main guest bedroom has an en-suite bathroom attached to it, so I seldom see Bryan now, except for the occasional mealtimes when he chooses to be at home, and a frosty truce prevails for as long as it takes us to eat a meal. He's spending most of his time away from the house now, and while he's always been away a lot because of work, I now feel that he's actively avoiding me, as much as he can.

I know he is reeling, and struggling to accept that he's been such an unwitting participant in my long and miserable chain of subterfuge. He was also trying – and clearly failing – to square away my admittance, after the last time Matty was here, that his behaviour had caused me to wonder if he actually might be capable of killing someone.

It was a terrible thing to feel, and a terrible thing to have to confess, even to the one person you love the most in the world and feel safe with. There has to be one person, doesn't there, who you could say such a shocking thing to, without being judged or condemned? Isn't your spouse the one person you should be able to confide your greatest nightmare to, and have it held safe, even if not with understanding, at least with a scrap of compassion for the terror you feel, *and* for the fear in confessing it?

But Bryan hadn't got it, in the way I meant it. It hadn't been safe, to admit that to him, and I don't know how to feel less devastated that I don't feel secure with him anymore! I don't mean physically; I know that he would never raise a hand to me, or stand by while anyone else did. He once knocked a guy out, in a restaurant, who had said something very inappropriate to me. I don't feel I can connect with him *emotionally* now, and I never thought I'd ever get to that place; that *we* ever would, as a couple, where he would condemn me for my thoughts or refuse to talk about something seismic that's happened in our relationship.

It's almost as if he actually wants our marriage to fall apart. Even if he doesn't, he isn't putting up a fight for it; at least not yet. All he is putting up is a brick wall.

So why is he so reluctant to talk? Why is he looking at me like I'm something he's had to scrape off the bottom of his shoe? Am I really that much of a disappointment? After all these years, shouldn't we be able to communicate, and weather the worst of storms? Aren't we strong enough to survive this? If not, <u>why</u> not?

I've tried, several times now, to get him to talk about how he really feels, and say whether he wants to try and sort things out, to find a firmer footing, to see where we can go from here, if anywhere. Every time, I'm just met with stony silence. I feel condemned, judged, and occasionally actually *hated,* when I see the way he looks at me when he isn't aware that I can see it.

Teresa was hurtfully dismissive too, on the phone tonight. I had a couple of conversations with her, when Matty was first arrested, and his innocence seemed so impossible to prove. Teresa had been alarmed, but she stoically refused to believe that her brother could be guilty of murder. It makes me feel so much worse for having wavered in that, myself. I still can't believe my head even went to that place. I'm his mother, for God's sake! If anyone should have unshakeable belief in him, it should be me.

Tonight's conversation, telling Teresa about Ruth, was a lot harder. My confession was met with stunned silence, before she abruptly shut it down, saying we could talk about it all when she got back, but she wasn't about to have her holiday ruined, thank you very much, by a manipulative and self-indulgent parent. She made it crystal clear that she wasn't going to let me cast a shadow over her holiday. The conversation literally left me weeping.

My thoughts turn back to Ruth, now, and how she might be coping. To see someone you love confused and anguished, is tough at the best of times. Knowing that you've been the cause of it, well, that is a whole new level of wretched.

Poor Ruth. So much to deal with, so much to have to find a way to accept. A monstrous family, an even more monstrous memory returning, and finding out that the person you'd always thought of as a trusted friend had lied to your face about everything; it was a pretty tough task, to transcend all that. Ruth is resilient, there's no denying that, but how vulnerable must she be feeling right now? Relieved, yes, that her sister's killer had been found, and no doubt *hugely* relieved that she wasn't of that terrible gene pool, but there is a staggering amount to process and come to terms with, and my barefaced bloody lies are a big part of it all.

Only time will allow us to know what might be salvaged, I suppose, and whether we can ever have a friendship again. I've always hoped for so much more, in the event that the truth ever came out but, with it stampeding forward as brutally as it has, it's hard to see where we might go from here.

What if she never speaks to me again? What if, after going to such lengths to find her, I'm to end up losing her all over again?

There's a lot to forgive and it would be down to Ruth, now, to initiate contact.

If she never wants to, how will I bear it?

Emotionally spent, I lay down on the bed. A hot flush is starting, and flaring in my chest. I've been getting a lot of them lately, and a few bouts of unexplained tearfulness too but I guess, at fifty-one, it's inevitable. 'The change' is coming for me, and menopause is the last thing I need right now, on the back of everything else that feels like it's stripping my soul to its core, but Mother Nature doesn't care about timing, does she? She does what she wants, when she wants to do it, and all I can do about this is ride the waves as best I can and hope I don't end up drowning before I get to salvage something of myself.

It's my time; it's as simple as that. The rollercoaster of hormonal disruption has started, and I have to find a way to manage it. I already know a fair bit about the process, thanks to some online research, and a few friends who have started the change too. Some, like my friend Miranda, swear by HRT. Others won't touch it with a bargepole, and I'm very much on the fence. I'm not sure how I feel about flooding my body with fake hormones, to stave off the inevitable. I really don't want to do that, if I'm honest. But do I really want to be flying blind with this, at the same time as my marriage is heading south and my kids are all monumentally pissed at me? God help me, I haven't a clue what to do.

Hormones in freefall are vexing enough, but what's creating the most turmoil right now is the fact that I'm not sure anymore whether Bryan and I will get our marriage back on track. I was pretty sure we could, to begin with, but he's become so remote, so unwilling to concede a single thing. Last night, he stayed out all night. He only came home today because I called him to tell him that Matty was being released and coming over. When I asked where he'd spent the night, he said he'd been working late and had booked into a B & B not far from the construction site.

I'm not sure if Matty noticed tonight, that for the whole time he'd been here, his father never spoke a single word to me.

But *I* noticed, and the pain of how Bryan behaved towards me, in front of our own son, was unbearable. If he wants to treat me as a nobody, that's one thing. But it's not okay to do it in front of our kids, and I need to tell him that. For Matty and Teresa, we have to at least be civil. Surely we can manage that?

But, as it turned out, it doesn't look like I'm going to have a conversation with Bryan tonight about anything. My phone just pinged, with a message from him. He's calling into the office, won't be back until well after midnight, and I shouldn't wait up.

Our bed feels huge, without him. As I sit up in it now, with a cup of herbal tea, I think about the days to come. What will they bring? When might Ruth speak to me again, or will she ever, at all? Matty said, earlier tonight, that he wanted to reach out to her himself. He wants, in whatever way he can, to make a connection that might make them both feel better about everything that's happened. He wants to find a way forward with his new half-sister.

I want to ease Ruth's anguish too, but how can I make anything better, if nobody will speak to me? Gina made the situation plain enough.

'Stay away from us! You hear me, sì? Stay away from my family! Put your casa on the fucking market and move away, because we were here first and we don' want you next to us anymore.'

Sitting up in bed tonight, alone in the house, I decide that there is one thing I can do. I'm not completely powerless, am I? I can write Ruth a letter. If nobody is willing to talk to me, and I'm only going to get the door slammed in my face if I try to change their minds, the one thing I can do is write it down. I can still say everything I need to, straight from my heart.

All of a sudden, it feels like the *only* thing I can do, and it feels critical that I do it right away. I get up and pad downstairs, to the study, and rummage through the desk drawers until I find a pen and paper. It would be easier to write on the computer, I know, but I've always felt that a heartfelt message should be in pen and ink; putting something of yourself on the paper and, let's face it, this might well be the most heartfelt message I'm ever going to write in my life. As I sit down at the desk, I don't even give myself time to think about what I *should* say to my daughter. I simply begin to write.

Dear Ruth

I know I'm the last person you want to hear from, and I respect that, but there are so many things I want to say. Please allow me, through this letter, to say them.

I am so very sorry for everything that's happened in your life, and for how much of it has been my fault. There are so many things I wish I could change, about the past, but it is what it is, and I can't do anything except try to explain.

When I gave you up, I had no idea that you would have a terrible life. I let you go with every hope in my heart that you'd have a <u>beautiful</u> life; the kind of life I could never hope to give you, in my wildest dreams. I was from a working-class family, and there were many times when we didn't have two pennies to rub together. There were many times when all we did was scrape by, and occasional times when we didn't even manage to do that. As sad as it is to say, there were times when we went to bed hungry, and I wanted better than that for you.

If I'd known, even at fifteen, that you would end up being raised by a pair of the most depraved people on the face of the earth, I would have fought tooth and nail to keep you. I want you to know that. I knew nothing back then, of the kind of cruelty you were going to face. I knew there was evil in the world, but it never occurred to me, not even for a second, that any of it would touch my baby.

I fell pregnant with you when I was fourteen, after a boy not much older than me took advantage of my naiveté. Then I was sent away, and forced to keep a lot of things secret when I didn't want to. My parents denied me the most important choice of my life, but they did it so I could have a _good_ life. They did the best they ever could, for me, and when I met Bryan and he wanted to marry me, I couldn't believe my luck. I was so afraid of what he would do if I told him about you. I wish I'd been mature enough, even then, to have trusted him because if I had we could have found you earlier. He would have wanted to do that, and I know that now but, as a scared and ashamed young woman who couldn't believe a man like him would want her, I was too afraid of losing him if I told him the truth.

When Matty and Teresa started talking about going to university, I knew it would only be a matter of time before I faced an 'empty nest,' and that was around the time the urge to find you started pressing at me, and became too strong to deny. I think the prospect of them leaving for good triggered something deeply maternal and long-buried within me, that drove me to find out where you were. I never expected that, but there it was.

I didn't know where you'd gone, or who you were with. The adoption was closed, at the request of your adoptive parents, so it was hard for me to find out anything about you. I hired a private investigator, and when she found you, I can't tell you how excited I was! But I was terrified, too. What if you didn't want to know me? Or what if you did? How would I tell my family? I would have told them, I'd have found a way, because I couldn't have kept you a secret if you'd known about me too. That rediscovery; it would have been too precious a thing to keep secret if you'd known too. I can't describe it any other way.

But you didn't know you were adopted, and that made things impossible for me, because I couldn't be the one to turn *your world upside down. It wasn't my place, to say something that big, to you. It was up to your adoptive parents to tell you that. When I realise that they never had, I didn't know what to do.*

But once I'd found you, the idea of letting go of you again, and you being somewhere, 'out there in the world,' was not an option for me. How could I pretend I hadn't found you? How could I un-know the knowledge, that the beautiful child I had created was 'out there'?

So I bought the house next door. I told myself that if the best I could ever have was you as a neighbour, and maybe even a friend, and see from time to time, that would have to be enough. I did a lot of soul-searching, before I made the decision that it could be enough. If that was all it could ever be, for me, I decided I could take it. I just wanted to know that you were safe and happy, and to love you in any way I could, without anyone's life except my own being turned upside down.

Yes, I should have told my husband. I should have told my children too. But it was so hard to do, in the early days, and then when I found you I couldn't see a way to tell them then, and still protect <u>your</u> world. It seemed so unfair, to tell you!

I know what I am. I'm nothing but a cowardly woman who has painted herself into a corner, because she was selfish. But I hope you can see that even in my selfishness, I was still trying to keep you safe from knowledge that I thought would blow your world apart. I just assumed you had loving parents. I had no idea your world was so difficult. If I had ever known that, years ago, I'd have come and got you. I'd have battered down the door of Michael Stenton's house, barged my way in, and taken you away from that life.

But I didn't know. I couldn't have known. I found out, much too late, that you needed to be saved from that terrible life many years before you managed to save yourself. I'd have saved you. Even if you never believe another word from me please, at least, believe that. I'd have done whatever it took, to have saved you.

I said I was sorry for everything, but I'm not. There's one thing I will never be sorry for, and that is getting pregnant, and carrying you to term. In spite of the terrible challenges you've had to face, that I unwittingly condemned you to when I gave you up, you have grown up to be a spectacular human being. I'm so in awe of you, sometimes I struggle even to breathe. I created you, and I do think it's one of the best accomplishments of my whole life.

My heart sang, when I saw <u>your</u> life! A beautiful woman with a great career, a loving marriage, a beautiful child, and a happy home. It all seemed perfect, and my heart literally sang. It still does, for all that you have. All I want for you is happiness. I want you to have the life you deserve, and if that means you're happier without me being in it, I completely understand and accept that. I will do as Gina says. I will sell this house, and move somewhere else, so that you can have the peace you deserve.

I have loved you from the minute I knew I was carrying you, and the love that grew within me never stopped. It continues to grow, and I will love you until I draw my last breath, and beyond. I will never stop wanting and hoping for the best for you, my beautiful, golden, special girl.

Adie

The tears are pouring down my face now. I read the letter back, and I know that although it's little more than a jumbled mess and might not make the sense I want it to, and probably repeats itself all over the place, it *was* straight from my heart. It's authentic. It's *me*, in all my rawness. I quickly put it in an envelope and decide to deliver it tonight, before I can 'chicken out' and throw it in the bin, instead.

Baring my soul isn't something I do very often. It feels acutely uncomfortable, and a growing part of me is wondering now, if it really is the best course of action. Maybe I *should* put the letter in the bin. A lot of people say that it's better to do that; do the cathartic thing by getting it all out of your head and onto paper, but then burning or binning it rather than upsetting someone else with your thoughts. Maybe they're right; maybe no good will come of letting Ruth know how I feel. But in this case it feels like the most important thing on earth, that my first-born and abandoned daughter gets the full explanation she deserves. If she refused to ever speak to me again, how would she ever get it?

Even if nothing good comes of my attempt to explain, nothing worse will; of that I am sure. Ruth and Gina are as mad as hornets right now, but they're not cruel. I seal the letter inside the envelope, write Ruth's name on it, and decide to deliver it straight away, again before I 'lose my bottle.' Being a coward is something I've been far too good at, for far too long. It's time to step up, own everything, and take responsibility for it now, however unpleasant the consequences might be. The time for keeping secrets is over.

It's really dark outside. There are no stars tonight. The sky is cloudy, after a dull day, and the chill in the air makes me shiver. I pull the front door closed behind me and walk quickly and quietly across the patch of lawn that separates our house from Ruth and Gina's.

Their house is all in darkness, but a security light comes on, and it makes me jump. I quickly post the letter through the flap in the front door and scurry away again but, as I reach my own front door, I'm dismayed to find that it hadn't been on its latch. I've managed to lock myself out of my own bloody house.

It's the final straw of the day. I feel myself sinking to the doorstep, sobbing, as the full avalanche of recent events sweeps me away. It is pointless, and futile, to deny the grief that overwhelms me. Another hot flush washes across me too, and I surrender to that as well. As I curl myself into a tight ball and hug my knees to my chest, I have never felt more wretched, or more alone, in my entire life.

A sharp, strident, demanding voice brings me to my senses.

'*A'dienne!* What the hell is wrong with you? Why are you curled up like a foetus on your doorstep, and howling like a dog in the night?'

It's Gina. My letter coming through the letterbox flap must have woken her up. I don't have a clue how to answer, or even how to stop sobbing. Gina sighs heavily, and speaks again.

'*Mio Dio, A'dienne!* It is late! What the fuck are you doing out here, crying?'

I manage, through Herculean effort, to get a hold of myself, at least enough to respond. 'I've locked myself out,' I mumble. 'I was delivering a letter, and I forgot to snib the front door.'

Gina tuts loudly and sighs theatrically. She rolls her eyes. '*A'dienne,* you are such a *disastro ferroviario!* Wait here. We have a key to your house. I'll get it.'

She stomps off in her red tartan pyjamas and her orange Garfield slippers, back to her own house. Moments later she is back, with the key to my front door.

'Here is your key, and I think you should keep it now.'

I take the key gratefully, from Gina's outstretched hand.

'I'll get your key too then, shall I?'

Gina nods curtly. 'I think so, yeah. We might as well do that.'

I let myself in, and locate Gina and Ruth's key from the peg behind the front door. The keyring has a little plastic replica of an Italian pasta packet, on it. I hand it over, without a word. Gina narrows her eyes, as she contemplates saying anything further, She decides against being abusive and simply shakes her head, before turning and walking away.

'Wait, Gina. Will you let Ruth have my letter?'

Gina turns. 'Of course, *A'dienne*. What, you think I wouldn't?'

I look down. 'That's not what I meant.'

Gina sighs, rolled her eyes again, folds her arms, and taps her foot on the path. They are her trademark behaviours whenever she is struggling to find a level of patience that is usually beyond her.

'Ruthie is her own woman, *A'dienne*. It is for her to decide if she should read a letter from you. It is not up to me. And it will be for her to decide what she wants to do about it. But you should not hold your breath. She doesn't wanna talk to anyone, and even if she did, it wouldn't be you. You get it?'

'Yes, I get it. Thank you.'

'Goodnight, *A'dienne*.'

'By the way, Gina; what is a *disastro ferroviario?*' I understood the first bit of what she said, but the second word is a mystery, and even as I'm asking, I'm wondering why I even want to know. Maybe it's simply a last attempt to keep Gina engaged because I love her too; with all my heart. I love her as much as I love Ruth. Losing her too is just as horrible.

The tears keep coming, I haven't a hope of stopping them.

Gina's shoulders slump. When she speaks, her voice is softer. 'It means train wreck, Adie. You're a train wreck in Ruthie's life. And in my life too.'

And with that, she turns away and melts into the night as if she'd never been there at all. At least she didn't leave me on my doorstep to freeze all night! That's something, I suppose.

But the heavy blanket of wretchedness remains. Sleep won't come easy, tonight. It's going to be another in a long line of sleepless nights, wondering what could have been done to change the past, and worrying what the future will bring. Right now, it's hard to imagine how things might be fixed. All I can hope for is that my letter will resonate with Ruth, if she decides to read it at all.

Chapter Twenty-five
- *Ruth* -

I'm getting pretty used to not knowing what to think. I'm getting pretty good at taking body blows and pretending they don't hurt, at least until I can fall apart in private. The stiff upper lip; I came to came to be pretty good at showing that too, didn't I, in the life I had before?

The life I had before. Huh. Interesting way to think; considering its still the same life. It's simply been smacked into, and spun a long way off its axis, and I'm having to get used to everything being in a different position. That's all it comes down to, really; the new position of everything, and how I plan to get my head around it all. It's still the same life. I have the same *wife,* the same daughter, the same house, the same career.

I just feel different about it all, I guess. Kind of removed, like it's all a long way from me right now. I feel like I've been cast adrift from everything I felt safe with. But those familiar things are the rocks of my existence. I have to reach out and grab them, and hold fast to them. I have to do that, and draw strength from them as the things that *haven't* changed, and *won't* change, while everything else around me has. It is the same life. I have to keep trying to remember that, as I pull back together all the bits of it that feel like they've unravelled. Gina is holding fast onto me, so I have to hold on to her too, and let her strength start helping me rebuild mine.

It's almost as if my life is a smashed-up jigsaw, but the edges are still intact. If I look at it that way, I can trust that the edges won't break, and the jumbled mess in the middle can still be made sense of, but I know I won't do it overnight. God alone knows how long it will take me, to find the right places for the pieces that are left.

Sticking with this 'jigsaw analogy' it's probably more like a 'Wasjig;' what you end up with when you put it all back together is a different picture from the one you have in mind. There's a resemblance, yes, but what you have at the end, as the picture that represents your life, is nothing like what you expect.

There's a lot to piece together, and I suppose it's better to focus first on what's possible, as far as that goes. My erstwhile 'parents,' are gone from my life for good. My 'sister' is also gone. She is dead, and they may as well be.

There will be time later, to find a route to acceptance of that, and all that went before. What's more important now, I feel, is to look at the living; what still shines within the wreckage.

Adie's letter was more or less an echo of the explanation she gave me when I went over to her house. There were more details, and I was grateful for them, but I still don't know how to feel.

I'm trying to imagine being a young and vulnerable fifteen-year-old heterosexual girl, who has to tell her parents that she's pregnant. I'm trying to imagine what that must feel like; how terrifying it must be, to be pregnant at fifteen, and to know that you're going to be judged and possibly condemned by the people you really need to have compassion and love for you instead, when you tell them. I'm trying to imagine what it must feel like to have something growing inside you that you didn't expect and were in no way prepared for, and how you'd feel about it, emotionally or biologically. I'm trying to imagine what it might be like to want to keep that child, even though you're still a child yourself, with no power to stand against someone who's steamrolling you in your own 'best interests,' by refusing to let you do it.

What is it like, to give birth, after carrying a growing baby for nine months? I've heard that the urge to protect that child is instant and visceral, and that's as it should be. What must it be like then, to have that child taken from your arms; to be left behind, still exhausted from the battle of bearing it, to somehow find enough faith that it will have a better life than you know you can give it yourself?

And what must it feel like, years later, to learn the terrible truth about that child's life?

I've never had the urge to have sex with a man, or to have a baby. I've never wanted to be pregnant. The whole idea of pregnancy and childbirth nauseates me. I know it's a terrible thing to say, and I'll probably be condemned to purgatory forevermore for even *thinking* it, but pregnant women simply look grotesque, to me. When Gina was pregnant with Chiara, I didn't love her any less – not even one iota – but physically her growing belly repulsed me. And when she was in labour, and roaring and screaming, and giving birth amid seeping urine, spraying blood and flying faeces, it made my stomach churn. I could never admit that to her, nor would I *ever*, even now!

All of it was forgotten, of course, in the instant Chiara was born. The love I felt for that baby, in the moment she came into the world, is indescribable. I knew, in that moment, that I was capable of killing anyone who tried to hurt her, and she wasn't even biologically mine! There hadn't been an umbilical cord, or any other tangible tie, to make me feel that way; I just did. I know that Gina would even kill *me* to protect Chiara, if she had to, so what must it have been like for Adie, to have gone through all that, and to feel that way about her baby – me – and then have me taken away?

I know enough about Adie Bostock to believe how heart-centred she is. Fundamentally, she's a really good woman. I know I'm not wrong about that. Goodness radiates from her in everything she says and does, and nobody is that good an actress. If Adie had a mean or selfish streak, it would have shown itself long before now. But this is a woman who bakes and decorates a beautiful cake for someone's birthday, without being asked, and lies on the floor for hours with her arms wrapped around her dog. She does local charity drives, and I can't help chuckling at a memory that pops up for me now.

She once got hundreds of flyers printed, to put through everyone's doors, asking for them to put a plastic bag on the doorhandle of their front door with any old bras in it that they would be willing to donate to African women in need.

Gina and I had gone with her to deliver the flyers, and I'd gone with her to collect the plastic bags. We ended up with more than three hundred bras, of all shapes, colours and sizes, to send to women in Africa. I remember thinking that my plain and serviceable cotton Marks and Spencer's bras were pretty uninspiring, compared to some of what came in. Some of those tribal African women would, in their far-flung and barely civilized villages, be wearing bright pink push-up 'Wonder-bras,' black lace balconettes, and some rather extraordinary leopard-print items from an 'adult' chain-store that didn't look like they'd really fit *anybody*. We joked, at the time, about what their rough and ready African men would have thought of it all.

That was who Adie Bostock was; a woman who was happiest when she was doing something for somebody else, whether it was supplying a week's worth of freezable meals for an exhausted single mum who'd just come home with a brand new baby, or downloading and printing off her daughter's online holiday snaps to put in an album in chronological order, to present her with when she finally came home from abroad. Adie lived for 'being of service.'

As much as it pains me, and as pissed as I am at her right now, I have to admit that she doesn't have a harmful bone, and when she tells me that the last thing she ever wanted to do was hurt me, and the only thing she ever wanted to do instead was love me, I absolutely do believe her. But, after so much subterfuge and shocking revelation, it's a bit of a stretch to just say, 'oh well, okay then, come into my arms, Mummy.'

I'm not sure I can ever get there. Part of me wants to try, but another part of me wants to run away screaming, and never look at her again. The bit that's left, between those extremes, feels paralysed.

Gina has made hot chocolate, and brought it to bed. She's poured a good slug of amaretto into it, so its warming and comforting, and I guess it might help me to get back to sleep again when I'm ready, but that won't be for a while. She gets back into bed, sits up next to me, and sighs, heavily.

'*A'dienne* locked herself out of her house. I gave her back her key.'

'Um… well, okay, I guess. Did you get ours back, too?'

She nods, and a small door slams inside me. A rush of realisation suddenly hits me. I didn't want that. I didn't want our key back from Adie, and I didn't want her to have back the one we kept for her. I don't want any more doors closing on me, even small ones like that. There have been far too many finalities already. I'm not sure I can bear many more. I tell Gina that, and she immediately looks contrite and apologises.

'Ruthie, you are right! It is not just up to me to decide these things. *Mi dispiace, cara.* I don't wanna make things any harder for you. You know, your joy is everything to me. When the time comes for you to talk to *A'dienne*, I will support whatever you decide, and if you wanna do the key thing again, I'll be okay with it. I'm sorry, for assuming something so big. I had no right.'

'It's alright, Gina. I'm not sure how to write the script for the future, either. I know I have to talk to Adie at some point, but not yet. There's too much else to get to grips with first. I still need to mourn Rebekah.'

'Yeah, you do, and that's not straightforward anymore, is it? There is so much more to her story than you ever really knew, and I can only imagine how hard that is for you, *cara*. I think maybe you should see someone, you know, a counsellor or someone who can help you to accept everything and be at peace with it? But no more nightmares, huh?'

'I hope not. I haven't had one since I spoke to the police, but I'm sure I still have a lot to work through. Right now it feels as if there's a curtain covering it all, and I'm not sure how to pull it back.'

Things are misfiring, in my brain. Thoughts are pinging around, but finding no place to land. Everything is simply whizzing around instead, leaving me fraught with confusion. If Rebekah was being sexually abused for her whole life by her father, and couldn't sustain intimacy with a boyfriend, how could she engage in such outrageous 'group activity' with paid escorts? Did she really feel that she was of such little value as a human being, for that to be all she was fit for? Or did she do it because it was something she could control without pressure? Requesting the use of no condoms – did she truly see herself as worthy of nothing more than a disease that might kill her, or was it a desire to get pregnant, to finally have something of her own that nobody else would ever know to lay claim to, to love?

As a 'client paying for services,' she could say what she wanted and be sure she would get exactly that – and nothing she *didn't* want. It's hard for me, as a woman who has never been interested in men, to understand how someone could do what she did and keep her self-respect. Maybe Rebekah hated herself. She must have hated Michael, but I know that she loved him too. She said that she did, many times.

And how must she have felt about her mother, who always knew, and never saved her? Was that a love-hate relationship too? I know how she felt about *me,* and the fact that *I* never saved her, but how could she sit at a table every week with the woman who'd stood by, while her father helped himself to her whenever he felt like it all through her life? Rebekah never found the power to say no, until she did and it got her murdered! I find it almost impossible to believe that Margaret never helped her while there was still time to do it. What the fuck was going on in *her* warped brain? The terrible way she treated me was nothing, compared to that.

There is so much; *so much*, that I still don't understand, and I know that Gina is right. I do need to get some kind of therapy – and soon – to try and make sense of what happened in my seriously fucked-up 'family.' I haven't a hope of working out for myself what drove Rebekah, or how her mind really worked, but I feel deeply driven to know, because although I was of no help to her in life, I want to understand her now. While I don't believe in any kind of God who could let this terrible thing happen, especially through one of His so-called 'vessels of love and compassion for the suffering,' part of me does wonder if her damaged soul *is* still hovering in the ether, waiting to be understood before it can find the peace it deserves. If I can understand more about her, and how anguished she was, maybe it will still help her in ways I can't quantify. Maybe I'm just naïve in this weird belief system I've got going, that I can't even really articulate properly, but anything I can offer her is better than nothing.

I tell Gina what's on my mind and she puts her arms around me and holds me close.

'For what it's worth, Ruthie, I am also mourning the passing of Rebekah. It is a lesson for me, that there is always more to somebody's story than they want us to see. I knew Rebekah was in pain, but I had no patience with her. All I saw was the worst of her, and I reacted to it in a way that didn't help her. That is my bad, *cara.*'

It's mine too. I didn't get it, either, and although I can sit here and blame repressed memories until the cows come home, I have to live with the fact that I failed her. It doesn't matter that it wasn't my fault that I couldn't remember in time; that she went to her grave thinking that I knew and didn't care. If all I can do is understand now, maybe it's not just me that it will help.

'How are you feeling about those not-parents, Ruthie?'

I think for a minute. How *do* I feel? I try to explain. It's not easy. Every word I utter feels like one that's being torn from my soul, and I wonder how much of it I'll have left, at the end of this journey that still stretches so far ahead of me.

'All the things you'd expect, I guess. Relieved that they're getting what they deserve. Thankful beyond measure that I have no biological or emotional ties to them. Pleased that Rebekah has some justice, that her situation can at last be acknowledged, even though it's too late for her. Sad for the fact that it *is* too late, and she was robbed of the chance to fix what was broken and have a good life. Sorry that she never found the courage to talk to me, before it became too late. Full of self-loathing that I didn't ring her back, after those two missed calls, knowing that it might have changed everything. Lots of things, Gina. My head is a mess.'

'Ruthie, no. Nothing was different for you that night. She often called you, and you never returned her calls. That was *normale* for you, because it was never a good thing, to call her back. And anyway, nothing could have changed, *cara!* She was already dead when we came out of the cinema that night. It was already too late for you to save her. The police told you that, no?'

'They did, Gina, but it doesn't help. I know there was nothing I could have done that night, but it doesn't stop me from hating the fact.'

When someone is murdered, there is always a lot of soul-searching that happens, for the people they leave behind, even when there was nothing they could have done that would have stopped the worst from happening. Families, friends, colleagues and acquaintances all ask themselves if they could have been more in touch, kept connections stronger, appreciated them more while they were alive; *cared* more, and showed it. Blah, blah, blah. As much as everyone is a long time dead, the living are a long time coming to terms with the fact – especially if they hadn't been what they should have been, to that person, or what that person wanted them to be. Any time you fail someone, it's a choice. But once that person is gone, there's no choice about fixing *anything*, is there? That's gone for good too, just like the person who died.

Gina knows a good psychologist; someone who specialises in recovery from sexual abuse.

'His name is Peter Dean. I saw him a couple of times myself, if you remember, after I got pregnant with Chiara. He will be good for you, I think. I know you were not abused that way, but you are still affected. He will help you to understand

Cat's-Arse Face and *il mostro ipocrita,* and hopefully Rebekah too.'

I finish my chocolate, and turn out my bedside light. Adie posting her letter through the flap woke us both, earlier, but that's not a bad thing because Gina and I have had a valuable conversation tonight. As I drift off to sleep again I know what a wonderful thing it is, that in the midst of all the wreckage from this scarcely believable horror, that I have someone so truly, totally wonderful by my side, who will not let me fall, who will stand strong beside me, and be here after I've gone through the fire.

The last thing that goes through my mind as it quietly closes down is that there are, actually, *two* such people in my life. I don't just have the rock-solid Gina. I also have someone else who will do everything in her power to stop me from burning, if I let her; my mother, Adie Bostock.

Chapter Twenty-six
- Gina -

Okay, so we have a plan, or at least the start of one. We can make an appointment for Ruthie with Peter Dean. I think it should happen soon. Otherwise it is just too much. Rebekah, Cat's-Arse, *il mostruoso vicario*, murder, *adozione*, and *A'dienne* and her stupid secrets and lies on top of all of it! *Mio Dio*, what a mess!

How does *anybody* make sense of it all, alone? It is too much, even for a bystander like me! But at least the dust is settling now, and we can see how to go forward. It is all about *recupero*, now, and it's gonna take a while. Peter will help, and I also will do all I can.

Some of our friends have been *magnifici* too. Even though there isn't much they can do, and we all know it, that hasn't stopped them from asking the questions; 'I wanna help you, is there anything I can do? What do you need?'

That is a *real* friend; one who asks what they can do. One who asks Ruthie what she needs. So many people just say, 'oh, well, you'll get through this, they were terrible people anyway, it's probably all for the best,' and other meaningless things that don't help. That shit is all just noise she *doesn't* need. I wanna shake some sense into *le persone stupidi* like that. People who actually ask her what she needs when she is hurting like this, even if they can't provide it, and even if they know they can't, they care enough to ask. It means so much more. We are lucky to have such people in our lives.

Ruthie was calm about the letter from *A'dienne*, and she let me read it. It's a good letter, and it seems to come from her heart. *A'dienne's* heart is broken too, by everything that has happened, and I get it. My own heart hurts for her, because I can see how *impossibile* the situation was for her, right from the start of all this. But I have to take Ruthie's lead on how we take things, with her. I can forgive her in my own head, because I know what it feels like, to be made to do something *sessuale* that you don't wanna do, and then have to deal with the result. I at least had the choice to keep my child. *A'dienne* did not. She has lived a long time with all that, and I can see why she did what she did. I don't agree with it, but I understand it, and understanding is the first step on the road to *perdono*. I *wanna* forgive her. I really do.

If Ruthie understands and wants to forgive too, it's good. If she does not, I can only try to see why she would keep the door closed. But if that is what she chooses to do, I have to stand with it. What she wants is more important than what I feel myself, in all this. I feel that she now has a mother, or someone she can at least see as *materna*, for the first time in her life, and to me that is important because it is never too late to need or want your mama. I know this to be true. My mama means *everything* to me, and I wanna think Ruthie can have that too, if she wants it, with *A'dienne*. Maybe the damage is too much for her, but I wanna think not.

It will be what it will be. But tonight, as I saw *A'dienne* so broken, curled up and crying like a baby on her doorstep, it hurt my heart. I wanted so badly to tell her that everything is gonna be okay, but I don't know that it is, and I cannot lie, or be seen to forgive her if Ruthie can't.

You have to be loyal to your spouse. That is the number one thing. No matter how *in conflitto* I feel about any of this, I have to follow Ruthie's lead. It is too big a thing, to not be on the same page about. Whatever my thoughts are, I can only tell her if she asks and if she does, I have to be honest without trying to influence her to see it my way.

I like to have things my way. We all do, right? 'My way or the highway,' as the saying goes, and sometimes I can get a little *calda* if I can't go the way I wanna go with what I think. But not over this. Ruthie needs to do this her way. She needs to resolve what she has to in her own time, in a way that fits for her.

It should be straightforward, no?

Well, maybe. Everything has been explained, and it all makes practical sense, but nobody can say what the emotions should be. Ruthie is so fragile right now, it is terrifying to me. The sooner we can get to Peter Dean, the better. We need to do that so she can get some *prospettiva* before she makes any big decision about *A'dienne* because whatever she decides will have big implications for her life, and we will all be affected by that, whichever way it shakes down.

Lines will be drawn. It will be interesting to see where all of us will be, say, a year from now. I hope with all my heart that it will be a better place. We all deserve to be in a better place.

ONE YEAR LATER
- Matthew -

It's weird, being back at Mum and Dad's house, without Mum being here. She hasn't lived here for months now, and every time I come here, it's always uncomfortable. All her stuff is gone, and what she couldn't fit into her flat she put into storage. The place feels like a shell now. It's half empty of furniture, fully stripped of soul, and I'm glad it's on the market. I'm not sure where Dad will go, after it sells, but he always lands on his feet, doesn't he? Wherever he ends up, I'm sure that 'very lucky boy' will be just fine.

    I still have a key to the house and I call in, now and again, just to pick up the occasional bit of mail that still comes here for me. Dad sends me a text to let me know when anything's here and I try to come when he's not around, because seeing him is still pretty awkward. I know he's still struggling to come to terms with what's happened in his family, like my escorting days and Mum's lies and secrets, but it's like he isn't even *trying* to see through his own self-pity, and consider the bigger picture. I never had him figured for a hippo but there he is, wallowing in some curious combination of his own emotional shit and the kind of mud he can't seem to suck himself out of.

    It's like he's been dropped on his arse from a great height, and he can't get back up again. He still hasn't a clue how to pull his family back together, and that surprises me, because he's always been the most resourceful one of the family. He's always had a solution to any problem but, a full year down the line from everything imploding the way it did, he doesn't seem to know how to deal with *any* of it, and I've started believing he doesn't even want to.

    When he isn't blatantly ignoring Mum, he's still constantly belittling her, even to me and Tezzie, and that doesn't feel good for any of us. He's in his own world even more now than he used to be. Tezzie's given up on him and I think Mum is about to, if she hasn't already. I wouldn't blame her if she did, to be fair. She's tried pretty hard, but he's having none of it, and you can only batter away for so long, at a door that doesn't seem to want to open. Dad's playing deaf and, as far as I'm concerned, he's shaping up to be the worst kind of dumb.

I've no idea what's going on in his mind anymore. I know this past year has damaged him emotionally, but I've too much on my own plate now to want to try and figure out how to help him, especially when every time I've tried, he's bitten my head off. He's still so disappointed in his little boy, for being a male prostitute. He genuinely feels I have nothing to offer him, and that's bad enough, but I can do without the sneering and the lack of tolerance he always shows, whenever I try with him. So we don't get in front of one another much, and I'm learning to live with the weirdness. It's easier now, since I'm married with a family of my own.

Yeah, get me; a 'newlywed!' I met my wife Marie when I went for the job interview I had in my diary when the shit hit the fan last year. Getting the job was a double draw for me, because she was the receptionist there, on the front desk and, as soon as I clocked eyes on her, something clicked.

Something truly joyful just shines out of Marie. I don't know how else to describe it. She has an *aura*, I suppose, that draws people to her. She's also the daughter of the guy who runs the company, which doesn't hurt at all when it comes to job security, does it?

It's not a long story at all, really. Marie took a quick shine to me too, and although a lot of people thought it was bonkers, I knew within just a few weeks that she was the one for me. She felt the same way, and as soon as we found out she was pregnant, a few months later, getting married seemed like the right thing to do. We went to Gretna Green; did the whole elopement thing, and then came back and told everyone.

Nobody knew what to think, about that. Predictably, Mum cried. She's been doing a shitload of that lately – it doesn't seem to take much to set her off – and it's something to do with hormones, she reckons. That kind of explains a few things, but it's a conversation I'm way too far at sea to get involved in. She's on her own, with that one.

She said that while she felt a bit robbed of her chance to be Mother of the Groom, and wear a posh frock and a silly over-sized hat, she understood why we'd run off and got wed in private. She also said that all she wants is for me to be happy, and she's over the moon that I am.

Dad didn't have much to say about it, only something along the lines of hoping Marie would keep me on the straight and narrow, once I was a father it might grow me up a bit, and I should at least try to keep my nose clean after marrying the boss' daughter. Good old misery-guts Dad, who can't seem to say a single word these days that isn't squarely aimed at making me feel small.

Marie and I eloped because there had already been too much drama, and I really couldn't cope with being the centre of attention again so soon, even for something as happy as a wedding. With my family in tatters, and my parents' marriage on the rocks, it felt wrong anyway, to be calling for some big celebration. I thought Marie might be disappointed that she wasn't having a big shebang because, as I understood it, that's what most women want.

But she didn't. Understated is who she is, and that was what she wanted – a quiet, understated wedding that focussed on what weddings should *always* be about – two people in love making lifelong promises to honour and support one another. She loves her family and there's nothing amiss among any of them, but it really didn't matter much to her either, that they weren't there to see her get married.

She understood where I was at, and we still made it the best day of our lives. She wore a gorgeous dress (something of a maternity tent, but beautiful nonetheless) and she had the loveliest bouquet of flowers. A couple of our friends went with us to Gretna as witnesses, and we all went out for dinner afterwards, before Marie and I had our wedding night in a posh hotel. That cost me roughly the black-market equivalent of one of my kidneys but, as the saying goes, the joy is remembered long after the cost is forgotten. As weddings went, it was perfect in our eyes.

Marie's parents, Babatunde and Joanne, were more upset than mine, to have missed the wedding of their beautiful baby girl, but they understood the situation too. After we got back and confessed all, they organised a big, post-wedding 'celebration' dinner with other members of Marie's English and Nigerian family. Some of our friends came along too, as invited guests. It must've cost Baba a pretty penny, but like my mother-in-law Joanne said, a 'proper' wedding, with an eye-watering guest-list and an even *vaguely* upmarket venue, would have cost them a shitload more.

Not having any of my own family there was a bit weird but it was my choice, and I think it was the right one because everything was still so fucking awkward. I just didn't want an uncomfortable night, especially since Marie's dad was footing the bill for it. He's a lovely, smiley, generous man who didn't deserve to have a horrible atmosphere at his table, and I wasn't ready to try and pretend things were okay when they weren't, between us all. Dad was behaving like an asshole, and I still wasn't sure how I felt about Mum, especially after Dad had let it slip that there had been a moment when she'd wondered if I *had* killed Rebekah Stenton.

I didn't know how to feel about that for quite a while but, on one level, I did understand it because I'd been a pretty big asshole myself, that night they took me back from the nick and tried to help me. I was violent and abusive, and I don't even recognise *myself,* who I was that night. I'm only sorry I gave poor old Mum cause to wonder. Dad was having a harder time than I was, with her confession about that, but I was still trying to figure out how I felt about *anything*, in the family. Marie, our marriage, our child – they were the only things I felt sure about, so I stayed in the cocoon that we'd created, and that was all I could manage, at the time.

It's harder than you think though, to feel like shit about your family, because I'm a father myself now and I can't even imagine being ashamed of my own child and not wanting to spend any time with her. Milly was born just a few months after the wedding, and the way I feel about that kid is something else. I'd spend every minute of every day with her, if I could, and I'd forgive her anything.

Dad not wanting to look at me, or Mum; it feels unfathomable, and tragic. He's so disappointed in us both, but *I'm* disappointed in *him*, because I expected him to be able to manage things better than that, and I know Mum feels the same way. We don't talk much either, me and her, but I have picked up on that.

I sold my little place and with a bit of financial support from Marie's grandparents we scraped together a decent deposit for a 3-bed semi in a nice little tree-lined street in Epsom, in time for Milly's arrival. Our place was what you'd probably call 'the worst house in a decent street,' when we bought it. It needed full renovation, but I've been doing what I can, as time and money permit. Baba wanted to bankroll an immediate overhaul, but Marie and I said no. We want to do it by ourselves, bit by bit, so that's what we've been doing. Baba did say that if we ever get sick of living in a building site, munching on brick dust and choking on paint fumes, we just have to say the word and he'll take care of it.

Bless that man; I love him to bits. All he wants is for us to be happy, but like Marie told him, we want to put our own stamp on the place, and living in it 'as is' for a while helps us to decide what we really want to do. She didn't want to plough ahead with big alterations that would cost a bomb, that we might end up wishing we'd done differently if we'd had more time to think about it. It's just one of the ways she keeps our feet firmly on the ground. She's not just gorgeous; she's sensible too, about absolutely everything. She's *my* everything.

So I've already replaced the outdated bathroom with its seriously scary turquoise suite. I advertised the toilet, bath and basin on Marketplace for fifty quid, and some idiot ended up buying it for two hundred, after it turned into a bidding war! I couldn't believe how bonkers that was. It was the most hideous suite in God's creation but, apparently, retro is all the bloody rage now, and people are falling over themselves to put that shit *into* their bathrooms! Someone said if it had been avocado, instead of turquoise, I could have got four hundred. We put the money from that towards a brand new kitchen that was half-price in a sale, to replace what could only be described as a monumental eyesore from the 1980's. It means we no longer feel like we're living in some strange culinary time-warp.

Aside from the woeful décor, terrible carpets and (I think we counted seven!) layers of the worst wallpaper imaginable, the house has 'good bones,' and a decent-sized back garden. Once Milly is old enough, I can put a swing and slide set out there for her to play on. And I've got a shed. Matty Bostock's man-cave. It makes me laugh, now; the unexpected things that make me happy.

I reached out to Ruth, not long after Rebekah's murder was solved. It was pretty hard to try and imagine what she had to get to grips with, especially after the repressed memories started coming out. I knew I couldn't be of any *real* help, but I wanted her to know I cared, that she's my half-sister. The fact that we share some genes; that means something to me, and I wanted her to know that, so I did what Mum suggested and I wrote her a card. It didn't say a lot, just that I was thinking of her, and I was sorry for everything that had happened, and that if she never wanted to talk to me about anything that was okay, but if she did that was okay too.

She sent me a nice card back. That didn't say a lot either, just that she appreciated the overture, and would probably make a connection sometime in the future after she'd worked through a bunch of stuff. Given how scrambled my own head was, that made perfect sense, so I left it at that.

It's easier now, after a year or so, to look back with a different perspective. Marie is an excellent mother and I see, in the bond she has with Milly, what my own mum was robbed of, in having to give Ruth up. She was 'just' a kid who had a kid, but that doesn't mean it didn't hurt like hell, to be told she couldn't keep her. And, while the whole sorry story of how we all ended up as a family fragmented by shock and betrayal is understandable, that doesn't mean it's not tragic. That doesn't mean we should pretend that none of us is hurting or confused about how we feel.

But it also doesn't mean we can't rebuild. With Mum and Dad a million miles away from the faintest whiff of reconciliation, I don't suppose the family will ever go back to being what it was, but surely we can rebuild something, out of the wreckage? Surely we can all be friends, at least? That would be a good place to start, I think.

When Marie and I first got together, she asked me a lot about my work as an escort. She wasn't put off by it, like I thought she would be, when I first admitted it. As it turned out, she knew who I was anyway because everything had been on the news and in the papers, including my name, and there aren't too many Matthew Bostocks in the local area. She knew who I was as soon as she saw my name on the interview list, but she didn't see my previous line of work as seedy. She was *curious* about it.

She wanted to know everything; did I ever form attachments, did I ever find myself unable to 'perform,' was there any point where I felt like I was being exploited or taken advantage of, where I wasn't calling the shots? Lots of questions, but all born from curiosity. The only things she was a bit hung up about were whether I really had given it up for good, and whether I'd been properly screened for STD's and other 'nasties.'

They were fair enough concerns, and I made sure she had no doubts that I was done for good, that I was as clean as a whistle, and that I was as committed to her as any man could ever be, to a woman he was in love with.

And I am completely in love with her. I don't feel I can even *breathe* properly, without her. She's changed everything.

She's helped me find myself again, and I know that sounds like such a worn-out cliché, but it's true. This woman is the most amazing of creatures, with her milk chocolate skin and mega-watt smile, complete with perfect teeth. She's pretty, but she's never going to be a model, like her big sister Marla, and a lot of other Nigerian-blooded women. She's never going to walk into a room and be the woman all the others hate or feel threatened by, and that's a good thing. Marie narrowly missed out on being 'classically' beautiful, but *only* narrowly. She has a different kind of beauty; a much rarer and gentler kind – the kind that's in a completely different league from the ability to grace the cover of a magazine. Marie is sincere and real, and loving and sweet. The aura of goodness around her is something you can really feel. She is beautiful to me, in every way.

She also happens to be a cracker of a cook, an incredible mum to Milly, and she has the best sense of humour of anyone I've ever met. She gets my sarcasm, and my strange sense of the ridiculous, and she makes me laugh with hers. We click. We've got that indefinable 'something' that so many couples don't, and there isn't a day goes by when I don't thank my lucky stars that I found her. Or maybe she found me.

She has helped me keep the sex work in perspective. It would have been so easy to start hating myself, for what I did, because of the scrutiny and criticism I got, in the wake of Rebekah's murder. It was so intense. Insane, almost. So many people, even ones I'd never met or heard of, had a terrible opinion of me. I know people can be mean, especially on social media, but the trolling and vitriol went through the roof, not just for me but for my whole family. I really felt for Marie because she'd only known me for five bloody minutes when it all reached its frenzied peak. She could have tossed me into the too-hard basket, and walked away, but she didn't. With her standing next to me, I felt like I could get through anything, and I still feel that way. She is the rock of our family.

'It was just a job, Matty' she used to say. 'It wasn't sleazy or sordid. It was a service that women were willing to pay for, that you were hired to provide, and it's really no more complicated than that. What other people think is their problem, not yours.'

She was right, and I *don't* feel ashamed. The truth of the matter is that a surprising number of women make the choice to pay for sex, and they do it for different reasons. Some have husbands or partners that can no longer get it up, even with medical help, and they're not ready to sacrifice that side of their own lives because of it. Some of them use an escort with the *blessing* of afflicted partners! Other women want to gain sexual confidence, or have fantasies fulfilled in ways that their partners don't want to engage in. Others just want to experiment in ways they're a bit embarrassed to ask their partners about. Some are busy businesswomen who just don't have the time to meet men, or don't want the drama of unwanted ties. Not every woman wants a relationship. Some just want to get shagged, without being judged, or being asked to explain *why* that's all they want.

Patriarchal society and outdated stereotyping find it hard to accept that the modern, emancipated woman has those kind of choices. I suppose there's enough people who'd get a bit bent out of shape to know she might shell out some money for a decent bang, but its none of anyone else's business, is it, what she chooses to do with her time or her cash? And it seems that anyone and everyone feels they have the right to condemn the guy that gives her what she wants, even when he's well-educated and articulate, and can hold a conversation about almost anything in the world.

Most of us were of that standard, because being decent company in the time a woman pays for is about a lot more than just being able to produce an erection when she's ready for it. The agency made no bones about the need for us to be up to speed with current affairs. I read a lot of newspapers, while I was escorting! If we couldn't converse, as intelligent men, we wouldn't make the grade, and it's so ironic that most of the men who judged me weren't intellectually superior. In fact, some of those keyboard warriors showed themselves up to be as thick as bloody tree stumps, with just as few prospects. Marie said she thought they were just jealous. That made me laugh. 'Keep it in perspective,' she said, so I did.

Society is a strange thing. You can't do right for doing wrong sometimes, and no matter who you are or what you're doing, someone, somewhere, will find it upsetting and choose to say so. It seems to be an ever-more evolving law of life. But, as long as you follow the rules (and I'll never forget when I didn't), escorting is perfectly respectable. It fulfils real needs and, in my humble opinion, which is shared by every last one of the women who choose it, all who engage in 'paid prostitution' as mutually consenting adults should just be left alone to get on with it.

None of that's to say I want to go back to it. Even if I hadn't met Marie, and even if Rebekah hadn't been murdered, I know that eventually I'd have moved on to something more mainstream. The only box it really ticked for me was money, and there are other ways to earn a crust. I'm on much better money now, in my new job, and it doesn't hurt that I married the boss' daughter. Thankfully, money's not something I have to worry much about anymore. We're not rich, and we probably never will be, but we have what we want, and as long as we can keep paying the mortgage, give the baby what she needs, and have a decent holiday once a year, I'm happy enough. I'm certainly not as financially driven as I was before. Being happy is more important than having money in the bank. I'd rather die happy and broke than be lonely with a big stash of cash, and wondering about the motives of whoever did want to be in my life.

The other three lads I was working with at Rebekah's house, the night before she was murdered, have miraculously managed to keep their jobs. I'm glad about that; not just because it meant they weren't after kicking my head in, but because apart from shagging her without wearing condoms they hadn't done anything wrong. They were initially suspended, then disciplined. They were made to sign more stringent contracts, and put on long probation but because a lot of the details were somehow kept out of the press and never became public knowledge, their personal reputations hadn't been hung in the wind. The long and short of it was that they're good guys, and the agency knows their worth. Few men try out for that kind of work and, of the ones that do, most don't even *look* like making the grade. Decent male escorts are like gold, to an agency.

Christmas is coming, and it's my first as a family man. I'm excited for this one. Milly's still too little to care about Christmas or even understand what it is, but Marie and I are thrilled to be having our first one in this house, as a family. This time last year, it was all very different. I was still single, sitting at a table in Mum and Dad's house, in the most bizarre atmosphere, pretending we were a happy family on the one day of the year when the pressure to do that is too hard to ignore. Teresa came home for that Christmas, to surprise us all, but she only came for a week. She flew straight back to Australia, to her boyfriend and her job at a swanky Backpackers hostel, wishing she hadn't bothered coming.

'I can't believe I gave up a three-day full-moon beach party at Burleigh Heads for this shit,' she'd stormed, as I'd driven her back to the airport. 'Why didn't you tell me how bad things were between Mum and Dad? I've spent a bloody fortune on the ticket to come home for Christmas, and all I want now is to turn back the clock to before I did it. Talk about blow up in my face? What a waste of time and money this has been! I won't be coming back for the next one.'

She'd been as mad as I'd ever seen her, but I didn't blame her. Christmas Day had been excruciating, with Dad behaving like a bastard and Mum pretending it didn't matter. Tez was as confused and pissed off about everything as I was.

She's still in Australia, still 'loved-up' with Ross, and reluctantly making plans to come home. Her visa is running out, and it's almost time for her to come back and get serious about establishing a career.

It's going to be weird for her. When she left, I was single, in a different job, Mum and Dad were still together, and Ruth

Stenton was simply our next door neighbour. Now Tezzie's coming home to a busted family, no parental home, a married brother, a new sister in law and a niece, and a half-sister she kind of knows but doesn't. She'll also probably be suffering from post-travel blues. I hope she does bring that Ross guy home with her. That would give her a bit of stability, at least, while she got her feet back on the ground. Her world is going to feel a bit unstable for a while. She still hasn't a clue what she wants to do, so maybe I can help her find something. I can ask Baba if he has any temp work going at our place, as a start for her, until she finds something more permanent or suitable.

I can't wait to see my little sister. She's the one person in this whole family mess that won't be weird to be around. Having her back here might restore some sanity to this fucked-up family. It will give me something to hang onto at least – the one member of my family of origin who might just behave in a way that's vaguely normal.

- *Adie* -

The traffic is lighter than I expected, and although the idea of house sitting in the Lake District in a place I've never even heard of is daunting, to say the least, it could be exactly what I need. Like Miranda says, I have to keep an open mind, and see if this house-sitting 'gig' might 'get out of my funk,' as she put it.

This was her idea, my lovely friend, who never lets me down. 'Mand' has always been the staunchest ally anyone could ever want, especially this past year. I've leaned on her a fair bit, while I've tried to pull things together in whatever way I can. When she said she wasn't going to be around for Christmas this year, my heart sank. Everyone else is busy too, or so they're saying.

When she knew how upset I was, faced with being on my own at Christmas for the first time in my entire life, she invited me to go to Madeira with her and her latest squeeze; some young stud she's been seeing for a few months. I said no, of course, because the last thing *anyone* wants is to be a gooseberry! She insisted it wouldn't be that, but three's a crowd, no matter what anyone says.

When she suggested house sitting, I wasn't overly keen, but I looked online at the sites she recommended. Something tugged at my insides when I saw an ad for a frantic couple with a last-minute emergency. They were going to Australia at short notice, to visit family. I decided to answer that little tug I felt, and I made an enquiry. Within an hour of making a connection with Glenn and Sue Robinson, it was sorted and I was booked in, to look after a place called Teapot Cottage, of all crazy-sounding names, and take care of a spaniel named Sid and a tabby cat called Mittens.

I have to admit, I was daunted. I still am, but I'm a little bit excited too. I've never looked after someone else's house and pets before. I'd never even considered the responsibility attached to that, but something about this just feels *right*. There's almost a *pull*, to go there. Three weeks out of the world, tucked away where nobody I know will ever find me, and I can lick my wounds and figure out what's next. It sounds a hell of a lot better than staying in my stupid little flat, all alone at Christmas, and trying to pretend things are okay when they're not. As for heading to my brother's place, and spending the day with him and his horrible wife, who I've never got on with? Urgh! No thanks. I'd rather stick pins in my eyes.

So here I am, driving north to a tiny working a town in the Lake District called Torley, to have what feels like an adventure. And driving is giving me plenty of time to think.

It seems pretty clear that my marriage is over. I'm still hopeful that Bryan will come around and recognise the value of what we had but, if he doesn't, I'll have to find a way to accept that. After a year of hardly speaking about anything that matters, I'm still clinging to my hope that he will see the light. But how long do I hang on, waiting for my husband of twenty-six bloody years to care enough about our marriage to even *talk* about the things that have forced us apart in a way I once never believed could happen?

Yes, I did a series of terrible things. I kept lifelong, damaging secrets from the very people I should have felt safe to talk to, and it's no wonder Bryan feels betrayed. He can't get past the fact that I never felt I could trust him, let alone the fact that I carried on and manipulated him horribly, in ways he had every right to know about and didn't. I think the final nail in the coffin for him was that terrible moment; the one that will stay with me forever, when I genuinely wondered if Matty could have killed poor Rebekah Stenton.

I'm desperately ashamed of myself for thinking that, but it's true. *I doubted our son*; only for what amounted to a split second, but even with emotions running as high as they were, I still don't know how I could have thought that; how I could have wondered whether my sweet boy could have taken the life of another human being. But I did wonder, and it's *no* wonder Bryan can't forgive me for that. I can hardly forgive *myself.*

I know that haywire hormones probably had something to do with what my thoughts were doing, back then, especially since they're still all over the place now! I wasn't prepared for the effects of abruptly free-falling oestrogen. Most women experience a stage of 'peri,' where the body starts preparing for the change of life, but I never felt that flag. Without any real warning at all, I was flung headlong into the 'real deal' and forced to ride the rollercoaster of no two days being the same, wanting to spend entire days in bed crying, or feeling like punching people I don't even know just for being able to smile when I can't. My body still overheats at random until I wonder if steam will actually start seeping from my ears, and all sorts of other weird things have happened that have caused me to question my own sanity more times than I can count.

I'm still resisting succumbing to the Russian roulette of HRT. I'm not ready to jump on that bandwagon yet. On the one hand, taking it for a short while might help me cope until the dust settles on everything else. My doctor thinks it might be a decent short-term option but, on the *other* hand, I don't see the point in indefinitely delaying the inevitable 'change of life.' I might feel differently in a few months' time, when I'm exhausted by the full force of it all and its driven me halfway around the bend, but my feeling right now is that it's just something I have to go through, like every other woman, and I'll manage it the best way I can, along with everything else.

Whether the madness of my hormone-depleted emotions played a part or not, in how I felt about Matty, I really can't say. Unhappily, neither can anyone else, because the change of life affects women differently. Some mainstream symptoms are widely-shared and obvious but others – like paranoia or being unable to stop dwelling on the worst that could happen – are probably less common, and maybe less easy to attribute to menopause. I guess the impact of whatever goes on in a woman's head in that process might depend on what her life is like to start with. Hormonal deficit is no excuse for thinking the worst when I shouldn't have (and maybe otherwise *wouldn't* have?), but it might be something of a reason. Either way, I still feel wretched. No excuse or reason changes that.

But, hormonal ping-pong notwithstanding, and even with a year's worth of hindsight under my belt, there's still a lot of frustration around my relationship with Matty. He seems to have taken it on the chin, that I had that brief wobble about his guilt or innocence, but there's more to the story of how we all got to here, isn't there?

Nobody wants to have the conversation about his work in the sex trade, and until someone does, and we can figure out how we feel about it, we can't move past that, can we? I'm still slightly disgusted about it, if I'm honest. That feels terrible too but, more than anything, I'm just so sad that he felt compelled to do it! I'm still thoroughly confused about *how* he could do it, in the physical sense. Some of those women must be seventy, if they're a day. It makes me wonder how well I know my own son. I no longer doubt him, but I don't know him the way I thought I did, and I don't know how to feel about that either.

I *hate* feeling disgusted and confused about my own child. It's the worst, most gut-scraping feeling in the world, but *I really don't know how to get past it!*

Matty and Teresa are being barely civil, in spite of the fact that they're clearly unhappy with the way their dad has been treating me. Teresa's still away, and the distance seems to suit her, for now, and Matty's reticence is quite possibly driven by a bit of deflected shame that might still be hanging around. He's also very distracted, now that he's married with a baby and everything, but neither he nor Teresa know what to think, of me, of Bryan, or of the situation we're all in.

As for Ruth? Well, that friendship is more or less in tatters, and I don't know if she will ever get past the point she's at right now – wanting to try but being unable to move forward from how she's feeling, even after almost a year. She is still frosty with me, and its completely understandable, but I just wish we could break through that.

It's hard to believe that a year down the line, we're all *still* a discombobulated mess of guilt, outrage and shame. It's because nobody is willing to talk, except me, and I won't get very far having those important conversations just with myself, will I?

The Stentons got long sentences, and I'm glad about that. It's justice for their daughter, and it's reassuring for Ruth. I can only imagine how conflicted she feels, about that terrible, sad, doomed little family. I'm not naïve enough to imagine I can ever truly be the mother she should have had. She's a grown woman now, and she and Gina are well capable of figuring out their own life. They've built a great one, and in spite of the fact that so much unravelled in the wake of Rebekah's death, that well-built life still stands up. Ruth doesn't *need* anyone else except the spouse she trusts and adores, to guide her.

But is it ever too late, to want your mum? I wasn't close to my mother, and I think it was partly because of her age, but mostly it was because she robbed me of so much when I was fifteen. I know she did what was right, but even when you do what's right, it still can come at a cost. I wouldn't say I never *trusted* her to know what was right for me after that, but we never really connected, at least not in the way I connect with Teresa, and want to connect with Ruth. I think there was a very deep layer of disappointment on both sides, beneath Mum's and my relationship, that negated any fertile soil for us to grow close from.

They were different times, I guess. My parents were of a different generation, and I do think that if Teresea had come home pregnant at fifteen, I'd have handled things very differently. Maybe it's because of my own experience, but maybe it's also because there are more options now, for young mothers, than there were when I was at school. It was only very forward-thinking parents, back then, who'd offer those options to their kids. My mum and dad were very traditional.

It didn't occur to them that with the appropriate support I could have kept Ruth, completed my studies, and gone on to raise her myself and hold down at least a part time job.

Yes, it would have been a challenge, and my life would have been very different. But who's to say that it might not have been better? I wouldn't trade Matty and Teresa for the world, but if I'd never met Bryan, and never had them, who knows where my life would have gone? Raising a baby alone was a challenge I could have risen to, if I'd been given the chance, but it doesn't do to dwell on the things you can't change.

Am I sorry it's all out in the open? Hell, no. I'm sorry about the *way* it came out, and the hurt it caused, yes, but do I wish that Ruth had stayed a secret? Not at all, and I meant what I said in my letter to her; that if she chooses never to speak to me again, she at least knows where she really came from, and how loved she's always been. After the horror she endured at the hands of the Stentons, I hope that at least gives her some comfort.

She asked me a bit about her father, but there wasn't much I could tell her. He was just a boy I'd mildly fancied. As a vulnerable young naif, I had no knowledge of the world or the mistakes I could make in it, or how harsh the consequences could be. A few kisses went too far, and the rest is history. I wouldn't tell my parents who he was, because they were talking about having him charged with statutory rape. I didn't want that. To this very day, that grown-up boy has no idea he has a grown-up daughter.

I'm aware that he should know. I'm aware that he's yet another person I've hidden the truth from, for all of Ruth's life. I told her his name, and where he was the last time I ever heard about him, and I told her it's up to her, if she wants to track him down. I certainly wouldn't stand in her way. It might be useful, from the health perspective, to know something about that side of the family. She made me a promise that if she does decide to go looking for him, and she finds him and tells him everything, she'll be as sensitive as she can with it.

Whatever the consequences might be, if it ever comes to that, I'll deal with them too. After what I've had to own up to so far, coping with whatever he might show up and throw at me would be a drop in the bucket. On that, at least, I feel strong.

The day before she left for Madeira, Miranda and I met for one of our regular 'cocktail hour' evenings, where we'd always put the world to rights over a couple of vodka martinis. We'd exchanged Christmas presents, and as she was leaving she gave me a warm hug and some really good advice. 'Take things one day at a time, darling. Take them just an *hour* at a time, if that's what you need to do. Look after your own needs. Put that priority before everything else, for a while. The kids will be fine. They'll come around.'

Miranda has faced some terrible disappointments in life, including a handful of failed relationships, and she has developed a very pragmatic approach to everything. She concentrates on meeting her own needs and wants, but she does it in full respect of the people she cares about, who care about her too.

I can learn something from that. 'Mand' isn't as happy as she wants to be, that's for sure, but she's content enough. She has made her own world as happy and comfortable as she possibly can, and she still has a big heart for her family and friends. She's had more than a bucketful of knocks, but she keeps getting back up, and she never feels sorry for herself for more than a day or two. She just knows how to take care of herself, in every way she needs to, and she doesn't let anything get in the way of that. Self-protection is important, and she's brilliant at it. I just need to take a leaf out of her book, stop tying myself up in knots worrying about what everyone else wants, and look at what I really need myself. I won't get better, if I don't, and then I'll be of no use to anyone, will I?

I know I need a decent period of time to grieve, regroup, and try to make sense of the new direction my life might now have to take. For now, I'm still clinging onto that faint glimmer of hope that Bryan might see sense, and decide that a marriage of twenty six years is worth saving but, whichever way that goes, I need to get ready for whatever might happen next in my life when the dust finally settles. Right now, I don't feel at all prepared for *anything*. All I do know is that I can't carry on with the status quo. This limbo state is becoming more and more toxic and corrosive. It will be the death of me, I know, if I can't somehow manage to get everything into a different perspective and, in the absence of any familial support, that is something I have to bloody-well do by myself.

I just have to try and look forward to the next three weeks. In a different location, away from prying eyes and family censure, I can use this time to contemplate a very different future from the one I always assumed I'd have. Nothing is certain anymore, apart from this little house sitting job, where someone I don't even know is willing to trust me with everything they hold dear, while they go to the other side of the world!

I find it extraordinary, that they would do that, and of course I can't let them down. This opportunity is a privilege. It's a gift. If I want it to be, it could be the first step in building a brand new life that *doesn't* involve disappointing the people I care about, or keeping devastating secrets from them.

Getting out of my poky flat feels like a small, but significant step forward. Spending Christmas alone, with all this crap in my head, is going to be excruciating. I'm dreading it but, since nobody except Miranda knows or even cares where I am, it means I can't have any expectations of anyone over the festive season. Quite simply, I have to get through it alone and one way or the other, I will.

I wind down the window to bring some cold air into the car, as another hot flush washes over me. The satnav reckons I still have two and a half hours left to drive, to get to Torley, and to Teapot Cottage. The Robinsons said they might be gone before I get there, and they've told me where to find the key, but I hope I can make it before they leave. It would be nice to actually meet them, before they bimble off into the sunset. I hope their little house will be as sweet, comfortable and quiet as it looked.

All of a sudden, I'm feeling a little lighter, and I quite like the idea of having a cat and a dog to cuddle, because I do miss my darling Creole, who stayed with Bryan after I left the house. He's started taking the old boy to work with him, so he's not on his own all day. I wonder if he misses me, but I push the thought out of my mind. He's safe and looked after. His living arrangements can be sorted out later on. I want to have him back with me, if I can figure out a way.

A decent chunk of quiet time to myself without any distractions other than the ones in my own head won't go amiss. Maybe I'm not such a horrible person that I don't deserve to have something to look forward to.

The hard knots of fear and dread that have been sitting like blocks of concrete in the pit of my stomach for months now have slightly shifted. They haven't disappeared, exactly, but they've moved, and become ever-so-slightly less heavy. It feels like the beginning, of something quietly 'unlocking,' for want of a better word.

I put my foot down and increase my speed a little, as I drive towards the Lake District. All of a sudden, I can't wait to get to my new little temporary home.

- Gina -

I look at Ruthie's new haircut, and I decide that I like it. She looks *alla moda* now; up-to-date and chic. She had it cut short just this morning, for the holidays, and she had the grey bleached out into highlights. Her hair looks a little more blonde now, and it suits her.

It's one of many changes we have seen in the past year. What a year! *Mio Dio*, it was something. We have been through a fucking fire, and no mistake.

Ruthie is the bravest woman I know. She is a *nuova* woman too, in almost every way. She changed her name by deed poll, around eight months ago. She is no longer Ruth Stenton, but Ruth Bird, and when I asked her why she chose that name, she told me it was because birds fly free, above the shit that always happens below them, but it was also because of a university lecturer she knew, *quando era una studentessa*.

She said he was a wonderful and clever man, and he influenced her the most, when she was trying to figure out where she wanted to go with her degree. She greatly admired him, and she was devastated when he died of heart failure one day in his office at the university. She decided she would thank him for his help to her over many years and remember him well, as someone who really understood her, by adopting his name. I thought that was a nice thing to do.

She didn't wanna be associated anymore with the Stenton stain on society, and I get it. Who the hell wants to share a name with the worst of human *mostri?*

They don't hang people now, but if I'd had my way, *il vicaro ipocrita* would have gone to the fucking gallows, and so would his Cats-Arse wife. They do not deserve to live, and

I take no comfort in knowing that they are in *unità di segregazione*, where they are kept away from 'normal' prisoners who wanna kill them. *Il bastardo* is in Whitemoor, and la *puta* is in Foston Hall. I wish the guards in those prisons would unlock the doors, maybe accidentally without thinking (oops, sorry!), and maybe turn the cameras off for a while (hey, they broke for a bit, okay?), so the people who wanna kill those two scumbags can go right ahead and do it, with *impunità*.

Ha! I guess that makes me a terrible person, no? But I don't care what anyone thinks, especially not about that, because I am just one ordinary woman, on a list of probably millions of other ordinary women, who could kill Cats-Arse for allowing her own child to be abused for so long by her husband. And as for him? *Quel stronzo*, I would just put him in a room with a handful of mothers, and see how long it took them to beat that son-of-a-bitch to death.

The ghosts have been a while, in putting themselves to bed. Ruthie has bad dreams still, and flashbacks too, but fewer now, and none that can't be explained. They are more annoying than scary now, and she gets over them quickly, but the fact that they are still coming tells me there is still a way for her to go, to be at peace. I guess we can't expect much more. We always knew this was gonna be a road to travel. There is no such thing as an overnight fix, for what has happened in her life. You don't get over that shit in a couple of weeks.

She doesn't talk much to me anymore about everything that happened, because she feels it's not right to do it. She is right about that, but it's not because I don't care, or don't want to know. I do. But I don't have the skills to help her rework a lot of the stuff she is thinking. I think it is some kind of treatment *cognitiva* where your beliefs get challenged and turned into something that's easier to live with. That's not a job for me. It's a job for Peter Dean, and he is doing okay with her, I think. The last thing I want is to make her thinking any worse by not understanding it enough to say something helpful. I'm just a woman who calls a spade a spade, and I know sometimes that kind of honesty is more destructive than helpful when someone is already hurting. *Diplomazia* is not a big talent for me, and the last thing I ever wanna to do is hurt my love by saying something wrong about it all. I am here for her, in other ways that really matter, and she knows it, and she says it is enough.

But now and then, she will say a random thing to me, like she wonders what Rebekah might think about something, or whether she is at peace now; that kind of stuff. One time she asked me if I thought some souls were beyond redemption. I told her I thought all souls can be redeemed, but only if they wanna be. So, with the questions, and the little things she says sometimes, I know a lot of things are still on her mind.

I often think back to the night we went to the Stenton's house. I had never seen Ruthie so angry, or so *eloquente*, and sure of herself. Something got woken up in her, that night, and I don't think that was a bad thing at all. She has always been the quiet one, some say the 'perfect counterfoil' to me. I know I have *la volatilità* at times, and sometimes it is funny to people and sometimes not so much. Ruthie has always been so much calmer and more measured in her responses. And, even that night, she controlled herself so well *after* she threw the phone against the mirror and made such a terrible mess.

I didn't see that happen. It was the crash that made me run. I thought someone was gonna die in that house if I didn't get in there fast. But a part of me wishes I *had* seen Ruthie lose her shit, because I don't imagine I will get another chance to see anything like that again from her. But, of course, after she did it, she was calm again. She was Ruthie again but finally, for once, with the important upper hand. She needed to have it, that night, and she claimed it and stepped into her light. *Lei era magnifica.* She had never been more beautiful, to me.

She stepped into her light and power, and it was wonderful to see that. I am so proud of her for that, and for how she has handled everything else that she has suffered and had to find a way to deal with. She has amazing dignity and grace. I could only ever hope to be half that amazing.

The Bostocks have blown apart, and I'm sad about that, because in spite of everything that happened, they were a nice family. But you can't keep big secrets in a family; not if you want it to stay as a family. When trust falls away from a marriage, sometimes it's too big a job to pull it back, and it seems to be the case for Bryan and *A'dienne*. It looks like they are gonna get a divorce. Even if they don't, they won't be living here. Their house is for sale, and I think that's a good thing. Even if Ruthie and *A'dienne* go on to have a relationship, it's better that *A'dienne* lives somewhere else. Over the fence is too close.

Ruthie is looking forward to our holiday, and Chiara can't keep still. She is going to *la casa de nonne*, where she will be spoiled and treated like a princess by her big Italian family, and her uncles will be like willing slaves to her. We are all excited! We need this time, to stop and catch a breath, and being in the Giordano bosom will help. It is a big, noisy, happy, crazy family, mostly, and there is always something to laugh about. We have a plan, to hire a car, and drive around the South coast for ten days. We will also spend a little time in *Sicilia,* and when we're not doing all that, we can sleep late at home, visit the local markets, and cook all day with *la mia mamma*, if that's what we wanna do. She will love that.

Nobody in my family knows anything about what happened here, in our lives this year. I asked Ruthie if she would want them to know, and she said no. She doesn't think they need to know about such dark things. She wants to have this holiday as a time when nobody wants to either have or avoid the talk about horror, or *incesto,* murder, or recovery from having a blown-up life.

I get it. I don't feel the need to share what it was like for me too, all this. We are okay, and we are getting over things, and we don't need *la famiglia* to help us do that. We can, instead, just enjoy being in the midst of the Giordano clan, and taking each day for what it is.

Chiara has been impacted as little as we could get away with, throughout the *turbolenza* of the past year. We have shielded her from most of it, but she too has felt the strain at times, of things that were too hard to talk about, and she has some trouble understanding why she doesn't see *A'dienne* anymore.

We all need this important time of *tregua*.

It is my hope (that I still keep to myself) that Ruthie and *A'dienne* will have a relationship of some kind. *A'dienne* and Chiara are nice together, and Ruthie could do a lot worse than have another woman in her corner who wants the best for her. I do believe *A'dienne* does, and I think in the end there may be something for the two of them if they both want it.

But I look at Ruthie now, and my heart swells, like it always does. We have made it through the storm, and we are standing, and walking forward, and we have everything in the world to look forward to. It is a good feeling. Ruthie is free, from all of the terrible things that were dragging her down, and casting such a big shadow over her life. Some of those things, she didn't even know about.

Am I sad that she had to remember? Am I sad that she has had to go through this fire? For me it is a hard question to answer. You never wanna see your loved ones suffer, or to be in any kind of pain, or *tormento emotivo*, but if Rebekah hadn't died, nothing would have changed for Ruthie! She wouldn't have found a way to be free, to know what life would be like without the shadows of her monstrous family making her cold inside all the time. They way they all treated her, especially Rebekah, would have stayed the same, and she would still be trying to get their approval, and spending her life in anguish, and the worst kind of confusion, about why they hated her so much.

Maybe she would have lived her whole life being miserable about it. And maybe Michael and Margaret Stenton would have gone to their graves never having atone for their terrible crimes.

I believe that Ruthie had to go through the fire to figure out *how* to be free. As painful and *devastante* as it all has been, she is in a better place now because of it. Sometimes you have to go through a fire to come out clean, to have the demons burned away that weren't even yours, even though they stuck to you like shit on a blanket. I think this was one of those times, and yeah, I hate that she had to do it, but she is already in a much better place, with many of the mysteries gone, and heading for an even better place, in her own mind.

For me, a lot of questions drove me crazy, and it's good to finally have the answers. What I want now is for us to start again with a clean slate, and that starts here today, with our holiday.

- *Ruth* -

We're packed, and ready to go. Gina has booked a private car to take us all to Stanstead for our afternoon flight to Lamezia Terme airport in Calabria, where her family will be waiting to meet us. This Christmas we're going for three full weeks, so we'll be there for New Year as well, which is always fun. Italians know how to put on a good show at *Capodanno*, with the most spectacular fireworks you could ever hope to see, and we'll be spending a few days in Sicily too. It should still be warm enough, during the daytime at least, to enjoy a bit of the island. We plan to look around and find a nice resort to book into for a longer stay next summer. This past year has been too crazy, on every level, for us to have taken the time to go when Gina first suggested it.

The house next door – Bryan and Adie's – is on the market. Their marriage collapsed, and she moved out a few months ago. I don't know the ins and outs of it, and I really don't want to. All I know is that they stopped being able to talk about anything at all, despite Adie's best attempts, and they called time on their relationship when it looked like there was no way back. That's a pretty big thing, after twenty-six years together. I'm sad for them, that they couldn't get over what happened. It just goes to show; sometimes even the rocks that look the most solid can have a crack in them.

It wasn't just the lies Adie had told, that busted them apart. I think it was a lot of other stuff too. We all found the press intrusion hard, with journalists more or less camping outside our houses, and hounding us all the time for comment. Even though they wrote some terrible things, we couldn't face trying to correct some of what they published. It was just too overwhelming for us all. We were too traumatized, too battered, to stand in front of anyone and try and defend ourselves. It was all any of us could do to even reconnect with the people closest to us, and the Bostocks have failed miserably at that – so far at least. Adie still has hope for her and Bryan, but I don't know how realistic that is. By all accounts, he has turned into a lump of immovable granite.

Matty's name was unfairly dragged through the mud, and I know they all found that hard, along with the hostility they had to deal with because of what he'd 'done.' His work was legitimate, but it wasn't exactly palatable for the masses, was it? The nastiness aimed at the whole family was off the scale but – sadly – depressingly 'normal' these days, in a world that seems to seethe with ever-more open hostility, and people itching to scream at strangers with little in the way of provocation. None of that helped the Bostocks much. When things are already close to unbearable, it doesn't take a heavy straw to break the camel's back.

Matty sent me a nice card, a few weeks after the dust started to settle. It was a sweet communication. He said he'd like us to talk sometime, now that we've discovered we're related, but he'd understand if I didn't want to. He just wanted me to know that he was there for me in whatever way I might want him to be, and I appreciated that. I sent him a card back, to tell him so.

None of what happened was his fault. He knows that, but I'm sure he is devastated on lots of levels too, especially at the implosion of his parents' marriage. I know he would probably value the chance to talk to someone like me, who's outside his own family but still may have a vested interest in it. If I can get myself to a place where I think I could help him to make sense of the shit that's gone down on *his* side of the fence, I'll certainly try. Him reaching out to me the way he did meant more than he will ever know.

He's married now, with a baby! Everything happened super-fast for him, but I guess he just needed to re-establish his life in meaningful way. I hope he's happy in the new family *he* has become a part of; he deserves to be. He's a good kid, at heart. Hearing about his marriage made me smile. It gave me hope that when recovery is good enough, life can be meaningful and joyful again.

Bryan is still friendly, on the rare occasions when we see one another. He always asks me how I'm doing, but he doesn't talk about anything that's going on in his own family. I haven't had a conversation with my new half-sister, Teresa, yet. She's still away travelling, so that might be a while, but there's no rush, is there? I guess we'll eventually get around to that, supposing *she* wants to.

Adie now lives in a flat on the other side of Guildford. We've met for coffee a couple of times in town, just her and me. It was horribly awkward, both times, and I guess it takes more than a couple of quick caffeine-fuelled catch-ups, to move forward from the place we were before, when we weren't even speaking, but I know we both wanted to try. Things *are* a little better, but we're still a long way from the comfortable rapport we used to have, and I still can't see her as my mother. It worries me a bit, if I'm honest, that I'm not sure if I ever will.

I want to; I have decided that, and I often think back to the time when she came to our house to tell me that Matty was being held on suspicion of Rebekah's murder. The urge I had, to throw myself into her arms and cry like a baby while she held me, was so powerful and strong that it really freaked me out at the time. It worries me, though, that I haven't had that feeling since. I *want* to feel that connection again. I *want* to have a relationship with my real mother, and I'm not sure why I can't. For what it's worth, I don't think that sense of connection has been lost; I do think it's still there. It's just still buried under everything else I'm still processing and dealing with.

Peter Dean, my therapist, said it's a bit like having everything in a bottle, with the good stuff at the bottom. It's sitting under a heap of bad stuff that you have to weed out first, before you can get to it. He sees that day coming when I can embrace the good in all this, stand up straight, and let the silver lining bathe me in its light. But for now, it's still that big pile of shit someone else described it as, that I have to wade through to get to the other side.

Analogies. Some of them are a bit of a stretch, and others are faintly ludicrous, but they do work. They are useful, in helping me to visualise the journey I'm on. The opinions of professional people who *know* I can get through it help too. Peter Dean tells it like it is. He's honest. He is certain I'll get to a comfortable place eventually, and he is always keen to reinforce that. It all helps.

What I can't do – at least not yet – is explain it all to Adie. I know she's been hoping I'd connect with her more, but I still have a wall around me, and while the bricks are coming down, it's a frustratingly slow process. I know I have to learn to walk before I can run, and I can only hope she can keep being patient until the wall comes down enough, for me to see whether a positive connection *is* possible again. Right now, as hopeful as I am, I really can't say for sure. She says that's okay, and Peter Dean says it is absolutely 'normal,' given everything that's happened, but it's frustrating for me, that even after some pretty intensive therapy that is helping to 'fix me' on lots of levels, I still can't quite seem to turn that all-important page that will put me on the same one as Adie.

There's been a lot to come to terms with. The biggest thing – and the most unexpected – was the *shame* I felt, for having longed for the love of someone *I* once loved, who I didn't know was capable of abusing and murdering someone *else* that I loved! That shame was all-encompassing, at the beginning. It extended so far, and cast such a huge shadow over me. I was ashamed of being unable to remember what my so-called 'father' had done, in enough time to save my sister. I was also deeply ashamed of my failure to cope with everything better; of feeling virtually incapable of lifting myself back up off the floor. I even felt bad for being unable to let Adie back into my life.

I was almost paralysed by the humiliation of my own weakness. I've worked on that a lot, and I no longer feel so pathetic, but some of my shame is still there, and it sits alongside so many other emotions I've had to try and battle through; the deepest sense of heartbreak imaginable, at Rebekah's entire life of terrible torment, and the fact that I lost her. I felt so much rage too, jostling for position with the utter disbelief, that my adoptive mother could have been so heartless and cruel. I still feel profound regret too, and I probably always will, that I didn't try harder to understand *Rebakah's* rage. I can't stop telling myself that if I did, if I'd only tried to talk to and understand her, instead of doing everything I could to avoid her all the time, I could have saved her. And I'm still confused and slightly scared about what happens next, and what sort of person I might end up being, at the end of this process.

This miserable journey of discovery and acceptance has felt, many times, like a long and incredibly steep ascent to the top of Mount Everest. It also occurred to me, somewhere along the way, that there aren't a lot of people in the world who love me enough to want to help me get there. I have Gina and Chiara, as my loving little family, and I have a handful of very good friends who care a lot. They always have bucketloads of positivity to offer me. There are plenty of hugs, lots of encouragement, and very little prying or unasked-for advice. I'm incredibly lucky to have people like that.

But that's it; just a small handful of people on the entire planet who care enough to want to keep supporting me through this journey. I do know that rebuilding a good relationship with Adie will help me too, in climbing this mountain. It has taken me a while to realise that there are many complex reasons why her being in my life is important. The fact that she *wants* to be a part of my support system counts for a lot. We both just have to be patient with the process that I hope will eventually allow me to feel more comfortable about inviting her in.

Gina, bless her, has *endless* patience, especially with me, and all my unpredictable emotional quirks and bangs. For her, that is nothing short of unbelievable. Her fuse is typically very short, and it never ceases to amaze me just how strong she has been for me, this past year or so, while I've started coming to terms with my life as it's shaken down. She's had to hear some pretty horrible stuff, but her 'take' is that it answers a lot of questions in her own head, as well as mine, about my family, and the effect they had on me.

In typical Gina-fashion, she's pulled the best out of all of it. She has a wonderful way of building something shiny and beautiful from smoking wreckage. She has enough hope and energy for us both, that I can get to a good place and, like she says, I just have to trust her and follow her lead.

She has brought me to fully understand, feel and *appreciate* what I already knew, but only at a superficial level. Contrary to what I first felt, as the overriding emotion, my entire life *hadn't* been a lie. A lot of it was, but the really important parts were all true, and solid, and real. Gina's and Chiara's love for me is still as real, strong, and solid as it ever was. The love my friends have for me is real. The respect my students and fellow academics have for me – that has always been and continues to be real. The bricks and mortar that contain our beautiful family and its immense and awesome love, *those* are solid and real.

I always knew they were, but I did find it hard to hold on, when everything else was falling apart. Gina held on for us both, and she held me hard. She stopped me from drifting away, in my head, to a place I couldn't come back from. It wasn't easy for her, seeing me go through all that. When your loved ones hurt, you hurt too, don't you? You hurt for what you can't fix; for what you know they have to somehow find the courage to fix *themselves*, in all its heartbreaking, terrifying truth. Gina is inherently positive and life-affirming. I couldn't ask for a better wing-woman, to go through life with, and I certainly couldn't have got through all *this* without her.

Michael Stenton was finally sentenced to a whole-of-life term of imprisonment, but only a couple of months ago. The delay was frustrating, and I don't think it helped at all, in the initial stages of my therapy. It was such a big thing, to not have a proper full stop at the end of such an important 'sentence left hanging,' while we waited for the *real* sentence to be handed down. It felt like Michael was standing in the shadows, staring at me from a place just outside the edge of my vision, where I couldn't actually see him, but I felt like he was there. It kept me in the weirdest place; in a kind of frozen suspension, while I battled to stay on the rollercoaster of my own emotions and sort through the jumbled mess in my head.

The wheels of justice took a long time to turn, largely because there was a lot of stuff to sift through, going back many decades, including a few statements from a handful of female ex-parishioners who had come forward with allegations of historical abuse, galvanised by the fact that Michael was being exposed. That was another thing I had to try and assimilate; those poor young girls, as they'd been, dealing with a terrible thing and being too afraid to speak of it.

I'm glad they found the courage to have their day in court, and hold him accountable for what he did to them too. Since the statute of limitations doesn't apply in historical sexual abuse cases, the Crown took their sweet time in compiling enough evidence to ensure they could throw the book at him with such might that he had no hope of escaping the worst.

That was what they planned, and that was what they got. When Michael finally had his day in court, the judge told him that he'd grotesquely abused a high-profile position in the community that people should be able to trust. It wasn't just his own child that he'd defiled, degraded and ultimately killed. Nor was it just the women who'd been violated by him as children. The entire community that had looked to him for guidance and succour had also had their belief in humanity tested to the limit and, in some cases completely destroyed, by his heinous actions. The judge said that what he had done was so far beyond forgivable, to so very many scarred and traumatised people, there could be no acceptable alternative to him spending the rest of his life behind bars.

I didn't go to court, to witness his condemnation.

Margaret Stenton was also sentenced, in a separate hearing, to seventeen years in prison for being an accessory to incest, rape and murder. That stunned me. It was a heavy sentence, considering she'd turned Michael in. In return for blowing the whistle and entering a guilty plea, and sharing some of the details of her life with Michael (in which it became clear that the sad bitch *was* just as much a victim as a perpetrator), she did manage to escape a whole-of-life sentence, but it wasn't much consolation, considering she'll be coming out as a very old and socially shunned woman, with nowhere to go and nothing left to look forward to in life.

I didn't go to court for that either. My not-parents, the monstrous banes of my existence; they were already dead to me, and not in a way I could mourn. It's funny, how people still think that no matter how awful someone was, the respect for the 'dead' should still stand. I struggled, for a long time, with the guilt of not feeling a scrap of compassion for either of the Stentons, but I finally got over that. As warped as their view on life might have been, with the sick sense of twisted entitlement that underpinned it, they were grown-ups who still knew right from wrong. Everything they did was a choice.

I did wonder, for a while, whether things would have been any better if we had been related by blood. But it didn't take me long to get my addled head around that one. Michael didn't consider the 'sacred' blood tie while he was consistently abusing his and Margaret's daughter, and Margaret was passively condoning it, did they? No thought was given to the meaning of a blood tie as he was throttling Rebekah to death, either. My gratitude is a thousand times bigger than Everest itself, in knowing that I share genes with Adie, Matthew and Teresa Bostock, who are good people. Anything is better than sharing them with human abominations like the Stentons. I've no idea how I'd live with myself, if they were my flesh-and-blood parents.

I changed my name, and there was a lot of power attached to that. It was my way of calling the shots, on who I want to be to myself and *my* family, instead of being endlessly ashamed of all that I couldn't be to someone else's. I chose my own identity, and even just a few months into having a different name, I feel it was the best move I've ever made. Sadly, I couldn't get my degrees reissued in my new surname. I don't know why that's not possible but, as they say, 'them's the rules, baby.' As far as everything else is concerned though, legally and otherwise, I'm now Ruth Bird; free as one, and flying under my own steam, without the pathetic need for acceptance from the worst of people, to provide the wind I thought I'd need, beneath my wings.

Is blood really thicker than water? I suppose on most levels it is, when you're a normal person, undriven by a bent and monstrous agenda. You'd always put your family first, and protect them from the evil in the world, in whatever ways you ever could. But I desperately wanted to be a part of a family that wasn't really mine, for a long time before I knew it wasn't. The connection I felt to Adie, when I wanted to hurl myself into her arms, and I couldn't explain why – does that have something to do with shared genes? And let's not forget that the towering, all-encompassing love I have for my daughter, who isn't biologically mine either, transcends anything that could simply be validated by being a 'blood tie.' You can hate your relatives and cherish your friends. Just because someone is your flesh and blood, it doesn't mean you have to love or even like them, and just because someone isn't, that doesn't mean you can't or shouldn't.

So it's not an easy question to answer, is it? I guess what it comes down to is where you feel you belong, and feel safe and loved. I never felt safe and loved with the Stentons, but even as Adie's neighbour and friend, I felt safe and loved by her.

I still want to feel that. I want to get back to that place where I felt like throwing myself at her, back when everything was uncertain and we were all just battling to stay afloat, even as our hurt, our suspicions and our bewilderment were all but drowning us. I needed her, in that moment, and I think on some level I need her now. There's little enough love in the world, without us turning our backs on what there is, and if Peter Dean, believes that I'll eventually be able to salvage something meaningful with Adie, I choose to believe *him*.

Rebekah got full justice in the end, but what I learned, in that whole miserable process, was that even when justice is served it doesn't lessen the pain one iota. I don't know what I expected, after the sentencings, but it wasn't to still be in a confined space in my own mind, where I was still trying to figure out how to live with the fact that if I'd only remembered things earlier, or if she'd had the courage to talk to me, she could have kept her life, and we could have made it better.

Getting out of that space is taking time. Peter Dean says I have to be patient with myself, while the wounds take their time in healing, but he believes that one day I will be able to think about Rebekah without feeling this crushing guilt and sadness that robs me of my breath, and leaves me in pieces, every time.

I choose to believe that too.

Adie has sent us a Christmas card, and I'm taking it with us. It's a fairly innocuous little card, nothing 'loaded' or 'heavy,' and I know she would have deliberately chosen it for that. It's the kind of card you'd send to a friend, someone you don't know well but want to send a heartfelt wish to. I didn't send one back, and I'm thinking I probably should have, but it's too late now. Maybe I can give her a quick call from Italy sometime over Christmas, and maybe next year we will be in a place where we can each send a card, and make them a bit more personal.

Only time will tell. And, of course, if we can get to a good place, there is a possibility of a bigger family to be a part of. All I've ever wanted was to be an important part of a loving family, and it never happened, despite my best efforts. But, after all this terrible upheaval and the worst kind of fire, there's finally a chance for me to have that, in some form at least, with a woman who genuinely loves me. How ironic it is, though, that the only thing stopping me now is *me*.

When all is said and done, Adie Bostock moved mountains to find me. She turned her own and her family's lives upside down, to find her way to me. It means more than I can find the words for, so I'm hopeful for *all* our hearts, that they'll survive this maelstrom and something good can grow from it, for us all. Who knows? Maybe I *will* have that longed-for extended family in the end, hopefully with Matty and Teresa too, and maybe even with Bryan, if he and Adie can ever get their shit together again.

Gina buttons Chiara's coat up, then turns and puts a gentle hand on my arm.

'Earth to Ruthie. You are miles away. Are you ready, *cara?* The car will be here in two minutes now. Is there anything you need to do before we leave? You wanna pee or something?'

I shake my head, and pull her into a hug. 'I love you,' I murmur, into her hair.

She squeezes me softly. 'I love you too, *cara*. This is gonna be a good holiday. We deserve it, all of us.'

She is right; we do, but this break away is not a full stop. It's just a semi-colon, because there is still a lot to be written, but it gives me time to breathe, and figure out how I want the rest of the story to run. It's my story, and for the first time in my life I feel like I can influence how it goes. After almost a full year of being terrified about what that really meant, I now think I've got the pen in my hand, and I choose to make my story exciting instead of wretched, interesting instead of dull, and free of the terrible shadows that forced me to keep so much of myself in the dark.

It's too late for Rebekah, but it's not too late for me. And in spite of everything, when I think back to when we were little, and dreaming of our futures, I do believe that she would want me to make the best of mine. So I will, and I'll do it for *her*.

As that thought goes through my mind, I hear a faint but familiar childish chuckle in the ether, out there on the wind.

'Do it for yourself, sweetie,' she whispers, and something inside me quietly moves, and lifts, and gently hugs my heart.

Glossary of Italian Words

accessori	accessories
agitato	upset
amante gelosa	jealous lover
aspetto adulto	adult appearance
bagno	bathroom
bastardo	bastard
bigotto	bigot
borsa	handbag
Cagna triste	sad bitch
calda	hot
Camica	shirt/blouse
cani battuti	beaten dogs
canottiera	camisole
casa disgustosa	disgusting house
catalizzatrice	catalyst
cattiveria	viciousness
cavalla nera	Dark horse
cerebrale	cerebral
che tipo di madre permetterebbe a sua figlia di essere così violato?	what kind of mother would allow her daughter to be so violated?
chioccolato	chocolate
Colomba di Pasqua	Easter cake
Consensuale	consensual
cosa magnifica	something wonderful
cucciolo	puppy
depravata	depraved
desolato	desolate
detestabile	detestable
devastante	devastating
diplomazia	diplomacy
dogmatico	dogmatic
domani	tomorrow
donna ridente	ridiculous woman
è contorto	twisted
è la vita.	That's life
farsesca	farcical
finito	finished
flagrante	flagrant
furioso	furious

Giustizia poetica	poetic justice
il bastardo depravato	the depraved bastard
imbecilli stupidi	stupid imbeciles
importanto	important
in conflitto	unacceptable
inaccettabile	incest
incesto	conflicted
incredulo	disbelieving
indifferente	indifferent
indignazione	indignation
inganno	impunity
intollerabile	intolerable
intolleranza	intolerance
Ipocrita	hypocrite
irritato	irritated
isterico	hysterical
la casa de nonne	her grandparents' house
la megera	the shrew
la mia amore	my love
la polizia	the police
la stupida	the stupid one
La tua onestà è troppo tardi	your honesty is too late
loro incompleto	incomplete/unfinished work
le prostitute	the prostitute
lei era magnifica	she was magnificent
lo strazio	the torment
madre	mother
Madre di Dio	Mother of God
Madrina	Godmother
materna	maternal
Mi disgusti	I'm disgusted
mi dispiace	I'm sorry
mia cara	my loved one
mio Dio	my God
miseria	misery
momento orribile	horrible moment
mortificato	mortified
mostri	monsters
mutandine	panties or knickers
nemici	enemies
non posso sopportare di guardarti, donna egoista	I can't stand to look at you, selfish woman
non sono preparato	I am not prepared

non ti interessata a nessuno tranne te stessa	you are interested in no-one but yourself
patetita	pathetic
perdono	forgiveness
perfetto	perfect
pessimo	terrible
pigiama	pyjamas
povera ragazza stupida	poor stupid girl
prospettiva	perspective
provocare	provocation
provocatorio	provocative
Psicologa	Psychologist
puta	whore
quando era una studentessa	when she was a student
quel stronzo	that asshole
questa e un a celebrazione	this is a celebration
questo è intollerabile	this is intolerable
reazione pragmatico	pragmatic reaction
recupero	recovery
resoluta	resolution
rosso	red
scena ridicola	Mother of God
sessuale	ridiculous scene
sessualità	sexual
sfigurata	sexuality
sincero	sincere
Spettacolare	spectacular
stereotipo	stereotype
tedioso	tedious
tormento emotivo	emotional torment
tregua	respite
Tu donna egoista	you selfish woman
Turbolenza	turbulence
umiliazione pubblica	public humiliation
un cane sgridato	a scolded dog
un'anima torturata	a tortured soul
unità di segregazione	segregated units
uomo stupido	stupid man
vetriolo	vitriol
violata	violated
volgare	vulgar
volgarita	vulgarity
volatilità	volatility

Note from the Author:

If you enjoyed *Thicker Than Water*, or any of my other books, I'd love you to leave a review on Amazon or other reader's platforms.
It would mean a lot!

www.anniecookwriter.com

Facebook: Annie Cook Writer
Instagram: anniecookwriter

Bouquets...

To my truly amazing husband Kerry. You are my biggest champion, my inspiration, the rock of our family, and my very best friend in all the world.

To the survivors of familial child abuse who shared their stores with me. Your trust, in doing that, is the biggest privilege of my life. There are no words to describe how beautiful you are.

To Adoption UK, and Ramsden's Solicitors for the invaluable information you provided about the issues around closed adoptions. It is important to get things like that right for the reader, and your help has made that happen.

To Dawn Walter, Jean Jones, Katherine McDiarmid, Robyn Gell and Yvonne Raymond, for the unwavering enthusiasm that helps me to keep going, on days when my brain would rather I left it asleep under the duvet. Everyone needs champions like you guys.

To Aisha Jamil at Chainzown for the inspiration in graphic design. Your idea was a thousand times better than mine. Thank you for your vision for the compelling cover of this book.

To Gwen Morrison, at PublishNation, for helping me with the all-important nuts and bolts of bring my work to life. Thank you for your ongoing support.

Read Annie Cook's other novels; available now…

No Small Change
A Teapot Cottage Tale (#1)

**The 'change of life' means menopause.
But what if it also means reinvention,
with the help of a little bit of magic?**

Adie Bostock is a self-confessed 'basket-case.' She's fifty-two, at the mercy of her haphazard hormones, and struggling to face the end of her marriage. Alone for Christmas and fed up with family drama, she lands at Teapot Cottage where she plans to wallow in guilt and self-pity in private.

But the cottage, with its mysterious healing energy, has other plans for Adie and she soon finds out that it takes more than one person to make things fall apart, and more than one to put them back together.

Confirmed widower Mark Raven is a rough-edged farmer determined to hide his heart. He's battling with grief and ageing, and keeping his rather dreamy daughter at least partly in the real world. Romance is not on his radar.

Adie and Mark want to keep things purely platonic, but an unseen influence is nudging them in a different direction. Then Adie's husband decides he wants her back. It's what she's been praying for, but is it still what she really wants?

Escape to the Lake District with this magical, life-affirming story about overcoming adversity and finding love again later in life.

The Power of Notes and Spells
A Teapot Cottage Tale (#2)

Every woman dreams of finding the love of her life. But what do you do when yours brings baggage that can hurt you and your family?

Feen Raven is often described as more than just a little bit barmy. The young 'white witch' has finally found her soulmate, but old family wounds are opened again when she finds out who he's involved with.

Gavin Black is on an unhappy errand that forces him to reconnect with his estranged mother. All he wants is to claim what's his and go home again, without any complications.

Carla Walton can't let go of a grudge. After a lifetime of pushing everyone away, she is isolated, bitter, and blaming everyone else for her problems. She wants to be left alone so she can keep ignoring her demons.

But Teapot Cottage, with its mysterious ability to heal the broken-hearted, always has a more complicated agenda for people who don't want to rake up the past. Pretty soon, Gavin, Feen and Carla come to question everything they think they do and don't want in life.

Will love and a little bit of magic help them find a way forward? Or will old family fractures be too hard to heal?

Come to the Lake District, to a gentle place where a beautiful blend of music and magic can heal the hardest hearts.

A MORAL SWERVE

Nobody comes home expecting to find intruders -
But what would you do if you did?

Alison Jones is single, lives alone, and doesn't have a lot of self-awareness. But, after coming home to find burglars in her house, she does a terrible thing without thinking, and is forced to confront some ugly truths about herself.

Darren Davies is a petty thief, stuck in the revolving door between small-time crime and prison. After he makes the biggest mistake of his life, he is compelled to re-evaluate the path his life is taking, and deal with the demons that drive him.

When Darren and Alison's lives intersect, they each find themselves on a soul-searing journey, as they struggle to come to terms with the catastrophic impact of their acts and omissions. After stumbling through the wreckage, the future for them both becomes crystal clear, but it's not what either of them expected.

As one door opens and another slams shut, choices expand and diminish.

At the crossroads of Beginnings and Endings,
who decides to go where?

WHEN IT'S MEANT TO HAPPEN
A Teapot Cottage Tale (#3)

Having a baby is something most women dream of and plan for. But what does it mean if you can't make it happen, no matter how hard you try?

Debby Davies longs for a family of her own. She is desperate to have a baby with the husband she adores, but fruitless years of trying to conceive have left her feeling like a failure. It's starting to make her crazy, that she can't seem to achieve the one thing she always felt destined to do.

Darren Davies is at his wits' end with his wife. Her simmering resentment is changing her in ways that really scare him, and the horrible way her parents treat him is starting to take its toll. He's beginning to question whether their marriage can survive what feels like a never-ending series of storms.

As their doubts take hold, that their love can survive, they know they're in the last chance saloon. But Teapot Cottage, with its mystical ability to pour balm on battered souls, has plans for Debby and Darren that show them what's possible in ways they could never have imagined.

Can they stay together and face a very different future from the one they had planned, or will they find the challenges too great, and go their separate ways?

Run away from home for a while! Come to the Lake District, to a place where miracles can happen, with the help of a little bit of magic!

RUIN, REINS AND REDEMPTION
A Teapot Cottage Tale (#4)

Everyone makes mistakes, and some of them are hard to come back from. When you've taken someone else's life, and destroyed your family in the process, where do you begin, to pull things back together?

Stuart Thomson is a disgraced lawyer whose catastrophic error of judgement has all but ruined his life. By the time he leaves prison, after six years, he no longer has a career, a home or a marriage, and his troubled teenage daughter is barely speaking to him.

Meghan Thomson is almost fifteen. She's a mixed-up mess of anger and confusion, and she has no idea how she feels about anything at all, especially her father. When he books a holiday to the Lake District together, to reconnect, it's the last thing she really wants to do with a man she doesn't trust.

On holiday, father and daughter both struggle to understand each other. But Teapot Cottage, with its enigmatic way of turning troubled lives around, reveals an amazing opportunity they once could never have imagined. The future on offer means a whole new level of faith and commitment from them both, to make it happen.

Stuart and Meghan desperately need a new start. Can they trust themselves and each other enough to make it happen? Or does the heartbreak of the past make the leap of faith too tough?

In Torley town, in a very special cottage, lives are often transformed with the help of 'a little bit of love and magic.'

Coming soon…

THE STUFF YOU FAIL TO NOTICE
A Teapot Cottage Tale (#5)

You can live your whole life without knowing what's happening around you. But how can you stop the things you haven't even seen from blowing your world apart?

Minty Cartwright is peri-menopausal, and reeling from the discovery that her husband has been having an affair with her closest friend from childhood. She takes refuge at Teapot Cottage, a quiet holiday house in the Lake District, while she considers her next move.

Fiona Winterson hates herself with a passion she once never knew she could feel. Her selfishness has shattered the heart of the 'soulmate' she's known and loved all her life. But faced with the worst of circumstances, she discovers that she needs that woman's help.

With decades of love and trust destroyed, Minty and Fiona are thrown back together in a sea of shame, fury and fear. Both women are forced to reconsider the value of a friendship that has influenced their entire lives.

Will the mysterious, healing energy of Teapot Cottage help them rediscover what's important to them both? Or is it all too painful – and too late – to even try?

Come back to friends old and new in the Lake District, where shattered lives can be gently pulled back together, with the help of 'a little bit of magic'

Milton Keynes UK
Ingram Content Group UK Ltd.
UKHW031100231024
450082UK00012B/619